COUP DE GRACE

BOOK 2 OF THE GIFT OF GRACE SERIES

FROG AND ESTHER JONES

Impulsive
Walrus

EXCERPT FROM COUP DE GRACE

"You want me to *what?*" I asked, incredulous. We'd moved from our normal training session into something much weirder.

"Help me move into a place down there in the Valley. In fact, I want help making it look like I moved in quite some time ago." Grace's voice was cool, but the crinkle on the side of her mouth told me she was stifling laughter. Originally, I'd thought that tone existed just to irk me. Now I realized that it signaled her being amused with *herself*, and guaranteed that Grace had another of her crazy ideas.

I had yet to see one of those ideas work as intended, which is why I immediately began to get nervous.

"Grace... Isn't living in town kind of a bad idea?"

"Oh, yes. I imagine the cops will be on me almost immediately." Again, that voice. It was almost as if she *wanted* to be raided by the police.

"Immediately? Probably not. But someone's going to notice you."

To Liz Vann-Clark and Tim Martin: Thank you for years of support, and your friendly rivalry to break Frog first with the number of panels and weirdest topics at conventions....
He remains unbroken.

CONTENTS

ROBERT

APPARENTLY SPOKANE HAS WINERIES. I never knew that.

I filed that fact in the back of my head, just in case I lived long enough for someone to ask me what I'd learned today.

I stood on a hard concrete floor in a high-ceilinged room with white walls, looking down a long aisle. On both sides, high shelves of oaken wine barrels formed a wall of aluminum and wood. Occasional drains interrupted the otherwise continuous cement gray in the floor, and the room's slightly chilly temperature gave me goose bumps. To my right, a rack of hanging wine glasses protruded from the wall, its glass stalactites forming a small, upside-down, translucent forest.

My attention focused on the seven-foot-tall woman in the middle of the aisle. She wore a single piece of white cloth, draped over her shoulder toga-style. My eyes went immediately to her exposed left breast.

Stupid, teenage eyes.

The only other article of clothing on her appeared to be a live snake wrapped about her head like a tiara.

She carried a long staff with clusters of small, yellow flowers on it, wrapped in ivy. A pine cone sat atop the stick, almost as though it had grown there naturally. Some sort of sticky substance coated the shaft, but from my vantage at the head of the aisle I couldn't identify it.

Her head came up and her eyes met mine. A milky film coated those eyes, obscuring the pupil like they'd been layered over with years-old cataracts. Her face, so smooth it could have been polished marble, broke suddenly into a crooked grin. Without moving her eyes from mine, she swung her staff at one of the wine barrels above her.

The staff struck, opening a small and unnaturally perfect circular hole in the wood. Bright purple wine began a thin stream from the barrel. The woman lifted her face to the wine. I expected her to raise her lips to it like a child to a ground spigot, but instead she positioned her mouth directly under it. Not a drop hit the ground after she began to drink.

"Well, looks like we've got ourselves a party girl," said a female voice behind me. I grimaced and threw a look over my shoulder at my backup.

Amy Milankovich looked back, one side of her mouth twisted into a wry kind of smile. "Sorry, just trying to inject some humor into the situation. That is what Grace does, right?"

Amy stood a full six feet tall, with the body and face of your average eastern-European supermodel. There's a point on the female hotness scale where a guy like me simply fails to respond because the hope of achieving anything has been dead and buried. In a magazine, I would have stared at Amy and fantasized all day long. In person, I preferred not to talk to her.

So, instead of answering, I shook my head and turned to focus on the task at hand.

It was right about here that I took a calculated risk, and did nothing.

I wasn't really a drinker. Don't get me wrong; I don't morally object to the consumption of alcohol. As a foster child, I made my way through the world on my wits alone. Anything that muddled those wits I viewed as a personal danger. As a result, I didn't quite know how much wine it would take to make a person completely, falling-down drunk.

I was, however, pretty sure that downing an entire barrel would do it.

As if to answer my thoughts, Amy gave a slight giggle behind me. "Well, it looks like you get the easy job today."

I turned back again and arched an eyebrow at her.

"I find them," she said. "You make them hold still. I banish. If that's the deal, and she's just going to drink herself silly, then making her hold still should be a cinch, right? I found her, I'll banish her, you sit there and watch her drink. That sounds like the easy job to me."

"Whatever," I said. "I'd still rather have Grace here." I turned to look at the statue-still woman with wine pouring down her throat.

My mentor, Grace, could have handled this alone. In a fight, Grace had held her own against any number of threats that I'd seen. Her knowledge of the runes summoners use to direct their energy verged on encyclopedic. Being next to her in a fight felt like riding a hurricane: fast, powerful, and ultimately dangerous. Grace would have handled this situation easily.

"Grace has her place elsewhere; she trusts us to handle the little stuff. I can banish this thing; I just need a little time." Amy's voice was insultingly calm.

"Easy for you to say. I'm the one that has to *buy* that time."

"She's getting drunk. It's a milk run today. Stop whining, sit back, and watch the demon do your job for you." Amy's voice came out a little sharper than I was used to.

I had to admit, she had a point. This was shaping up to be a milk run.

"Besides, *you* could be banishing demons if you had just paid attention to your instructor." Amy just couldn't help getting that jab in.

"I pay attention! I'm just not exactly good with runes."

Amy sighed. In front of us, the wine petered out of the first barrel. The demon moved to a second, opened up the same kind of perfectly round hole, and started to drink.

"Robert, you've got one of the biggest Senses out there. You use it

3

as well as any summoner I know. But if you don't start focusing on your rune work, you're always going to be half-baked."

"Look who's talking—it takes you all kinds of time to banish these things." I regretted saying that almost as soon as I said it. Amy wasn't Grace, and it was Grace I was angry with. I *felt* the icy silence Amy gave me, colder even than the dank concrete room around me.

I fought; Amy banished. Our little Mickey-Mouse demon-banishing team worked, after a fashion. *Grace* could have simply banished the demon with ease. Since Grace was out drinking martinis with her buddies, I got to risk my life on these little excursions instead.

Behind me, Amy pulled a small yellow pad and a ballpoint pen out of her purse. She scribbled something down; by the dab of her hand I knew she was sending a letter out to somewhere. A minute or two went by. The giant demon-chick cracked open another barrel with her flower-staff. The temptation to tell Amy to simply start the banishment struck me, but I feared that as soon as she began, we'd be attacked. Better to let the demon drink.

"Umm...Robert?" Amy said behind me.

"Yeah?" I asked, still gawking at the woman guzzling red wine.

"Look at this." Amy handed me a piece of stationary. It looked classy, embossed with the logo of an expensive Vegas hotel, but written on it in a hasty scribble was the following note:

AMY,

By the description, you've got a Maenad on your hands. Should be pretty easy. Just don't let her near any alcohol and you'll be fine. Stop bothering me for the little stuff—I'm busy here.
Grace

"So...WHAT if we've already let her chug two and a half barrels of wine?" I asked Amy.

"No idea. *Probably* not a good idea to let her keep going, though."

I took a deep breath. "For the record? This is *not* the easy job."

❧

I DREW a small throwing knife from under the rune-covered bracer on my wrist. Grace could summon all her weapons when she needed them, but my runework was nowhere near fast enough for that. Instead, I had to make do with what I could carry on me.

I brought up my Sense and shifted the steel along the knife's blade minutely, sharpening it to an almost molecular edge.

Summoning, directly through the Sense, or indirectly through runework, is simply the ability to move a thing from point A to point B. You can't *create* anything new; you can only move it around. That said, it's actually pretty easy to generate kinetic force by moving an object upward and letting it fall naturally.

Using my Sense, I summoned thirty of the wine barrels up to the ceiling; they immediately began falling towards the floor. Before they hit, I used my Sense to steal their kinetic force, allowing the barrels to settle gently to the floor with no damage.

I now had the momentum of thirty filled wine barrels, which I shaped behind the knife. I then threw the knife at the Maenad, using all the force of the barrels to accelerate it.

Round figures, here: a gallon is roughly ten pounds of liquid. Each barrel contained fifty gallons, or five hundred pounds. That's fifteen thousand pounds, and they accelerated over twenty feet of gravity. In other words, the kinetic force I stole from those barrels and applied to my little throwing knife came out to three hundred thousand foot pounds, give or take.

The point is, BMG .50 caliber ammunition, one of the deadliest pieces of ammo out there, produces a muzzle energy of between ten and fifteen thousand foot-pounds. My little throwing knife had roughly thirty times that stopping power behind a molecular edge when it slammed into the Maenad's side.

Which is why I was very, very chagrined when it splintered against her ivory skin, leaving not even a mark.

5

Her head spun gracefully away from her stream of wine, which then flowed down her chest. Those cloudy eyes fixed on me once again. She pointed the pine cone-topped staff at me, moving it in a delicate, intricate set of patterns. Her power was immense but her strategy was flawed. I could Sense the alcohol she tried to summon into my bloodstream, and I turned it aside easily.

The next attack wouldn't be so direct. She'd shown herself to be a summoner, of sorts. I had to get a handle on that power. I didn't see any runes, though; something else must be directing the power.

I summoned wine from the barrel still leaking around the Maenad and added some miniscule sharpened fragments of the concrete floor beneath me to it. I grabbed a wine glass from the tasting rack and summoned this slurry of sharpened dust and cabernet into it. My left hand swirled the glass slowly to keep the concrete in suspension.

Holding the glass with my right hand, I reached out with my Sense again. Once more the wine barrels appeared at the ceiling and dropped, and I grabbed their force for my own purposes.

I streamed the wine and sharp fragments through her staff at a massive pressure. *She* might be invulnerable at the moment, but the staff wasn't. It fell to pieces. She dropped its remnants to the floor.

Then she dropped into a crouch and sprang at me, her fingers spread and bent like claws. I summoned a barrel in her face; she collided with it, spraying wine all over the place in a bright purple shower. It gave me time to sidestep her assault.

I am not a trained hand-to-hand fighter. Over the past year, as these demonic appearances have grown more and more frequent, I've developed some good instincts for getting out of the way, but I'm no martial artist. That said, you don't need to be great at hand-to-hand when you can steal your opponents' kinetic force and use it against them. The Maenad whipped her arm out at me. I felt for the kinetic force behind the hand, intending to steal it.

And felt nothing.

Crap! I should have expected she'd be warded, too. I didn't have time to make a different move; her hand slammed into my side and gripped hard, cracking my lower rib and shooting pain through me.

She lifted me by my ribcage with one hand and flung me into the whitewashed cinder-block wall.

The pain ripped through me, jarring my concentration and forcing the Sense out of my grasp. Behind me, Amy gasped. The Maenad turned toward her. I slumped to the floor next to the wall and fought to maintain consciousness.

The Maenad moved fast, but all she had was speed and strength. As I sat on the floor, eyes closed, I took a deep, painful breath. The Sense rose back up within me, and once again I became a part of the Weave, that over-arching construct that is everything around us.

Amy had retreated along the wall, running at full speed. The Maenad streaked towards her, one arm up in the pre-grab position. She was almost out of the range of my Sense when I opened the floor underneath her. I summoned a chunk of the floor from beneath her to directly above her; her foot landed where she expected ground, and she got nothing. She tumbled into the hole I'd made, six feet down. The earth and concrete I'd displaced fell on top of her. I wrapped rebar from the concrete floor around her like a snake, tightening the bonds until they immobilized her.

Grace had once used a magnum-sized version of this trick with a field of rune phrases, but I didn't need the kind of power Grace had pulled there. This demon bitch just needed to hold still for a bit.

I coughed into my hand and looked at it. No blood; that was a good sign. "Now," I choked out at Amy. "Get her out of here."

The Maenad strained against the rebar, but to no avail. Amy performed the banishment. To do this, she constantly referred to her Grove Book, scribbling her runeset. After that came a dollop of blood from a Styrofoam container in her purse, and another minute's worth of concentration. I kept my Sense up throughout this, ready to respond if the Maenad did bend the rebar, but Amy finished with her runes and sent the wine-drinking bitch to whatever world she'd come from.

The cold wall pressed against my back as the pain took me.

∾

I WOKE up in the passenger seat of Amy's car. We sat parked in front of the Denny's on Pines Avenue. Amy held out a small jar of pills.

"Ibuprofen?" she asked. She passed me the bottle; I swallowed three or four pills dry and handed it back. She tucked it away in her purse.

"I figure I at least owe you dinner for that one," she said. I shrugged.

Amy hadn't spent a lot of time with me before Grace's vacation. In the short time Grace had been gone, I'd done a couple of jobs with her, but I didn't really know her. Still, I wasn't going to pass on free breakfast-for-dinner, so I followed her into the restaurant. My side hurt but I couldn't do much about it. The bruise would be pretty impressive later, and my ribs were going to hurt for a month, but I'd taken worse. At least this injury was easily hidden under a shirt.

We took a booth and ordered coffee, then both made a show of staring at the menu instead of talking to each other. Thankfully, the waitress interrupted our awkward silence. Amy ordered a nice, light sandwich. I ordered the biggest breakfast platter I could. The waitress took the menus and Amy and I sat looking at each other, with absolutely nothing we could talk about in a public setting.

Oh yeah, this was a great idea.

"So," Amy tried gamely, "how's school?"

Why is it that any time an adult tries to open a dialogue with a teenager, they go to that question? Generally, school is not something we enjoy while we're in it. It's certainly not the sort of thing we like to think about when we're *not* in it. Why do adults assume that it's the go-to topic of choice for starting a conversation?

"Um, fine," I said. This is the stock-standard, teenage response to this question. It is generally followed by a period of awkward silence, which is exactly what happened next.

"So, Grace is going to be back in a couple days," said Amy, trying again.

"Yeah," I said. I tried to hide the bitterness in my voice, but it didn't really stick. "I hope she had fun."

"Fun? Why would you think she's having fun?" asked Amy. She

8

seemed genuinely startled by the comment.

"Hmmm... Let's see. Grace gets to stay in a free hotel room in the middle of Las Vegas. Yeah, I would say she's having fun. *I'm* getting the crap kicked out of me, and she's on vacation."

"You know there's more to it than that."

"Not really. Oh, sure, there's all the business conference stuff, but those are just excuses for people to expense cool trips. One of my fosties—I think it was three sets ago—used to take them all the time."

"Robert, Grace is working very hard right now. She's gone to protect all of us. The last thing she needs is a surly teenager on her hands. Give her some support."

"Support?" I asked, my voice raising a little more than was perhaps prudent. "Both of us came very close to dying today. As it is, I'll be coughing for the next month. Did you feel like we were *supported?*"

"Yes," Amy said, softly but firmly. "Grace left me with ample support. You."

I rolled my eyes and dropped my voice to a harsh whisper. "Oh, sure," I flung at her. "*You're* supported. Of course, *I'm* the one with the cracked ribs and the concussion. You know, if Grace were here, we'd have been fine. I get cracked ribs so she can go on vacation. That's just not right."

Amy looked hurt. "That's not fair. If we don't get more help, all three of us are going to be in trouble. Grace is trying to get that help."

"And trying to get help *just happens* to mean Grace goes on a Las Vegas vacation. Where she can't be bothered by us or the 'small stuff.' Right. Look, I think I changed my mind. I'm not really all that hungry." I stood up and stalked out of the restaurant, leaving Amy to cancel my order. My stomach complained that the fosties were unlikely to provide anything better, but my pride overruled it.

I ended up sitting at the bus stop waiting for a ride home. Better to be on the bus than thrown under it. I had to listen to Grace because no one else would train me, but she had tossed me right under the wheels. Today I had managed to get away with a cracked rib. Tomorrow might be worse.

All because my master wanted to try her hand at the craps table.

9

GRACE

I TOOK the bus to Vegas using my shiny new ID, which proclaimed me to be Alice Harrington. It was a cramped, nerve-wracking way to spend one and a half days, but I expected that. Flying would have been much faster, but as a theoretically dead person, at least to the authorities, I didn't want to risk the airport security. At least at a bus depot, security was less worried about hijackers or terrorists and more about what mind-altering substance some teenage punk might be trying to smuggle on in their luggage.

Since summoners were the government's boogeymen and scapegoats for everything from the Great Recession to natural disasters, I really didn't want to be attracting their attention for the second time in six months. According to the police files, I was dead. I'd prefer to stay that way—at least on paper.

I'd also abandoned my usual loud colors and flashy bangles for this trip. I wore non-descript gray sweats with my dark hair tied up under a plain and subdued head scarf. The last thing I needed was some clueless tourist recognizing my unique fashion style or face. I'd been on every six o'clock news alert across the country as a murderous summoner with no regard for human life for weeks straight. Supposedly, I had summoned a large demon to carry out the largest public hit against the Grove organization in U.S. history. Oh, and since I'd also saved Robert, I'd also been labeled a kidnapper. I can't forget that part.

Since the laws in the United States categorize summoning as a felony of the worst kind, the Groves operate not unlike a very large underground mafia family or gang syndicate. Reality is that, without us, the world as we know it would cease to exist. Summoners mend tears in this reality and keep it from leaking into others—and vice versa. Maybe if what we did wasn't so vital, we would have given in to the pressure to eradicate summoning a long time ago. No matter how bad the punishments, the alternative was still worse.

Holding in a deep sigh, I picked a seat in the far back corner of the bus and laid my duffle bag on the adjoining seat. If my cover ID somehow failed drastically, I at least had a chance of busting my way out the back of the bus without hurting anyone. The other deterrent I'd brought was a thick book of the break-your-toes variety. I kept my nose buried in it the whole trip, surreptitiously making sure no one paid any attention to me. Thankfully, the bus trip proved long and boring.

Seattle Grove Director Phineas Brandiole was waiting for me at the Las Vegas bus depot. He was technically my "sponsor," for putting me forward as the interim Grove director for Spokane, and my mentor at the Cooperative Council Meeting. The Seattle headquarters served as a hub for the whole northwest region, after all.

This was the first one of these shindigs I'd been invited to, and I was a bit nervous. No doubt there'd be political crap to deal with, so I just wanted to submit a petition for backup and get out.

I still hated Director Brandiole after the way he'd sent me to face a demon alone last fall, but I admit it was kind of nice to see a familiar face at the end of such a long journey. A short flunky in a tidy gray suit stood to his left, a frown creasing his bland, spectacled face. I hadn't met *this* one before. Then the director opened his mouth and reminded me *why* I loathed him.

"You're late," he grumped at me. "We've been standing out here in the heat for the last half-hour. Did you have trouble with your ID?"

"No. Talk to the bus driver if you want to complain about the delay. He's the one behind the wheel." I looked at him more closely. "If it's that uncomfortable, why didn't you go sit in your car or something?"

"If I'd done that, you would have blown right past me and gone to the hotel by yourself." He made it sound like an accusation. I took a closer look.

Perspiration stood out on his brow, plastering his dark copper curls to his forehead, and his dress shirt was drenched with sweat under his light sport jacket. He did indeed look really uncomfortable. I admit it: it gave me a small happy that I'd repaid him a fraction of the inconvenience and discomfort he'd cost me during the last few months. It couldn't match the spine-numbing fear or near-death experiences he'd also gifted me, of course, but still... My lips twitched and his brow drew down into a deeper frown. I cleared my throat and tried to smooth my expression into something less obviously amused.

Director Brandiole heaved a sigh and gestured to the man standing beside him, who took a step forward. "This is Thaddeus. He is also part of the Northwest Council's delegation. He's currently on loan as my aide, courtesy of the Boise Grove."

Thaddeus held his hand out for me to shake. "Pleasure to meet you, Ms. M—ah—Harrington. I don't think there's anyone at this meeting who hasn't heard of you. Quite the adventuress, aren't you? Your reports read better than some fiction tales."

I shook his hand a bit hesitantly as I returned his greeting, unsure whether he meant that last bit as a compliment or a dig. I decided to let it slide for the time being

"I appreciate the escort." I flashed a smile, attempting to change the subject. "But what's the big deal if I show up by myself? It can't be that easy to get lost here. This is supposedly the biggest Agricultural Show in the western United States, stuck smack dab in the middle of the City that Never Sleeps. Anyone would be able to point me in the right direction."

Brandiole actually groaned. He pulled out his key fob, and a black shiny car in the nearby parking lot beeped. He opened the door to the passenger side and motioned me in.

"Director Moore," he said to me as I climbed in, shocking me by using both my name and my title, "that is exactly what I'm afraid of." Then he slammed the door and circled to get in on the driver's side. My eyebrows lifted in surprise.

Thaddeus slid into the back seat, his eyes shining a little bit too much. I had a horrible suspicion he not only knew that Brandiole and I hated each other, but was secretly enjoying the fact.

The interior of the car smelled of shiny black leather and an overpowering car cologne. As Brandiole turned the key in the ignition, he glowered sideways at me but didn't explain his earlier remark. Nor did he move to pull the car out of the parking lot. The interior of the vehicle filled with the hiss of the air conditioning and the quiet rumble of the engine, but no one said anything for a good two minutes. We all just sat there.

"Nice rental," I said finally, to break the awkward silence. Brandiole's gaze narrowed further as his brow furrowed downward in poorly concealed irritation. He opened his mouth, caught Thaddeus' expectant gaze in the back seat, and shook his head, snapping his jaw shut. He put the car into gear and started backing it out of the parking lot.

"I am so glad you find the mode of conveyance acceptable." The words were bland, and yet the undercurrent in the car was anything but. The atmosphere vibrated like a guitar string that was about ready to snap.

Maybe I was just being hyper-sensitive. I had just put in thirty-six hours looking over my shoulder, expecting the Feds to pounce on me any minute. Anyone's nerves would be shot after that. Still, I couldn't shake the feeling that something wasn't quite right.

I glanced in the rear-view mirror. Thaddeus sat quietly and neatly in the back seat, like some southern debutante. Even the air around him seemed proper. I watched him curiously as the buildings started to flash past out the window. His eyes caught mine in the rear-view and crinkled slightly at the corners.

"Have you been to Las Vegas before, Ms. Moore?" he asked conversationally.

"No, I haven't. I'm not really into gambling and all that." I realized I could be taken as staring, and felt a small flush crawl up my cheekbones. I refused to look down, though.

"Now, that's not true." Thaddeus still smiled at me, but it sparkled with frost around the edges. "From the report I read about Spokane, it sounds like you like to gamble quite a bit. Fortunately for you, it seems you had some beginners' luck."

I opened my mouth to issue a scathing rebuttal. Director Brandiole cut me off with a hand on my arm and a sickeningly avuncular tone of voice. "Thaddeus, you know Grace is one of the Seattle Grove's best and brightest. I'm sure there was no gambling involved. Of course, there's always room to second-guess after a mission is completed, but you have to trust your expert on the ground. Every strategy student knows that. Director Grace just got here. She must be tired. Let's give her a chance to rest and freshen up before we talk business, eh? Plenty of time to get acquainted later."

Thaddeus straightened his mouth into a tight smile. "But of course. I wouldn't want to make the interim director uncomfortable."

Apparently the devil known as Phineas Brandiole was on my side this time. Now why didn't that make me feel any better?

I OPENED the door of my hotel room to find Brandiole on the other side, this time without Thaddeus or any other flunkies in tow. He shouldered his way past me without so much as a hello.

My irritation with him ratcheted up another three notches. "Do come in. Make yourself at home. Obviously, mi casa es su casa." I shut the door a bit more sharply than was strictly necessary behind him. He paced quickly across the sitting area and then spun to face me. One of his hands braced his hip; the other flailed about in wide arcs as he utterly failed to articulate whatever had brought him to my door. The meetings didn't start until tomorrow, so it was really unlikely I was late for something, or that I had missed an important meeting already. I settled myself in the chair near the door and waited to see what would happen.

"Do you realize the situation you're in?" he asked suddenly. So much for a greeting or preliminary attempt at pleasantries. "The situation you've put us both in? It is highly important to me that you not do anything while you're here to upset the balance I've worked so hard at achieving."

Ooookay, so what were we arguing about here? Me, presumably, eschewing mischief and all other general riffraff? I believed I could do that for four days without the obligatory pep talk.

"Excuse me? I believe I'm here to represent the Spokane Grove's interests and needs."

"Oh. Is that all?" he asked in an unmistakably sarcastic tone. "Let me ask you this: I sent you into a volatile situation, which you proceeded to make more volatile and more public. Do you actually think appointing you as the Spokane Grove Director was a popular move? That the other directors applauded my decision?"

"I assumed they appreciated the fact that I stopped an overcharged Cornuprocyon from paying them all a visit. Single-handedly saving all of their butts from Cythymau seems pretty applause-worthy to me." I put my hands on my hips and glared back.

"Well, it wasn't a popular decision. In fact, you can say it was hugely *unpopular*. So much so, I've almost rescinded it several times. But whether you are in Spokane as director or not, the other Groves still hold me accountable for your actions. Your response to the Spokane Grove damaged *my* reputation. Appointing you Grove Director was the only move that allowed the Seattle Grove to save some face and avoid us having to expose more Grove assets to law enforcement. Did you think I wanted to give you a promotion for that public fiasco? To most Grove officials, myself included, Director Moore, you are a necessary inconvenience. To a few of them, like the Great Plains's Ryan Wilson, your existence as a director is a weakness in the Northwest Council he plans to exploit to gain power. He's already got his protégé crawling all over me. Well. You met him earlier. Thaddeus is such a delightful man, don't you think? And Director Wilson insists on pushing him forward as the only suitable leader for Spokane to anyone who will listen. I would prefer that Wilson doesn't succeed in replacing you with Thaddeus, as it would then give him an opening to remove *me*."

"If my situation is so precarious, and I'm so unreliable, why even bring me here?" I asked, flabbergasted.

"If I didn't, the opposition would see it as an admission you can't be trusted, and gain more support."

"But apparently you don't trust me!"

"I trust you more than I trust Ryan Wilson," he grumbled.

"That doesn't seem to be saying much." I crossed my arms over my chest and waited.

"It says a lot," Director Brandiole retorted. "If you weren't politically blind as a bat, you could see that. Just don't do anything to draw more attention to yourself or embarrass me for the next few days. If you go down, you're dragging all of the Pacific Northwest with you. We're surrounded by piranhas, and those who aren't piranhas are sharks."

"Since when did this become one of those fear-based reality shows?"

The quip slipped out before I could stop it. I was too busy trying to calm down my suddenly hammering heart. I wished my biggest worry was still how to attract a few more summoners to a Grove that currently had few resources and no fringe benefits. Damned if I was going to admit to Director Brandiole that I was less than confident, though. I threw him a mocking smile. At this point, I wasn't even sure if I was mocking him or myself.

"Oh, a reality show would be vastly preferable at this point, I assure you. Those shows deal mostly in smoke and mirrors. Our position has nothing to do with illusion."

"So, is someone going to try to mug me in the hallway?" My stomach did a lurching somersault despite my glib words. "You may want to warn them I'm really handy with pepper spray."

"If they don't scare you, they should," Brandiole answered dryly. "If this conference goes poorly, a mugging would be preferable. That, at least, would be over one way or the other in under a minute. The people here can make both of our lives very uncomfortable for a long time into the future."

I crossed my arms over my chest and resisted the urge to roll my eyes. It felt like I'd been through this discussion before. Oh, right. I had.

"Your apprentice is a subject for a whole other discussion, and none of it's in your favor," he added.

"What's Robert got to do with this?"

Brandiole waved his hand dismissively. "We can talk about him another time. I'm more worried about what *you're* likely to do right now."

"Well, I'm not going to stride down the hallway knocking heads together for fun, if that's what you're asking. I will be the epitome of a reliable Grove director."

"See that you remember that when you talk to the other Grove delegates and directors in attendance." He gave me a sidelong look. "And try not to get us all killed. While we're on that subject, do something about your appearance. We wouldn't want someone accidentally recognizing you after all." He moved back toward the door and gave my dirty gray sweat pants one last look of distaste. "I sincerely hope you brought significantly more formal clothes than that. If not, arrange some. And don't let any of the other directors see you like that. You'll set yourself up to be bullied."

"You're joking," I said flatly.

"No, Director Moore. That was advice, whether you believe it or not. *Try* not to start any more catastrophes. I'll see you tomorrow."

As much as I hated Director Brandiole, I heeded his advice and changed into a long, sleeveless black dress before going in search of the buffet. I'd packed much more conservative clothes for this trip that didn't match any of the descriptions from my manhunt last summer. I had purposely left behind anything that would make me look like a "demented gypsy," as Robert so delicately put it. My giant all-purpose shoulder bag had even been switched out for a much less cool handbag. If anything, I thought of my new look as more "classy schoolmarm." I really felt naked without my bag and bangles, though.

I shut my hotel room door behind me and braced myself to walk down the hotel's pretentious hallways. This town might not be on my top ten list of places I wanted to be, but at least there was one thing here where I knew exactly how I stood. Time to go hide out in the buffet.

Out the hotel's large windows I could see giant puzzle gardens that must have taken obscene amounts of water to maintain in the desert, and more casinos off in the distance. The whole hallway was coated in opulent mirrors and lush velvets. Why seeing yourself and other tourists from three angles is considered something desirable or chic is beyond me.

The buffet turned out to be monstrously huge, taking up four room-length tables, and absolutely decadent. I loaded up a plate with calamari, shrimp scampi, crab legs, and a flatiron steak, with some token greens. My very own custom surf-and-turf, with cheddar garlic biscuits on the side. It looked just as good as anything I could get on the waterfront in Seattle. I took my treasure to a small two-person table in a corner of the dining room and proceeded to savor the best thing that had happened to me all day.

As I sat, I watched the people flowing through the buffet line and back into the casino. The front for this meeting was an agricultural convention, but I had never seen more high heels, suits, and evening gowns. I guess folks really do like getting their glamor on, although I've never really seen the point.

Supposedly that's why so many events like this one take place in popular locations. You get better attendance. In the Grove's particular case, I guessed it had more to do with Nevada's reputation for being friendly to organized crime—Sin City and all that.

Don't get me wrong; the authorities knew something was going down, but the agricultural convention gave everyone a valid reason for being here. Think of the opening wedding scene from *The Godfather*; it's the same idea. They might be suspicious of a larger gathering full of people of interest, but without someone actively breaking the law, they couldn't do anything about it.

Me though, I needed to keep off their radar altogether, or I really would be taking a one-way ride to maximum security. I narrowed my eyes as I watched the crowd.

Some of the overdressed people flowing past my table could even be the ones who wanted to remove me as director. I munched on a shrimp absently as I pondered the implications of that. I didn't want to believe Brandiole, but I didn't see why he'd lie about it either. It couldn't hurt to act with caution for now. When I got home, I'd see about some further precautions. I just needed to focus on getting new members for the Spokane Grove while I was here and get the hell out. *No fights, Grace,* I reminded myself.

I felt a note pop into existence in my pocket. Curious, I pulled it out and found a question from Amy. She and Robert had found a hole in the Weave, and something had come through. I read her scribbled description and breathed a sigh of relief. Given the staff she was describing and the manner of dress, it was a minor follower of Bacchus that they should be able to handle without too much difficulty.

The stupid handbag I'd brought to Vegas with me didn't have any of my standard necessities in it, up to and including a pen. Vegas is the center of the service industry, though; the waitress at the nearest station loaned me a pen and a bit of stationary. I scribbled a quick note back and grabbed a stall in the powder room to send my reply.

It did reassure me to know that no matter what happened here, they had everything under control while I was away. My plate contained enough just getting through this political minefield with everyone intact. If I got extremely lucky I might also find us some more resources and gather a few new members, but at this point that was looking like icing on the cake.

When I came back into the dining room, someone else was sitting at my table. He was kind of a squat little man, not fat exactly, but stocky. He wore a tux, but the way he wore it resembled an eight-bit penguin—blocky and awkward. The designer couldn't have intended that look. It was not helped by his substitution of a bowie for the more traditional bow tie. His thinning brown hair culminated in a small, shiny bald spot at the back of his head. He watched me come out of the bathroom and waved me toward the table with an affable sweep of his arm. I almost turned around and looked to see if he was gesturing to someone behind me, but he was already seated opposite my food. Since he obviously knew it was my table, I'd just end up looking stupid and cowardly if I tried to ignore him and walk past. Fresh from all of Brandiole's warnings, my nerves jangled in spite of his beaming face.

Never present your back to a potential enemy, Gracie.

"Director Moore, it is a pleasure to meet you. Forgive me for interrupting your dinner. I've heard so much about you, I just couldn't wait to talk to you until tomorrow." The man got to his feet as I approached the table, and pulled out the chair next to my plate. "Please go back to eating and don't let me disturb you." He threw me a wink. "I promise I'm a pleasant dinner companion."

I hesitated for a fraction of a second, but really, my only two options were to sit down or snub him. Since I had no idea who he was, the latter seemed like a bad knee-jerk reaction.

I smiled and held out my hand for him to shake. "I was just thinking I'd love some company for dinner. It's very kind of you to volunteer." I moved around to sit in the chair he held out. "Sadly, I don't know you by sight, sir. I'm afraid I'll have to ask for a more mundane introduction." He slid my chair back up to the table and resumed his previous seat. I picked up my fork and tried not to look quizzical.

"No worries, my dear. I'm the Great Plains Council head and the Kansas City Grove Director. Just go ahead and call me Ryan. No need to be all formal-like. I'm sure we will be great friends. You are, after all, a hero to some here."

My smile froze in place. Of course. The one person Director

Brandiole warned me to avoid was the first one who sought me out. Just great.

Purely on auto-pilot, I murmured a pleasantry in response, my brain racing. If he really did want his protégé in my shoes, what in the world was his goal in approaching me first?

"I am most impressed with you, Director Moore. It isn't everyone who could get into the situation you did and walk out alive. Or rescue a young untrained boy—who in your circumstances was little more than a liability. You must be the eternal optimist."

"It's true the Seattle Grove sent me there by myself, but they didn't send me without support, sir—"

"Please call me Ryan."

"Um, Ryan." I cleared my throat and started again. "While I was the only summoner physically there, the Seattle Grove did provide a lot of support and resources to my mission. Also contrary to what the rumor mill seems to be spreading around, my surprise apprentice turned out to be a lot of help."

He raised his eyebrows. "Ah, am I to understand you had everything under control then? Honestly, when I saw the news reports, I fear I blamed Phineas for sending someone in so woefully underprepared."

The food which had brought me such joy just minutes before suddenly caked in my mouth like sawdust. His words obviously contained a trap, but how to avoid it? I held up a finger, signaling a pause, and reached for the tall water glass by my plate.

The glass's heavily condensed shape shook slightly in my hand as I scrambled for an answer. Admitting I wasn't prepared threw Brandiole under a bus and called into doubt my current ability to maintain leadership of the Grove. On the other hand, brushing it off as having the situation under control last summer would make me out to be a callous killer of civilians and flouter of Grove rules. My continued leadership of the Grove would still be called into question —just for different reasons. The cold heaviness of the glass served as an anchor; I left my hand loosely curled around its base after setting it back down and tried for a response that split the difference somewhere in the middle.

"As with any emergency situation, unexpected circumstances can arise, but I did the best possible job I could with the resources and people I had available to me." As a rebuttal it wasn't great, but it was the best response I could think of. Damn all these politics. Give me a demon to banish over this kind of political doubletalk any day.

"Oh, I have no doubt that's true. But surely you didn't mean to end up on evening news alerts all over the country. It's made your face very familiar to a lot of people, not just me. If I were you, I would resent the Grove for putting me in a situation where that outcome was inevitable." The question rankled, but even if I did feel slightly resentful of Director Brandiole, Ryan here wasn't someone I wanted to confide in.

"No outcomes are inevitable," I replied, my pique making me clip my words a bit shorter than usual.

"I am so very glad to hear you feel the outcome in Spokane was not inevitable. Please do enlighten me. I am awash with curiosity."

Well damn. I walked right into that one.

"Like I said, some unforeseen circumstances arose," I repeated woodenly.

"Unforeseen circumstances? Like running into a young and out-of-control boy with more power than sense? Are you saying your apprentice forced you into making those public displays?"

Under the subtle, hostile pressure in his gaze, my blood pressure was slowly inching up, but I fought to keep my composure, temper, and tongue under control. I tightened my hand on the water glass of sanity and took a deep breath.

"I'm not saying that at all, sir. Robert is not responsible for any of the events of last summer, except perhaps showing extraordinary courage in using power he didn't know he had to save people he hadn't met."

"But it can't have been the demon that was unforeseen, surely? I mean, the Seattle Grove sent you to investigate with their resources at your disposal. A reasonable person would assume they expected to find something powerful. That leaves the boy as the only X-factor."

"That's false. It leaves Cythymau as the only X-factor."

"Ah, the mysterious demon from another Weave who is apparently set on world domination," he drawled. "Yes, I was wondering when you'd bring him up. And what concrete proof do you have that this Cythymau even exists?"

My ears rang with the effort to keep my suddenly surging frustration and anger in check. The hand holding the cool slickness of the water glass tightened to a death grip.

Fuck this dude. I didn't put my ass on the line last summer so I could come back and have politicians doubt whether the events in my report ever even happened. The arrogance and small-mindedness of it just floored me.

"I spoke with him," I forced the words out through gritted teeth in a passably civil if somewhat frayed tone of voice. "Robert went to his Weave and was almost captured by him." I envisioned the ice water from the glass in my hand flowing over my temper and sending up billows of cooling steam. This man was a pompous ass, but he wouldn't get my goat. I wouldn't say anything stupid.

"I believe you misunderstand me, Director. I asked you what concrete evidence you have that this demon exists. I believe that *you* believe you conversed with a demon named Cythymau, but that is not concrete evidence. That's belief."

"Robert *saw* him," I said again.

"And now we're back to your unvetted, untrained, and—from everything I've read—frankly unreliable apprentice. Has it not occurred to you, Miss Moore, that your apprentice would do anything to keep himself in the good graces of the Grove, given his history so far?"

My jaw clenched harder. Wilson had managed to demote me to a naive and stupid female and insult Robert all with one question. And he wasn't. Done. Talking.

"Let's think about this for a moment. According to your apprentice, he came back from a supposed encounter with this dastardly and overpowered mastermind completely untouched. That hardly seems possible given the *supposed* power level of your apprentice and this hypothetical demon. Which again leaves me with no concrete evidence, and only two questions. One: Did your apprentice lie about the existence of Cythymau to save his own skin? Or two: Has his stint in the foster system left him so mentally unsound that he's convinced himself he met this figment to save his own skin?"

A white, buzzing haze of contempt and anger for the man in front of me filled my head. Robert and I didn't survive just so he could be judged by small-minded dirt bags like this guy. I jerked to my feet so I wouldn't yell.

My anchor hand moved automatically as well.

The dining room spun in my vision as I turned and walked stoically out of the room. I wouldn't say anything. Nothing. It wasn't until the mirrored hallway showed me the glass still clutched in my left hand that I realized it was empty.

I noticed the pointing and whispering about the same time a drenched and coldly furious Ryan Wilson strode out the door behind me, making straight for the elevators. He did spare a venomous glance in my direction. My hand tightened reflexively on the glass; in one of my less honorable moments, a chuckle of dismay and satisfaction started to bubble up. Yeah, I rocked at this politics thing.

Somebody get me the hell home.

～

I WENT BACK to my room to change clothes for the second time that day. My stomach still protested my abbreviated meal, so room service offered an attractive alternative.

My new theory pretty much said that if I stayed in my room for the rest of the evening I couldn't attract as much trouble. Even if the spectacle earlier didn't manage to upset the 'delicate balance,' as Director Brandiole put it, my original hope of winning more support for the Spokane Grove seemed rather anemic.

I ate some lovely Eggs Benedict, flipped through the channels on the TV, and ended up staring at the ceiling, wondering how I would protect Robert and Amy if this all went south.

It was still much too early in the evening to be cooped up in my room flailing about Grove politics. The elaborate gardens outside my window finally made up my mind. I'd go down to get my mind off the things I couldn't change—at least until the meetings tomorrow where I could make my case for help.

The sun was low in the sky as I stepped outside, but the air hit me like a living thing. Heat rose from the asphalt until vanquished by the shady and graveled paths of the garden. The shrubs and plants were artfully arranged with long airy paths, little grottos, benches, and gazebos. One of the gazebos in the middle of the garden, set beside a small fountain that sent a little stream flowing through it, called to me. Even in the heat, it felt good not being cooped up. I stretched my feet out in front of the bench and closed my eyes for a few minutes. That is, until someone inconveniently cleared his throat behind me.

Director Brandiole stood glowering over me. Once he had my attention, he moved into the gazebo to sit opposite me.

"I can't believe I leave you alone for less than two hours, and you already get in a fight with Ryan Wilson." He sighed. "Can you really be that inept?"

"Hey, I just went down to get some food. He showed up at my table and picked the fight. The aggression was all on his side."

"There are forty or fifty witnesses who say otherwise. Half the Council saw you throw a drink in Ryan Wilson's face. Not very suave, to say the least, and now you have a reputation for explosive temper tantrums. You can see why that's a less-than-desirable quality in a new director, I hope?"

"I dunno, I could have really lost my temper and shoved my foot all the way up where he deserved," I countered, baring my teeth in a wolfish grin.

"If you ever do that, I am washing my hands of you and handing you and your apprentice over to all of your haters and be damned about it. Why that encyclopedic knowledge of yours had to be coupled with such a damned difficult personality is one of the world's greatest mysteries." Brandiole sighed again. "Obviously, he's one of the more vocal of the parties opposing your elevation to Grove Director. Try to avoid encountering him in the future, if at all possible, for the sake of my sanity."

"What the hell!" I exploded. "What I want to know is how any of this political fiasco can be an acceptable response to my request for aid! We have three people, Brandiole, *three people* to maintain the Weave for three hundred and forty thousand square miles and keep Cythymau on the right side of it. Not even you are supporting my request. One person is all I asked for—one person from each region. What a load of bullshit."

He grabbed my shoulder and gave me a little shake, shocking me all the way to my shoes. "Look at me! I know you thought you could come here and get people for your Grove. But I told you it wouldn't be that easy. You can't do anything for Spokane if you get removed as Grove head. Just focus on staying away from Ryan Wilson."

"We're here to participate in negotiations with other Groves," I protested. "How can I avoid meeting him?"

"He's one of the big players. You're not. Don't sit next to him. If he sits next to you, think of an excuse to leave and return to a different seat. No matter what he says, don't engage, and don't get in a shouting match with him. If he's standing there smiling and you're shouting, you're the one who looks stupid. You understand me?"

I nodded. These political intrigues really confounded the hell out of me, but anyone could see that it was better not to give more ammunition to an opponent. By appearing to talk with Director Wilson, I'd given credence to the fact that he might know something worth listening to, then compounded that assumption by publicly fighting with him. Damn.

Brandiole gave me a considering look before surprising me by leaning in to give me a slap on the back. "Oh well, no lasting harm done. It's possible you may have even gained a few fans by throwing that drink in his face. Tons of people have wanted to, but you're the only one to really do it. Just don't do it again. Once can always be shrugged off as a heat-of-the-moment fluke. Twice, and it's a pattern. Remember that next time you get the urge to do something impulsive like this, because no one else is going to forget."

"I hope I'm not interrupting?" A middle-aged women in a navy blue pantsuit stood just outside the gazebo, dark-skinned, with hair beginning to gray at the temples. Her lilting accent had a disarming quality, but trust came hard today.

"Director Brandiole, I would very much like an introduction to this young lady." She stepped over and grasped my hand in a firm grip. "It is a pleasure," she said.

"Director Moore, please meet Director Abigail Diaz of the Las Vegas Grove. She's been instrumental in setting up this council."

She nodded. "I have very much wanted to discuss the events from last summer in person with you. There is much debate and heat over the events in the Cooperative Council, as you might expect. While any formal conclusions must wait for the internal investigation, I would still like to hear the events from your own perspective."

Fearing another incident like earlier, I looked at Brandiole, but he seemed to be waiting for me to plunge in. So I gave her the thumbnail version, downplaying Robert's role in the opening shenanigans as much as possible, while highlighting his assistance in the successful defeat of the super-juiced Cornuprocyon demon that tore up Spokane last fall.

Director Diaz took several moments after I had stopped speaking to consider. Finally she turned to Brandiole and said, "The Seattle Grove and the Las Vegas Grove have enjoyed many mutual interests over the years. I've heard rumors lately that Director Wilson has his sights set on your eastern border, Phineas."

"If his former apprentice breathing down my neck isn't a good indicator of that, I don't know what is," Brandiole grumped. "You hardly need the rumor mill to make that deduction. I'm not letting that go anywhere."

"Well, see that you don't. I don't want him breathing down *my* neck next." Abigail straightened her jacket and leaned in. "I am hearing that the Mexican, Prince Rupert, and Midwest Groves have all agreed to back Thaddeus if a vote arises. The Eastern Seaboard, Quebec and New England are still undecided. And that vote will arise by tomorrow, going off the reactions to the scene in the dining hall earlier."

Brandiole's face turned a little pasty. "Has the opposition grown so large that you think they'll be able to force a vote on Grace's removal?"

"I'm not sure how many votes he has, but I would say it looks to be a close-run thing. I expect they'll make their decision in the morning, and either way, they *will* be pushing for a vote. Whether they get it or not, well… If I were you, I'd talk to Director Ahren of the Texas Grove and see if you can use him to shore up some support. Even better, don't give Wilson any more ideas to use against you to gain more momentum. Although it may already be too late, considering that whole display earlier today. I should be going, though. Best of luck to you both."

I watched her leave with a surreal feeling that my jaw must still be on the ground. A vote to remove me as interim director? That fast? I just got here.

"Do you think that was sincere advice?" I asked Brandiole, hardly believing that I was trusting him for direction. He shrugged.

"As sincere as you're going to get here. Abigail Diaz has been a high-ranking council member for many years. You don't get there or stay there without being a very canny judge of political climates. It can't hurt to at least seek out Director Ahren and discover his views before tomorrow's meeting. I believed we had enough support coming into this weekend to at least maintain our status quo, but if Abigail Diaz says it isn't so, then I have to give her opinion some credence."

He stood up, looking more like the frazzled Director I remembered from my last fateful meeting with him eight months ago.

"Well," I said, "I guess we'd better go find this Director Ahren then."

~

THREE COORDINATORS, two bellhops and four personal assistants later, we'd found out that Director Ahren planned to relax in the Casino's spa after his last engagement. The hell with being cautious. I was going to talk to this guy if it killed me. Brandiole must have seen that move coming, because he leaned over and hissed in my ear, "You can't accost him in the spa! You'd be a stalker! That's just creepy. Plus you suck at politics. What are you planning to say?"

"It's only creepy if he knows I meant to run into him in the spa, and you forget two major assets I'll have on hand that you just don't have."

"What?" he asked.

"Boobs."

I winked at him and waltzed through the door into the spa before he could stop me. Once inside though, it was obvious there was one large flaw with my plan. It was split into a men's side and a women's side. There would be no bumping into Director Ahren unless I managed to catch him just as he was coming in or going out. So much for my brilliant idea.

"Miss?" the man at the spa reception asked. "Can I help you? Did you have an appointment?"

Dang.

"No, that's ok." I smiled at him, "I've just remembered it isn't until tomorrow. I just got turned around. Thank you, though."

"Why, Director M-Harrington!" a male voice behind me exclaimed. I turned to find a tall, tanned man with shockingly blonde hair. I didn't recognize him. "How do you do? I'm Luke Ahren. I hear you've been trying to find me."

He turned to the man at the check-in counter. "Justin, you wouldn't mind pushing my appointment back just fifteen minutes, so I can talk to Ms. Harrington, would you?"

Justin was happy to oblige. I'd wanted to talk to the director. Now I had the opportunity.

"Is that little side room being used right now? Wonderful. I promise we'll be right out. Only take a minute." He placed his hand on the small of my back and smoothly but inexorably ushered me into a small waiting room.

The only problem was that I didn't actually know what I wanted to say to this person now that I'd found him, other than that I needed him to support me, and save both me and Robert. Blurting it out hardly seemed like an option.

The waiting area consisted of two overstuffed leather recliners facing a small table. He motioned me into one of them and sat down in the opposite one. I sat upright, my cold hands on my knees, waiting for a genius plan to hit me upside the head.

"Well, Ms. Harrington. It is a pleasure to meet you, and you definitely have my attention. What can I do for you today?" He leaned back in the recliner, completely relaxed, his ankle resting on his knee. His weathered skin had crow's feet around his eyes that crinkled when he smiled. But that smooth smile hid a keen political mind. Every word he spoke had been weighed before it hit the air. I took a deep breath.

"Director Ahren, I came to ask if you would help the Spokane Grove and the Pacific Northwest Region protect their autonomy in the current situation. We would, of course, help the Lone Star Grove in any way we can in return."

"I am still not convinced how immediate the threat presented by this demon in another Weave really is, but in Texas, we've always been big fans of autonomy. How does protecting your autonomy actually help my members? Fancy words about assisting us is fine, but—" He leaned down before continuing bluntly. "I've seen your roster. You only have two summoners and one apprentice in your Grove. Not much help in a pinch, if you ask me."

"We're helping you right now," I said desperately.

"Well now, is that so?" he drawled, leaning back into his chair again. "How do you see that?"

"I have Ryan Wilson's full attention at the moment. If you leave me where I am, I'll make sure I keep it. Summoner's honor."

He steepled his fingers and thought for a moment. "I'll keep that in mind tomorrow. Nice to meet you, Ms. Harrington. Now I really must be going."

Well, so much for my first stab at political negotiation. I guessed that after this, it was time to let the chips fall as they may and hope I'd hedged my bets right.

DIRECTOR DIAZ WAS UNCANNILY accurate in her predictions. Wilson's supporters were calling for a vote to remove me before breakfast, and by dinner the next day, they had it. The evening's meetings were pushed out a day under the reasoning that it really was a waste of time to let me make any petitions or ask for arrangements until the question of who spoke for my Grove was put to rest.

I entered the hotel's executive conference room and sat next to Director Brandiole while I waited for my fate to be decided with cold and clammy hands.

Director Diaz stepped up to the podium and cleared her throat. "We've heard the arguments both for and against confirming Director Grace Moore in her position on the Cooperative Council the last two days. Significant reservations have been voiced by a substantial number of council members. Her qualifications and experience have been brought into question. Therefore, we will first have a vote on whether to rescind Director Moore's interim director status. If you have not yet put your ballots in the receptacles at the back of the room, please do so now."

After several tense moments while the ballots were counted, Director Diaz stepped back up to the podium. "Director Grace Moore is re-affirmed in her position as interim Grove Director of the Pacific Northwest Region's Spokane Grove on a probationary basis. This council will reconvene and evaluate her appointment to full-time Grove Director at the next Cooperative Council scheduled for January, or as necessary if other circumstances which affect Grove Council interests arise."

Thaddeus stood next to Ryan Wilson with a smugly satisfied look on his face. We'd won this match, but looking at their slimy grins, I suddenly wondered whether we were actually winning whatever political cat-and-mouse game they were playing.

That tore it. I needed out of here ASAP. Whatever thin welcome had met me in Vegas had just very nearly missed hitting its expiration. If it came to another vote with these folks, lady luck just might run out on me. I hoped for all of our sakes that what happened in Vegas, stayed in Vegas.

ROBERT

THIS TEST DIDN'T REALLY MATTER.

I mean, it was the last set of tests in our senior year of high school. The teachers made a big deal about them, but everyone knew it was bogus. I'd already submitted my application to Eastern Washington University and been accepted; as long as I scraped a "D" on these tests, enough to squeak by, it didn't matter.

My fellow students and I had basically been lighthearted about the whole senior-finals endeavor. It wasn't like *actually* taking tests, it was more *going through the motions* of taking tests. Acting like high school students for just a bit longer, because that is what society expected of us.

The point here is, I wasn't thinking of them as tests. I hadn't cheated on *any* of my previous tests. I knew that using any tricks in class would just get back around to Grace, and I didn't want to think about what would happen to me if she found out I'd been abusing my "gift." *Tests* were sacred things; I didn't use my power on tests.

I had worked all year to make sure that I was a good little nerd. If a bully picked on me (and they did), I didn't do any unnecessarily cruel things. I'd already done that once, and the amount of trouble it had caused me just wasn't worth it. With the exception of my extra lessons with Grace, I lived my senior year of high school like any normal foster kid. I spent my time in the band room with my saxophone, and kept my head down when walking the hallowed halls, though my power had hummed in my head, pressuring me to get out and destroy the bullies who mocked me. I could've joined the basketball team and made every shot, or played baseball and hit nothing but homers. That primal desire to show up each and every one of the smirking faces surrounding me had been eating away at me all year, and I hadn't given in.

But I'd wanted to. The knowledge that I *could* had festered in me all year long, and now we were doing something that had all the appearance of a test but none of the consequences. And since this test was consequence-free...

I closed my eyes and called my Sense to me. The classroom was quiet; only an occasional cough punctuated the constant scratching of pencils. That made it easy to concentrate and fall into the Sense.

Bringing up my Sense is always an intense experience. When I use it, I become aware of everything within roughly fifty feet of me. I can feel how everything is connected, and it all becomes a part of me. Every student in the room, the sparrows nesting under the eaves outside the classroom, the pencils, the paper, the lights and the current running through them...I felt them as easily as one feels the parts of one's own body.

I bored my thoughts down to the answer key sitting on Mr. Higginson's desk. This was a multiple choice test; the key was nothing more than another copy of the answer sheet with holes punched through the correct answers.

Using my mechanical pencil, I placed a light mark on each of the correct answers on my own sheet. Then I let my Sense drop, and my consciousness slammed back into the confines of my skull.

I looked down to my answer sheet and filled in the circles with the light mark. I was a B-minus or a C+ student generally; today it was going to be perfect marks across the board. I looked to the front of the classroom where Jeanelle, my former girlfriend, sat. The temptation to change all of her answers to the wrong ones hit me strongly, but I shrugged it off. That might even affect her status as our salutatorian. I had already taken far too much revenge on that score. There was no reason to continue.

Besides, she'd know what had happened. Jeanelle had been quiet about Grace and me. She owed me one from last fall, and I'm pretty sure Grace terrified her. Even so, if I started harassing her, she'd turn on me. Petty teenage vengeance was no longer worth it to me; better to let the sleeping dog lie.

Even if she was a real bitch.

I turned my perfect test in half an hour before time was up and casually strolled out of the room. Mr. Higginson had a confused look on his face as he glanced up above his bifocals, but graded the paper with his key as I walked away. I didn't even stop to learn my results.

~

"YOU ARE A MOTHERFUCKER," whispered Jake as we stood in line in the school cafeteria. "A really grade-A son of a bitch, you know that?"

Jake was one of the few people in the world who knew about my alternate course of education. He and Jeanelle had figured it out during last fall's adventures, and he'd seen me use it on a couple of occasions since then. I'd even manage to screw up a perfectly good double date he'd set me up on around Christmas.

"Look, we're graduating in, what...a week? I've already been accepted to college. That grade doesn't make a hamster's fart worth of difference in any of our lives." I tossed this off casually, attempting to play it cool.

The line continued to advance, and we stepped along with it without noticing.

"Yeah...so why pull that shit on it? How could that possibly be worth it?" Ah. Jake didn't care about the fact that I'd cheated; I should have seen that coming. Instead, Jake was worried about my use of the dark arts.

"It's not like I was going to get caught. Mr. Higginson was confused, but he's not going to start a police investigation about it."

Jake's understanding of my powers was both limited and tainted by the indoctrination we all get growing up, that summoners sell their souls to the forces of darkness for power. It's not true, but even I had taken some time and some trauma to accept my power. I wanted so much for Jake to accept it, too, so I tried to keep things casual.

Jake's voice dropped to a whisper. "Motherfucker, you know that's not what I mean. Why sell your soul for a grade that don't even matter?"

I swung my head around, but everyone else was wrapped up in their own conversations.

"Jake, I've tried to tell you...there is no soul-selling. That's a myth. Hype. Propaganda, right up there with Hitler and the Jews."

"Godwin's Law—you mentioned Hitler, you lose."

"Shut up. Anyways, my soul is no worse for the wear, and I've always wanted to do that. I waited for a test that didn't matter, and then I aced it. 'Nuff said."

Jake rolled his eyes, but realized I wasn't going to budge on this one. He stuck with me anyway; there's a reason Jake is my best friend.

We came to the front of the line, where we signed our names on a list, then received an envelope with three tickets. The gym's limited space made these last a necessity; I considered my tickets an overabundance.

"Oh, hey...got any plans for graduation?" he asked, calmly.

"Plans? I was planning to, you know, graduate. I'll give one of my tickets to Grace, let the others go. What other plans are we talking here?"

"Tickets? Who the shit cares about our tickets? I'm talking about *after*, man. Some folks are throwing parties. I figured we'd make the rounds, find some hotties, have a good ol' time."

"Hotties, huh? Tell me, what makes you think that, after four years of trying, graduation is the night in our high school careers that we find hotties?"

"'Cause it's not our high school careers, bro. It'll be the first night of the *rest* of our lives, and really that's more important."

~

WHEN I ARRIVED at my foster parents' home, I knew I was not in for a fun afternoon. A Spokane Valley Police car was parked outside the house. There were no lights or sirens, which meant only one thing.

One of the Valley's finest was in the house, waiting to have a word with me.

I wasn't wrong. When I entered, the slightly rotund figure of Captain Carlenos, head of operations for the Spokane Valley Police branch of the Spokane County Sheriff's Office, sat at the kitchen table, a steaming cup of tea in his right hand. My foster mother appeared to have exited the room in some haste, as her own cup was half-poured and the kettle left on the stove next to the counter.

"How did you even find out?" I was pretty sure Captain Carlenos wasn't going to arrest me; he'd have done it already if he wanted to. Still, it was strange that he even knew about my little stunt on the algebra test.

"We've got all your records flagged. You know you've been a person of interest ever since that business in the mall last September."

"Business in the mall" was a very polite description. A twenty-foot long raccoon demon (not the technical term—that's a Cornuprocyon) had chased Grace and me through the Spokane Valley Mall. In my panic, I'd named it Rick; not a terrifying name, but it had stuck. Rick had left a trail of devastation and security footage in his wake. Afterward, I'd used my illegal magic to handcuff Captain Carlenos to his own filing cabinet and hold him hostage while Rick savaged his precinct office.

Good times, right?

"So you're tracking my every move, then?" I should have figured on this, of course, but having it confirmed still managed to raise my paranoia hackles.

"Pretty much." Carlenos took a long drag of his tea, then stared at me. After several seconds of awkward silence, he leaned back in his chair and said, "History tells us that you people always go bad. You've got a pass with us for the moment, but we don't want to get caught with our drawers down again."

After the mall, Rick had performed a stunning encore wherein he killed roughly a quarter of the law enforcement officers in Spokane County. Grace and I had (barely) managed to send Rick back to his home plane of existence. Since we had basically saved their bacon (pun absolutely intended), local law enforcement was looking the other way when it came to Grace and me. At least for now. I wouldn't say it was an easy truce for either side. Officially, Grace was dead and I was simply a kidnapped victim of all the fuss.

I couldn't blame them for watching me out of the corner of their eye. Fair enough, really.

"Captain, it was one test. And it didn't even matter; I'm already slated to graduate and go off to college."

"College? Which one?"

"Eastern."

"Oh. Well, good for you. Know what you want to do yet?"

That was a complicated question from a law enforcement officer. What I *wanted* to do was keep training with Grace and become a badass summoner. Of course, telling a cop that your ambition is to become a summoner is a lot like telling him that you really want to be a mob boss or a drug dealer when you grow up. That answer was right out.

I had argued with Grace about college. After all, if I was going to be a powerful summoner, why did I need a bachelor's degree? She had responded by telling me, very sharply, that she would train me no further until I agreed that I would head off to college. Apparently I knew enough now to not get myself killed; any further instruction would simply give me more power. To Grace's mind, that was strictly optional.

So no, I had no idea *why* I was going to college. I was doing it because someone who was, legally, dead had told me it was my responsibility to go. I was as honest as I could be with Carlenos.

"Nah. Just seemed like the next step."

"Huh," said the Captain. "Well, you could always try criminal justice." That drew a laugh from me. Carlenos's eyebrows climbed at my laughter, and he shook his head slowly.

"I ain't kidding. Someone like you could go far in the Department, long as you ducked IA."

"Yeah, right. I'll think about it."

"Ok, kid. Meantime, get your head back down. Anything you do has to be pushed up the chain, and there's talk that the Feds are looking into Spokane. I'll bury this test thing in with a whole bunch of other worthless info and make it seem like nothing, but I can only do that once. You pull the attention of a Fed, and there ain't much I can do for you."

"Ok, ok. I hear you."

"Also, I'm letting Grace know. Consider that your punishment." I winced. This wasn't going to be pretty. Still, Carlenos had his police-officer-do-not-argue tone of voice up, so I was just going to have to deal. I nodded. Carlenos finished his tea and stood up. My foster mother, ever the hostess, walked into the kitchen to see her guest off. She showed him out, then returned to me.

"Robert, what was that about?" she asked in a deceptively calm tone.

I could never peg how much the fosties had figured out about me. Last fall had been hectic, and the cops were clearly paying additional attention to me. The fosties had simply been calm, kind, and *there.* They gave me a home, and they really tried to be supportive.

I hadn't treated my foster parents well, to tell the truth. Prior to the Rockfords, my fosties had either been shallow do-gooders, out of their depth with a child like me, or strict, Bible-and-child thumping types. As a rule, I didn't trust fosties. I also didn't get close to them; they came and left my life in short order.

Francene and Donald had made a genuine effort over the last year, and I credited them with it. Still, soon I would leave for college. They'd find some other troubled teen to take in and I'd be a speck in their rearview. They were good people, but that didn't mean I wanted to grow close to them. That meant sticking to my strict policy of communicating in as few syllables as possible.

Which is why I answered Francene with not so much words as a grunted, "Eh."

"What does that mean? You aren't in trouble again, are you?"

"No."

"I mean, you just got taken off probation for that theft back in December." Petty theft; I had been trying to impress a girl and Carlenos had twigged to me.

"Yeah."

"It wouldn't be good to get back into trouble right before you graduate, you know."

"Yeah."

Francene gave me a hang-dog look. We had fought this battle before: her trying to establish a connection, me fending her off. I used to do it because I thought she wasn't genuine. Now I fought her off because I knew she was, and that was going to hurt all the more when it was gone.

"Okay, well, as long as you're keeping out of trouble. Are you excited about graduation?"

"Eh." It wouldn't do to show her that I was very excited; better she receive the noncommittal response.

"Do you know when Donald and I should be there?"

My head shot up at this. It seemed Francene was going to force at least this much. I tried to shrug it off.

"Not that big of a deal; you two can stay home if you want."

Francene made a little "hrmph" sound. "I don't think so, mister. You only graduate high school once in your life. I may not be your mother, but I stand in her place since she can't be here. And she would be proud of you, and would want to watch you graduate. I skip your graduation, I dishonor *her*. You tell me not to come, and you do the same. I know you don't want to do that, so when should Donald and I be there?"

I was stunned. Francene never used that kind of directness with me. She took this one pretty seriously, though; no fighting it.

I pulled the smooshed envelope of tickets from my front pocket and handed her two. "Family's supposed to be there at five o'clock for pictures. The rest of the audience gets there at seven."

"Very well. We'll be there at five."

I turned my face to hide my smile from Francene. Then I shuffled upstairs to my room, and brushed the tear out of my eye.

THAT NIGHT, a note appeared on the desk in my room with a quiet "piff." I glanced over at it; it simply read. *"I'm back at your uncle's place. Come see me."*

Ah, Grace had returned. Lovely. I snagged my keys from the desk and left. As I walked out the door, Francene asked where I was going. I ignored her. She had one victory already today, and I wasn't about to give her a second. I jumped into my old beater of a Volvo and took off for the mountains of Northern Idaho.

Grace sat on the split-log bench outside of Uncle Herman's cabin as I pulled my car up the dirt road. She appeared to be eating dinner from a Styrofoam container; no telling which of her exotic takeout places it had come from.

"Hey," she tossed at me. "Heard you had some fun at the winery."

Fun? Her little vacation had almost gotten me killed.

"Yeah. Next time you go off to shoot craps, you might want to leave someone who knows what they're doing in charge here. Amy...is a bit of a flake sometimes."

"Amy's not a flake. And you two did just fine."

"By 'just fine' I assume you mean 'no permanent injury or death.'"

"What other standard would you suggest I judge by?" She had me there—it was a fair point. I sat down on the bench next to my mentor and looked out at Uncle Herman's property. My property, really, but I didn't think of it that way.

"Look, it scared the hell out of me, ok? Going off to Vegas to gamble when we're so shorthanded is just...it's irresponsible."

"Oh, that's rich. *You're* lecturing *me* on responsibility now? Hey, how'd your algebra final go?"

"Carlenos talked to you already, didn't he?"

"He has my cell number. No reception up here, but he left a voicemail. You know that was stupid, right?"

"You have a cell phone? Why don't *I* have your number?"

"Not the topic, mister. Do you know what you did was stupid?"

"Yeah. But I'd always wanted to do it. It should count for something that I waited until the test didn't matter to pull it off."

"It does, a bit. Still stupid. If someone in that class had noticed you..."

"Jake did. I'm fine."

"Not the point and you know it. Carlenos *has* to investigate you if someone else reports, and he's going to bust you if he does."

"No one noticed. I was careful."

"No, you weren't. Careful would have been not doing it at all."

We sat in silence for a bit. I had to concede the point. It had been a stupid teenage bout of recklessness, but on a scale of my bouts with recklessness, it wasn't all that bad. Grace finished her dinner, some form of pasta in a white sauce that smelled hot with garlic, as I sat in silence.

After Grace finished, I passed her a graduation ticket. A warm smile crossed her face as she read it, then stuck it in her bag. She looked me in the eye and changed the subject.

"I've been researching this Andrea girl," she said softly.

I perked up. Andrea was a beautiful girl held hostage in an alternate universe; just the thing for my overly-romantic fantasy mind to churn on. I had only seen her once, and I knew that she was strapped to a table having her power slowly siphoned away by a demon named Cythymau. I also knew she had long, auburn hair.

And every few seconds on this world was a few hours on the world where she was being held.

I looked at Grace expectantly. We were getting down to business, and it was time to serious up.

"It looks like the Tri-Cities Grove lost an Andrea—a really new novice, from the looks of it—in the mid-seventies. She vanished after an attack on the Grove by a Lycaon, which is a kind of—"

"I know what a Lycaon is." I had been attacked by one on entering Cythymau's world; our personal nemesis had used the attack to build trust. I could still hear his soft, pleasant voice. *Andrea here agreed without getting the full terms. Much more congenial. You, I'm afraid, still must agree. I wish it wasn't this painful for you, but there you have it.*

Cythymau must have used the same trick: loose a magical beast on the world, then promise to help fight it in exchange for some unknown service. Andrea had taken the bait, thinking that it was the only way to help her Grove.

I had almost made the same mistake.

Andrea had been in that world since the mid-seventies. If every second here was an hour there, then every year here was thirty-six hundred years there. Andrea had been stuck in that world for over thirty-five years. Here. Over one hundred and twenty-six *thousand* years there. That was staggering. Andrea's life-span was longer than history by over an order of magnitude. She had been strapped to that board for far, far longer than, say, King Tut had spent in his tomb.

I knew it had been bad. I didn't realize how bad. I could do nothing right now but put my head back, sigh, and gather it all in. In the time it took me to compose myself from that news, Andrea watched two more days sail by.

"You know," said Grace conversationally. "I think it's time to get you a training partner."

GRACE

MATT STARED at me with a pasty white face and a nervous twitch that suggested he might rethink this whole idea and rabbit at any moment. His stocky build had gotten a little heavier, and his acne had cleared up since I last saw him, but apparently his skittish personality hadn't changed. His dress shirt and slacks hit me as incongruous next to Uncle Herman's mountain-man cabin.

Matt was the only survivor of the original Spokane Grove attack who had actually stayed in town. Not that there were many survivors to begin with. When I'd met him last summer, Matt told me he didn't have any summoning ability, so he assumed that must be why Rick hadn't killed him during the initial massacre. I couldn't say he was entirely wrong; the only other people who had escaped had been young apprentices with little training. The rest of Matt's family and friends had died that day, and he hadn't been able to do anything about it. But given Rick's fascination with chasing Robert last fall, that probably indicated only summoners with a certain level of power caught his attention.

I'd had Amy look Matt up for me as soon as I got back from Vegas, so I could act on my nagging gut feeling that, much like a younger me, he had written himself off too soon. I'd also gotten permission from the Cooperative Council to take him on as a second apprentice if he did have the Sense. My real genius happened while I was talking to Robert last night—realizing that if Matt did have the potential to Sense, I could be training both boys at once.

Summoning—as near as I could tell at least—was genetic. It always ran in families, even if it did appear to "skip" individuals occasionally. Based on personal experience, I thought maybe the Sense just didn't manifest as strongly in those particular individuals. A Sense could be so small that it wouldn't show up on our standard tests. Most summoners' Sense extended between ten and twenty feet from their bodies. When I'd been young, mine extended half an inch—and that was on a good day. Mom had saved me from an "ungifted" fate by holding her scarf to my back and having me Sense it. Then she'd made sure I had a chance to be a true summoner by spending long nights studying complex rune phrases with me. From the outside, it probably looked like I'd been skipped ahead of everyone still doing Sense-only exercises.

In reality, if I hadn't gone to such lengths researching runes to compensate for my natural abilities, there's no way I could've kept up with my peers.

Even now, my Sense barely extended two inches compared to Robert's fifty feet.

After the dismal reaction to my request for aid at the Cooperative Council, no option could remain unexplored in my search for new summoners. No one else would send me anyone. *I* believed Matt had the right genes to Sense, even if no one else saw it.

The crux of my theory hinged on a simple true or false—whether Matt possessed the Sense or not. To test that, much like my mother had done for me, I handed him a fortune cookie and told him to read me the fortune inside without breaking it. His face wrinkled in concentration before he shook his head slowly.

"I can't see it."

Undaunted, I broke the fortune cookie, and held the slip of paper to his back. "Ok. No problem. Try now."

He closed his eyes, and his face broke out into a slow grin. "It says

'Good luck follows in your footsteps.' Totally untrue, but I can't believe that worked."

He had the Sense. I'd worry about its size or potency later.

"Knowing you have the Sense, however small it might be, is only the first step. Now you need to learn the runes and how to use them."

"I know a fair bit already. I used to look over my siblings' primers. Will I really be able to become a true summoner?"

"That depends on how much you're willing to work. But yes, I think so."

"Oh, I'll work for it all right."

Along with the Sense, Matt also had a huge dose of survivor's guilt, and the training I offered represented something constructive he could do with it. Hopefully. He had the rune primers, and he had the opportunity. It was up to him how far he'd take it now.

I STOOD on top of the log bench in front of Herman's cabin that afternoon, my hands poised on my hips, and tried to infuse my speech with the military assurance and authority that still sometimes crackled in my Uncle John's voice. Matt and Robert both stared back. Matt showed his usual pale uncertainty; Robert no doubt *thought* he was concealing his impatience. I needed the two young men in front of me to learn. And I *needed* them to do it as quickly as possible.

Getting a spirit of competition going between them should do the trick, right?

"Starting today, the two of you are going to partner up for rune activities and testing once a week. We'll do a brief run-through of the runes that I gave you"—I raised my brows at Robert. Knowing him, he'd probably only made a cursory attempt at memorizing them, since he still had difficulty using runes to channel his Sense—"and then we'll do some activities that test your knowledge. The winner gets a prize, as chosen by yours truly."

"Great," Robert grumped. "We already know that means you'll summon some sort of crazy gourmand item so you can eat it, too." He leaned toward Matt with a knowing smirk. "It's her go-to for everything."

"You'll just have to do your best so you can find out," I said, refusing to take the bait. "The person who *loses* gets extra patrol duty with Amy, since he'll obviously need extra practice. Motivation enough for the both of you?" Totally an empty threat—no way Matt would be ready—but maybe it would light a fire under Robert.

Robert grunted, his arms folded over his chest. Matt nodded solemnly.

Robert *needed* someone to compete with to motivate him into learning all these runes. Otherwise he'd continue to be lackadaisical about his rune studies, doing just barely enough to get by.

With that monstrous Sense of his, narrowing his focus down to a point small enough to channel through the runes was difficult. He had to figure it out on his own, though. None of my books or experience would help him with that. Lectures could only take him so far before we reached a point where no amount of talking was going to get past his mental block. Logically, he might understand why learning to use the runes was important, but runes were still painfully slow for him. Somewhere in the back of his monkey brain he clung to his Sense as more reliable. Within fifty feet, it was. Beyond those fifty feet, it left him defenseless. Oh sure, he could still summon something in blind, but that was exactly the kind of move that got us summoners a bad rep in the first place. One word: Chernobyl.

As for Matt, he burned with the need to prove to himself he could really be a summoner. Not just the unfortunate "ungifted" relative.

I didn't really know if he'd be up for my rune-intensive way of summoning long-term, and I had a lot on my hands to even think about training someone else. Juggling two apprentices wouldn't be easy. Summoning is not a kind science to begin with, and even with some small spark of Sense, I couldn't guarantee Matt anything. But I desperately, desperately needed more feet on the ground to mend tears in the Weave. Even with his *almost* non-existent Sense, Matt had potential.

Besides, Robert was so far behind with runes that they should be at the same level in that regard. Robert would have to step up his game if he wanted to keep up. Matt might even have a slight advantage, since he had grown up seeing runes all the time.

"So what bizarre food-based torture have you thought up this time?" Robert asked in that teenage I'm-pretty-sure-I-know-but-I'm-going-to-ask-anyway tone.

"This challenge actually has nothing to do with food. Shocking, huh? We're going to do something completely different. Have you guys played Boggle before?" Matt nodded. Robert shrugged.

"Boggle is a game where you make as many words as you can out of a chain of adjacent letters in a grid."

I tried to make my voice sound cheery and exciting. Not that it works on kids over eleven, so it failed miserably. Neither boy looked impressed.

"The person who finds the most viable summons within three minutes wins. You can't use the same tile twice in one rune chain. We'll do a set of three matches; the person with the most points at the end is the winner."

They both took a writing pad and pencil for jotting down their phrases. Since Robert hadn't played before, I did a quick demonstration, linking the adjacent Thurisaz rune to Kano to Dagaz to Eihawaz. "Remember you can't rearrange the runes. You have to use them in the order they appear. Once you find a chain, write it down and go on to the next one. I'll go over them after the time limit. If a rune phrase doesn't work, I'll subtract a point from your final score." I waited for them both to nod, shook the board to reset the tiles, then set the timer. "All right, go!"

Their heads bowed over their writing pads as they stared at the rune grid with concentrated intensity. The sun glinted off Robert's mousy brown hair, emphasizing the shaggy tufts around his face. Matt picked a spot slightly more in the shade, frowning thoughtfully as he drew each rune. Robert, on the other hand, was scribbling furiously, occasionally erasing with a wide gesture.

"All right, time," I said as the timer beeped. "Let me see what you guys have." I glanced over their rune constructions. They were pretty

48

evenly matched as points went, though they had found a few slightly different phrases.

"Okay, looks like Robert came out slightly ahead on that one. Matt, you're not far behind though. There's only five points difference. This is anyone's prize still. Next match!"

Robert's mouth turned down a little as he shot a considering look at Matt. Matt flipped the page on his notepad and poised his pencil above it, tensely waiting for me to shake up the rune tiles.

"You don't have to take it so seriously," Robert said to Matt as he flipped the page on his notepad. "The prize is just going to be another of Grace's stupid desserts, and the whole patrolling thing is a bluff. We'll get roped into that with Amy anyway."

Matt's face shuttered, going blank for a moment. Then he met Robert's eyes directly. "I'm not doing it for the prize," he said. "But I am taking it seriously. Everyone I cared about died before you and Grace ever got pulled into this. I don't want to be in that situation ever again. Since Grace is willing to teach someone as weak as me, I'm going to learn everything I possibly can to become stronger. I already decided that last fall. I just didn't think I'd ever get a chance like this."

"If you were a trained summoner last fall, you'd be dead, too. My Uncle Herman was a total badass, and he's still just as dead."

"That may be," Matt answered, "But at least I wouldn't feel like such a worthless coward. All I did that day was panic and run away. Never again. I'm the only one from my family still here."

"You're not the only one without a family anymore," Robert said, stung.

There weren't a lot of good places this conversation could go. I decided to cut it short.

"This is all water under the bridge, boys. I'd appreciate it if you'd concentrate on what's in front of you." I jostled the rune tiles and reset the board. "Round two, start! You only have three minutes, so you'd better get going."

~

I FINISHED ADDING the results of the three rune boggle matches, and my mouth fell open. "Huh. What were the chances of that?" I double-checked my math, just in case. "You two actually managed to tie. The total number of points between the three matches is exactly the same. Robert did manage to win two of the three matches, but Matt had a substantial lead on his one win, so it all evens out."

"I still won two," Robert pointed out. "That should count for something." Despite his assertions that it didn't matter, I could see he was thinking of the extra patrols.

"No," I said slowly as I thought it out. "I said we were going to do this off the total number of points. Matt has been in training less than a day, and he still managed to tie your points. I think we need a tie-breaker."

"We'll just tie again if we do another round. I guess you can say we both won," Robert said hopefully. "That seems fair to me."

A thought hit me and a smile broke across my face. "No. I know the perfect tie-breaker." I reached down and picked up the rune tiles, lining up a simple summon for a smallish-sized rock.

"If neither of you can summon this stone using the runes, then it's a tie. If one of you can, that person's the winner. But the summon only counts if you can manage to get the rock using the runes."

"I don't see what the big deal is." Robert rolled his eyes in typical teenager fashion. "My Sense is way bigger than his. So what if I can't use the runes that well?"

He knew better. "If that's really what you think, you aren't looking at the big picture. Without runes you are absolutely defenseless outside of fifty feet. You can't do a long-range summon at all. That cripples you."

He started to protest. I gave him a hard look. "If you keep summoning without runes," I said bluntly, "Someday there will be something so important that it would be worth breaking all the Grove's laws even though it's outside that fifty feet. That will get you killed. That will get me killed. And now that Matt's with us, it might get him killed. Don't forget that."

Gods, I didn't know the best way to deal with this kid. He was so powerful and yet at such a disadvantage without runes. His Sense just wasn't like anyone else his age I'd ever heard of. Maybe there weren't other summoners like him. His huge Sense made him akin to his own species as far as teaching went. I had a lot more tricks up my sleeve that Matt could use. Robert, not so much.

Blood and runes make up the bedrock of a summoner's tool box. The blood acts as a connector, and the runes become a targeting system—allowing a summoner to send his Sense through and pull in an item from outside his normal Sense range. Or at least, that's how it's supposed to work. Despite his ridiculously large Sense, Robert had been having connection issues.

"You're hoping I lose the tie-breaker," he accused. "You know I suck at runes."

I held a finger up. "Hold on, Matt. Robert and I will be right back."

I pulled Robert over to the side of the cabin away from Matt.

"Look. Matt is brand-spanking-new at summoning. There's every chance that neither of you will be able to summon the stone. But I need you to try. This is something you have to keep working at to master. Whatever is holding you back from using runes, you *will* figure it out. You're a smart kid. You can do this."

His head dropped, and he gave it a shake in denial. I tipped his chin back up with a finger, realizing how much taller he'd gotten in the last few months. He'd always been taller than me, but now it felt exaggerated. "You can. And the next time you pull a stunt like this on me, trying to accuse me of somehow setting you up, I'll kick your ass." I held his gaze to make sure he saw how deadly serious I was.

"You *will* be a power to be reckoned with, and you will do it with runes. Don't you ever doubt it." He gave me a small jerky nod. Good.

"Now I need you go get back in there and focus. Can you do that?"

"Yes," Robert said hoarsely. I realized suddenly he was trying not to cry. Dammit. I hadn't meant to do that. I gave his arm an awkward squeeze.

"Okay." I marched us back to Matt. He was studiously looking at nothing off in the distance. Not subtle at all. I guess Robert was officially the teacher's favorite now. Oh, yeah, this two-apprentice thing was going to work out great. I had a sinking feeling in my stomach that I might have already created a little too much rivalry. Yep. Another genius plan from the desk of Grace Anne Moore.

I plowed forward before I mired down in self-doubt about my teaching abilities.

"Ok, let's do this. Who wants to go first?"

Matt shook his head and motioned Robert forward with his hand.

Robert grabbed a vial of the local butcher shop blood from the small cooler outside the cabin's door. Flipping up the cap with his thumb, Robert walked up to the rune phrase, splashing the blood across the runes with a flourish and striking a dramatic hero pose.

Unfortunately, that pose did not actually bring the rock to him. Possibly he'd decided if he was going to fail, he was going to look cool while he did it. I could feel the Weave tremble as he struggled not to use his Sense to forcibly bring it to him, as he would have when I first met him. He stood like that for what felt like half an hour, but was probably more like ten minutes. I didn't try to rush him. Finally he gave a gusty sigh, and just as he started to drop his hand to step back from the summon with a shrug, the rock appeared in his right hand.

He looked down at it with a stunned expression. A smile slowly spread over his face; he brought the rock over to me with a swagger. Matt clapped faintly a couple times, his expression even more unreadable.

"Good job! I told you persistence would pay off."

"It still wouldn't be worth anything in a fight." The words were negative but the timbre of Robert's voice was anything but.

"Let's see if we have another tie. Matt, go ahead and give it a try." I reset the rock and cleaned off the rune tiles.

Matt stepped up to the rune phrase, his brow wrinkling in concentration as he swiped blood across the runes. He stood there for several minutes, tension in every line of his body as he tried to move the small rock toward him. It trembled for a second, but in the end, stayed stubbornly where it was.

Matt opened his eyes, shaking his head in disappointment, his face turning paler. "It's too heavy. I could feel it. I knew where it was, but I still couldn't bring it to me. I should have known."

"Matt, you're just starting. It's great that you could feel it. Don't—"

"I had it, Grace," he said in a voice that cracked just a little. "It should have come to me. My Sense went through the runes just fine. But it felt like an anvil. I couldn't *lift* it." He turned his back to the runes and started to walk away. I'm not even sure if he knew to where.

"Hey!" I said sharply, going after him. I made a grab at his arm, bringing him up short. "A little hasty much? This was your first attempt at a summons. It didn't work. Maybe you're right and that rock's too heavy for your Sense. Even so, that doesn't mean your Sense can't do anything. And anyway, you can practice to make your Sense stronger. Maybe it'll never be super-strong, but you can't just give up after your first try on your first day."

I jabbed my finger into his chest. "What this proves is that you actually have the potential to do it. You *felt* it. You're over here." I pointed at the ground where the rune phrase still sat. "It's over there. Capische?"

He nodded slowly. I frowned. Damn. If Matt's confidence was this weak, my dual training plan wouldn't work. What would show him that *small* didn't automatically equal useless?

I pulled my rune board out of my purse and quickly set up a new rune phrase. Turning the board, I presented a new rune phrase to Matt. "Try this one."

"This better not count toward our score," Robert muttered.

"Hush. Try it." I told Matt again, holding the board out to him insistently. He took it reluctantly, looking down at the summons.

"Is this for a piece of paper?" he asked skeptically. "What good is summoning paper?"

"If you can summon it, I'll show you something immensely powerful you can do by summoning just grams of stuff." I crossed my arms over my chest and waited.

He took a deep breath, blooded the runes, and concentrated. The tag paper appeared in his fingers a bare second later. So he was probably right. His last summons had fizzled due to his weak Sense. Now to show him that a underdeveloped Sense didn't automatically doom him to being powerless.

I quirked an eyebrow at Matt. "See? You can do this. Now, you might not be able to do things through brute strength like Robert over there, but with runes, you don't need to. Runes make it all about creativity and finesse, not strength."

"Hey!" Robert objected. "I have finesse."

"You blew out the wall to a police station using several thousand pounds of raw kinetic energy and caused a multiple car pile-up."

"With finesse," he insisted.

I turned back to Matt. "Anyway, are you ready to see what havoc you can create with just rune knowledge and a little ingenuity?" Excitement started to bubble up in my chest. I knew *exactly* what I could use to show both boys how powerful runes were. Besides, this summon was one of my favorite works-in-progress.

"Just runes?" Matt repeated dubiously.

"Yup." I took the tag paper from his hand and smoothed it out, uncapping a pen with a flourish. "What do you know about nuclear fission?"

"I—what?" Matt sputtered.

"Nuclear fission. The chemical reaction that drives power plants, and by the way, also weapons of mass destruction. That fission reaction relies on an unstable uranium isotope, U-235." I started scribbling runes on the paper, the pen moving faster as I really got into the science of what I was doing. "But uranium as it naturally occurs is almost totally U-238 with a very minuscule amount of U-235 mixed in. U-238 is actually very stable and not useful for causing reactions. Or at least on the scale needed for generating a lot of power. This is usually where the process of enriching uranium comes in. You guys know what enriched uranium is, right?"

The question hung in the air for a second, but neither one gave me a response. I was on a roll now, my pen skating over the paper. I gave them the explanation, anyway.

"U-235 is heavier than the U-238 surrounding it. The uranium is spun in giant centrifuges to attempt to get a higher concentration of the good, highly reactive stuff. Uranium that is five percent U-235 will fuel a power plant. If you can get uranium up to twenty-five percent U-235, then you're starting to get into weapons-grade quality fuel. That's why there's so much debate when places like Iran start enriching uranium. They could be trying for power, or they could be trying for something with much more oomph."

I finished the row of complex runes and turned the finished summon around to show Matt and Robert. They squinted at it with confused faces. "Of course, as a summoner, you really don't have to worry about centrifuges. This little baby will summon one gram of pure U-235 from one of the decommissioned fuel rods at Hanford. One gram of one hundred percent U-235, also known as the ultimate super fuel." I finished my object lesson with a smug feeling of satisfaction.

"And you call me the reckless one?" Robert whistled under his breath and raised his eyes to mine. "So what exactly does one gram of pure U-235 do?"

"Well, on its own, not much." I admitted. "But—" I dug around in the bottom of my purse and came out with a giant scroll that I unrolled on the ground in front of us. Three feet of complex runes that represented years of knowledge and study stared up at us.

"If you bring it together with fifty-two thousand other grams gathered from fuel rods all over the world, then you get a nuclear weapon on par with the one that leveled Hiroshima. All you need is the knowledge of how to do it. Like what's laid out here." I patted the paper fondly. I was rather proud of this little masterpiece.

"No way." Robert interrupted. "You've been carrying a nuke around in your purse? You're still pissed about me causing a car wreck with my Sense last fall, and now you're trying to show Matt how to summon a fucking nuke?!"

"Wait." Matt piped up. He'd knelt beside the scroll I'd laid down and was reading over the runes.

"This summon brings together fifty-two thousand grams of U-235 from all over the globe simultaneously?"

"Yep." I beamed. The super-complexity was one of the things I loved about this summon. It really was a feat of mastery.

"Also known as fifty-two kilograms?" He pressed.

"Yep. It's still about the size of a pop bottle, though. U-235 is incredibly dense."

"I couldn't move that rock," he said, pointing, "How in the world would I move fifty-two kilograms at once?"

"This summon isn't about actually doing it," I insisted, feeling a little deflated. "It's the fact that you could *theoretically* do it."

Matt's lips curved up in a smile, and he started chuckling. "But I couldn't do it. This relies on being able to move all this U-235 into the same space at once to cause the reaction. I'd still need to pick up fifty-two kilograms and put it in one place, which is never going to happen. You probably are the only one that could get this to work. It's insanely, stupidly complex."

"Doesn't this summon all of the U-235 right on top of you?" Robert chimed in. "How do you protect yourself from the blast?"

"Um, you don't. Yet. I'm still working on that. Like I said, this whole exercise isn't so much about what the summon does, but what *you can do* with runes if you put your mind to it."

"Riiiight. So let me get this straight. In the name of summoning, you are currently carrying around a scroll that can not only incinerate you but everyone in a six-mile radius? Yeah, that seems like a great example." Robert quipped. "Why would you even want that?"

Matt hid a smirk behind his hand.

Robert waved and headed back to the rust bucket he called a car, still laughing. He'd probably be cackling for hours. I let him go. No matter what he said, this summon was still cool. Nevertheless, I started rolling it back up.

I hadn't gotten the reaction I wanted from either of the boys. So much for my wise-sage role.

Matt turned another laugh into a cough as I stuffed the scroll back in my purse, and pretended to be studiously looking at something around the corner of the cabin. I sighed.

"You still made a lot of progress today, Matt. Even if the example was a bit flawed, I hope you understand what I mean when I say you don't need a lot of power to excel. Just find your strengths, and you'll catch up to Robert and everyone else in no time. Let me see if I can think of any other pointers for you."

"Uh, that's ok. I think I got the gist of today's lesson." He stared at my bag like parts of his world had just been turned completely upside down.

"What?" I asked, after he'd been silent for a while.

"I think I finally understand why normal people can think we're scary," Matt answered.

"You're just catching on to that now, huh? People always fear the unknown. But summoning is still just a tool, like always. It's what *you* do with it that really matters." I grinned and slapped him on the back. "Since Robert decided to cut out early, let's get revenge on him by eating some absolutely amazing dessert without him. I know a bakery that makes a pecan caramel torte drizzled in chocolate that is just to die for. We'll eat some and gloat, as Robert would put it. My treat."

THE CABIN WAS cool and quiet. Robert and Matt had headed off to their respective mundane lives. Tomorrow we'd do it all again and try to get different results. I'm pretty sure I'd just provided Einstein's definition of insanity, and I couldn't really disagree with him at the moment.

"Grace, you got a minute?"

I looked up from my papers and saw Amy standing worriedly in the late sun slanting through the cabin doorway. She usually stopped by a couple times a day, but since she was my eyes and ears outside the cabin, she had her own place in town.

"Sure, what's up?" I pushed my stack of unwanted Council advice, complaints, reports, and memos over to the side and ran a hand through my hair to ease my headache, no doubt causing several curls to stick up at odd angles. "More unexpected Visitors popping in and creating havoc? Where this time?"

My fingers moved almost against my will to rub over the runes engraved on the Weave-mending bracelets on my right wrist. These little babies had already gotten way too much use since last fall. Without them, the impossible task of keeping this reality intact became even more impossible. I sighed and closed my eyes for a second, hoping it wasn't too big an infestation. Despite my threats of double patrol duty, in these few days before graduation, I was trying not to rely on Robert too much. That left just Amy and me trying to hold the Weave together, hoping all hell didn't break loose.

"Um, there is a visitor," Amy said hesitantly. "But not in the way that you mean. I think Detective Allen just pulled up outside."

"What?" My head jerked up and I suddenly felt much more awake as a surge of adrenaline hit my system. "How many deputies are with him? Does it look like he's trying to signal us to clear out?" I started grabbing papers and notebooks, stacking them in a pile on my desk with the intention of piffing them to a safe house. Looking troubled, Amy shook her head.

"He's in an unmarked car, and it looks like he's by himself. I didn't think the Sheriff's office knew where to find you. What do you want to do?" She twisted her strawberry blonde hair nervously around a finger.

"He shouldn't know where to find us," I said grimly. "I didn't want the Sheriff's office having too much information. What they already know would put them far on the bad side of the Feds. The only reason they have a phone number to contact me *at all* is for leverage with Robert when he acts out."

I felt my brow furrow as a new line of worry worked its way across my forehead. "Whatever it is, it's so serious it means he took the time to find me. Even scarier, if he can find me, who else might be able to? I guess I'd better go see what's happened." I closed my eyes for a second as a thought occurred to me. "I really hope Robert didn't do something stupid. He wasn't too happy about the training earlier."

Amy's eyes got round. "You don't really think he did something?"

"Maybe. But I doubt it. I don't know. You stay here. If the detective hasn't gotten a good look at you, I don't want him getting a better one.

I don't know what his reaction to finding out there's another summoner in town would be, but let's not test it." I levered my feet underneath me and Amy took my chair.

Time to go see what catastrophe was trying to swallow us all.

I stepped through the doorway, shutting it firmly behind me. Frank was on the edge of the property, looking almost comically torn for the hard-nosed detective I was familiar with. He took two steps toward the cabin, turned around, strode back to his black sedan, reached for the door, then paused. Spun back around, took five steps toward the cabin, and stopped again. He looked up at the sky, apparently deep in thought. It appeared as though he was completely unsure if he really wanted to be here.

That, at least, I could understand.

He let out a long sigh. It wasn't until he abruptly muttered, "I already decided. Just do it, Frank," and jerked his head down to resume marching toward the cabin that I realized he'd been preoccupied in arguing with himself.

I couldn't help it.

"What's been decided, Detective?"

He flinched so badly that he almost turned his ankle on the gravel of the driveway. "Don't startle me like that," he barked, fixing me with his penetrating cop's eyes. He glared at me for several moments, then his brow relaxed and he let out another tired sigh that seemed to come up from his very toes. What could be so serious that it brought him out here against his better judgment?

My heart squeezed a little tighter in my chest.

"It's good to see you," I offered tentatively. "I'm glad to get a chance to thank you for everything you've done for Robert this last year in person. And for me, of course." I indicated the log bench outside the cabin. "Why don't you come sit down? It's a bit of a drive to get here from Spokane."

Allen lowered his weight onto the bench with a gingerness I didn't expect. His movements suddenly reminded me of a very old man, which was at odds with my memory of the spry and tenacious detective from last fall.

"Are your legs still bothering you?" I asked in concern, staring at the lower leg of his trousers as if I could see through the heavy fabric. His legs had been badly broken in that final fight with Rick, but he had still managed to buy me the time I needed to finish the fight.

He rubbed his left leg absently. "They twinge occasionally," he admitted, "but they're not bad. Not at all bad, considering I thought I might never walk again when it happened."

"I'm glad to hear they healed well." I couldn't help wondering if he had come to announce the end of our unorthodox truce. Although, if he already knew where I was, he really didn't have to come in person at all. All he had to do was tip off the Feds and wash his hands of the whole thing.

"Last fall when this all went down and you saved my deputies, I thought you might be trying to play an angle. Throw the old dog a bone and maybe he goes peacefully off into retirement; or hell, dies of his injuries and ceases to be a problem. Then you show up at the hospital with your 'friend' and pretty much guarantee us all speedy if not miraculous recoveries. You're one hell of a puzzle, Grace Anne Moore."

"It's not so big a puzzle, Detective. Our goals just lined up a lot more than you originally thought they did. We both wanted to get rid of the big bad monster endangering the public. I started with the bonus knowledge that the big-bad wasn't me or Robert. I'm just sorry I wasn't more effective at banishing it before people got hurt."

Frank snorted. "I'm well aware that without you, there's no way we would have gotten rid of that thing on our own. I'm also damn sure I wouldn't be on active duty right now if that special doctor hadn't done whatever she did to heal my legs. You went out of your way to help law enforcement. I'd been doing my damnedest to hunt you down. I've thought about that over and over this last year. I kept expecting you to try and call in that favor, so I could report you to the Feds with no regrets."

"If you want to turn me in, Detective I don't see why you haven't. I did call in that favor. I asked you to let Robert stay where he is. I'm well aware *just that* could cost you and your deputies in the future."

"If the kid truly acted up, it would be a huge favor, and I might have turned you in. But the only two times he's landed on my radar since last September, he was attempting to stop a robbery in progress and cheating on an algebra exam. Those are not the types of favors I expected." Frank paused. "I don't get *why* the kid would want to risk his soul for a few math problems, but teenagers aren't my shtick."

"Well, probably because Robert doesn't see it as risking his soul." I didn't know why Detective Allen was here, but since he had engaged me in conversation, I might as well try to make the most of it. "Summoning is a tool; it's the person behind the tool who is good or evil. Much like all the firearm arguments, the questionable part comes in with who wields that tool. I won't try to convert your way of thinking, but honestly, you can't think Robert and I are in thrall to 'the Dark Arts'; otherwise I really doubt you'd be here. All you'd have to do is 'discover' I faked my death, pass along my whereabouts, and I'd be totally busted. No muss, no fuss."

"This is personal," he admitted. "And I thought about busting you a hundred times, but in the end I always came back to how hard you tried to keep me and my men alive. I decided, based on that, that I have to believe you when you say the demon would have been here whether you were or not."

He stared at me with those flinty cop eyes. "Given that assumption, I'll bet my badge that no one gave you orders to try and protect everyone. Keep off the radar and try to keep civilians from getting harmed? Sure. But I bet no one *ever* told you to save the bullheaded detective and his men in spite of what they might do to antagonize a demon. I don't think there's a Grove in the world that would give that order. The kid, too. I wager whoever you report to wasn't too happy you were dragging around an untrained liability. That's all you."

He kept that all-too-perceptive gaze on me and waited for my reply. He still had that same razor-sharp intellect that had so frightened me in our previous encounters.

He said he wasn't here to bust me, but this was starting to feel a little too much like our dance in the interrogation room. His take on the Grove's view of Robert was too close for comfort. It might be time for a distraction.

"I just did what I thought was best, Detective. Trust your person on the ground and all that, you know. There's something I'd really like to ask you, too. You want to tell me how you found me? GPS in the cell phone number I gave Carlenos?"

Allen scratched his head, pursing his lips. The wind rustled through the trees as I waited for him to answer. GPS was unlikely, because that would involve way too many labs and technicians, but you never know. He ran his hand through his hair again, sticking it up on end in gray tufts. His suit matched; it was rumpled like he'd slept in it, or rather hadn't slept at all. My lips pulled downward as I considered his general appearance of exhaustion. Maybe he was just having trouble thinking. I doubted he'd slept recently. That might explain his silence and his bizarre inner argument.

He put his hand back down on the bench. I reached out and picked it up between mine on impulse, and then didn't know what to do with it. My knee provided a convenient if somewhat awkward landing place. His dry, weathered fingers looked out of place between mine. But he didn't take his hand away, which was also unlike him. I half expected him to snatch it back and snap something like, "I don't hold hands with anybody." That didn't happen.

"Frank," I said gently after a few minutes. "Why are you here?"

He was really scaring me. Frank Allen was a shrewd detective, a gruff adversary and a genuine good guy, but he'd never had trouble being uncomfortably straight with me before. He tended to be a plainspoken type of gent.

"This place belonged to Herman Lorents," he said, suddenly looking up and around.

"Yes," I said guardedly, not seeing where this was going.

"It's how I found you." Frank finally took his hand back and smoothed it down his face. Then he shifted on the bench so he could see me better. "I had a file on Herman. It didn't say exactly where this place was. But I knew he died in the massacre last August, and that he'd lived in Idaho. I lost a bet to Carlenos about Robert being related to the old guy. Herman didn't have any other relatives besides Robert, or I *would* have known about them. Add the fact that the showdown last year happened on I-90 coming out of Idaho, and you're from out of town but had to go into hiding fast... It makes sense that Robert either knew of—or provided—your hideout. So anyway, I looked up the estate of Herman Lorents on the Idaho State Courts website, and got the courthouse to let me look at a copy of the file. The address for this place is listed in the inventory."

"You, sir," I said, torn between admiration and abject terror of the implications, "are scary good at what you do. How concerned *should* I be about others finding me the same way?"

"They'd have to know the connection between you and Robert, and know that Robert's uncle *is* one of the recently deceased summoners, but if a few out-of-the-box thinkers do enough digging in the existing reports, there's a chance the Feds could be knocking on your door instead of me."

My guts flopped around a little at that. "Thanks for the warning."

While not good, that didn't sound like news that should cause him to come all the way out here like this. There had to be something else.

"You have more bad news, don't you?" I asked.

He nodded, and held my gaze. "The Feds reopened the Valley Mall investigation a few weeks ago. Yesterday they confiscated all of our reports and records concerning it." His left hand clenched on his knee, his knuckles slowly turning white.

"What does that mean?" I forced the question out from behind the sudden lump of trepidation in my throat.

"Most likely, it means that something has tipped them off that you aren't dead. The fact that they've confiscated our records and cut us off from the investigation means they're worried someone in our department is altering records and/or providing information to you. I don't know what you did, and I don't want to, but I'll bet my badge they know you're alive."

"You're about to be implicated for hiding me," I said slowly, putting it together. "They'll hang you...and Captain Carlenos...out to dry."

He gave me a nod of grudging respect. "I'm not worried about me.

63

I'd do it again for the aid you gave our deputies. I'm an old dog, and I'll take my lumps as they come. But Carlenos, he's young. He's got kids and a wife who depend on him. And now, because he looked the other way to give you and the kid a second chance, his own kids might grow up without their father."

His eagle-eyed gaze was back. It bored into me.

"I won't ask for me. And I don't want you to hurt anyone. But if you can think of a way to get Carlenos out of this, I'd be grateful. I'll take responsibility for my decisions and give you and Robert a chance to vacate town before the Feds. You've made me believe you're a fair-handed and conscientious, *decent* person. Don't make Carlenos and his kids pay for our little agreement. I'd have to hunt you down myself. Even if I have to wait to get out of jail to do it."

I believed him. My lips compressed into a tight line. The suddenly huge weight of this new information filled my head until it threatened to burst.

"How close do you think they are to implicating you?"

"The discrepancies are there if you look hard enough." He saw my blank look and added, "If nothing else happens, maybe a week. No more."

"What will they do to you?" I didn't want to ask, but I had to.

"I don't know. Nothing good."

Whatever he saw in my expression made him frown. "Don't worry about me. Worry about Carlenos," he said, almost angrily. The very fact that he was hiding something from his superiors went against his grain. I knew that. He was a good detective, and a good officer. Spokane couldn't lose such a force for good because of me. It would be impossible to get myself out of the Feds' crosshairs, but I might have a way to keep Frank and Carlenos out of this mess.

To Frank, I just said, "I'll think of something."

He stuck his hand out for me to shake before shrugging back to his feet. "I'm counting on it."

After he left, I sat on the log bench for a long time, meditating and thinking but feeling strangely empty. No time to throw a fit. Not enough warning to even indulge in a good bout of self-pity. The overwhelming pressure of being hunted again pressed down on me. Finally, I pushed it to the back of my mind and got to my feet, secure in the knowledge that I would do anything in my power to protect what was mine. Call me arrogant, but Detective Allen, Carlenos, Robert, Amy, Matt—they were *mine*. Mine to protect. I'd do whatever I needed to in order to keep them all safe. I took a deep breath and opened the door.

"Amy, I'm going to need Robert. Tell him to get back here, ASAP."

ROBERT

"You want me to *what?*" I asked, incredulous. We'd moved from our normal training session into something much weirder.

"Help me move into a place down there in the Valley. In fact, I want help making it look like I moved in quite some time ago." Grace's voice was cool, but the crinkle on the side of her mouth told me she was stifling laughter. Originally, I'd thought that tone existed just to irk me. Now I realized that it signaled her being amused with *herself,* and guaranteed that Grace had another of her crazy ideas.

I had yet to see one of those ideas work as intended, which is why I immediately began to get nervous.

"Grace... Isn't living in town kind of a bad idea?"

"Oh, yes. I imagine the cops will be on me almost immediately." Again, that voice. It was almost as if she *wanted* to be raided by the police.

"Immediately? Probably not. But someone's going to notice you."

"Well, as I'm going to have you call the cops for me, I imagine someone will."

"You're going to have..." My voice trailed off. Grace's eye held a twinkle normally reserved for harrowing life-or-death situations. She planned to intentionally pick a fight with the cops. Lovely.

"I thought we were on friendly terms with the good captain." I knew she was fishing for a reaction, so I was playing it cool here.

Grace sighed. "Too good, as it turns out. The Feds are breathing on our boys in beige."

I began to see. If Captain Carlenos got into a fight with Grace, it might pull some of the pressure off him. Sheriff's deputies would respond based on an anonymous phone call; she'd attack them and make her escape. It was just the kind of theatrics that Grace liked to claim she hated.

"Don't hurt him. Or yourself," I suggested.

Grace shrugged. "I'll be going for a couple of flesh wounds. Make it believable. Mostly, though, I'll evade arrest. Since I know it's coming, I should be able to get away clean."

In an actual fight, assuming she had time to prepare for it, Grace would be able to lay every cop that tried to take her down out flat. I had learned, since last fall, that her summoning was every bit as unique as mine. I had a massive Sense, and I had begun to realize that Grace's Sense was somewhat smaller than average. She compensated for it with beautiful, elaborate rune constructs. The longer and more convoluted the rune phrase, the harder it was to slip your Sense through it; that didn't hamper Grace, as her Sense was just small enough to nimbly slide through, while still being strong enough to hook onto whatever it was she wanted. Once she had it hooked, her elegant phrases would do most of the work bringing it back.

That meant a Grace who had fully prepared for an encounter was a frightening thing. She was going to be able to pre-set all her runes, and for Grace that was the difference between being given a fantastic edge and being at a stunning disadvantage.

I did not place good odds on the cops.

"So, you want the place to look like it's been lived in for a while." Of course she did; that way, the Feds wouldn't bother to trace her back here to Herman's old cabin.

"Got it in one. I have—acquired—the keys to an empty house that's on the market. I need this house to go from zero to trashed in one night. If that's not a job for a teenage boy, I don't know what is."

I smiled in spite of myself. Jake was going to *love* this.

~

"I DID *NOT* EXPECT SUCH a blatant disregard for authority from you, motherfucker," said Jake. As anticipated, he was grinning at me. "How'd you get the keys?"

Jake didn't need to know the full reason he was doing this. In fact, the less Jake knew about why we were doing this, the better. Besides, a party was, in Jake's eyes, reason enough. "A friend of mine has special access. Anyway, empty house, no adults, and graduation incoming. What do you say to a pre-commencement hootenanny?"

We stood in line in front of a set of tables where gowns and caps pretentiously claiming to be "one-size-fits-all" were being handed out to our entire graduating class.

"Party at your place, eh?"

"Yeah. You think you can round up some other people to come grab some 'za or something?"

"Keg?" Jake asked.

I winced—Grace wouldn't want to be responsible for that, but it was expected at these gatherings. Plus, a keg could pay for itself and then some. "Go ahead. I'll chip in twenty as seed. Get what else you can."

Jake grinned at me. "Sweet. I'll hook it up with my keg guy. You want this thing going down tonight?"

"One night only," I said, reaching for my plastic-sealed robe and hat.

"All right, then. I've got some calls to make." Jake's smile had a manic edge to it.

There had been a time, not long ago, when the prospect of a covert party in an empty house would have given me that kind of a rush. Jake was, no doubt, looking forward to a magical night of music, dancing, beer, and (with any luck) light petting in some upstairs walk-in closet.

Don't get me wrong, here; I was looking forward to those things too, though I'd begun to realize that the dream of the closet was oft-pursued but rarely grasped. I also preferred to nurse a beer and stay on guard rather than get blindingly drunk, but my compatriots didn't really need to know that.

"You know," I said wryly to Jake, "I'm not sure that 'one-size-fits-all' is all that accurate." The robe I had tried on resembled something more like a sundress than a graduation robe, its hem falling just above my knees.

"Yeah." Jake said, looking at me. Jake was shorter, so his robe fell to between his knees and his ankles. "Maybe you shouldn't go naked under that thing after all."

I rolled my eyes at my friend. "Go make your calls."

"Aye-aye," he said, flashing me a salute.

I watched him scamper away and brought my head back to focus. The party would be fun, but I'd be there to work.

"THESE SHOULD DO THE TRICK," said Grace to the thrift store salesperson. We were furnishing her house on the cheap, bouncing from thrift store to thrift store.

"Ugh," I said. "That couch looks heavy."

"It's an old hide-a-bed. The cast iron frame'll do that." said Grace. "I'm sure you and your friends can manage."

That "friends" line was undoubtedly for the benefit of the salesperson; I knew she meant me alone. Grace had decided to call it "practice," though I was a little skeptical on that note. Actually, come to think of it, I wasn't the only one who should be out here "practicing."

"Hey, where's your golden boy?"

"Hm?" asked Grace.

"Your new apprentice, Matt. Why isn't he helping me lug all this stuff inside?" Matt had been showing me up in all the academic testing on runes, and he'd only just started training with Grace. I really wanted a crack at taking him on in a task more suited to *my* strengths.

"Well," said Grace in a cool tone of voice, "to begin with, he isn't the one getting a free party out of it."

I sighed and helped Grace load the monstrous couch into the back of our rented truck. We climbed to the privacy of the cab and I waited for the truck doors to close before I turned on her.

"It's not like I'm 'getting' a party either. You've got me pulling evidence out. I can't leave a trace of anyone else there. One of my friends has a single hair found by the cops, and they're in hot water. I've gotta spend the whole evening Sensing stuff, and that means I can't actually have fun at the party."

Grace cocked an eyebrow at me but didn't say anything. I realized that my voice had descended into a whine, and took a breath to compose myself.

"I'm just saying, this *isn't* going to be a fun night. You've got me working double duty, and you let Matt do whatever he wants."

"Well, that's not true at all," Grace said. "I'm using you for field work. I have Matt doing...other things."

"Oh really? What's your boy wonder up to then?"

"He's generating all my fake records, of course. Bank accounts, a couple of mutual funds, some loans, a charitable gift to certain politicians..."

"Never figured you for a political donor," I said.

"I'm not. But I may as well let it be publicly discovered that some of the ones I don't like have been taking cash from me," she half-cocked a smile. I rolled my eyes in response.

"I see. He sits at his desk and does paperwork while I lug around furniture." It was pretty clear who'd gotten the cushy job here.

"Well, you have a tendency to cheat at the paperwork," said Grace, smiling. "We're here. Let's unload."

I LEANED back into the secondhand couch and closed my eyes, letting the stillness of the Sense wash over me. As always, complete awareness of everything happening inside the bubble surrounding me flooded my consciousness. I had work to do here, and I knew I needed to start, but I took a moment to enjoy the absolute peace that being enveloped in the...

"Hey—are you passing out already?"

The girl who knocked my focus away with this question was, I decided, kind of cute. She wore a tank-top, giving me a great view of what little cleavage she had. Her tight jeans outlined her legs, sleek and firm. She was also sitting next to me on the couch, leaning toward me with an almost drunken sway.

Of course. The *one party* where I was busy. This was going on the ever-lengthening list of favors Grace owed me.

"Nah, just...listening to the music," I said. I had been, too. Actually, the kinetic vibrations of the music had been just one part of me as I extended my Sense, but that was a little too much to go into.

"Oh. You like this band?" Damn her persistence. I felt a stirring in the more primal areas of my consciousness, prodding me to drop what I was doing and pay attention to that smooth, high-pitched voice. Those primal sections of the teenage boy? They are powerfully strong. Hard to shake off. It took me a moment to compose myself before I gave her a shrug.

"Don't really know them. They sound all right."

"Yeah. I prefer Squirrel Thump to these guys. Better bass lines. Who's your favorite band?" Crap. I shouldn't have used the music as my cover; it was clearly an invitation for my new companion to seek more contact, not less.

Her hand came to rest lightly on my upper arm, a signal as unmistakable as it was inconvenient. My hormones cut a burning path through my focus, but if any trace of these kids' identities was discovered by the Feds, it would mean trouble. I ducked my head down and closed my eyes again, willing my temptress to take the hint.

"What's the matter? You shy?"

"Uh...yeah," I said, going with the presented excuse before I thought it out. I knew it was a mistake as soon as it left my mouth.

It was, too. She leaned her head in toward mine until her beer-scented breath grazed my ear as she whispered, "You don't have to be.

Jake said you could use the company. I think you're cute, and he says you're a great guy. No reason to be shy with me."

Goosebumps shot down my right side; an involuntary shudder escaped me as I struggled for breath. I simultaneously cursed and praised Jake's name.

"Look, I think you're really nice," I said, trying to put some distance between us.

"But?" she asked, falling back to her place and sticking her lower lip out into a pouty-face.

"But... I'm really busy tonight," I tried desperately.

"Busy? You were sitting here doing nothing. If you don't like me, fine. Just say so. You don't have to be full of bullshit about it." The brunette stood up, shook out her hair, and flounced in front of me. She wiggled her rear end as she walked by in a deliberate show of what I had rejected. I made a note to ask Jake about her later; maybe I still had a chance to mend that fence.

To business, though. I closed my eyes again. I had to wait for my raging hormones to calm and my base desires to subside before the focus needed for the Sense came to me. Stepping into that kind of universal awareness shocked me like a cold shower. The knowledge of everything around me drew my attention away from my own sense of longing. Once again, the serene bliss of...

"Hey, fucker, what the hell just happened with Shawna?"

Son. Of. A. Bitch.

"Jake... I'm trying to do some shit, here."

"What, exactly, are you trying to do that's more important than a solid make-out session with Shawna? I got her all primed and everything, and you blew her off. What the fuck could you be—"

Jake cut off immediately when he saw the hard look in my eyes.

"Oh," he said. "Really, dude? At a party?"

I gave him a slight nod of my head. He shook his. Jake was never going to be comfortable with this sort of thing.

"Look, asshole," he said. "You do what you gotta do. I don't wanna know. I'll go try to mend things with Shawna. You get free later tonight, you let me know. Willy's got some seriously good Ex flying around here, we can grab some chicks, have a good time."

Ecstasy? I didn't even know Jake was into that sort of thing. No time to deal with it now, though. I gave him a noncommittal shrug; I was going to be busy all night, and I would get nowhere moralizing with him.

"Sweet." Jake smiled and popped off the couch to follow other, more party-like pursuits.

At last, I slipped into the Sense and immediately began to clean things up. Hair, saliva, blood, and semen were all transported to the fire pit in the back, which had a roaring fire. The blood was from someone who had cut himself on an open beer bottle; the semen was from the walk-in closets and I didn't want to know.

As the night progressed, I found out anyway. I felt every heady feeling of a party in full swing. Every dancing gyration, every lurching stomach whose contents I then had to clean up, every awkward grope in every shaded corner and, yes, every closet, pounded their way into my consciousness. This clearly ranked as one of the best parties of high school, and I spent it feeling other people having a good time around me.

I heard a story once about a guy who was punished by the gods. They placed him neck-deep in a cool stream and gave him a powerful thirst. However, any time he lowered his head to drink, the level of the water dropped to just out of range of his lips. I felt like that, walking around the revels of my peers, feeling them all, but not participating.

Yeah. Grace owed me big for this one.

Even so, throughout the night I maintained my vigil.

THE NEXT MORNING, I kicked Jake awake. I was not, perhaps, as gentle as I could have been. I didn't care.

"Rise and shine, my slumbering friend," I said in as falsely cheery a voice as I could muster. "It's time to go to school." Most of the others had already departed, but Jake had gone on a pretty serious bender after talking to me. That opened up all kinds of opportunities for payback.

"Rrrrrhhhhhnnnn," Jake moaned. "Go...go fuck yourself."

"Now, now, my little magpie, who needs that kind of talk?" I said in a falsetto, imitating an old maid as I pulled blankets down off the window, letting the sun's rays hit Jake directly in the face.

He sat up slowly.

"Yup. You people *are* evil," he grumbled. "I'm gonna grab a shower."

"Ok, but don't expect me to cook breakfast."

Jake said nothing, just waved his hand at me as he entered the bathroom. His hand was, of course, clenched, save for a single finger. It was the most fun I'd had for a while, and the most I was likely to have for a long time now that Grace was picking a war with the Feds.

After Jake showered and left for school, I made one last round, cleaning up anything I had missed. I surveyed my handiwork. The house was clean, but lived in. The carpet was trampled; some dishes were used. The keg had left with its purchaser, and most of the liquor bottles and pizza boxes had been disposed of as well. I left some for show. The toilet had a very used look about it—I didn't think that urine or feces was subject to analysis, and if it was, there was such a jumble in there, good luck pulling any one sample.

All in all, we had done it. The house looked like someone had lived in it for a while.

There. My job was finally finished. Grace could handle it from here on out.

I had to go rehearse the end of my high school career.

GRACE

"AMAZING WHAT ONE night's hard use by a herd of teenagers can do," I commented, my lips quirking upward as I surveyed my new "hideout." The main door of the house opened into an entryway that led into the living room. To the right of the living room, the house divided into a dining room with access to the upstairs, and a small alcove that had entrances to a downstairs room, the bathroom, and the kitchen.

Grungy traffic patterns were ground into the beige carpet between the couch and the kitchen. The whole house sported smudges and grime that usually would have required months of surreptitious use. I slapped a tag on either side of the front entryway before climbing up on the couch to affix several more to the middle of the ceiling in the living room. The tags went up in the kitchen next, even though it required climbing up on the counter to fix runes to the wall opposite the entrance above a once-white sink.

"You sure you're ready to do this?" Robert asked.

I hopped down from the counter and looked up at him, surprising a fleeting expression of concern on his face. We'd planned this event for the early evening, since that seemed the most likely time to get the cops to respond immediately and still give me darkness for most of my escape. Given the limited time window before Allen and Carlenos landed in hot water with the Feds, today also happened to be the day before Robert's graduation. Robert's uncertainty with this plan might be justified, but I just didn't have time to get into a long discussion with him about it right now. We'd already spent most of the day on prep work as it was.

Thinking back to my own high school graduation, the whole time leading up to the ceremony had been an uncertain, limbo-like period for me. If anything, I'd bet that was adding to Robert's sense of unease.

"Of course I am," I answered finally, my voice full of brisk bravado. Turns out, learning the Feds knew I still breathed and psyching myself up to wave my person in their faces engendered two entirely conflicting mindsets. At this point, I wasn't even sure if it mattered who or what had tipped the Feds off. It could be any number of options: another Grove sold me out, someone recognized me in Nevada, or even someone had noticed me here in Spokane. Either way, flaunting my continued existence would guarantee me their immediate and undivided attention. The problem was what to do with that attention once I had it. I sure wouldn't be getting rid of it very easily.

All for a good cause, Grace, all for a good cause, I told myself.

"We owe it to Allen and Carlenos to keep them out of this if we can. If we wait, it doesn't stop the Feds from looking for me any way they can. It just ups the likelihood that Allen and Carlenos get outed for helping us."

I reached up to ruffle Robert's scruffy hair as I added, "You just make that anonymous phone call and worry about your graduation tomorrow."

It spoke volumes about his inner unease that he didn't even offer his usual protest about keeping my hands to myself. No words would fix what was bothering him, and the limited minutes we had left to pull this off today were ticking away. My nervous energy took me back through the living and dining rooms to the stairs. There should be tags all the way up to the second floor as well. These stairs had two steps and then turned at a ninety degree angle before the rest of the flight. That should come in handy. Robert followed me up.

"You sure you'll be able to be there after all this?" he asked, gesturing at the tag-coated walls.

I climbed the last few steps and smiled for his benefit. "It's at seven, right? I'll be there with bells on." I reached the top of the stairs. A large closet took up the area opposite them. Immediately to the left and right stood two more doorways. I poked my head in the door to the left. The room's window looked out the front of the house.

"Even if that's true, won't someone recognize you?" Robert asked skeptically. "If the reaction's anything like last year, they'll have pictures of you everywhere."

I switched to the right-hand door. This room's window looked out on the back yard.

"Hey, let me worry about that," I said. "You just focus on graduating tomorrow and getting your butt to college. Speaking of that, aren't your foster parents planning on some big dinner for you tonight? I've got this under control, so you should get moving. Just give me about another ten minutes before you make the call. See you later."

I shooed him back down the stairs with a wave of my hand. Robert's lips compressed in an unhappy line, but he vanished around the bend in the steps. The sound of the front door slamming reverberated through the half-furnished house as he left.

Yup, he wasn't happy, but I'd deal with that tomorrow after I'd successfully executed my diversion—and he'd gotten through his graduation.

This room to the right of the stairs had potential. Along with the back yard, a small section of the downstairs roof was visible through the window. The asphalt shingles sloped gently downward, then changed to the corrugated metal of the covered patio roof. It appeared like the whole thing might be sturdy enough to walk on. I opened the window and stepped tentatively out onto the roof, testing the footing all the way down to the patio. This then, was the room I wanted to stage my escape from.

～

ALL THE WINDOWS throughout the house were shrouded with heavy drapes. There were no gaps where anyone could see in. Even so, I felt curiously naked sitting by myself in that living room.

I'd taken care of my last-minute preparations and tags as soon as Robert left; Matt's meticulously drawn-up red herring papers were stuffed under a book in the desk upstairs to make it look like I'd forgotten about the documents in my haste to leave. Mixed in with them were Carlenos' and Allen's alibis along with an insurance plan for Robert, hinting that I had been framing them the last few months to take heat off myself. Matt might not be powerful, but he was already showing a knack for summoning original paperwork and, umm, altering it.

I desperately needed this to go smoothly for a number of reasons, not the least of which were the lives and well-being of certain members of the County Sheriff's department.

Unlike my last big confrontation, I didn't have access to the Seattle Grove's resources or arsenal this time around. That might actually be for the best. This stunt was going to ruffle enough feathers as it was; I didn't want to compound that by getting called onto the carpet for breaking one of Seattle's favorite toys again. No sense adding extra scrutiny from officials on both sides by burning through tons of illicit weaponry. Not to mention that I didn't want to seriously hurt anyone; big weapons made that difficult.

I'd had to get creative.

The Grove heads wouldn't be happy that I'd chosen to expose myself to protect people they didn't see as assets, but I was confident that I could lay out my reasons in a persuasive manner. Allowing them to be exposed would be an even worse alternative in my official incident report.

This situation definitely demanded asking for forgiveness rather than trying to wade into the mire of glacially moving red tape an interim director would have to go through for permission.

The whirring of the surveillance chopper's blades came first. Nervously, I readjusted the shoulder strap holding my blood vials and the straps fixing the rune board to my arm. I found myself staring at the dark red liquid sloshing against the confines of the small glass tubes while I waited.

Blood formed the conduit for summoning, but contrary to a lot of crazy rumors, it didn't have to be human in origin. Cow's blood tended to be my blood of choice since it could be obtained without too many questions at a butcher's shop. Hell, larger Groves usually had a butcher shop or two under their control, making obtaining blood even less of an issue. So far the Feds hadn't figured out a way to legally differentiate the regular butcher shops from the summoner-run ones. This batch of blood had come from a butcher shop this morning and I'd kept the vials chilled until needed for this fight.

Taking a deep breath, I rearranged the runes on my board, sending out a summoning to locate the direction Carlenos and Allen were driving in from. When it found them, they were already really close. Moving the drapes a miniscule fraction, I freed a sliver of window to see out. On cue, Detective Allen's vehicle turned onto the road running in front of the house. The law enforcement cars quietly started to roll in, setting up a perimeter. Carlenos left his vehicle to block access at the turn-off and changed to a different vehicle two back from Allen. More cars rolled silently in. My sliver of view reached its expiration. Too much activity got blocked out by the curtain.

I let the curtain gently sway back into place and summoned the light reflections to my eyes as if I stood in the front yard. On the road in front of the house sat shadows of five county patrol cars, a SWAT van, and several more plain cars which I assumed were the Feds. So, a total of approximately twenty armed-to-the-teeth individuals currently camped out on the lawn. No sweat, right?

Of course, that's what they considered me, too. Not armed, but totally dangerous.

Buck up, Gracie, I told myself. *No heroics here, just make it convincing and get out.*

The SWAT members began deploying to the front and the back to block the exits, signaling to me that they were committed to breaching the house. That was my cue to de-ass the first floor. I let my Sense drop and ran for the stairs.

This house had the low steep steps of older houses, easy to charge up two at a time but deceptively cardio-intensive. Panting, I made it to the top and braced my hands against the right doorframe to catch my breath just as the front door splintered open.

On the count of three, I thumbed open a vial of blood and slammed my hand down on the first tag at the top of the stairs. My Sense flicked through it to the tag in the entryway closet.

The first two deputies into the house were pelted with sharp pieces of kinetically enhanced basalt. Loud curses filled the downstairs. The force of the impacts could be heard through the floorboards along with the frantic yelling of the SWAT team. I winced and hoped I hadn't misjudged the amount of force. I'd only used up to softball-sized pieces of rock, but with the force and the jagged edges... My goal for today was zero fatalities, but it had to look convincing for this tactic to be worth anything. I re-summoned the light reflections to my eyes, checking the results of my first gambit.

Once the rock stopped flying, those injured exited for medical attention. As another five deputies stumbled in and tried to kick clear the loose rockfall in the doorway, I dropped my current summons and splashed blood across a second tag. Immediately, the stairwell writhed with a giant nest of rattlesnakes just above the turn in the stairs.

Looking at all those snakes made my stomach do somersaults, but it should definitely slow down anyone's attempt to pay me a visit with assault rifles.

I moved into the room to the right of the stairwell, leaving the door slightly ajar so I could still peek through to the stairway.

A deputy rounded the ninety-degree corner and bit back an epithet before hastily withdrawing to the living room. The plan was working as it should for now.

Splashing a vial across the runes, I activated another tag. A low-riding rain of one-inch nails swept across the downstairs. The summon targeted the deputies below waist height, avoiding...other vital areas. A nail or two in the calf or thigh should be plenty debilitating. Most of the deputies caught more than two. I winced as several men thudded to the floor, yelling and clutching their legs.

Quickly rearranging the runes, I blooded another summon, looking for Carlenos and Allen. Allen stood on the road in front of the house manning a command position. Carlenos, half-crouched, slowly moved toward the front door with his weapon drawn. He'd almost made it to the front porch steps.

Quietly I closed my door the rest of the way. Now, to provide convincing proof that Carlenos and Allen weren't in cahoots with me in any way. I wiped sweaty palms on my skirt and took a deep breath while I waited through a count of ten. These pre-set tags only worked once; for it to be effective, Carlenos needed to be well into the front room by the time it triggered. I reached ten and swiped blood across the runes, filling the downstairs with an angry swarm of wasps.

It would be best if none of the deputies were allergic to bees—and I hoped they weren't—but even if they were, Matt had already confirmed for me that the squad cars carried a standard issue medical kit that included a shot of epinephrine. Absolute worst-case scenario, the Valley Medical Center where Frank had been treated last fall was only a few minutes away. Any of the deputies who had a severe reaction should be able to get medical assistance in time.

I acknowledged to myself that this tactic still gambled with their lives. But it was a really convincing ploy, with minimal true risk.

It got harder for me to remember that once the screaming started. I winced. Pretty rough pay back for all of Carlenos' understanding with Robert the last few months. *You'll have time to feel bad about this later, Grace,* I chided myself. *Right now you need to close the deal.*

The Seattle Grove's weapons might be off-limits this time, but that didn't mean I was completely disarmed. I fine-tuned the runes on my board and powered my next summon, sending a hail of arrows at the Feds and deputies outside the house with deliberate, pinpoint accuracy. As they flew, I spent a breath praying that no one would move wrong in the fraction of a second it took for the projectiles to find their targets.

Two shafts pierced Frank in his left thigh and one just below the knee in the same leg. Arrows punched into the Feds on either side of him, taking them in strategically non-vital areas: the outside shoulder, upper arm, lower arm, outer thigh and lower legs were my prime targets of choice.

Well, Grace, I told myself snarkily as I watched the results of the summon, *Frank already owes you the use of his legs. At least this time he's only injuring one of them. Here's hoping he remembers that after this little stunt.*

As the wounded began to hunch over and the less-wounded to scatter and take cover, I sent another volley, puncturing the vehicle tires and windshields.

Deputies poured out of the house, trying to avoid the wasps. To be absolutely thorough, one last summoned volley of arrows should do the trick. My carefully aimed arrows fell in a seemingly thick carpet, wounding Carlenos and several of the less-hurt deputies. My fingers flicked over my rune board, changing the phrasing to summon the outside light to my eyes and double-check my handiwork. Every single law enforcement official out front sported some type of injury. Nobody appeared to be dead or mortally wounded. Regardless, they should be slowed down enough or too busy finding medical help to pursue me.

No matter how careful I'd been or who it protected, this really didn't feel like a good day's work.

I opened the window a crack and slid my small frame out onto the back porch roof. Time for me to leave.

My head was starting to twinge from using my Sense so much in a short amount of time, but this should be my last big summon for the night. The giant owl spirit, Hyctea, appeared next to me. The wind created by her condor-like wing span pushed my hair back from my face. Hyctea was a guardian spirit tied to the Moore family through the Visitant Pacts, and right now I really could use a protector.

Most of the Visitant pacts are older than dirt really, but new pacts are made on very rare occasions. My family's pact with Hyctea dated to so many centuries ago as to be almost impossible to count. Guardians have their own home Weaves and can be tied to a person, family, place, or Grove. Hyctea had entered into my family's pact in return for a service, but she had her own reasons why she negotiated and valued the exchange.

The new pacts are generally for ancestral spirits, and occur when a summoner dies. Summoners can leave behind a runic avatar in their chosen Grove book after they pass on to the afterlife. As much as I loved my spirits—especially Hyctea, Sir John, and Redwood, coming back to this Weave as a spirit was an awfully big commitment to make. With my chaotic life, when I died, staying dead sounded pretty darn restful.

Hyctea knelt to allow me to scramble onto her broad back. Hugging her feathered neck, I braced myself as she busted up away from the back window, putting more distance between us and the chaos ensuing out front.

A lone deputy standing guard on the back porch surprised us. He saw us clear the window and gave a shout. He swung around his assault rifle and fired. Hyctea pumped her wings, angling upward sharply. The bullets missed me, rattling off the armored feathers on her underside with little effect. Spirits tend to have more resilience and strength than was anticipated by your standard firearm manufacturer. As long as we didn't run into any large ordinance up here, we should be home free, and I'd start worrying about getting myself to tomorrow's graduation.

Just then, as if to mock my cocky thoughts, a bullet shot through my skirt and scored along my outer hip. I choked back a shriek, though surely the gunfire would bring anyone who was still mobile from the front of the house at any moment.

I spotted the police chopper coming closer out of the corner of my eye, still a bit off to our right. "Climb as high as you can!" I gasped to Hyctea. "More will be coming, and we want to avoid being seen from the ground. Try and get away from that helicopter."

She gave a low hoot in affirmation. Hunched over her back, I slid the rune tiles into place and summoned most of the fuel out of the helicopter's gas tank. It splashed down over part of the roof, and I considered lighting it up. It was the last house on the street before the dead end, after all. But then, Matt's carefully constructed documents would go to waste if I did, so better not.

The helicopter crew attempted to pursue us for a few more seconds before they realized what had happened and made an emergency landing in the empty field behind the house.

Hyctea flew up and away from the crime scene until the ground became a blurred tapestry. My hip burned. I hunched over her back, hugging her neck, sick to my stomach with pain, cold, and self-doubt. This had been my only option to protect Detective Allen and Carlenos. I didn't regret it exactly, but the reality of what I'd just done left me feeling inadequate to deal with the inevitable backlash from authorities on both sides of the fence.

HYCTEA and I flew north over Mount Spokane State Park to avoid populated areas. Just when I thought I might be able to congratulate myself on a clean getaway, something large and explosive hit Hyctea low on her underbelly.

She turned, managing to shield me from the worst of the blast, absorbing most of it into the down stroke of her wings. The shock wave still vibrated through me like a live jolt. Heat and black stars wove in my vision, gifting me with a brief moment of disorientation.

Groggy, I didn't see the second blast that knocked me sideways almost off Hyctea's back. I struggled to right myself, desperately clutching her armored feathers. I caught the military jet streaking toward us out of the corner of my eye. Before I could even shout a warning, its rotary cannon strafed us.

Hyctea wheeled. Her wing swung up to protect me. She caught most of the gunfire on her armored underside, but the bullets tore through my fluttering skirt like cotton candy, missing my feet by such a small margin I could actually *feel* the air they displaced.

Hyctea blocked one last blast by rolling so that she was between me and the jet. She shuddered with the impact, lowed one last guttural hoot and then completely disincorporated from this Weave.

I fell.

The wind rushed past my ears in an endless whistle. The foliage blurred into a green haze below me. I tried to gauge how much time I had before I hit the ground in a gruesome human pancake. The remains of my skirt flapped in my face, tangling with my arms. I unbuttoned the waistband with numb hands and let the air resistance rip it away from me.

Free from the entangling fabric, I could finally move. I forced my fingers, stiff from the cold, over my rune board, painfully sliding the rune tiles carefully into place against the friction of the ferocious air current. The magnets that held them to the board stuck more than usual, and I worried that one might whip off the board if I tried to pry it into place faster.

Gritting my teeth, not trusting a vial of blood against this wind, I dug my fingers into the bullet score on my hip to reopen it. I spread my own blood over the summoning, holding onto my willpower with a grim determination. If I screwed up now...this fall would end in a very final and epic landing.

A large mountain of feathers popped into existence on the ground below me, denuding several poultry farms' worth of chickens in the process. Despite my imminent mortal danger, a commercial flashed through my mind extolling the farmer's friend, the pre-plucked chicken.

I landed at near-terminal velocity in a giant plume of feathers, exhibiting none of my namesake. For a stunned moment I lay cocooned in that soft, fluffy crater, just thanking the gods for my survival. As the blizzard of plumage started descending back toward me, my sluggish brain registered the idea that it might be a good idea to get moving, and not just because a manhunt was surely headed this way. Breathing in that fuzzy avalanche would be an issue. Awkwardly flopping around, I tried to get upright. The feathers slid under my weight the moment I attempted anything resembling leverage.

After two episodes of thrashing, coughing, and choking on feathers, it became apparent that standing up in the normal way just wasn't going to happen. Flailing, I floundered forward in a crude parody of synchronized swimming, using my hands to scoop out a pathway in front of me. Eventually I emerged, whiplashed, covered in tufts of feathers, and possibly slightly concussed from the fall, but alive. My ankle twinged fiercely, but upon experimentation, held my weight. Good enough.

I heard the whir of another helicopter's blades somewhere in the distance. Kinetically increasing my speed with momentum stolen from the Spokane River's Bowl and Pitcher rapids, I headed to the east, away from the tell-tale noise, using the trees as best I could to hide from any search parties.

As the copter blades got louder, I wove through the thinning trees. Wincing, I added a little more kinetic energy to my summoning, attempting to get through the clearing before the copter got closer. A gunshot suddenly interrupted the rhythm of the chopper blades. The bullet sang past my shoulder, obviously meant for my head or my neck.

Not that it really mattered what part of me they were aiming for. Any of those targets would put me severely out of commission. Not to mention the implications, since I still couldn't see the copter. I assumed that meant some very powerful fire arms and scopes had been put to use. I wasn't a true fire-arms expert, but it seemed safe to assume the Feds had brought in the heavies—also known as anti-summoner squads. Not good. With my right hand, I dug into the outside pocket of my bag, searching for the ring that held the runes for Redwood, one my family's most trusted guardian spirits. He was not only a protector but a friend. The ring was wedged up against the seam at the very bottom. I fumbled it onto a finger and brought my hand out in a fist so it wouldn't fall.

I jagged through the next set of trees, altering my trajectory and hoping it would throw my pursuers off the scent.

It didn't.

Another bullet cracked into the trunk of a spruce only six inches from my head. At this moment, my only saving grace was my superhuman speed. It made me a much harder target to hit. I switched Redwood's ring from my right hand to my left, jammed it into the sluggish bleeding on my hip, then pushed my Sense through the flare of pain in my head and my hip and into the summons.

A flash of lightning and a sudden gust of wind told me Redwood, two hundred feet of majestic old-growth forest incarnated, stood at my back. I couldn't stop to double-check, but with the scent of green needles and ozone masking the now stormy weather, I didn't really need to. Another gunshot cracked through the night, and I didn't even have to explain the situation to him. The winds snapped violently and the bullet went wide. I kept moving. Redwood would have no trouble catching up with me, and he was much better at knocking speeding bullets off trajectory than I could ever hope to be. Besides, with Redwood's ferocious thunder now splitting open the night, the crack of gunfire got muddled. Even with his support I couldn't afford to be a stationary target.

Good thing I kept moving, because a second copter joined the first. Not even Redwood could keep both of them off of me. Not without knocking them out of the sky, and I'd never ask him to do that.

No matter how I zigged or zagged, my copter stayed right with me, taking a shot whenever it got an opportunity. My strength was starting to flag. If I wanted to make it through this, I needed to do something, and fast.

Obviously, the gunner didn't have a lock on me all the time, otherwise they'd be taking many more shots. That meant they were tracking me another way. I scrambled through my limited knowledge of military sensors, and decided the most likely was some type of infrared, since there really weren't any other sources of heat in this area of the forest except small animals which could easily be filtered out.

A large, granite outcropping, surrounded by thick pine growth, gave me the opportunity I needed. I remembered someone in the hazy past saying the first rule of evasion is looking like someone no one's looking for. Or in this case, some*thing* no one's looking for.

The bottom of the outcropping formed a small crevice. Re-arranging the runes on my board, I widened the crack and summoned enough dirt away to make a ten-by-ten-foot hole. Stepping into the opening I'd created, I summoned most of the rock back into place, sealing myself in. A small gap low in the rock face let in fresh air, so I wouldn't suffocate. The pitch-black interior pressed in oppressively, but I needed to finish making it a truly effective hiding place before worrying about light. Summoning a layer of permafrost from the arctic, I inserted it into the rock above me in a thick layer, lining my small hiding place with its ice to mask my body heat from any sensors.

The condensation in my breath hovered thickly in the suddenly chill air of my refuge. My head felt about five times too big and my hands shook with reaction to the cold. I pushed myself to summon a small battery-powered night light, a warmer set of clothes, and a first-aid kit. I stripped, shivering, and examined the wound on my hip. It still bled sluggishly, but didn't really scream "life-threatening" to me. Hopefully I'd be all right for now. The first aid kit provided gauze and a self-stick plaster for my hip. Then I summoned a thick blue sweater and loose sweat pants and shrugged into them. The sweat pants were the loosest warm clothes I had available, but stretching them over the wound was still a new kind of torture.

Reassured that my hiding place was as secure and secret as it could be under the circumstances, I summoned a slip of paper and scribbled the rune Algiz, giving Redwood the all-clear signal. Sketching another quick summons, I sent it to him; he would know that rune meant I had found refuge, and he could safely return to his own Weave. Since the Feds used mundane weapons such as guns and explosives, it would be very difficult for them to kill or permanently harm a guardian spirit like Redwood or Hyctea in this Weave, but that was no reason to leave him hanging.

That taken care of, I figured it might be a good time to find out what the authorities had up their sleeves. Closing my eyes, I felt out the runes and started forming the compound phrases to start looking for the closest team of searchers. After several minutes of tweaking my summon, I found what I wanted. The hand radio appeared as a sudden weight in my lap. It crackled and buzzed due to the stone and earth's interference, but it should work well enough for me to eavesdrop. Or at least, that was my hope. If they realized one was missing, they might decide not to use the radios or send fake information. If that happened, I'd just have to come up with a new plan. But right now, listening in seemed like my best option.

Even if I did manage to get something useful out of the radio, I'd still need backup. The search teams weren't likely to just up and leave the area any time soon.

Given the speed and thoroughness of the Fed's response, I'd no doubt they were setting up road checks, blockades, surveillance, and the whole works. Getting out of the Mount Spokane area and into the Valley would be like trying to sneak out of one police state into another. A police state where I'd actually promised to attend a graduation ceremony in just under eight hours...

The radio crackled to life, confirming some of my suspicions. They were systematically blocking all the roads out from my last sighting and slowly expanding the search area. If I could provide a decoy and get them to concentrate their efforts in one area, I might still be able to slip through. Grabbing a piece of paper out of my bag, I scribbled a note to Matt asking him to fabricate a false "summoner sighting" compelling enough to draw the Fed's attention to the northeast.

I just might make Robert's graduation yet.

ROBERT

GRADUATION IS, at its heart, a relatively simple ceremony. One stands in a long line outside a gymnasium. One walks in this line, slowly, to the chairs set up *in* said gymnasium. One sits. At a certain, specified time, one stands back up and continues to stand in line until one's name is called. Then one walks across the stage, grabs one's diploma case (the diploma itself will arrive in the mail), and then walks, in a line, to sit back down.

That's it. That's all that's required at a graduation ceremony. I guess the valedictorian has to make a speech, but that had little to do with me.

I contemplated this simplicity as I stood outside the gymnasium in my line, and wondered why I felt nervous. I realized that, subconsciously, I was envisioning scenarios in which I *didn't* graduate. What if they had a pop chemistry quiz for everyone before they let us get the diplomas? Could I remember enough to get through? I knew it was silly, but my heart began to race and my breathing quickened.

Looking around, I saw others in the same predicament. All my classmates were twitching, or giggling, or losing focus in their eyes. Graduation is a very simple process, but it wasn't until I stood in that line that I realized *it has to be.* Any more complicated, and the mess of humanity standing around me could never pull it off.

The music started. "Pomp and Circumstance." For once, I wasn't sitting in the sweat-drenched balcony with the rest of the band, and that made me smile. This song becomes the bane of any high school band geek's existence. Like the ceremony itself, it is painfully simple. In fact, my part as tenor sax consisted of nothing more than quarter notes. I hated it. Even now, standing in a line and about to go through the most important moment of my academic career to date, all I could think about was how glad I was not to be playing that friggin' song.

The line began to move. Slowly. The graduation walk is a very slow, formal walk. One foot goes in front. The other foot drags up to the first one, then stops. A beat later, that other foot goes forward. I'd been in marching band, and I knew it was possible to march to music much faster than this. Still, the whole line proceeded with a step-pause rhythm.

Once in my seat, I craned my neck. The graduates were seated on folding chairs on the floor while the audience sat in the bleachers normally used for basketball games. The graduates were coming in from the back of the gym; two more doors flanked the stage at the front for use by the public, but they were masked by the stage itself. Only a small gap separated bleachers and stage, about as wide as the doorway itself. The stage filled the entire end of the gymnasium, a gaudy behemoth whose only purpose was to be walked across by every student on the floor. This was going to take a while. I sighed.

I managed to spot Francene and Donald in the stands. Francene was fanning herself with her program. I couldn't blame her; it was sweltering in here. I didn't see Grace, but I assumed she was keeping a low profile. That relieved me; if I couldn't pick Grace out of the crowd, no one else could either.

Last night's flap had been pretty spectacular. The news reported that the summoner had been confronted by the police. Detective Allen had been interviewed, and said some pretty nasty things about Grace. I guessed he was acting; otherwise I'd already be under arrest.

The lady from the Feds whose name I couldn't place also had

some screen time, and she talked about how Grace was considered a "high-priority" target or some such. The Feds weren't clued in to Grace's connection with me, though, so security here was non-existent.

Speeches. I imagine that every commencement address ever made looks exactly the same. Somehow, wearing the square cap and the blue robes made the speeches meaningful. Tomorrow, the rest of my life really would start. It finally clicked that it wasn't the ceremony I felt nervous about; it was what came after. My classmates and I sat, rapt, and listened to this simple truth given to us by Megan Reeser, our valedictorian.

I had seen Megan once or twice in the halls, but really never knew her. She wasn't the stand-out type. Still, as I sat, she spoke to me. She let us know that we had made it through, and she bolstered our courage for the future. In that moment, Megan Reeser was amazing. We drank her words as though she were a prophet. Then she sat back down, primly, and the ceremony continued.

The diplomas began, each row rising in turn to be presented with their cases. Some kids struck an exultant pose, some cried something unintelligible. Most scurried across the stage, anxious to get their diplomas and rejoin the faceless mass. Being an "L," I was staged in the middle of the pack, and my breathing began to quicken as Principal Stevens worked through "J" and then "K." Halfway through "K," my row rose and stood in line.

"Larsen...Larrien...Lerman..." Gulp. "Lobson..." Here we go. "Lorents."

I ascended the steps to the stage, my heart leaping into my throat. I looked at Francene, saw her clapping wildly, and couldn't help but smile. Her excitement about me warmed my heart a little; I had to remind myself that I was trying to keep my distance.

Halfway across the stage, I realized that Principal Stevens had missed his mark. He was supposed to keep reading names; instead, he had stopped after mine. I shot him a look and was surprised to see it returned. His face set into a twisted grin; as I passed him, he leaned his head down to whisper to me.

The voice was not Principal Stevens's. It belonged to a horror instead.

"Whuft! I did not expect for there to be so much applause for one such as you, boy."

My eyebrows shot up in recognition. Immediately my nerves became very, very real. Cythymau's voice haunted my worst nightmares; this was the last place I expected to hear it. I took a breath and snapped my Sense into place, preparing for what was coming.

Principal Stevens was not there. In fact, no one was there; Principal Stevens was an illusion of light and force. It was a complicated summons, intricate and almost perfectly done, but his voice carried no breath as he whispered in my ear.

"Yes, boy. Get ready. Well done. I couldn't let you go through a... *commencement*...ceremony without adding my own, special, test."

I stole a glance at the crowd. The ceremony, so simple in nature, had been disrupted. Everyone stared back at me; I noticed Francene clutching her program to her chest. Grace was somewhere out there, and as soon as things started to get weird she'd start prepping something. I needed to stall. The more time she had, the more effective she would be.

So I went with mockery.

"You know," I said, mimicking Cythymau's detached, pleasant tone, "it's never really been personal between us. You want to invade my plane of existence, I want to stop you, etcetera. All professional and businesslike, yes?"

"Whuft! Yes, business. I offered you a deal once, do you remember? Business! But you turned me down. You did not want to do *business*."

Cythymau had offered to let me join Andrea in slavery in exchange for sparing the Spokane area. Not the rest of the world; that he would have conquered with ease had I agreed. But Spokane would have been safe.

"I got better terms from a Cornuprocyon," I said. I had, too. Rick the Cornuprocyon had burst in on our negotiations, attacking Cythymau and freeing me.

"Whuft! Did you, boy? Did you indeed? Because the Cornuprocyon bought you only your own freedom. You could have bought the safety of *all* these people." He gestured out toward the crowd, and his whisper became fast and harsh. "But you did not. You spurned me, and left these people defenseless."

"Not defenseless. Just not under your protection. There's a difference," I said, baring my teeth. I didn't know what was coming, but I knew Cythymau wanted to get the last word on me. The rustling in the crowd let me know that people were starting to realize there was a problem. Grace was undoubtedly one of them. I knew the tags for the heavy artillery were even now being set. Cythymau's attention was focused on me, and that was a tactical error. The more he spoke with me, the bigger the blindside was going to be. I almost felt sorry for him.

"You see, I've been practicing. These people are not under your protection, they are under *mine*." I flashed him my teeth. "And you are nothing more than an illusion."

"True, true. Illusion, yes. On your side of the world. That matters little, now. I am not unreasonable. Businesslike, as you say. Yes. So I offer again: these people will be safe, for all time. No harm comes to the people in this"—he paused, accessing Andrea's memories —"county. You see, I extend the boundaries of my protection, so generous am I. No harm to all, in trade for you. Just you. Yes?"

And all I would have to do in return was submit myself to Cythymau's slavery, doubling his power base and dooming everything that *wasn't* Spokane County. It was a fool's deal, but it tempted me for half a second.

Still, I held the advantage here. Cythymau could only send a handful of his beasts through, and Grace had been in the audience during our little tête-à-tête, laying an ambush. Cythymau thought I was alone here; most of my battles recently had been solo. We had him.

"You know, it's tempting," I kept at him. "After all, most of my friends and the people I call family are here. Heck, if you're including the county, then I still get my college over in Cheney. What more could a guy ask for, right?"

The face that belonged to Principal Stevens lit with hope. I knew I was making the right choice when I said, "But you tipped your hand. You let me see what was in store for me, and I don't want a piece of it. If you're going to fight me, then fight me. But you attack this gathering here, and we're not businesslike anymore. You make it personal. It won't be the Grove you fight, it will be me. And I will hunt you and make whatever bargain with whatever power out there I need to in order to destroy you. So either bring your attack, or get the hell off the stage, because it turns out there is no business between us."

"Very well," sighed Cythymau. "But you choose this. I am sorry you do, but the choice was yours. I will not seek it again. I am sorry, Robert of Lorents. Goodbye."

The image flicked out. A collective gasp rose from the audience. I jerked back. I was alone on the stage. No one was calling names. Everyone leaned forward in that silence just before the panic set in.

Our blue-painted friend struck before any other reaction.

A rift in the Weave opened in the back of the gym and three large, wolf-like creatures slipped through. I had encountered one of these in my abortive trip to Cythymau's realm; he had called them "Lycaon," as I recalled. Lycaon. Essentially, large wolves. They were big, and powerful, but I did not remember them exerting anything but physical strength and speed.

I didn't want to get caught in any crossfires, nor did I want more attention drawn to myself. A manhunt was already on for Grace; let her be the flashy one to draw the gasps from the crowd. I stood back, waiting to see what she did and how best to add my power to hers. The Lycaon leaped to their prey in the stands, and I waited for the blast from Grace that would send them back.

It never came.

Then the screaming started.

IT TOOK me a full second to realize Grace wasn't there.

That really doesn't do the time frame justice, though. Let me put it to you in terms with a little more meaning.

In the time it took me to realize Grace wasn't there, four people died under the lightning-fast jaws of the wolf-monsters. In addition, one lady lost her leg; by the look of it, she was going to bleed out soon. One man had most of his arm torn off; he began gripping the torn flesh wrapped around his shattered humerus.

In the time it took me to realize Grace wasn't there, a general panic crashed through the gymnasium. Audience and graduates alike began a general press away from the beasts towards the exits by the stage. People became bottlenecked in the trampling, the sudden crush of the crowd.

In the time it took me to realize Grace wasn't there, Cythymau was able to send one, last, chuckling message. "Your choice, boy. Now protect what you can." His voice grated against me.

In the time it took me to realize Grace wasn't there, the rift behind the Lycaon closed, trapping them in this plane of existence. The trick we had used on Rick the Cornuprocyon, throwing him back into the other world, wouldn't work without that rift. We were—no. I. *I* was stuck with the beasts.

All of that happened before it hit me. I was the only person here who could fight. Once again, it was Robert versus the Beasts. And this time, I had already failed. People were dead.

I launched myself off the stage, jumping for the stands. My Sense was still up; I stole kinetic force from the mob below to boost my jump, clearing the space between the stage and the stands. It looked athletic, but not impossible.

Heading for the top row of the bleachers let me avoid the press of people trying to squeeze through the narrow gaps the other way. I barely heard a female voice say "Robert?" as I streaked past; it registered as simply one of the many things open to my Sense. Vaguely I pegged it as familiar. The woman who uttered it began running after me. No time to argue, though; I had to make it to the Lycaon.

As I approached the one on my side of the gymnasium, I had to dodge to the left to avoid a flying body. I caught my breath as I recognized our former basketball star and my personal rival. I had risked my life time and again to keep Duane alive last fall; now it looked like I had simply managed to buy him another nine months.

Time for that later. I slid into place in front of the first Lycaon. Its head swiveled to meet me. The woman from the bleachers was still behind me, charging up fast. I didn't know what she was thinking, but I didn't have time to find out. I had to deal with this one quickly; the other two were still tearing into my classmates and their families.

The Lycaon lunged for me, its jaws dripping with saliva. I began siphoning off force from the lunge, pulling it around my fist and preparing for—

The woman behind me grabbed my upper arm, startling me out of my focus. My Sense slipped away from me as Francene pulled me away from the Lycaon, placing herself between me and danger.

Danger took a bloody chunk out of her side in exchange.

Stupid! Why did she have to—

No time. I forced my emotions down, steeling myself back into my focused state. The Lycaon was coming down on her again, and this time it would finish the job. Francene's eyes were beginning to glaze over with shock. As it lunged, I once again stole its force to pull around my hands. I stepped in front of Francene as the teeth came snapping in and delivered an uppercut to the bottom of the Lycaon's jaw. My force-wrapped hand shattered bone as it plunged home, and the wolf-monster let out a little yelp.

The Sense is, most of the time, a blissful calm. Not this time. This time, it pounded through me, riding my rage. I grabbed a shattered, protruding jawbone; the wolf fought me but I stole all its force and put it into a neck-snapping twist. The Lycaon collapsed under me. I ripped the lower jaw free of the corpse.

One down.

The second Lycaon was surging into the graduates, who were now just a mess of blue gowns and square hats. I ran at its flank, snarling, holding its pack mate's lower jaw in my right hand. Behind me, the rest of the corpse vanished as I summoned it to the gym ceiling above me. The force of its fall added to the force of my swing as I rolled under the second beast, swinging the tooth-lined jaw as I went.

I hooked and tore open the creature's abdomen. Its entrails began to fall to the floor; blood poured onto my head. It craned its neck back toward me but I was already moving. I rolled to my feet on the far side of the beast—and came face to face with Jake.

He looked uninjured; that was good. A hint of worry formed in my gut, but my rage carried me past it. I gave him a wild, berserker grin as I flashed past. His face never slipped from a shocked stare.

The second Lycaon stumbled as it tried to chase me, falling off its feet. It let out a barking growl that turned into a wheeze as the last of its life drained from it. I wiped its blood from my eyes as I made a beeline for the third and final of the beasts, which had dealt a significant amount of damage to the audience on the far side of the gymnasium. The bandstand was above it; I sent a silent thank-you to whatever gods could hear me for the fenced barrier that separated my friends in the band from the chaos below.

The third Lycaon turned and stalked me slowly. It had seen what had happened to its pack mates, and it was trying not to give me an opening. My Sense, though, was solidly attached to my berserker fury. This beast was *mine*, and if it sought a slow death, then so much the better.

I summoned jagged chunks of three large planks of the bleachers out from underneath it. The Lycaon gave a high-pitched yelp as it fell into the resulting hole.

The remaining, sharpened ends of wood held it in place by its chest and hindquarters. Its feet thrashed wildly for purchase and found none.

I further sharpened the three large planks I had summoned as they came crashing down. I compressed the wood, adding density to the tips until they were almost like metal. I grabbed whatever force I could from the press of the crowd and the thrashing legs of the Lycaon to add to the gravity already driving my improvised spears downward.

They impacted the Lycaon on the hindquarters, the torso, and the neck, driving through without mercy. It died on impact. Its thrashing calmed. I looked around wildly for something else to kill.

A hand grabbed me by the shoulder. I whirled, grabbing force and preparing to attack. Then I saw Jake. His face was pale, but his eyes met mine.

"It's over, man."

I took a deep breath and let the Sense fall away. Three Lycaon, three targets, all dead. I struggled to bring my rage under control.

"Snap out of it, fucker," said Jake, his voice trembling as he tried to make a joke out of his fear.

I shook my head, coming to grips with what I'd seen.

"Come on," he said, pulling me through the hole in the bleachers I'd just made. "Here, take my robe. Leave yours under here. There're enough witnesses that saw me, I'm fine. If you've got a clean gown, there's no way you're the student that trashed the place. Ditch yours here."

I smiled at him, shook my head, and brought my Sense back, this time embracing its calm. The blood that coated my robes and body I simply summoned off, leaving me pristine. I pooled it under the body of the Lycaon, then let it drop.

Jake inhaled sharply, then exhaled slowly. "Still not used to that," he said as he led me out the back end of the bleachers. Once free, I ran for Francene.

She was where I had left her, on the bleachers. A large chunk of flesh had been removed from her side and there was a lot of blood. It looked like her abdominal cavity was still intact; I thought that was a good sign. She was unconscious, and it looked like she had broken something in her fall. I stripped off my now-clean gown, held it to her side, and waited for the sirens to come.

GRACE

It's hard to stay awake after sitting by yourself for five hours in dim light. The adrenaline that first drove me when I made my hiding place had long since evaporated, but I couldn't afford to sleep either. The chatter over the radio hadn't been helpful for the last two hours or so. Since the Feds had to be aware that I had one of their units now, that wasn't shocking.

I stifled a yawn and felt a note piff into my pocket. Matt's handwriting marched across the page in tidy rows.

Feds took bait. They are moving in for a possible apprehension near Newport. There are still some law enforcement teams in your area, but the air support has already been moved. The rest of the ground teams won't move until they confirm an actual sighting (which they won't), so you'll have to deal with them if necessary. You have an hour at most before the Feds figure out that you aren't where they expect. Break a leg.

Time for me to get moving too, then. I strapped on my rune board just in case, and unsealed my hiding place. I couldn't see the sun through the trees, but the light was blinding after my dim refuge. No movement caught my eye in the immediate vicinity.

Ten hours underground hadn't been kind to my clothes. I brushed the worst of the dirt off my sweater and sweats. A light wind ruffled through the tree branches, carrying a hint of pine needles and rain. The breeze felt wonderful against my skin after my cramped hidey hole.

The Feds should still be searching in the national forest to the east. I wanted to keep it that way, at least until after I sneaked in for Robert's ceremony.

My hiding place was only about fifty minutes away from Robert's school by highway, but since the back roads would be safer, it could take closer to two hours. To be there anywhere close to on time, I'd better head out now. If I headed east, I should eventually hit Highway 206 and be able to take that south, losing myself in the throngs of civilization again. It occurred to me that in some ways I was trying to return to the scene of the crime. Or at least the city of crime? In this context, my hazy plan to sneak back through all the law enforcement wasn't brilliant. But I had promised Robert.

I struck out resolutely for about four steps. Something snapped and rustled in the bushes. Not breaking my stride, I adjusted my bag on my shoulder and slipped a hand inside to my rune tags. This was a wildlife refuge after all. It would be silly to escape the Feds just to become an early-morning snack for some nocturnal predator. Realistically, it could just be a moose—but anyone who thinks a moose won't kick your ass because it strikes their fancy hasn't met many moose. Unfortunately, since living at the cabin, larger wildlife and I had had a few less-than-pleasant meetings. I poised myself to summon a tranquilizer gun and fire on whatever came out of the bushes. Not wanting to make any sudden movements, I left my hand in the recesses of my purse, thumbing open a vial of blood. Then I waited. Once it broke through the brush there would only be a fraction of a second to fire. My nerves thrummed in time with my Sense headache.

Something charged into the clearing from my left. I spun, powering the summons and bringing the tranquilizer gun up to my shoulder in one fluid motion. My finger tightened on the trigger; I fired the dart before I'd even really had time to get a good look.

That wasn't a moose.

The state trooper crashed to the floor of the clearing, the brightly colored tufts on the end of the dart sticking out from the bit of his right shoulder not covered in bullet-proof armor.

A gunshot cracked behind me. Instinctively I dropped flat. The bullet thudded into a Ponderosa pine behind me. I glanced over my shoulder. Two more troopers were advancing into the clearing with their weapons drawn. I had no idea how they'd managed to find me, but I didn't have a lot of time to think about that now.

Abandoning the dart rifle in the dirt, I started rearranging the runes on my board, still lying flat. The blood splashed over the runes and a burst of focused kinetic energy knocked the next shots off trajectory. I snatched up the dart gun, jumped to my feet, and used the last of the summoned force to propel myself to the tree-line and back into the forest, zigging and dodging to avoid their gunfire.

Running in a jagged arc around the clearing, I summoned a new pack of tranquilizer darts and turned with a fresh dart loaded in the breech of the gun.

One of the troopers was kneeling next to the man I'd shot with the tranquilizer, feeling his pulse. The other was standing a few feet away, reaching for his radio as he scanned the area.

It would be catastrophic if they gave the Feds my exact location. I couldn't stop the beginning of the transmission, but I could stop him from relaying exact coordinates.

Belly-crawling up to the edge of the clearing behind a large boulder, I put the gun to my shoulder and squeezed one eye shut, aiming for his thigh. The gun went off with a puff of air.

Immediately I reached for a new dart and started reloading the rifle.

The trooper's cry of pain cut off his report mid-sentence. He stared incredulously at the dart in his thigh before slowly crumpling to the ground.

I got the other trooper in the upper arm as he turned to look, his hand on his weapon.

Crouching in the classic action-movie run, I sped back into the clearing and checked the pulses of all three officers to make sure they were steady, and then went through all their pockets. The first paper turned out to be my mug shot from the booking last summer. Well, I guess that part of the ploy to save Carlenos and Detective Allen had worked. Go me.

No matter what decoy Matt had come up with, the Feds were going to be re-deploying at least some of their forces to these men's last known location. I fished the nearest trooper's key ring out of his pocket. There must have been twenty keys on it. I fumbled through the silver keys looking for a vehicle make or some other identifying tag. These guys should have at least one vehicle nearby, and I was going to use it to leave the vicinity before they reset the road blocks. Finally I found a key marked "Dodge #5." Bingo.

If these guys were here, an access road couldn't be too far away. I trekked out the way they'd come. A faint trail cut through the grass and pine needles in vaguely the right direction; I followed it until it turned into what appeared to be a forty-five degree slope covered in a green leafy canopy of tightly packed bushes.

I'd missed the trail branching somewhere though, because the path I was following gave out right before the ledge. There was no obvious way down through the bushes. To add insult to injury, at the bottom of the ledge, only about fifty feet away on the horizontal plane, I could see the access road and a government Dodge four-wheel-drive police vehicle pulled off next to a trailhead.

Now if only it wasn't also about thirty feet down vertically.

I hunkered down and watched it for a few minutes to see if it was the right one. A trooper walked out around the car, talking into a radio. Damn. No one else joined him in the next few minutes, so I decided my best option was to crawl carefully down through the bushes and try to tranquilize him too. Even if it was a different squad's cars, this guy should also have keys. Most likely though, he'd come with the patrol I'd already put out of commission. At least, I hoped so. I did *not* need more complications if I wanted to make Robert's graduation ceremony on time.

Favoring my injured hip, I carefully slid down over the ledge in front the bushes. The blanket of waist-high leafy foliage looked steep but not impassable. The idea here was to get down there quickly while making as little noise as humanly possible, so I could quietly and efficiently knock out the trooper and be on my way. Unfortunately, the bushes had other ideas.

I crept forward into the green canopy, and dropped a very abrupt six feet as the ground cut off sharply underneath me. I tried to tuck and roll, only partially successfully, as I bounced painfully on several unknown protuberances on the way down. The ground and incline found me again with an abruptness that knocked the breath out my lungs, before smacking me up against a slightly giving surface that stopped my momentum cold.

I took a moment to gather my spinning senses and assure myself I still had all of my limbs—and that none of them had decided to bend in directions the gods hadn't intended. I'd be sore for days, but it didn't feel like I'd actually broken anything.

Taking a deep breath, I finally evaluated where I'd ended up. The top leafy "bushes" were now a good foot above my head. In front of me, a forest of tightly woven stalks supported the leafy canopy above me. Well, fuck.

The green stalks were about an inch wide, and appeared to be covered in a velvety white fuzz. Speculating that at that width they'd be flexible, I reached out, attempting to part them in a breaststroke motion. Fire raced up from my palms, and I jerked my hands back. What I'd taken for "velvet" was actually millions of tiny little stickers which were now embedded in my palms. Grimacing, I extended my Sense and pushed the needles out of my skin into the dirt behind me. It felt much better, but my hands still smarted.

So Plan B, then.

Rearranging runes on my arm board, I summoned a pair of gloves and a pair of pruning shears. Not subtle, but I needed to get down off this mountain. Given my tiny frame, I should be able to keep the path relatively small, but eventually there would be a noticeable line of cut fuck-bushes (actual genus unknown) going down the mountain and pointing straight at me to anyone who looked up.

The only saving grace was that their thick canopy of foliage above my head still kept me mostly hidden.

Excruciatingly slowly, I cut each stalk, tested the treacherous incline and then squeezed myself into the small space I'd created between the tightly woven plants. Then I repeated that process again, and again, and again.

The tight profuseness of the bushes even prevented me from seeing how far I had to go to my intended target—or if he'd noticed the slender, approximately four fuck-bush-wide scar now running down the ledge toward him.

It was truly a mind-numbing process. After I'd done it for about the hundredth time, part of me was lamenting the fact that my own ethics wouldn't let me fire this part of the mountain and burn all these stupid bushes to the ground. It would be a catastrophically stupid thing to do on many levels, of course, but setting these fuck-bushes aflame would be very personally satisfying.

I finally reached the edge of the bushes and crawled out of them into the shallow ditch before the access road. Color me sweaty, exhausted, and triumphant.

The trooper had moved around to the beginning of the trail and was peering up it, talking into his radio and checking his watch.

Good. That meant he was turned at least obliquely away from my current position. I re-summoned the tranquilizer gun and loaded the dart, waiting for him to finish up reporting before I shot. Whatever he was saying probably wasn't good, but I didn't want him to cut off mid-transmission. After all, his ride was my only way out of here. He put the radio back in his belt holster, but as he turned to walk back to the vehicle his gaze swept over the tiny line I'd just traversed down the side of the mountain. He frowned. His hand reached for his side arm. I shot first.

The tuft of bright feathers stuck into his shoulder above the elbow. He crumpled to the ground. At least *one* thing had gone right today.

I dragged the unconscious trooper into the shallow ditch beside the road I'd just hidden in, so he wasn't obvious to everyone driving past on the access road. Next, I took his keys and radio and threw his gun into the bushes.

Time to de-ass this place with speed. I slid in behind the wheel of the car, adjusted the driver's seat to midget size, and inserted the key into the ignition. I took a deep breath and tried to turn the key. After a tense moment the engine leaped to rumbling life. Realizing I still hadn't released my breath, I exhaled and threw the car into gear.

Lights, sirens, and speed got me past the first two checkpoints that had been set up blocking the north-south roads. It had been maybe twenty minutes since I knocked out the last trooper and stole the car. I needed to be off this road and gone to ground before the Feds found those unconscious men; otherwise, this vehicle would become a deathtrap instead of a boon.

I took the first north-south turn-off that was unblocked and not dirt or gravel. The sign said Heckler or something. It went by pretty fast. I continued for a few more miles and then used a turn-off to pull over. Strapping my rune board back on, I sent out a summoning to the road ahead and made sure there was no roadblock where it met up with Argonne. For now, the coast appeared clear.

That last run-in with the troopers had cost me in both time and cover. I couldn't afford to draw any attention to myself while the Feds were regrouping. I took the time to summon my janitor-lady disguise (complete with wig, spray bottle, and dust rag) and changed yet again.

I threw the patrol car keys onto the seat, summoned all of my fingerprints and DNA out of vehicle, and set the runes, sending it back where I'd found it. In all likelihood it wouldn't keep the Feds from figuring out what I'd done for long, but it would buy me a little more time after they found the troopers. The several tons of metal and plastic were actual pretty easy to move once you knew the correct runes. Runes did all the heavy lifting, not my Sense.

Matt might scoff, but he was still a small grasshopper when it came to summoning. By this time next year, moving a rock would probably be small beans for him. Smiling at the thought, I summoned my own car, and started the long, circuitous drive back to the Valley to attend my other apprentice's graduation. I was going to be late.

~

DURING THAT DRIVE BACK, pulling over every half-hour to scry for road blocks, I had a long time to plan what I was going to do after Robert's graduation. With the Feds' reaction, Spokane was much too hot for me now, even though it seemed that the law enforcement presence really thinned out once I got into the suburban areas.

Actually it was *a lot* quieter in town. More so than I ever would have expected given the outlying roadblocks. I didn't even see any patrol cars. Matt must have realized I'd been sighted and come up with another diversion.

I didn't really trust Uncle Herman's cabin anymore, since Frank had found me there. Really, it might be time for the Spokane Grove headquarters to relocate once again. Once Robert graduated, he'd be in Cheney at Eastern, and Amy and I could find accommodations that didn't have any ties to last summer.

Several blocks away from the school, an ambulance passed me going the other direction, its lights flashing, siren wailing. Then another, and another. By the time I'd pulled over to let the fourth and fifth ambulances, both going my direction, pass me, foreboding had settled heavily in my stomach.

Sure enough, as soon as the high school came into view, it was apparent that Robert's school was crawling with emergency personnel and wounded on stretchers. All those patrol cars and Feds I hadn't seen earlier were concentrated here. I parked my car a block away so as not to hinder the emergency personnel and slipped through the confusion to the front of the school. With all the shell-shocked and injured students and families trying to find their graduates, people hardly noticed my janitorially-clad figure.

One white-faced student gave an account to a young deputy I didn't recognize. He must be one of Valley's new rookies, hired after the deaths last September. The teenager's words reached me while I struggled to walk unobtrusively past.

"The principal disappeared and then these freakish, giant wolves came from nowhere and started killing people. When the principal disappeared, I thought it was some new senior prank. You know, like a magic show. But then people started dying."

My pace instinctively quickened, following the "This way to Graduation!" signs down a narrow hallway toward the door marked "Gym." My head already felt like it was full of razors after the workout I'd put my Sense through during the last twenty-four hours. I didn't know how I'd pull any more summoning out of my battered Sense if necessary tonight. But Robert should be here somewhere...unless he was in one of the ambulances that had passed me on the way here.

Only one demon would have targeted this *particular* public gathering. I'd assumed Robert would be safe in a public place while I drew off the Feds. How wrong *that* was turning out to be. I'd badly underestimated Cythymau's fascination with him.

Robert should have been able to protect himself if he'd been attacked here, but he also would have been handicapped in front of so many witnesses.

As I got closer to the gym, I found more and more clusters of people with deputies or Feds at their center giving statements in a confusing cacophony of sound and bodies. EMTs burst out the gym door with another person on a stretcher between them. I slipped through the door before it slammed shut behind them and ducked around the corner into the gym.

It was everything I'd secretly hoped *not* to find. The scarlet swaths of blood stood in brilliant contrast to the waxed polish of the wooden floor. Medical personnel worked over a long line of injured individuals, some of them with bones visible through broken legs or arms.

If these were the people who hadn't been transported yet, I didn't even want to think about the more seriously injured who had already left. I turned my face away, and was confronted by a long row of bodies under a blue plastic tarp hastily thrown over them. No medical personnel hovered over these bodies. Too many graduation gowns with young legs in fancy shoes or loafers sticking out from under that tarp drove the air from my lungs. My ears rang from the lack of oxygen as my eyes tried to comprehend the horror in front of me.

Even last September most of the dead had been adults, not children; in the cold nights when I couldn't sleep, I could at least comfort myself that I'd done everything I could. These deaths already reproached me in ways those never had. The casualties last fall gave me nights of pain and regret, but these children swamped me with guilt. *I was supposed to be here.*

My stomach rebelled. I fought to keep my gorge down. I needed something constructive to do. A demon had done this, and where there were demons, there had to be a rift nearby.

Demons and tears in the Weave I could handle. What I *couldn't* do was stand here speculating about whether any of the legs under that tarp belonged to a certain apprentice.

I backed up to a clean spot of wall partially hidden by the bleachers and reached into my bag. Covertly activating the runes on my Weave-mending bracelets within the confines of my purse, I closed my eyes and focused my Sense. It sent a spike of pain through my head in protest, but showed me what I wanted.

The Weave in the gym twisted and strained like a snarled skein of yarn. Someone—Robert—had forced it to flow in directions it wouldn't naturally go. Traces of his power colored the Weave, but rather than the bright rush of power that usually accompanied his talent, they looked dark and stained. Several of the worst snarls in the Weave centered around one of those stains.

Everything pointed toward the damage having been done by Robert's Sense, but if he'd intentionally done this to the Weave, something was very, very wrong. I'd seen this kind of warping from a rogue before, but not even Robert's first, most misguided, untrained attempt at using his Sense for revenge had corrupted the Weave like this.

Whatever he had done in here had forced the Weave into unnatural patterns, or bent it with such unnecessary force that it left an impression: a bruise, not unlike a thrown peach or piece of memory foam that's been punched. It also left the Weave much more vulnerable to tears and incursions.

I opened my eyes. The wooden bleachers opposite me to the left were shattered as though a giant wrecking ball had smashed through them. Suspended in the jagged gap by their sharp rent edges sprawled a Lycaon corpse, with three more planks speared through it from above.

Parents and students waiting for medical attention lined one wall. The seriously injured had been laid out in an area swept clear of debris, presumably for that purpose. Three teams of paramedics still worked furiously over them, stabilizing them for transport.

That last line of bodies, ominously still under the tarp, lay a little farther away, waiting for *someone* to have time to move the dead. As I watched, a paramedic approached that line, carrying a slight body in a graduation gown. I recognized Jeanelle's pale, perfect features in the moment before he covered them with that ugly blue plastic.

I looked away, staring at the banners on the wall without really focusing on anything. That, particularly, seemed too cruel. Jeanelle had been Robert's first love, first heartbreak, and the reason why he'd done something so outrageous as to catch Rick's attention last fall. Now she was dead.

I took a deep breath, lowered my gaze to the swarming mass of people in the gym, and finally located Robert's scruffy brown hair. He was slumped over with his elbows on his knees on one of the few intact bleachers across the gym. He stared at his hands, seemingly unaware of the chaos all around him. It surprised me that one of the paramedics or officials hadn't moved him out into the hallway yet.

Unless they knew he was involved.

He wasn't in handcuffs or custody, though, and with all the Feds present, no one would be lenient.

Carlenos and Frank weren't here. They would've known Robert was involved immediately, but they must still be recovering from the fight yesterday. Since putting them convincingly out of commission had been the goal, that was not shocking, I suppose.

I walked over and quietly got Robert's attention. He lifted his eyes to mine almost mechanically. Fire sparked in his expression as soon as he saw me. I motioned him over to a secluded corner of the gym slightly behind the raised podium and stage.

"What in the world happened here?" I asked him. "The Weave looks like you took a meat tenderizer to it. You almost tore it open."

"What happened here? *What happened?*" Robert exploded. "I'll tell you what happened. Cythymau showed up, and I counted on you. You told me you would be here and you weren't. And guess what? That makes you just like everyone else in my life, because when I needed you to be here, you were nowhere to be found. No warning. No 'Sorry, Robert, I can't make it.' Not even a fucking note." He took a shaky breath, but that only seemed to refuel his anger.

"I guess when you say you'll be there for me, it's only lip service, just like all the other fakes. But when I count on you, and you aren't there, it's different. It's even worse. People die. People I could have saved if I hadn't been following your rules and trying to lie low. You promised you would be here, so I *waited for you to take care of it* before I acted. I worked so hard to save Duane, to make up for my mistakes, and now it doesn't even matter because I only bought him a couple of months. Another monster came to get me, and this time he paid the price. You're always telling me I have to get out, to blend in as long as I can. These people are hurt or dead because I tried to be a normal teenager. You were supposed to *be* here."

The last words hissed out of him.

I rocked back, blasted by the heat and frustration rolling off him in waves. I opened my mouth to try to talk to him, to figure out how much of this anger and frustration was due to today's events or if this knot of rage had been festering, but something in him had burst. He cut me off before I got a word out.

"You know the one person who did try to help me? My fostie. She tried to protect me. She stood between me and a demonic Visitor that had already hurt and killed people. Then she tried to stop it. You can imagine how that went for her," he added harshly. "The Lycaon took a chunk out of her. She's in the hospital, probably dying. It turns out if you really care for me, it's a death sentence. First my parents, then Uncle Herman, and now Francene. Maybe I should be glad you're a fake, or you'd just die on me too."

"Hey, wait a minute here," I tried to cut in. "I am sorrier than you can know that I wasn't here and Cythymau attacked, but even if I'd been here sooner, there's no guarantee who would have lived or died or gotten hurt. I don't know if I could have stopped Cythymau or the Lycaon faster than you—"

"The three Lycaon," Robert inserted tonelessly. "Count the corpses."

I turned and found the other two lifeless Lycaon that had been hidden by the press of people and emergency personnel.

"Three, then. Maybe I could have stopped them more effectively, or maybe even more people would have died in the rush trying to get out. It sucks that Duane died in the attack. It *sucks* that people died trying to get away. It *sucks* that the attack happened at all. Neither you or I have control over what Cythymau does. He probably would have tried a whole different tactic if I'd been here. You can't know what the outcome would have been."

"I know I wouldn't have tried to stall Cythymau, waiting for you to react, if I'd known you weren't even fucking here. I gave him all the prep time he needed to just wade through all my classmates and their parents, like I'd presented them on a platter," he said in disgust.

"They were supposed to be graduating, going on to the bigger and better things in life. Instead, because I was in their class, they get to feed the worms. Our valedictorian, the person who got the best grades, who just gave a speech about hopes and futures—she was supposed to grow up and be a doctor or a scientist—just died. All because of me, but only, *only* because I counted on you to back me up. I should have known better."

"I was just a little busy shaking the Feds off that diversion you helped me set up for, remember. Listen, Robert—"

"I'm done listening to you. Yeah, I saw the news, and that you were having a hard time of it, but it didn't look any worse than anything we haven't already run into. When I didn't hear from you I *assumed you were running on time.* The last words I heard from you were you *assuring me* nothing would keep you from being here. So, no, I'm not listening to you ever again. In fact, I don't even want to look at you."

"I understand you're frustrated I wasn't here. That's on me, but it's not your fault Duane and Jeanelle died," I tried desperately. "Or that Francene got hurt. It's not something I had control over, either. That blame lies at Cythymau's door. You can hate me and blame me for not being here, but you did your best, and you *saved* a lot of people."

"I do blame you. And I didn't save enough people. Not more than I put in danger by being here."

His head jerked up suddenly. "Wait. Did you say Duane *and Jeanelle?*"

He gave me a shocked glance and ran from our sheltered corner, stopping short of the line of corpses. Then he walked forward and lifted the edge of the tarp to see the face that belonged to the delicately sandaled feet on the end.

Crap. He hadn't even known. And I'd just thrown it at his head like that.

Robert shot me a cold look that pierced me all the way to the core, his face set in hard lines that made him look much older than eighteen. He put down the tarp as someone tried to tell him he shouldn't be there, turned, and walked slowly from the gym.

I followed him out, also feeling shell-shocked. I took a few steps, wondering if I should go after him, totally confounded as to what I would say if I did. A hand fell on my shoulder.

I looked over, half expecting to see a Fed or someone in uniform.

A stocky new graduate, his gown bedraggled and slightly blood-spattered, stood at my shoulder.

"You better let him go," he said. "No talking to him right now. He's too raw."

I threw him a startled glance.

"Yeah," he said. "I know who you are. And I know you're some scary, super badass summoner. But you let him down hard today, and you know Robert. That fucker don't trust anyone easy in the first place." I dug around in my memory for the name of the friend Robert always hung out with.

"Jake?" I asked.

"Yeah. And don't do anything freaky with my name neither. I just wanted to lay some knowledge on you about our man. See people—

people always leave Robert. He has some hang-ups about it." Jake took his hand off my shoulder and stared at it for a moment as if he couldn't believe he'd just touched a boogieman.

"Some?" I asked.

"Some." He rubbed his hand on his jeans. "He's had four foster families in the last three years. Can you blame him? I'm the closest thing that fucker has to stability, God help him. And you not being here when the shit hit the blender just emphasized that. If you really care about him, you'll give him some time and cut the bastard some slack. But don't expect him to come looking for you. If you want to fix this between him and you, it's gonna have to be all you."

I nodded, not feeling amused. The kid had a foul mouth, but I got his point. I hadn't meant to stand Robert up, and I definitely hadn't meant to put his classmates in danger. But to Robert, what I meant to do didn't matter. To him, all that mattered was that he had trusted me, and his trust had been betrayed. Again.

ROBERT

HAVE I mentioned before that I hate hospitals?

I was becoming all too familiar with the sterilized halls of the Spokane Valley hospital. I gave a friendly nod to Barb, the receptionist at the front desk. In the days following Rick's last attack, I had visited people here often. None of them were close friends, but I bore some of the blame for them being hospitalized.

I didn't have to use the elevator this time. The emergency room was on the first floor; Francene had been taken there. I didn't know if I could see her at the moment, but I could wait. It's not like I had anywhere else to be.

Donald, Francene's husband, was in the waiting room already. He sat on one side of a couch, reading a newspaper. I wasn't sure how he'd managed to get clear of the traffic around graduation so quickly. He nodded at me gravely. I returned his nod and sat next to him in a fluffy chair. He retreated behind his paper and resumed his inner thoughts.

Donald had always been the quiet sort, which I appreciated in a foster parent. Francene wanted to form a connection with me; I got the impression that Donald just wanted to get through the day. He was not particularly interested in being my father figure. As I had no interest in being his son, we had a good working relationship with each other.

We sat in awkward silence for a minute or so before I finally asked him if there had been any news.

"They've got her in surgery now. We'll know more once they're done." Donald's tone was gruff, and he did not make eye contact with me. I went back to my silence.

The most excruciating thing to do in a hospital is nothing. As my foster father and I waited, I did everything else there was to do. I made a run to the snack machine and ate a stale Moon Pie. I walked into the bathroom only to realize I didn't have to use it; five minutes later, I returned. I read a four-month-old copy of a gardening magazine and learned several good tips for improving the health of my rhododendrons.

I have never in my life raised a rhododendron.

The clock dragged its way around in ever-maddening circles, and even I ran out of things to do. I sat beside Donald, staring at the ceiling and waiting for word. I tried extending my Sense a couple of times, but she was out of my range.

When a doctor in blue scrubs finally marched through the door, lowering his surgical mask, I jumped to my feet almost on reflex. Donald simply lifted his head to the doctor and asked, "Well?"

"She's stable, but critical. She lost a lot of blood, and we're still worried about infection, given the size of the wound and the involvement of the intestines, but we're cautiously optimistic."

My breath rushed out of me in relief. I went to shake the doctor's hand. Donald gave him another of his terse nods.

"Can we see her?" I asked, my voice tight with pent-up anxiety.

"Not at the moment. She's resting now. I would come back in three or four hours. She may be conscious by then."

Donald calmly folded the newspaper, stood, and made to leave. "You going somewhere?" I asked.

"Cup of coffee," Donald said. "Back in a while."

I shrugged; if he wanted to abandon our vigil, that was his business. I wasn't about to leave Francene here alone. Enough people had left me alone during my life. I wouldn't pass that disservice on to her. When the time had come, she had proven she wouldn't leave me. That kind of thing was valuable.

Stupid, of course. There was absolutely no need for her to take the hit that she did; I could have taken the Lycaon. I *had* taken the Lycaon. The wolf-demons hadn't had a chance against me. Francene's sacrifice had, in the end, been completely unnecessary.

The thing that got me, though, was this: she hadn't known. She had thought I was vulnerable, and she took the hit for me. Francene had spent most of the last year trying to form a connection with me. I had driven away many foster mothers who tried to bond with me. She had managed to break through, but I had forced her to pay a terrible price for it.

The least I could do was stay. I resumed my place on my fluffy chair and continued my monotony.

"ROBERT?

My head jerked up; I had managed to doze off in the waiting room. One of the nurses—I think her name was Lori—lightly tapped my shoulder. Guiltily, I tried to shake myself out of my nap and responded by raising my hand.

"She's asking for you," said Lori. Laura? Lorinda? I couldn't remember.

I looked around for Donald and didn't see him. "Not Donald?" I asked the nurse.

"She keeps saying 'Robert.' If that's you, come on back. It'll do her good to see you."

I glanced at the nametag as I brushed past her. Leanne. She informed me of the room number as I strode toward the elevator. I did not look back.

Francene was in a room by herself, hooked up to a number of machines, but her eyes fluttered in recognition when she saw me.

"Rob—ert," she croaked. She was clearly on some heavy-duty painkillers; just speaking my name had taken a significant effort.

"Shhh," I said. "I'm right here. I'm ok. They didn't get me."

I didn't imagine telling her exactly *how* that had happened, and she was in no condition to ask. She smiled and nodded at me. I took her hand in mine, and was rewarded with a gentle squeeze.

"Yeah," I whispered hoarsely. "I love you too." Her smile widened, her eyes closed, and her head tilted back. We sat, her hand in mine, until I was sure she had fallen asleep. Then I stood up, looking at the nurse in the doorway. She gave me a half smile. I hadn't noticed her; she'd made her entrance quietly. As I stepped out of the room, I saw that Donald was coming down the hallway.

"She's asleep again," I said.

"Mm," agreed Donald. I made to head back to the waiting room, but he held out his hand to stop me.

"So, boy," he said quietly. "That's that. You've seen her. Now head home and start packing."

I whirled on him. "What?" I tried to keep my voice low for Francene's sake.

"You're eighteen. You're out of high school. You're done. Congratulations on being an adult. Get out of my house." Donald's voice remained low and solid.

"Where am I supposed to go?"

"Don't know. Don't really care. Francene wanted you to stay for the summer to set you up for college. You almost got her killed this time. Next time you might finish the job, or come after me. Can't risk it. Get out." Donald's voice was firm.

"You think this is my fault?" I asked. Deep inside me, an inner voice reminded me that this *was* my fault. Cythymau had sent those Lycaon to punish *me*. He had succeeded.

Donald grabbed me by the arm and dragged me in close with a force I did not knew he had. "Boy," he growled, low and tight like an angry pit bull. "You think I don't know about you? Cathy from the police department stopped by at work to tell me about this. She told me all about your little magic tricks. Are you honestly going to try to tell me those things weren't there because of you?"

I lowered my eyes to stare at the floor; I couldn't answer. If Donald knew the truth, there was nothing more to say. I knew, deep down, that he was right. I did present an ongoing danger to him, to Francene, and to everyone who knew me. I had offended Cythymau by declining his little deal, and he had chosen to take his revenge out on me personally. So long as I was a target, no one around me would be safe.

Wait a minute.

"Who was it you said told you? I've met most of the Valley cops, and I don't know a Cathy."

"Really," said Donald, in a rare fit of deadpan sarcasm. "She told me she'd worked with you personally. You're trying to say you've never met Deputy Maru?"

Deputy Maru. Deputy Cathy Maru. Now things made sense.

"Oh, right," I said. "Deputy Maru. I'm not sure what it was exactly she told you, but I'm not dangerous. Not on my own, anyway."

"Not dangerous? My wife is in the next room fighting for her life because of your...*corruption*." He spat the word. "This discussion is over. Go home, pack, leave. Don't be there when I get back. Goodbye."

I spun, my face hot, and kicked the wall opposite Francene's room before stalking off. I thought I'd found a place to call home. You'd think I'd have learned by now that there is no such thing. I jumped into my Volvo and headed home to pack.

Cythymau. I kept thinking of that little, mild-mannered, blue-swirled demon as I packed my few belongings. He had killed the one girl who had ever called herself my girlfriend. He had simultaneously shown me that someone did love me, and taken it away. He had informed Donald of my talent in the worst possible terms. Come to think of it, I would bet that "Deputy Maru" had triggered the Federal investigation of the Valley Cops too. He had done *all* of this to strike at *me*.

He had succeeded, too, I thought, as I opened the door to the house I had almost called home. I briskly moved through the kitchen, then the dining room, not pausing to look at the pictures of Donald and Francene. No nostalgia; that was the trick to ditching fosties. Don't get attached. Without attachment, you can just pack up and leave. My moment with Francene in the hospital had been for her benefit, not mine.

Or so I told myself.

I clumped up the stairs. No. That wasn't fair. I did love Francene for what she'd tried to do. In fact, I was pretty sure that Francene would have stuck up for me in front of Donald. But Donald had the right of it in the end; I would endanger them as long as Cythymau threatened me. That made the equation easy. I needed to go after Cythymau.

In my room, I paused and took a deep breath. This had been a good room. It was a safe, homey sort of place. My old secondhand desk and rustled bed beckoned me to lie down and be comfortable. The used stereo system Donald had picked up for me at Goodwill itched to play some jazz tune. I was going to miss this place.

No nostalgia, I reminded myself. In and out. I grabbed my bag and started packing. The first things in were my rune-covered bracers, an inheritance from my Uncle Herman. Clothing followed, then my copies of Uncle Herman's summoning notes. Finally, I grabbed my saxophone case. There was no practical use for my beloved instrument, but I refused to leave it behind. Some things are important.

I looked around the room; there was little else here that I could actually claim as mine.

More here than anywhere else, really. Those bracers and notes were my most treasured possessions. The notes, especially, now that they were all I had to study. I knew Grace had opened the portal last fall based on what she'd read there; I now needed to do the same. Once through, I could deal with Cythymau for good.

I had nomadically wandered from foster home to foster home for so long that I had no impulse to put down any significant roots. I took one, last look around, slung the strap of my bag over my shoulder, then left the last foster home I would ever have.

Leaving was easy; I had practice. Figuring out where to go next, that was a little tougher. I did own the cabin, of course, and if I felt like seeing Grace again I could return and crash there. Technically, I could even kick her out, but doing so would involve law enforcement. I wasn't on good terms with Grace at the moment, but I wasn't about to serve her up to the Feds on a platter, either.

Jake's was the easiest answer. His single mother was rarely, if ever, home, so crashing with him was a semi-regular event. He'd take me in, I was pretty sure. The problem with that was summoning. Jake got the heebies over very simple summons, and what I was about to do went far deeper than that. More importantly, I didn't want him to be a target any more than I wanted Francene to be one. I began to see why Uncle Herman had lived in a remote cabin. I needed to isolate myself.

That's when it hit me. The original rift in the Weave, the one Cythymau had attacked through originally, was in an abandoned factory. Not the homiest of lodgings, but exactly the sort of place I'd need if I wanted to re-open the Weave. I slid into my Volvo and began driving down Sullivan. For the next couple of days, I was going to live in an aluminum plant.

THE ABANDONED factory had all the charm of a little French chateau. This is assuming, of course, that said chateau was in eastern France, circa 1916. I threw my bag down in the corner and pulled out Herman's notes.

They were, as ever, incomprehensible. Herman used a jargon that I hadn't even begun to learn. Oh, I'd been training with Grace for the better part of a year, but I hadn't even started on these technicalities. By Grace's reckoning, I was about as advanced as your average ten-year-old. I could use my Sense, but it took me forever to use a rune set.

That wasn't actually true. It took me forever to use a rune set *properly*. The proper form of rune use was to send your Sense through the rune, hook it to something on the other side, and pull it back.

There was, however, a second way. If you pull on a rune with your Sense hard enough, it pulls something through from the other side. You can never tell exactly what you are pulling, though; it'll be the nearest thing out there that fits the rune.

I needed someone who could interpret these notes for me. Amy couldn't, Matt was barely above me in ability, and Grace was out for other reasons. I drew a couple of runes on the floor. The sets for father, brother, and spirit came easily. I threw in Wunjo more as a habit than as an actual safeguard. Not having any other blood, I used my Sense to first clean, then sharpen a piece of scrap metal on the factory floor. I cut my finger, letting the blood flow over the runes. Then I closed my eyes, raised my Sense, and pulled at it.

I had to pull very, very hard, but eventually there was a sense of the Weave giving out a small bit, and Uncle Herman's spirit stepped through.

He looked...younger. Much younger than I remembered him. He was dressed in bell-bottom jeans and a paisley shirt, with his long, brown hair pulled back in a ponytail. This was not the old, crusty mountain man I remembered from my youth.

This was Herman as he remembered himself, a flower-powered hippie. It came as a shock.

"Hey, it's Robert! You found the book, did you? Good, good, well done. Knew you could do it." Herman's voice was younger too, but still his.

"Hello, Uncle. What book?"

"*The* book. Up in the woods. Your Grove book."

"Oh, that. No, it's cool. Grace lent me one of her family's."

Herman's eyebrows lifted. "Grace? Who is Grace? No, never mind," he said, thinking better of the wasted time. "What I really need to know is how you summoned me without the book."

"Oh, that." I shrugged, and pointed to the runes on the floor. "I figured calling you my father's brother would be good enough."

"That's...not my summoning rune set. How did you make the exchange through the Weave?"

"How did I what?"

"Make the exchange. You were bringing a soul here from the realms of the dead; you had to *send something back*. What did you send?" Herman's voice was beginning to grow a bit agitated.

"I didn't bother with anything like that. I just drew the runes, applied my Sense, and pulled you on through. No problem." I knew he wouldn't like the way I'd gone about it, but that was just too bad.

"Who the hell's been training you, boy? Getting something through the Weave is a balancing act. We send *before* we receive. Not only did you damage the Weave before you did it, but you sent some random item the equivalent of *a soul* through. You'll get it back, of course. But it will have been in the lands of the dead. Guess what can't live there? Anything."

Oh. That was going to suck.

"Also, you need to repair the Weave, boy." Herman's voice had that same authoritative ring.

"Repair?" I asked.

"Yes, repair. What have you been taught? We summon because we need to manipulate the Weave. That lets us repair it. Where there's a hole, we mend it. We do not—and it is very important, you understand—we *don't go around making new ones*." It wasn't that his voice was loud, it's that his voice became much slower, more intense. His eyes met mine in a harsh glare. "Now, bring up your Sense and start putting the Weave back together."

I took a breath and drew up my Sense. He was right. Underneath the physical substance of everything around me, there was another layer. I hadn't noticed it, before, because normally it would be totally smooth and completely worked into the fabric of reality itself. Here, assorted pieces fell away, unraveled and worn.

I began rethreading reality back to itself, my uncle looking on. He offered no direct aid, but he seemed to be able to Sense what I was doing. Occasionally he would butt in with a "No, boy, the other way," or an "Ok, now you've got it." I'd never manipulated the Weave at this level before. It was strenuous; a cold sweat broke out across my face as I struggled to keep my focus on the cracked shards of reality.

I'd lost track of time before I managed to slide the final piece back into place. As soon as I did, the Weave faded from my Sense, melding itself into the physical presence. I dropped my Sense, breathing heavily. Herman was smiling.

"Ok, boy," he said abruptly. "That's enough for today. The book is below the old rock pile downhill from the cabin. About forty-five feet below. Go Sense it, grab it, read it, summon me *correctly*, and we'll talk. Good day."

Before I could stop him, my uncle had faded from view. That was all right, though; he'd given me a starting point. Now that I knew how to bend the Weave itself with my Sense, it would be that much easier to break it.

GRACE

I SAT for a long time on the log bench in front of the cabin, smelling the trees and the wood smoke as I tried to reset my priorities. My focus had been so zeroed in on the threats presented by Cythymau and the Feds that I'd forgotten Robert was really still a kid, and a troubled one at that. In almost any situation, he was just as capable as any adult. I'd been treating him as one, without much regard to his feelings or his youth. If my schedule couldn't fit his, he'd manage.

Well, he'd managed, all right. But at what cost?

What type of mentor did that to her student?

An inch-high stack of messages from other Grove councils waited for me in the cabin. They wouldn't be love notes, given my recent actions. I picked up the first one without enthusiasm.

Director Brandiole condemned my "ill advised" show for the Feds, and warned me he'd withdrawn his support of my interim directorship. Not even Thaddeus Neilson would want to come down here, what with the Federal investigation still ongoing, so as threats went, it could be worse. Yet another worry, but I threw it on the back burner.

The rest of the messages followed pretty much the same lines. They read like someone had come up with talking points and then passed them out to everyone on the Cooperative Council. Maybe they had.

Collectively the council denounced me for aggravating a pending Federal investigation, endangering the Grove system as a whole, allowing my apprentice to act independently, and continually alerting the public of Grove activity with my overt and blatant disregard for Grove rules. You'd think someone had passed around a list of anti-Grace talking points. Maybe they had.

Amy burst in the door, her hair crazily askew. It had obviously started the day as a perfectly tidy bun, but fallen further and further afoul as the day progressed. She ran her hand through it, trying to push the straggling wisps off her forehead, and managed to pull the bun even farther off center.

"Grace! What is going on? Did you really pick a fight with the Feds? Spokane Valley and the surrounding areas look like a military state right now. It took me two hours just to get from the Mall to the freeway."

"I really did," I said wryly.

"Why?" The word burst out of her on a wail.

"Well, things have gotten a bit dull around here since we got rid of Rick, don't you think? Or it *could be* I had a good reason." I was suddenly feeling defensive and a little silly. It was surprisingly hard to tell her I had staged this because I wanted to protect my favorite two law enforcement officers *from* the law. No one was reacting to my decisions favorably today.

"You know I love you like a sister, but what kind of good reason could there possibly be?" she asked skeptically. "These are the *Feds*. They won't stop looking for you now. And it's not just you. What will you do if they find all of us? Robert, me, Matt? Aren't we good enough reasons not to do something like this?"

She gestured widely and looked at me, waiting for an answer. Might as well fess up, after all; I was going to look silly either way.

"The Feds would be after me no matter what. They had already found out I didn't die last fall, God knows how. They started an internal investigation into the Sheriff's department. Carlenos and

Allen were about to be implicated for letting me go. I attacked in order to give them a cover and distract the Feds from looking for moles in the Sheriff's department."

"Well, you certainly succeeded in that last one. The problem is that the Feds look primed to try and take on the whole Grove system in a way that hasn't been seen since the Inquisition," she said bitterly. "Have you even watched the news since last night?"

I blinked. "What? No, I haven't yet. Why?"

"You should," she said flatly. She dug around in her purse and handed me a shiny black rectangle. Her tablet, I realized. "I saved some of the more standout news stories for you." She waited a moment, opened her mouth, shut it again, and stalked out the door.

I watched her leave, a bit bewildered. Surely, she hadn't come all the way out here for that short conversation? The drive out to the cabin wasn't easy, especially when you tacked on the extra two hours she had said it took her to get through the checkpoints.

Time to find out what the news media was saying about me, though I'd rather not. Much like reading internet opinions, you rarely read anything flattering. I'd start with newspapers and whatever Amy had saved to the tablet; those at least I could stay home for.

I SWITCHED OFF THE TABLET, my stomach now a lead weight in my abdomen. The popular theory, given the public nature of the attacks at my "hideout," the high school, plus the mall last fall, seemed to be that I was staging a full-out war on the public in the Spokane Valley. The news sources I read weren't sure if I would bring forth a manifesto or a demand list before the attacks would stop. Speculation ran rife, though. Everyone believed I must want something.

Ok, maybe not everyone. There were also the people who fervently believed I enjoyed killing people for fun and giggles. "I didn't kill *any* of the deputies," I muttered. Not only did I, reportedly, revel in killing people, but I was generally bad at it.

Cythymau's death toll at the high school had come in at over fifty people, however, and since I got the credit for that too, that's what everyone focused on.

I also found out my newest, most dubious honor. America's Most Wanted had a new top star. Me.

Yup, what a *great* role model for Robert I turned out to be. No wonder he was always flying off the handle.

I frowned at a decided shimmer starting to hover in the air of my living room. Swiping blood across one of my Weave bracelets, I reached through the runes to feel the Weave. A tear opening up in the cabin would be the last straw. Through my Sense, the Weave looked intact. But just because the warping wasn't a Visitor from the other side didn't mean someone (or something) potentially dangerous *wasn't* about to manifest itself in my home.

I backed up as far as possible in the small, hewn-log room. The bark from the back wall scratched against my shoulder blades through my blouse as I adopted a defensive stance. The summoning continued to solidify. After Robert's run-in with Cythymau, my nerves thrummed. I was not ready to go back up against that guy in a one-on-one fight; not yet. That situation required a sure-fire solution first.

Please let it not be Cythymau.

The figure fully coalesced. I did a double take. Part of the tension I'd been holding left my body. The person who appeared to be standing in my living room was familiar, and while I did not expect our conversation to be pleasant, it probably wasn't dangerous either.

Or at least, not in the physical sense.

When the summons completed, Annalisa Miller, Seattle Grove Historian, gave me a grumpy hello from where she appeared to stand in the cabin.

The summons really was cleverly done. I assumed she must have a way to hear and see me as well, or it would have been pointless. I needed to learn how to do that. Not that *now* would be a good time to ask.

"To what do I owe the pleasure?" I asked her. As always, the Grove

Historian looked like a prim and proper business woman, on the slender, smallish side, with birdlike features.

"The fact that you even need to ask shows that your brain has turned to mulch," she said, her voice tart and disparaging. "Which, given the events over the last few hours, is, I suppose, only to be expected. We at the Seattle Grove were at a loss to explain your actions to the Cooperative Council. Aren't you a bit young to be suffering from dementia? Or is it just that power has gone to your head?" she finished acidly.

I grimaced. I could only imagine the type of day she'd been having. My situation was bad, sure, but I'd take a straightforward fight over political squabbling any day of the week. Still, I'd defend my actions against all comers if I had to. "I think that's putting it a bit strongly. I did the best I could with a bad situation. No one else would have done better."

"Oh, really?" she snorted. "Well, let me recite the reports we've received about you, and you can inform me if they're accurate. Then you tell me what conclusions you would draw about that summoner's reasoning powers."

I opened my mouth, but she cut me off by plunging right in. "First, you openly provoke a fight with the local law enforcement, in broad daylight in a residential neighborhood."

"The house was deserted, and there were no neighbors."

"Still, you don't deny that you intentionally provoked a confrontation with law enforcement, with full knowledge that the Federal presence in Spokane was still strong?" She raised her brows.

"The Federal investigation had already discovered somehow that I hadn't died. The confrontation was a diversion."

"I suppose, now you are going to claim you were inside the Federal investigation, looking at their notes?" she scoffed.

"No, I had a source," I said, beginning to get angry at her snide attitude.

"Really." She frowned. "Let me guess, your source was one of your pet sheriffs? Did it never occur to you that you confronting them in any way makes the Feds' job much easier? That it obviously was a trap to get out of the awkward position you put their whole department in? Really, you are so simple sometimes. Think about it."

"It wasn't a trap," I ground out.

"Tell yourself that if you like," Annalisa's voice dripped with icy scorn and condescension. Wow, she was in a bitchy mood today. Usually she was one of the more reasonable of the Seattle Grove Council.

I trusted Frank Allen with my life. If he had wanted to turn me in, he could have done it any time these last few months. *But not without implicating himself and Carlenos,* the unwelcome thought trickled to the front of my brain. He'd said the heat from the Feds was bad. I shook my head again. He'd left what I would do about it up to me. He hadn't asked me to confront the Feds head-on. I'd come up with that myself.

I took a deep breath. "My source didn't even know what I was going to do with the information he gave me." I tried to keep my voice level as my hands clenched and unclenched by my sides. I wanted to hit her. And I sensed we'd barely even started what was going to be a very long conversation. Maybe it was a good thing she wasn't really here in person.

"I don't see how that helps your case," she sniffed. "Actually, that's worse. Are you sure you want your official statement to be: it wasn't a trap, you weren't misled? You just triggered the biggest federally mandated witch-hunt on the Grove system since the stock market crash in 1929 because *you thought it was a good idea?* With no outside influence, you provoked the Federal government into the harshest public policy *ever* against all suspected summoning activity because you thought it would make a 'good diversion?' What were you trying to divert? What asset or reason could possibly be worth this type of fallout? Did you even think at all?"

With each of her words the real-world ramifications of my actions crashed down around me.

I cleared my suddenly clogged throat. "The Feds declared a national emergency," I whispered. "That's why the military responded and the blockades were able to be set up so quickly."

Annalisa smiled for the first time since she'd appeared, but it wasn't a nice smile. "I see you are catching up with the rest of us, now. Do you still wish to state that local law enforcement didn't lure you into making the show of force that precipitated the 'national emergency'?"

I frowned. "I really don't see where the distinction matters," I said. "Regardless, I did what I thought best, as the director, for the good of the Spokane Grove and its allies."

"Let's just leave that for the moment then, and proceed to the fact that you then engaged the military in a wild-goose chase across eastern Washington and northern Idaho, thus causing them to flood both Washington and Idaho with anti-summoner personnel and strike teams. This caused great hardship and impeded the business and stability of other Groves in those two states, including the Seattle and Boise Groves." Despite being a summoned manifestation, Annalisa still managed to look over her glasses and down her nose at me as she said the next part.

"Please explain for the official report to the Cooperative Council your reasoning for overtly engaging the military."

My mouth fell open a little at this point. I felt my face heat with incredulity. "You'd prefer I let myself get captured?" I asked.

"We'd *prefer* you'd never alerted the Federal authorities or the military to your presence. But since you did, we would like your reasoning for further engaging the Federal forces."

"I never *engaged* the military. They engaged me, and I only used summoning to aid myself in running away. I don't even know if my summons were observed. Although," I was forced to admit, "I left some evidence that would be rather difficult to explain without the aid of summoning."

A giant mountain of white feathers in the middle of an otherwise chicken-less forest and a newly dug, then collapsed, hideout full of thawing permafrost came to mind.

Her lips compressed. "We are aware. We are also aware that your apprentice's high school was attacked by as-yet unreported assailants while you led this goose-chase. Your apprentice, whom you left *completely* unsupervised, then further damaged the Weave. As well as scarring the Weave, he allowed many civilians to be injured or killed in his failed attempt to banish the Visitors. Your absence from that emergency is as conspicuous as the casualty list."

"You can't be blaming Robert because uninvited Visitors killed members of his school. He's only an apprentice, and he managed to save almost everyone there." My skin prickled with anger on his behalf.

"No, we blame him for the wonton destruction he inflicted on the Weave while combating them. It was completely unnecessary. And we blame you for your obvious neglect of the most basic control tenants in summoner training. Your apprentice is an unmitigated disaster waiting to happen."

"He was by himself in a situation where he could not openly summon, against a much more powerful opponent. He had also just seen the Lycaon killing his classmates. He was understandably distraught. That is by no means indicative of how he usually wields his Sense or his power. He managed admirably well for a teenager who has less than a year of training under his belt. I have already spoken to him regarding the unnecessary force he used on the Weave. It will not happen again."

I said the last part with more conviction than I felt, given the way Robert and I had parted, but that was a worry for later.

"Nevertheless. I thought this Grove made perfectly clear last fall and again at the conference that your appointment by the Cooperative Council was of an interim nature, and at the convenience of the Council. Your apprentices were also only tolerated under the assumption that you would be keeping them under control and providing supervision. Had the Council realized you were mismanaging the first one so horribly, we definitely would not have granted you leave to take another. You have made your appointment as interim Grove Director untenable for everyone involved."

"The Seattle Grove is withdrawing its support of the Spokane Grove?" I spluttered.

"The Seattle Grove, and all other Groves are withdrawing their support of *you*," Annalisa corrected. "You are hereby removed as the

Spokane Grove director and placed on inactive duty for the near future. You are by no means to attempt to leave the area or return to Seattle." She didn't say it, but the implication was clear. *We don't want you.* "Please, *please* cease drawing Federal attention to yourself and thereby to the rest of the Grove system. If you do not, the Groves will be forced to…more extreme disciplinary measures."

"Shouldn't there be some kind of a hearing or inquiry before you just decide to remove me?"

"Oh, there will still be an inquiry," she said. "But with the hornet's nest you've stirred up over there, it will be delayed indefinitely. I don't think you realize what a colossal fuck-up this was, Grace."

My jaw went slack. I'd never ever heard the Grove Historian swear. She wasn't through. "The Cooperative Council voted unanimously to remove you from leadership," she said, "revoke your acting director authority, and sort out what further measures were to be taken later. A new Grove Director has been dispatched and should be arriving shortly."

"I thought you said no one can get here with the crackdown?"

"It is not easy for anyone to get in or out of Spokane, that's true. But with the various issues currently running amok over there, it was decided it was worth the risk to dispatch a summoner of utmost repute and power level."

"Okay, so who are we expecting?" I thought I was holding on to my temper rather well, seeing as I'd just been summarily fired.

"I believe you've met him before. His name is Thaddeus? He should be there by morning at the latest. Try not to self-destruct before then."

Oh joy. He and I had gotten along dandy at the conference. This was just going to be a riotous barrel of laughs. Or possibly just a riot.

ROBERT

THE TRICK to being a runaway is twofold. First, if you can, don't have anyone who wants to find you. That was usually easy enough for a foster kid. I'd managed to push away Grace and the fosties in a single day, so mission accomplished.

Second, lay low. It doesn't matter if anyone wants to find you or not; if you're young and wandering the streets in the middle of the night it's not going to go well for you. If you're lucky, you get hassled by the cops. I was eighteen now, so at least I couldn't get taken in as an at-risk youth. That said, they'd still hassle me. If one of them searched me I could be in a world of hurt—not all the cops in Spokane County were as forgiving as Captain Carlenos.

I knew where to find the weakness in the Weave. Since moving around was going to be difficult, I simply set up shop in the old factory. It wasn't the most comfortable place to live, but I'd been in worse. It was quiet, and that gave me the study time I really needed to punch through into Cythymau's world.

I pored through Herman's notes. Many of them were historical, mentioning (of all things) the Neanderthals. It appeared Uncle Herman had a particular fascination with anthropology. Not useful. His other, more arcane notes seemed to be more in line with what I was looking for, and I spent days pondering their meaning, trying to wring some basic concept from them.

As far as I could figure out, the number of worlds out there was countless. I sifted endlessly through his notes, but had no idea how Grace began to figure out how to find the right world. A couple of pages had her notes scribbled in the margin as well; those I paid particular attention to, but even then the jargon was so thick and heavy that grasping it seemed impossible.

Several days in, my cell phone rang. I picked it up hesitantly.

"Hey, Robert. It's Jake." The voice on the other end sounded quiet. Somber. Also, he didn't open our conversation by calling me "fucker." This, then, was something serious. I responded in kind.

"Hey man, what's up?"

"You going tomorrow?"

"Where?"

"Shit, fucker." Ah, now this was more like it. "You been living with your head in the sand?"

"Uh," I said. "Close enough."

"The funeral's tomorrow," Jake said, growing solemn again.

"Wait, funeral? Which one?" I ran down the list of casualties I knew about from graduation. Duane and Jeanelle were only the start.

"All the students, man. They're doing a big group funeral. The rest of our class is going to be there."

Oh.

I knew I should go. After all, they had died because of me. On the other hand, what if Cythymau attacked during the funeral? If I went to this one, I'd have to make sure *Graduate Funeral II: Electric Boogaloo* was not in production.

"You there, man?" I had forgotten I was on the phone with Jake.

"Yeah. I'm here."

"You should be there." Jake seemed certain.

"You know there's a risk, right?"

"Fucker, I've been taking that risk all year. What makes you think I'm going to stop now? Now get off your ass and come say goodbye to your dead friends, you son of a bitch."

Ah, Jake. Ever the wordsmith. He was right, though. I agreed, he called me some more names, I insulted his mother, then we hung up. I rooted through my bag and tried to find some clothes worth wearing to a funeral. I came up with unripped jeans and a polo shirt. Good enough.

~

Funerals are, for the most part, events of extreme boredom punctuated by moments of crippling emotion. I watched as the family and friends of each deceased classmate ascended to the podium to tell their favorite stories of whatever child I'd killed. I cried at times, but for the most part I simply wanted the cursed thing to *end*. Eulogizing eleven students at the same time just took waaay too long.

Worse, this was turning into a political event. People who never even knew these kids showed up, most of whom were running for some office or another. These speakers talked about the students' "brave sacrifice." I wondered, idly, what it was they had collectively sacrificed for. Oh, some of them had thrown their lives away to protect another student, and I do not mean to belittle that. But Jeanelle had died in a human crush. Exactly who did that benefit?

Brave sacrifice. I held back the urge to run up on stage, whip out my Sense, and sacrifice *them*.

The general theme to the politicians was "summoners bad." That was one of those givens, like making a lawyer joke or saying we needed to create jobs. No one offered specifics on what it was the politicians wanted to do about us, but that was fine. Their general statements were enough.

This was becoming a circus, and I was becoming disgusted with it. I looked at Jake, seated to my right. He shook his head.

"This is fucked," I whispered to him.

"Yeah."

"How the fuck are we supposed to get closure at a goddamn campaign rally?" I asked.

"I guess fuck us," replied Jake eloquently. I nodded in agreement. A moment passed as the asshole currently occupying the stage talked about how, if elected, he would "purge this scum from the face of our fair city." Mayor, then.

"Sooo...abandoned factory party?" I asked Jake.

"Robert, I am shocked that you would even suggest that." Jake's tone was pious. I waited for the other shoe to drop, trying to look nonchalant. "Shawna's folks are out. She's already throwing a party. It would be rude of you not to go."

I smiled at him, nodding. "Is Willy going to be there?" I asked.

"Willy? I think so. Why?"

"Because I would very much not like to feel anything by the time this night is over."

Jake grinned at me. "That can be arranged, fucker. That can be arranged." His arm came up and slapped my back in the closest thing to a hug Jake and I ever had.

"Good," I said.

IT WAS POLITE, of course, to stay at the reception after the funeral for a short, but still unbearable, length of time, and I resigned myself to doing so. As I fished some punch out of a rather large bowl, a female deputy came to stand next to me.

"Hey, Robert," she said. Her voice was low and hoarse, and it caressed my name in a way that gained my immediate attention. It seemed wildly incongruous coming from a uniformed deputy. Briefly, I considered the possibility that Jake had gotten me a stripper, but not even he could be so uncouth as to unleash a strip tease at a funeral. Could he?

The deputy stood up, and I looked for the nametag. It read "C. Maru."

I dropped my punch cup and slammed my Sense into place, looking wildly around the room, waiting for the next attack point.

"*Whuft*, don't be so uptight," the unspeakable evil giggled. "I'm not going to attack you. I know you've been looking for me." She slipped her arm around my shoulders, pressing her ample bosom into my side. "Well. You. Have. Found. Me." Each word was punctuated by a pouty lip and a slight shift in her torso, causing one breast and then the other to collide with my midsection.

It was an illusion. My Sense was up, and I could tell that Deputy Cathy Maru was simply a projection of force and light, just like my principal was. But it was a damned convincing illusion, and it had very firm, supple breasts. Those parts of me that rarely have good ideas had another really bad one.

"I'm not looking for something that...*shallow.* Sorry, Cathy. I'm holding out for *the real thing.*"

Cathy—damn it, Cythymau—giggled at me again. "Of course you are, you silly thing. I wanted to help out a little bit with that. Here." She handed me a small slip of paper with a series of runes on it.

"What's this?" I asked, guardedly.

"Well," said my demonic foe in his/her very best vapid-girl voice. "It's my address. Don't you like it when a pretty girl gives you her address? Come and get me, Robert. You. Just. Come. And. Get. Me." The staccato poutiness returned on that last sentence, as did the breasts, but the illusion rose and walked away from me, leaving only the rune slip in my hand.

Okay, I wasn't a complete idiot. Obviously it was a trap. Even so...

I slipped the rune tag into my wallet. This was obviously neither the time nor the place to do anything with it. I had some forgetting to do, and to do that I needed to get out of here.

To Shawna's house.

IT IS A VERY, very good thing that summoning requires mental focus. That's really the only thing that saved me from outing myself that night.

Jake and I rolled up to Shawna's house and were treated to the sight of Shawna herself holding a red plastic cup out to us in each hand. She smiled at me, which I returned warmly. It didn't look like she was still mad at me. I took the beer, gratefully, and tipped the cup to my lips. The light, yellow comfort made its cool, clear way past my lips as I chugged it down. Then I crinkled the cup against my head and sounded a thunderous belch.

"Holy shit!" Jake exclaimed. "*You* are not *fucking around* tonight!"

"Nope," I replied. "Fuckin' A."

Jake slammed his beer back as well. "Fuckin' A."

We got fresh cups from the keg set up in Shawna's kitchen. Bottles of liquor lined the counter as well, another welcome sight. Jake, ever the showman, grabbed a bottle of cheap, dark rum and stood atop the central island in the kitchen.

"Fuckers!" he shouted. It took away some of his presence that his voice cracked right in the middle of this. "Listen the hell up!"

Surprisingly, the party began to grow quiet. The loud thump of the stereo continued from the living room, but the normal drone of conversation that accompanies a party died away.

"Raise 'em high, fuckers." Jake said, slowly lifting the bottle in his right hand. "Raise 'em up high. Here's to ya, graduating class of University High School. Here's to those that didn't make it through." A silence followed, and I noticed for the first time a tear rolling down Jake's cheek.

"Here's to all the good times. Here's to our valedictorian, who makes a much prettier speech than I can. Here's to being looked down on by the Homecoming King and Queen. Here's to the lucky bastards that got to die young and pretty. Here's to those of us still stuck on this earth. When we go, let it be in half so much style as them. And here's to the crazy son of a bitch who killed those things—"

I took a sharp breath. Surely even a drunken Jake wouldn't out me here.

"Whoever he is, he may be a damned summoner but he saved some lives. Including mine. Here's to living our lives hard, so's we have as much fun as they would have had. So raise 'em high, fuckers. Raise 'em high for one last salute to our fallen comrades, then tip 'em back so we can forget. We'll join them in Hell soon enough."

A forest of arms holding plastic cups and shot glasses raised up in the air, and then on some unseen cue, we all drank.

The rest of the party gets kind of blurry in my memory. Here's what I know: I drank as much as I could, as fast as I could. Willy, presumably per Jake's instructions, handed me a couple of pills. To this day I have no idea what they were, but he told me they'd take away all my troubles, so I took them.

I do have a relatively vivid image in my head of me standing on top of Shawna's coffee table and shouting, *"Which one of you motherfuckers wants to see a magic trick?"* I think—though I am not sure—that this was met with general acclaim, whereupon I immediately fell *off* of Shawna's coffee table—no, wait. The table broke? Or was it...well, whatever happened, I ended up on my ass, to raucous applause and laughter.

I can't say for sure, but there's good odds I was trying to summon something. I couldn't, though—I had no focus at all, and that's probably for the best. Definitely. It's definitely for the best.

I ended up in bed with Shawna. It wasn't like when I made out with Jeanelle; there was no emotion in it. With Jeanelle, I was always feeling the great romantic thoughts any time we ended up making out. With Shawna, we were both driven by a desperate, consuming need not to feel anything at all. Before I knew it, we were naked and clumsily progressing our way away from anything that could possibly resemble love.

The first time you have sex had been, to that point, heralded as one of those pinnacles of existence. Boys had been talking about the Loss of Virginity as though it were this mythic, perfect thing ever since we learned that our penises had a function other than urination. I had wanted to lose my virginity to Jeanelle, but we had never quite gone that far. Oh, there was some heavy petting, to be sure, but not that one, sacred act.

Of course, Jeanelle had been in love with Duane.

With Shawna, though, I hardly think I was her first. Once naked, she straddled me quickly and guided me into her. It was startlingly quick, and my reaction was...also startlingly quick. I suffered my orgasm within seconds, then my clenching muscles caused me to vomit. *That* embarrassment, no amount of alcohol or drugs can purge from my mind, no matter how much I may want them to.

Too embarrassed to talk, and with the room spinning about me, I decided that the best thing I could do was pass out.

~

I AWOKE to a pair of rough, burly hands grabbing me by the upper arms. They dragged me up and away from the bed. My head lurched, and seconds later my belly disgorged yet another round of contents onto the bed covers.

"Holy shit, it's Lorents," a voice said. The voice sounded older than my fellow partiers. "Get the Captain."

Captain? That didn't sound like a party term. I looked around.

I was still naked, though Shawna was nowhere to be found. That was probably for the best, I reflected, given my less-than-stunning performance earlier in the evening. Two men hoisted me between them and held me on my knees by my arms. My back was resting against one of their knees, and my head lolled first forward, then back.

"Captain? Captain!" shouted the voice. My head rang with the volume of it. I tried to tell him to quiet down. It came out as more of a moan than anything coherent.

"What the hell do you want?" asked a new voice. This one was familiar, but I was having a hard time putting my finger on exactly who it was. "Look, we can't peg *all* these kids with MIPs. Just break it up and send them on their way. If he's too drunk to stand, we'll take him to the tank for the night."

"But, Captain, it's fucking Lorents." Ah, that's where I'd heard the voice.

"Carlenos?" I mumbled, trying to make my mouth move correctly.

"Oh, shit," said Captain Carlenos. "All right, boys. Gentle now. We're going to talk to him nice and slow, and we're not going to make any sudden moves. That ok, Robert?" Carlenos's voice was calm and

141

slow. It had all the rhythm of someone trying to talk to a dog that was making up its mind whether or not to bite the speaker.

I wasn't sure what they were driving at. Of course that was ok.

"Lemme go back to sleep."

"Robert? We're not trying to hurt you. You can't try to hurt us. That's fair, isn't it?"

I nodded. It wasn't like there was a lot I could do at the moment anyway.

"We just want to make sure you're going to be all right. We're going to take you down to the tank for a night, ok?"

"Back...sleep," I insisted, gazing longingly at the vomit-covered bed in front of me.

"We're going to take you to a different bed, Robert. We're going to take you away from here, and put you in a nice bed down in the tank. Do you understand? We're going to take you to a different bed, and you're not going to fight us or try to hurt us, right?"

"Fine," I returned. "Just...just let me go back to sleep as soon as you can." My stomach was starting to churn again.

"Robert, I know Francene's in the hospital. Do you want me to call Donald to come pick you up? Or do you want to sleep it off first? Or..." His voice trailed off. I was pretty sure he had been about to suggest that Grace come pick me up, but that stopped short.

"Donald doesn't want me. Kicked me out. Let me go back to sleep," I begged.

"Doesn't want you?" asked Carlenos, surprised. "What makes you think Donald doesn't want you?"

"Tol' me so," I groaned back. "Tol' me thought I'm dangerous. Didn't want me around no more. So I left. Took my things, left. Went to live in a factory. Live in a factory now. No parents. No one left to leave me. All alone." I was rambling.

Carlenos had an oddly soft expression on his face as he jerked his head in a signal of some sort. The two deputies holding my arms helped me to stand, wrapped a towel around my torso, and began to walk me down the steps.

"Carlenos...wait, Carlenos," I said, and the deputies halted.

Carlenos came up to look at me. "I'ma get the sumbitch," I slurred. "He thinks he's so special but I'm better now. I'ma get him, for you, and Allen, and Jeanelle, and Duane, and fucking all your deputies and all my friends and shit. I'ma get him."

"Sure you are, Robert," Carlenos said gently. "Sure you are. But not tonight, eh?"

"No," I agreed, shaking my head back and forth, then instantly regretting it. "Not tonight. Sleep tonight."

"Sleep tonight," Carlenos agreed, and motioned for the deputies to remove me. They slowly helped me down the stairs and out to the patrol car, where I leaned my head against the back of the seat.

"Gonna...get...sumbitch..." I repeated, slowly letting sleep reach its hands around my consciousness. "Gonna...get..."

GRACE

WELL, this little announcement about my demotion and suspension was going just about as well as could be hoped. Which meant walking backwards over a live volcano would probably be more enjoyable right about now. It's not every day that the Grove Director calls a meeting to announce her own disciplinary proceedings. Amy and Matt sat on the log bench outside the cabin in the early morning light. Amy's face had set in grim and angry lines. Matt's expression looked gray and blank. I didn't know what had upset them more: the fact that I'd been suspended from active Grove duty, or the fact we had yet another crisis to deal with. We'd dealt with too many already.

"The main thing," I continued calmly, trying to push down my own roiling nerves, "is that the Spokane Grove will be getting a new director. By the time I learned of it, my demotion had already been pushed through the Cooperative Council. I'll try to appeal, but I don't hold out too much hope. For the time being, there will be new leadership coming in from out of town. From what I understand, the new Grove Director will be meeting us within the hour. Amy may remember he wanted the Spokane leadership position before. His name is Thaddeus Neilsen."

The silence stretched.

Robert hadn't shown up for this meeting. He hadn't replied to any of my summoned notes or apologies over the last couple days. Even after the talk with Jake I hadn't really expected Robert to completely cut me off. Ignore me and blow me off, sure. But he'd completely failed to respond to the emergency code I sent out last night too.

Nothing to do about it now. I just hoped I could spin his absence in such a way that it wouldn't be an immediate mark against him with the new director. It's not like our little Grove was big enough that you'd expect some people to be absent.

"I don't even see how the new director can get here. The roads in and out of town are locked down like they expect us to start bombing the civilians any minute," Amy said dourly.

"As grateful as I am for your concern"—the way the new voice drawled out this comment suggested he meant the exact opposite—"I assure you, I am capable of bypassing a few roadblocks with a skill far surpassing all of you. But then, I suppose that is why I was brought in. Let me introduce myself properly. I am Thaddeus Nielsen, recently aide to Phineas Brandiole of the Seattle Grove, originally of the Boise Grove, and now your new director effective immediately."

The voice belonged to the small, thin man in a gray pinstriped suit standing at the edge of the rolling driveway. He hadn't been there a minute before. We all turned to look at him in surprise as he started toward us. His eyes were the same as I remembered: steel gray, edged with a hardness that reminded me of flint. Where some people had smile lines around their mouth, he had frown lines. His salt-and-pepper hair looked a little whiter around his temples than it had a few weeks ago. The corner of his lip twitched upward as I watched, making him look dour yet smug. That bastard.

I forced myself to watch him with a façade of calm, despite my pulse thundering under my skin. I hadn't been comfortable with my position as the Grove Director, but I didn't appreciate being fired either. "We didn't expect you quite so soon," I said finally.

"Surely you didn't expect us to leave this Grove subject to your disastrous policies a second longer than necessary."

"My actions protected this Grove and its allies. You may not have made the same decisions in my shoes, but I stand behind my reasons," I shot back, stung. His disapproval hit me like a physical force, radiating off him in waves.

"Did your 'reasons' take into account the consequences of your actions at all?" His voice was deceptively mild, singeing me with hidden scorn. "Surely an all-out confrontation with the resources of the Federal government was not part of your original goal?"

I lifted my chin higher in defiance and maintained eye contact. "My actions preserved valuable Grove assets that would otherwise be lost."

He glowered. "However pure your motives may have been, the outcome speaks for itself about how misguided those actions were. I doubt your goal included protecting your Grove by crippling Groves all across the nation. However, it aptly demonstrates why the prohibitions against overt summoning exist in the first place. More troubling to me and the Cooperative Council, it shows your willingness to continue to flaunt Grove law—outside of the direct threat to life, limb, and public safety, which you used to justify your actions last fall. The Council let it pass last time on those extenuating circumstances. This situation bears little resemblance to your previous reports, except perhaps for your need to demonstrate your own self-importance."

I opened my mouth to protest, but he didn't give me a chance.

"I can quote each section of Grove law your actions violated, if need be. Shall we start? 'Chapter 14, Section 11.2(b). A summoner shall not, without the special dispensation for circumstances described in 14.3 of this chapter, summon in front of any mundane in such a way as to make the act of summoning visible, audible, or unavoidably apparent to the untrained observer.' Or 11.4. 'A summoner shall not provoke a confrontation of any kind with mundane law enforcement. Any grievances with mundane law enforcement are to be brought to the proper Grove officials through the channels described herein.' I would think the meaning of those two very basic clauses would be plain. Need I *really* continue? If you are shocked that your actions have brought about *any* of the results we now face, you are a fool as well as reckless." His voice stopped as if he'd physically snapped the words off.

Blood rushed to my face as my temper flared. He was trying to provoke me into an angry reaction to prove his point. I wasn't going to give it to him. Plus, he was right in one regard. The government's escalated reaction to my ambush of its officers shouldn't have come as a surprise. I *had* focused on protecting my little group without much thought to the bigger outcome. Sure, my original goal of taking heat off the Sheriff's department worked, but at the expense of transferring all that scrutiny to the Grove system I'd sworn to protect.

If I looked at it from his point of view, I was lucky I'd only been suspended.

Thad's clipped voice cut into my unpleasant thoughts. "However, I am not here to conduct the inquiry into whether or not your actions can ultimately be justified. That is for other, more advanced legal scholars than myself. I am here because the Cooperative Council decided this Grove is in crisis and sinking faster every day. As such, it needed a new authority immediately."

He fixed me with those hard eyes. "I think you will find I am just as displeased to be here as you are to have me."

I severely doubted that claim, considering how hard he'd tried to get in these shoes just a little over a month ago in Vegas, but I bit my tongue.

"However, I shall do my best to clean up this train wreck you have created as quickly as possible. You've been suspended from active duty pending the internal investigation. Your exact position in the Grove for the time being has been left up to the new director. Me. Do you accept the Cooperative Council's decision regarding yourself, and that the same has the authority to appoint a new director?"

He'd phrased that well. I couldn't say no without declaring myself above the Council's authority. I worded my reply carefully.

"While I don't necessarily agree with their reasons, I absolutely accept the Council's authority over myself. I do not seek to stand above the law."

"Could have fooled me." The sotto voice mutter came from an

unexpected location. I glanced at Amy and Matt. It had been low enough to make whoever said it indistinguishable. I couldn't imagine timid Matt piping up with that, but if it was Amy, she was *super* pissed. Way more than I'd realized yesterday. *Way to alienate absolutely everyone, Grace. Good job.*

It also turned Thad's attention to the rest of my little Grove. I winced as he raised his brows, considering them with those sharp eyes, "I see you are not the only one who has forgotten the respect due the Council." His brows lowered. "I was told there would be one more."

"With the short notice of your arrival, I was not able to reach Robert in time. He should be along shortly," I said. Amy snorted.

"Did you have something to add, Ms. Milankovich?" Thad asked.

Amy tossed her strawberry-blonde mane of hair over her shoulder and crossed her arms over her chest. I tried to remember if I'd ever heard her last name before. She was just Amy, my lab buddy. Gods, saying she was angry was the understatement of the century. She looked murderous.

"Robert has been avoiding Grace since he had to deal with the Lycaon at his graduation by himself the other day. I doubt he even looked at the summons." Amy's words came out clipped and short.

Thad looked at me. "Is this true?" he asked mildly. The even tone couldn't deceive me. I stood on the edge of a precipice here. As did Robert.

"I don't know if I would put it so strongly," I said instead. "It's true he was upset by the unpreventable casualties at his graduation, but to my knowledge, I just wasn't able reach him today."

Amy didn't let me get away with that evasive answer. "I wonder why," she slid in snidely.

My mouth dropped open. I'd always known Amy had a sharp tongue on her, but I'd never had it directed at me before. I stared at her. My sunny, scatterbrained friend had been replaced by a stranger. She gave me a look that was full of rage, but also hurt. I took a deep breath and tried to release the fist of pain suddenly lodged in my stomach.

"But were those deaths truly unpreventable? Either way, Ms. Moore," Thad said dryly, "it's obvious to me that you have exerted very little control over your Grove members. Perhaps it is only to be expected that such a loosely run ship would end up on the rocks so quickly. *I* expect all of you to please refrain from taking the rest of the Grove system with you in your attempt to self-destruct."

He straightened his suit cuffs before continuing in that cold, crisp voice. "Now that I am here, I can guarantee any outbursts against Grove authority, whether in word or action, will not be tolerated. I expect respect and discipline from you all. I will get it, or none of you will like the consequences."

"It's not Robert's fault that Cythymau targeted his graduation," I blurted. "Cythymau has focused his attacks on Spokane. Robert is still learning, and took the deaths to heart."

"Ms. Moore, I do not hold the deaths at the high school against your apprentice. It seems, under the circumstances, he reacted with much presence of mind and without, I might add, alerting the hundred or so people gathered there that he was a summoner. However, his methods of defeating the Lycaon leave much to be desired, given the *extensive* damage he inflicted on the Weave. I absolutely hold that against him; furthermore, I hold his actions to be proof that you have been criminally negligent in his training. As for Cythymau, Groves across the nation are being targeted by malicious Visitors every day. That you have your own pet bogeyman should not factor in to these particular decisions. The Council does not debate the potential for amazing power possessed by your apprentice, Lorents. However, we do debate whether such a power should be allowed to grow unchecked. Part of my task here is to determine if either of your apprentices are in fact, salvageable."

"Matt and Robert are *not* a threat to you *or* other Groves. They're both great kids," I choked out.

"That remains to be determined. Your protests so far do not inspire confidence. If I have to terminate either of them, make no mistake that my reports to the Council will hold you ultimately responsible."

Matt's gray face blanched white. He lowered his head to stare at his dusty shoes.

"As for you, Ms. Moore, I expect you to draw no further attention to yourself while I am here. You will remain here at this cabin and not go anywhere unless explicitly ordered there by myself. Is that clear?"

Deep breaths, Grace. Today is not the day to fight this battle. Whenever I spoke, the hole just got deeper. I nodded, rubbing my suddenly clammy hands on my bright skirt.

"Yes, sir." I barely got the words out past the constriction in my throat.

In the back of my mind I acknowledged that I might, in fact, be giving an empty promise. If Thad decided Robert needed to be "terminated," I wasn't going to abandon him twice. Or Matt, for that matter, though he was much less likely to come across as a threat. I didn't leave my men abandoned in the field, demotion or no.

"I am told that your specialty in the Seattle Grove was Visitor research and rune theory," Thaddeus continued.

"That's correct."

"While I do not believe the presence of this Cythymau is justification for your actions, I do wish to find out whatever we can about him given his continued attacks. You have my permission to continue your research into this entity. However, any books you require are to be cleared through me, and you are by no means to pursue any leads which would take you back out into the field. Those you will refer directly to me. If I find out at any point that you have gone against these orders, I will strip you of all privileges and remand you to the Council. Are we still clear?"

"Yes, sir." Feds, the Council, no matter which one got me, it wasn't going to be *pleasant*. I didn't want to pop up further on their radar either. He stood there weighing me with his eyes until I wanted to squirm.

My cell phone chimed from my handbag. I jumped. No one should be calling that. Not with the Feds all over me like white on rice. The only people who had the number at all were—

I swore without thinking, digging into my handbag. I pulled the cell phone out from the bottom. The phone number on the screen was unfamiliar, but that didn't mean anything. It had to be either Carlenos or Allen.

The phone was plucked from my hand. "Not good news, I take it?" Thad queried. He flipped it open and pushed the button to put it on speaker. He held the phone up between us and raised his brows, pressing me to go ahead and answer, or admit I didn't accept his authority. As the new Grove Director, he had a right to all my contacts. Unless I was willing to throw down with Thad right now, I only had one option. A part of me hoped it was another Visitor incursion, even as I acknowledged that it made me a bad person. *Please let it not be about Robert. Not right now.*

I cleared my throat. "This is Grace," I said, attempting to put my normal briskness back into my voice.

"Grace, thank God." Carlenos' voice was relieved. "After the stunt you pulled, I wasn't sure you'd answer. Look, I don't know what's going on exactly, but I have Robert down at the Valley Station."

"What?" My voice squeaked despite my best efforts. "He's in jail?"

"I've got him in the drunk tank. We scraped him out of the ruins of a party we broke up earlier this morning. I know this puts you in an awful situation, but I need you to send someone to come get him. He says his foster parents threw him out; they won't pick him up. I like the kid. I don't want to have to pin him to the wall unless I'm forced to. He seems to think he doesn't have anyone looking out for him anymore. Before he passed out, he said something about living in a factory. To be honest, he's a total mess."

My eyes met Thad's over the phone, my stomach dropping all the way into my toes. The muscles in his jaw stood out so prominently that I knew his teeth were clenched against whatever he wanted to say. Well, we were thoroughly in the shit now. There was only one answer I could give.

"I'm so sorry for the trouble. We'll send someone for him." Thad jerked the phone, gesturing back toward himself as he held it. I nodded in resignation. "You won't have met him before, but he's safe. He'll be the gray-haired man in a suit asking for Robert."

"Send him soon," Carlenos replied. "I can't hold Robert much longer without booking him or it'll raise questions. He doesn't look in shape to do anything at the moment, but he's making a few of the deputies from last fall, including myself, a little nervous. He's so out of it, we're afraid he might start blasting things accidentally. Oh, and tell your friend to bring some clothes. I don't know what the kid was wearing to begin with, but he doesn't have any now."

The phone line went dead. Thad considered it for a moment before closing it with a vicious snap and putting it in his own pocket.

"Not a good start, Ms. Moore, not a good start," was all he said.

Director Nielsen took spare running clothes of Robert's from the back of the cabin and directions to the Valley station, and walked down the drive with the bundle. He hit the edge of the property before his form seemed to shimmer and vanish. That was a nifty summons. I couldn't tell if Thad was still there or not.

I turned to Amy and Matt, at a loss for what to say.

What came out of my mouth was, "I should go after him and make sure Robert doesn't say or do anything stupid." I started to walk toward my car. A hand on my arm stopped me.

I looked over my shoulder at Amy. "Did you not understand anything that man just said?" she asked me in a strident whisper. "You can't go anywhere. If you do, you're toast. *We're* toast." She gestured to Matt and herself. "I don't get what's going through your head right now." Her eyes searched my face.

"Robert's my apprentice," I said. "I'm responsible for him. If I don't go, there's no one to stand up for him."

"If you go, you're not doing Robert any favors," Amy countered. "You really *must* think you know better than Grove law."

"I do not!"

"Then what the *hell* are you doing right now, Grace? You have been *suspended*. You're effectively on house arrest! There is no way you going to Robert right now doesn't break Grove law." She paused. "Are you sure you don't have some kind of weird crush on Robert?"

My lips turned down. "That's impossible and gross. He's, like, fifteen years younger than me. Besides, I'd do the same thing if Matt

152

was in trouble. And Matt would want me to back him up. Right, Matt?" I turned to my newest apprentice.

"I'm sorry, Grace," Matt shook his head. "But no. That guy just said he was here to judge whether to terminate both Robert and me. That scares the shit out of me. And I don't see how ignoring his authority puts anything but a black mark on either of us. Maybe you could help. Maybe you'd just get us killed faster. Director Neilsen doesn't seem to take insubordination well at all." He got up. "I'm going for a walk. If you leave, I don't want to know anything about it."

"I agree with Matt," Amy said. "You'll only make things worse for Robert if you go. Robert's situation *is* your fault. All of this is your fault. Did you somehow forget the Groves are supposed to be a *secret* fellowship?"

Her words knocked the breath out of me, and my will to argue right along with it. "It's your fault," she said, "but this isn't the way to fix it. Have a little faith in Robert, will you? If you go, I'm not backing you up this time. You're on your own."

Amy released my arm and followed Matt.

I walked over to the log bench in a daze, and sat down where they'd been. It looked like the vote was unanimous. The soldier out of step was me. Why, if they were right, did it all feel so wrong?

ROBERT

I WOKE WITH A POUNDING HEADACHE. I was lying on some sort of a cot, and the smell of an uncleaned bathroom filled my nostrils.

Oh, right. Jail.

I blinked, trying to rub the sleep from my eyes. My stomach lurched, and a foul belch forced its way up my esophagus. My skin was crusted with old sweat, my mouth dry and parched. I made a mental note to myself: drinking tequila out of a one-gallon milk jug was off-limits from here on out.

I'm not sure how long I sat on the bunk collecting myself before Captain Carlenos entered the hallway in front of my cell. "Robert Lorents?" he asked.

"Uhhhh..." I responded. For the state I was in, this was the pinnacle of eloquence.

"Officially, you're charged with trespassing. That's what we're giving all the kids we couldn't tag with drugs or MIP directly. I've got your paperwork here. It's your first adult offense, so I don't imagine you'll get too dinged by it."

"Nrrnnh," I replied.

"Still feeling it, huh?" Carlenos' voice was almost sympathetic in its softness. I nodded.

"We're on camera here, just to let you know. Also, your ride is here."

"My ride?" Had Jake come by to pick me up? Before Carlenos could answer, a new voice cut into the conversation.

"Hello, Robert." A short man stood at the entrance to my cell, wearing an immaculate gray pinstripe suit. His posture was still and formal, as was the pitch of his voice. A pair of horn-rimmed glasses framed his eyes. His hairline was receding, but not too severely. All in all, he had a crisp formality about him that I immediately recognized.

"This my lawyer?" I asked Carlenos.

"Ah. No," said Carlenos. "If you need counsel, you'll have to apply for it at your arraignment. This man responded to a call from me to—"

"Suffice to say that I am the man who is picking you up," announced Suit Guy. "All else will be explained on the way."

"Captain, this dude isn't my legal custodian. Can you really release me to him?"

"Robert...you're eighteen," Carlenos reminded me. Crap; I didn't *have* a legal custodian anymore. The Volvo was probably still parked outside Shawna's place. I wasn't really sure who Suit Guy was, but Carlenos seemed to trust him. I shrugged my shoulders.

"All right, I could use the lift. Let's get out of here."

"Um, about that," said Carlenos. "You don't have anything in property."

"Well, good. That should make the check-out pretty quick."

"No," said Carlenos. "You don't have *anything* in property. Usually we send you out of here wearing the clothes you had when you came in."

"Yeah, so what's the—oh." Memories of the night before slowly intruded. "So when you say I don't have anything in property..."

"I mean *anything*," confirmed Carlenos.

"Captain Carlenos," said Mr. Pinstripe in his icy tone. "I have brought Robert his clothing. Perhaps while you begin the booking-out process, I can go use the restroom and then fetch them?"

"Really?" asked Carlenos. "Because when I called—" A sharp look from Suit caught Carlenos, who shut up immediately. Interesting; this guy scared my good friend the Captain, and that was hard to do. "Oh, of course," said Carlenos. "Yes. That makes sense."

The good Captain led me out of my cell and down to booking to begin the process of checking me out of the jail. Midway through signing my various forms, Not-a-Lawyer joined us, a bundle of my clothing in his hand.

It was the spare clothes I kept at Uncle Herman's cabin. Now I knew what had scared Carlenos. This man was another summoner. Grace had called in reinforcements. Hallelujah. If getting this kind of help was her way of extending an olive branch, I was willing to take it. I was going to need all the help taking Cythymau down that I could get.

I stepped away and changed my clothes, signed my last form, and walked out the front door next to my new friend.

"Robert Lorents," said Suit Guy. "My name is Thaddeus Neilsen. I am the new director of the Spokane Grove. Pleased to meet you." He had waited until the car door shut on both of us to spring this on me.

New director? "Did something happen to Grace?" I asked, concerned.

"Ms. Moore has been reassigned to her normal research duties. I am here as her duly assigned replacement."

"Research? Grace?" I chortled. "How long do you think that's going to last?"

Mr. Neilsen was less than amused by my joke, which I took to mean he didn't know Grace very well. "Oh, come on. She'll be out in the field in no time. Her beef with Cythymau is almost as big as mine, after all." Almost.

"If she acts outside her assignment, she will be dealt with. For now, her reassignment should keep her away from fieldwork." Mr. Neilsen's voice was still unwavering and official. Cold.

"Look, Mr. Neilsen, Grace is a pretty amazing—"

"Mr. Lorents, I do not believe the judgment of a half-trained apprentice is going to sway my assignment decisions." Mr. Neilsen started the car and started down Sprague. I was silent for a while; it was pretty clear that this new guy wasn't interested in socializing.

"Hey, before we head back to the factory, can we swing by Shawna's? I need to pick up the Volvo."

"Mr. Lorents, there is a lengthy discussion the two of us need to have before I let you out of my sight. You will be allowed to pick up your vehicle at a time more convenient to the both of us."

Mr. Neilsen drove a direct course to the factory, and I led him to the area I had made my home. I sat on a giant, rusted-out, roller-machine-thingy, and gestured in a host-like manner for him to take his seat on another.

The furnishings in my new home were not exactly designer quality.

He ignored this gesture, standing straight as a post while addressing me. "Mr. Lorents, it would appear that you have encountered this Cythymau spirit more times than any other summoner at this Grove, Ms. Moore included. I have read Ms. Moore's reports, but I would prefer to come to my own, untainted conclusions by speaking directly to the source. What happened when you first met Cythymau?"

I leaned back, remembering. "Well," I said. "The first time I heard him talk at all, it was through the mouth of his pet Cornuprocyon. Actually, it was in the building you just took me out of."

"You were under arrest then, too? Is this a habit for you?"

"Ah, no. I've only been under arrest one other time, for shoplifting. No, it was Grace who was under arrest."

"Yes. Grace's report did mention that, although details as to your involvement were left...scarce. Begin there, and please fill me in."

I did, though I did not get too far.

"You launched a frontal assault on the police station itself?" interrupted Mr. Neilsen.

"Well, I blew in their back wall. I'm not sure you can call the assault *frontal*. But, yeah. I stormed the place."

"I see. And could you describe exactly how you, as you so put it, 'blew in' the wall of the police station?"

"Oh, I just used raw force. Here, check these out." I rummaged through my scant belongings and came up with Uncle Herman's...no. With *my* bracers. "See? I used this set, right here." I pointed to the appropriate runes etched into the bracers.

For the first time since meeting him, Mr. Neilsen displayed some form of emotion. His eyebrows rose, ever so slightly, as he took the bracers from me.

"Mr. Lorents, where did you get these?" The pitch of his voice had altered just slightly. He actually sounded interested in the answer to my question. I brightened, happy at having evoked a human response from this otherwise disturbing man.

"They were my Uncle Herman's. He left them for me last fall when the Cornuprocyon got him."

"Do you have any idea how old these are?"

"Uh, no. Not really. I just figured they were something Crazy Uncle Herman made. He was always making stuff."

"No," said Mr. Neilsen, firmly. "These predate Uncle Herman by over a millennium. You've got a genuine pair of summoner's bracers from the Dark Ages here. They're an amazing piece, really. I've never seen a set in this good condition." His voice was accelerating with his excitement as he stared at my bracers, spinning them around to look from all angles.

"Huh. I never figured."

"Oh, yes. Look, you can see the maker's stamp in here. Let's see...oh." His voice fell away to a hushed whisper.

"What?"

"Vee-oh-lahnt..." he sounded out. "Old Germanic, see?"

I looked, and inside the lip of the bracers was stamped a word. It read *Wiolant*. "Ok," I said. "Wiolant. So?"

"You don't get it? No, I suppose you don't. Let me Anglicize the name for you; these bracers were crafted by Wayland the Smith."

I stared at him blankly.

"You have no idea who Wayland the Smith was?"

I shook my head. He sighed. "Well, anyway. These belong in a Grove museum, not on anyone's wrists. But we have a more immediate issue to address."

His face fell back into his officious mask and his voice resumed its icy crispness. "Using one of these archaic rune forms is absolutely prohibited under current Grove law. Why Ms. Moore allowed you to continue possessing artifacts of such danger is beyond me. These forms were made for a time when a clan's summoner would do battle alongside the clan. They are blatant displays of power, invoking which is limited to emergency use. I will confiscate these temporarily, for holding as property of the Grove."

"Look, Mr. Neilsen. You're a weird little dude. But those are mine; you can't just take them." I seized them back, pulling them away from his reluctant hands. A flash of anger burned on his face, then he took a breath and controlled himself, settling back into his cold, calm state.

"Mr. Lorents, I assure you I can. You are compelled to surrender them to me as a potentially dangerous artifact under Grove Regulation—"

"Oh, shove your regulations. Those bracers are one of the only things I have left from my uncle. You can't have them. End of story."

A silence fell. Mr. Neilsen lowered his face and stared at the floor for a good minute, not saying a word. Then his head snapped back up.

"Mr. Lorents, I wish you to know that this final insubordination of yours is merely the last in a string of incidents that has led me to my evaluation results," he announced. What the hell did that mean?

"I believe that Ms. Moore has irreversibly damaged your training. I do not think you are viable for continued apprenticeship or Grove membership," he said.

"Well, I wasn't really asking to train under you anyway, so that's fine. I'll stick with Grace for now."

"My decision binds the Grove," said Mr. Neilsen. "Goodbye, Mr. Lorents. I do apologize." He spun on his heel and began marching away, leaving me sitting on my roller-thingy.

So that was that, then. I wasn't going to be a part of the Grove system any more. No more obligations. That was fine. I had stuck my neck out enough for the Grove anyway. I did need their help with Cythymau, but I couldn't imagine the Groves not also wanting to take out the vengeful spirit, so I didn't worry too much about...

Wait. Something was wrong here. The Grove system was, by Grace's description, full of paranoids. It was, after all, an organized crime operation. Why would they simply cut me loose to follow my own path? Alone, I was far more of a danger than under their control. That was the explanation Grace had given me. Heck, even Matt, who had very little talent at all, had been kept in the Grove simply because his knowledge would be a liability.

When Mr. Neilsen paused almost exactly *sixty* feet away from me, I figured it out. I slammed my Sense into place just in time to feel and deflect the needle-sized piece of kinetic force hurtling at my skull like a bullet.

"Mr. Neilsen." I tried to adopt his cool tone of voice. "I must register an objection with your decision," I said, mocking him. As I strode toward him, he backed up; he knew the range of my Sense, and he wasn't about to step inside it. I couldn't feel any of his power inside my Sense; ten feet was about the maximum for him.

He produced a silenced automatic pistol from under his suit jacket, pointing it at me. I quirked an eyebrow at him as he pulled the trigger. I felt the bullet coming at me through the Sense, and immediately moved it to—nowhere.

The fucking bullet was warded. Fortunately, Mr. Neilsen's caution had put him back too far to make an accurate shot with a silencer on. His bullet grazed my left shoulder. White-hot pain followed its path over my skin.

He fired again, but instead of grabbing for the bullet, I began summoning chunks of scrap metal from around me to deflect them. Fool me twice, shame on me.

I summoned one of the massive machines to the ceiling and let it fall, using it to generate kinetic force. I applied the force to my pieces of scrap metal, sending them hurtling at supersonic speed back at Neilsen.

My scrap metal *wasn't* warded. He managed to use his Sense to direct most of them around him. One of them caught him in the ankle; he fell to the floor, clutching at his shin.

Success! I leapt forward, knowing I could get him in range now. As I approached, he took a small disc from inside his coat and threw it like a miniature Frisbee. Fascinated, I watched as he then summoned...himself. He disappeared from where he was standing and reappeared beside his Frisbee, which he grabbed. He had exceeded my range by a hundred feet or so with that stunt, and he was pulling out a tag to do something more complicated. I sprinted to make up the difference.

Teleportation. The thought of that frightened me. Do you know how many parts there are in a human body? A lot. No, really. Do you know what happens when you don't summon all of them together correctly? Nothing good, I assure you. Teleportation required a degree of complexity that I was pretty sure scared even Grace.

This was not going to be an easy fight.

As I ran, I re-formed the light around me, creating mirror images of myself. He slapped his tag into the ground, and a thorn hedge began to grow. It snaked toward me, ripping its way out of the ground at tremendous speed. I summoned chunks of it away, but it simply regrew itself, forming an ever-shrinking wall of thorns around me, slowly closing in.

This was going to take something outside of fifty feet to deal with. The thorns had surrounded me in the middle of the factory floor; he had drawn me away from the heavy pieces of equipment when he teleported. Damn, this guy was *good*. He knew exactly where my weakness lay, and knew how to exploit it.

Time to do the unexpected. I summoned a thorn branch to my hand and scratched the fire rune onto the floor: no set, just the rune. I was going to take a bit of a gamble here. Wiping some of the blood from my shoulder, I coated the rune, then slammed it hard with my Sense, drawing fire to it from anywhere.

I had been told, repeatedly, that slamming the Weave was the sort of thing for which the Grove kills a person. Clearly, the Grove had already decided to kill me. I felt pretty free of that restriction. Oh, I wasn't sure where the fire was coming from; I hoped I hadn't flared out any jet engines or anything. Still, I needed fire, and right now.

And I got it. The fire hit the thorns, which went up almost immediately. I used my Sense to draw water away from the thorns and around myself, trying to keep myself cool in the center of the inferno while the thorns went up. I shielded myself from the heat and the smoke as best I could, then began forming a path through the dying thorn bush to where I knew Thaddeus Neilsen was lying with a crippled ankle.

The advantage the fire gave me, other than handily getting rid of the thorns, was that I could Sense Neilsen through the smoke before he could see me. As I approached, I could feel his Sense, and as soon as I did I felt the panic in it. Eight feet. Immediately I summoned his little Frisbee to my hand. He tried to use his Sense to ward, but in a straight power contest between his Sense and mine, I held the upper hand.

After the Frisbee, I summoned every last rune tag on him directly into the fire. Then, to be certain, I did the same with his clothes. I blasted away the last of his accursed thorn bush that stood between us, then stopped nine feet away from him.

"Thaddeus," I said, crouching down to meet him eye to eye, "do you still feel as though I am not viable as an apprentice?"

"You—" he gasped, clearly in pain. "You are an abomination. Even if you kill me, the Grove will ensure that your existence does not continue to imperil our world. There is no hope for you."

"No hope, eh? That could be said of both of us right now, couldn't it?" I let my voice get a little cruel here. Neilsen's face blanched.

"Relax, Thaddeus. I'm not a monster, and I don't actually want to kill you. I work in self-defense. Very well, as you've no doubt seen. But I'm not a murderer—"

A blast of raw force hit me in the chest at point-blank range. I had let my Sense slip while talking; I hadn't even realized I'd done it. I thought I'd been standing outside his Sense range. Besides, where in eight feet had he pulled that force from? These are the things I thought as I struggled to breathe and to find my feet. He had knocked me backward several feet, and before I could bring my Sense into focus, he hit me again, rolling me back and away from him.

"You are undisciplined, Mr. Lorents. That is and has always been your flaw. It is what makes you a poor candidate for apprenticeship. I do so wish things were otherwise, but..."

I finally managed to get my Sense up before the third blast hit me. I stole that blast and wrapped it around myself, sending it back against its progenitor. It caught him high, slamming his head into the wall. He slumped to the floor, unconscious. I could still feel a steady heartbeat through my Sense; I hadn't killed him. Well, good. I didn't really want to kill anyone.

A quick scan of his person found what I was looking for. A complicated rune structure was tattooed onto his inner wrist in almost-microscopic form. Grace had one of those, too, only Grace's summoned a plate of duck curry. Thaddeus here was much more dangerous.

So, I was hunted by the Grove now. I was homeless. And I was already facing criminal charges. It seemed, to put it another way, that I was running out of things to lose.

GRACE

THE BOOK of runes lay open and ignored on my lap as I sat in Uncle Herman's cabin. Instead, my mind looped through the events of the past few weeks. Matt and Amy's words still rang in my ears. Grove law and hierarchy existed for a very good reason. Ever since Robert had started as an apprentice, beating obedience to the Grove rules into Robert had been a major goal of mine. The potential for world-altering catastrophe from one out-of-control summoner reached astronomical proportions on multiple levels.

But I also valued thinking for one's self. How did one decide if they'd really crossed over the border from slight maverick to rampant menace? I didn't feel out of control. *Obviously, no one else agrees with you*, the voice in the back of my mind pointed out wryly.

Had my defense of Detective Allen and Carlenos pushed me over some invisible line into rogue status? My knee-jerk reaction declared it preposterous. But while under an explicit and contrary order from our new director, I couldn't pretend—even to myself—that walking out and trying to fix the situation with Robert appealed to me as the more reasonable solution. Whatever was happening between Robert and Thad, Robert would need an advocate. I *did* believe I knew the situation and my own apprentice way better than any out-of-town Grove bigwigs.

I'd gotten to my feet, ready to say screw it and leave, at least five times, but second-guessed myself each time. By showing up, the consequences could be worse for Robert. Amy sure thought so. There was a possibility my mere presence might be a death warrant for both of us. But equally compelling, there was a possibility I could let Robert get killed by *not* showing up.

My instincts screamed at me to go. The more logical part of my brain told me that would be an act of open defiance against the Grove, likely branding Robert an outlaw as well.

But again on the other hand, Cythymau was a totally different kind of threat from the usual Visitors we banished. His attack last fall had been deliberate and focused. His ultimate plans and goals, the things he needed summoners like Andrea and Robert to accomplish, remained as much a mystery as ever. Now he'd shown up at Robert's graduation for seemingly no other purpose than to provoke or expose my apprentice. No matter what anyone else said, that demon *did* have an unhealthy fascination with Robert.

That's what finally decided me. I snapped the book shut and threw it on the bed. It shouldn't be impossible to get there. While there were still Feds and extra cops in the vicinity, things had cooled down considerably in the last week since my little diversion. I'd just avoid Thad noticing me if at all possible.

Carlenos had said Robert was holing up in a factory. The chances that Robert had found the time to scout new abandoned factories while he finished up his senior year were pretty slim. Not when he already knew of one conveniently and centrally located in the Valley. He'd definitely complained to me enough about not having time to do anything "extra" between school and training these last few months. My smile had more in common with reflex and less with humor. At least I had a really good idea where to start looking.

MY CAR ROLLED down the familiar streets outside the Mall in Spokane Valley, headed toward the aluminum plant with me (hopefully) inconspicuous at the wheel. My bag of tricks lay in the foot-well of the front seat, though its contents were much more limited than the last time I'd visited this factory. I debated for the hundred and fiftieth time what in the world I would say if Thad saw me very obviously flouting his orders. I really had no clue.

A fist of power slammed into the Weave so hard the repercussions reverberated through my skull even with my limited Sense. It also tasted very, *very* familiar. I cursed low and long under my breath as my foot automatically pushed down on the gas pedal. The Weave still shook with aftershocks. What the *hell* was Robert *doing*? Had Cythymau mounted another offensive? Or...some other bit of nastiness?

Either way I needed to get there—preferably ten minutes ago.

A few blocks away, a plume of dark smoke laced with fire shot into the air from the abandoned aluminum plant. Well, that should capture everyone's attention on both sides of the Weave. Perfect.

Teeth clenched, I slewed around the gravel corner outside the plant campus and sped down the last stretch of road on the far side. With the police station so close, the probability that several squads weren't already on their way approached zero. Any rescue attempt wouldn't have a lot of time. I scanned the sky. No sirens or helicopter yet.

I pulled the car up, spinning it around to face the way I'd just come. Anything to get out of here a little faster afterward—especially since it appeared Robert had already started something with our brand spankin' new Grove Director. If I had to abandon my new car, so be it, but I'd rather take it with me if at all possible. There were no other cars in the parking lot on this side of the factory, which worried me. Robert's rust-bucket Volvo should have been somewhere nearby.

In reality, putting myself in the factory easily qualified as a stupid move in the first place. Don't mind me; only America's most feared, most wanted criminal here. And instead of saving my own ass and fleeing the scene of the latest summoning catastrophe, I rushed to check it out.

I couldn't leave if Robert might be in there. Missing car or not, that had been his power slamming into the Weave earlier. With the force he'd used to bend the Weave, anyone with a spark of Sense would be able to feel it clear to Canada. Whatever he and Thad were into had to be heavy.

I hadn't come geared for a real fight. My bag contained some tags and a couple of vials, but nothing like what would be needed for a full-out battle along the lines of what I'd just felt. Well, I had the nuke. But that would take out me, Robert, Thad, and most of Spokane Valley. Not exactly a weapon-of-choice.

Still, there had to be something I could do to help. *Improvisation it is, Gracie. You're good at this stuff, remember?*

Yeah, I was *so* good at improvising, I was winging my way right into Rogue Summoner status. If it was Cythymau in there, he'd treat my lack of preparation with his usual contempt, and this time he might be right. Thad wouldn't approve of any actions I chose at this point. He would probably pop a couple of blood vessels the moment he saw me. Rage or contempt—really, which was worse? Rage *and* contempt, maybe?

I ran through the jagged hole Rick had made last fall. Trying to hug the wall, I plunged into the darkness. Nothing immediately tried to kill me, so two points for Team Gracie. Nor did I see any current action. Light seemed to be filtering in not too far ahead. No time to waste. I walked briskly toward it with my hand poised over my rune board, expecting to get jumped any second. Whatever had provoked Robert into that hellacious outpouring of power had to be lethal. The kid had a tendency to be a little hasty, but not stupid.

Machinery lined the long-disused hallway of the factory, beyond the spot where I'd fought Rick last fall. I turned a corner, and the hallway opened up into a large warehouse-like room with high ceilings. I stepped through the door and immediately knew I was in the right place.

It looked like the room had been hit by the bastard stepchild of the

O.K. Corral and a cyclone strike. Bullet holes and other divots lined the walls. Some of the cast-iron heavy machinery had been turned over. A burned ring of what may once have been some kind of bush stuck up in the middle of the open floor, rather incongruously. Tendrils of smoke still rose from it toward the ceiling. Whatever had happened here, it had ended very recently.

Assuming it was finished.

I scanned the room and waited a few moments to see if something was going to literally pop out of the walls or the floor and attack me. Nothing. Ok, then, until further notice, I would assume I'd missed the action.

Again.

Damn me for listening to Amy. I grimaced painfully and rubbed my arms. I didn't see anything to tell me who'd won or what he'd been fighting. Except... very few Visitors used firearms. Had the Feds figured out Robert's connection to me?

No. If they had, they'd still be here. Guns weren't Cythymau's standard modus operandi either. He was a little too old-fashioned. Nothing in the debris seemed to point to any one thing I'd fought with Robert in the past.

My frown grew deeper. Speaking of which, I didn't see Robert either.

"Robert?" I called tentatively, trying to keep my voice low. "You here?"

No answer. Clearing my throat, I tried again, a little louder. This time, something that might have been a groan sounded from somewhere in the shadowy room.

"Robert? Where are you? The cops will be here soon. We have to move." This time I heard a distinct groan from somewhere off to my right.

A lump against one wall I'd assumed was part of the debris twitched slightly.

As I edged closer, the shape resolved itself into a head, sagging down over what looked to be a bare chest. I swore, rushing over, then paused as I realized it couldn't be Robert. This person didn't have enough height. Plus, he had gray hair. A flush of embarrassment flooded my face as I noticed he also didn't have a stitch on him. Not one.

"Erhm, hello?" I knelt down to get a better look. The man's right wrist was bloody, and I picked it up in concern. A quick look showed the skin wasn't broken. The blood had powered a tiny kinetic force summons tattoo. The salt-and-pepper hair began to look familiar. So did his jaw. And there were horn-rimmed glasses on the floor beside him, one of the lenses cracked. My jaw went slack. What the heck? Director Thad?

I whipped a vial and some tags out of my purse, summoning a blanket to wrap around him. I put my hand to the pulse in his neck and was relieved to find it beating steadily.

"Director?" I asked. Still no response. His unconsciousness concerned me, but I didn't have a lot of options. If we were going to vacate this place before the police arrived, we didn't have much time. He'd groaned once or twice already. Hopefully, that meant he was headed toward consciousness sooner rather than later. I reached out and ran my hands briskly down his limbs. Nothing *seemed* broken. I hesitated half a second before running my fingers over his scalp. He did have a giant bump on the back of his head.

Screw it. Waiting would only get both of us deeper in the shit. Summoning a flatbed cart, I awkwardly positioned his limp form onto it and moved him away from the wall. Hastily wheeling it down the hallway, the first faint wail of approaching sirens finally reached me. We had thirty seconds to a minute at most before my already super-bad day took a turn for the even worse.

I scanned the surroundings, pushing Thad down an alternate hallway to the south of the hole where I'd come in. I quickly rearranged the runes to summon away the wall between the two supports closest to my car.

Groaning with effort as my Sense headache set in, I pushed Thad out into the parking lot. Once we were clear, I took a deep breath, blooded the runes, and replaced the wall. Only a thin line, easily mistaken for a hairline crack, remained of my impromptu door. My final summons dropped several gallons of gasoline on the lit embers in the other room, coating the remains of the fight.

Thad remained unresponsive as we traversed the last few feet of parking lot. His unwieldy bulk made getting him into the back seat a challenge. After a few false starts, I settled him hastily across the bench seat. Moving to the driver's side, I slid in behind the wheel, already groping for the ignition with my key. Sirens and flashing lights approached in the distance, too close for comfort. I couldn't do any complicated summons while driving, and if the deputies or the Feds caught up to me before we could get clear of the scene, this was going to get ugly fast. But I might have an idea.

My purse strap allowed me to clip a blood vial within easy one-handed access. A permanent marker waited for me in the glove compartment. I grabbed Thad's wrist and flopped it onto the arm rest between the passenger and driver seats. Scribbling runes furiously, I used the marker to modify his tattoo slightly. Then I headed the car north, my foot a lead weight on the gas pedal. The closest police station for backup was to the south, so with any luck they would be a little slower to set up roadblocks in the opposite direction.

The car was almost clear of the aluminum plant's campus before I reached over and bloodied the new rune phrase on Thad's wrist. Part of the plant wall on the south end exploded upward. With any luck the police and first responders would go there first. I pulled the car back into the traffic on Trent, slowly driving away from the latest summoner-incriminating scene. The explosion at the factory should help to delay and obfuscate the police response for a bit.

I drove steadily from the factory toward I-90, being careful not to attract any more unnecessary attention. Thad lay in the back seat like a bag of only slightly sentient potatoes. He'd been out for a while; I started to worry that I should veer toward the hospital after all. Wouldn't that just make my day?

"Ms. Moore." The voice coming from the back of the car sounded strained and groggy.

Bizarrely, my nerves uncoiled at the sound of his voice, even though it lacked its usual crisp edge. I'd actually much rather deal with Thad's possible ire and arrogance rather than his death within twenty-four hours of setting foot inside the Spokane Grove.

"I'm not feeling well enough to ask you why you are not at the cabin as directed. Why don't you just tell me what's going on here," he said.

"I was going to ask you the same thing." I quirked an eyebrow at him in the mirror. "Why don't you tell me?"

"My head is extremely painful," he said instead.

"I'm sure it is. It looked like you'd cracked it really hard on the wall when I found you. I'd guess you're pretty concussed. I'd summon you some aspirin, but I'm driving."

"What really interests me," I added, watching him narrowly in the rear view mirror, "is finding out what Visitor could knock you unconscious, and also what it has done with my apprentice. I assume you fired the gunshots, even though I didn't find the firearm."

I braced myself, waiting for him to say Cythymau (or something sent by him) had defeated him and taken my apprentice, or something along those lines.

"No one did anything with your 'apprentice,' Ms. Moore. Nor was a Visitor involved. If you did not find Robert where you found me,"—his brows lowered as if he were taking in the implications of that—"then I suppose your 'apprentice' has done something with himself. Your 'apprentice' perpetrated this outrageous attack on my person."

"Robert would *never* just attack you," I said angrily. I stopped. "*Unless* you attacked him first."

I pulled the car into the first parking lot I saw and parked it in the back corner, my knuckles turning white where they gripped the wheel. Furiously I reviewed the mess I'd seen in the factory.

I hadn't seen any of Robert's possessions, but he had been there. His essence slamming into the Weave had drawn me there in the first place.

"Did you attack Robert?" I demanded.

"Your apprentice is an uncontrollable menace. I did what I believed appropriate for the good of the Grove."

"You *did*. You bastard! He's just a kid. A mere kid you've known for"—I looked at my watch—"less than six hours."

"A mere kid would not have been able to knock me senseless," he said a bit bitterly. "And a well-trained apprentice would never have thought to try."

"You're going to say he wasn't well trained because he protected himself? According to that, a good apprentice would have just stood there and let you end him. That's commendable."

His brows lowered. "Nothing you can say will change my mind, Ms. Moore. After talking to your apprentice, I am sure he is a danger to us all. You will only do yourself and him further harm if you persist in trying to protect him. Don't think I haven't noticed that the only way you can have 'found me,' as you put it, is by blatantly disregarding my authority in regard to yourself. You are well on the way to convincing me you're just as dangerous as your protégé."

"Well, my acquaintance with you is definitely teaching *me* to think twice about pulling your unconscious, naked ass out of the remains of a summoner's battle. Next time I'll keep the fact that it goes against orders in mind and just stay home and let you get picked up by the authorities." I was suddenly so mad that if I didn't mock him, I'd scream.

Taking a deep breath to calm my nerves, I sighed, rubbed my forehead, and realized this was getting me nowhere. Robert's whereabouts should be the main concern here. Getting him somewhere safe before the trigger-happy boss in my back seat could off him became my priority. I pulled the car out of the parking lot and started back toward the cabin.

"So you and Robert fought, and he took off?" I finally asked.

"I was unconscious," Thad said with heavy dignity. "If he was no longer there when you arrived, I would assume so." The silence between us stretched.

"Let me tell you something about the Spokane Grove and Robert," I said. "The four of us here are outgunned, out-manned, and overworked. You will not get the support from the other Groves here that you are used to. At least not right now. Maybe you have enough political pull to fix that. I didn't." I gave a frustrated sigh.

"Before that, it was just Robert and me against an extremely powerful demon with unknown motives. I'll be happy when we finally get more summoners, and I would welcome all the red tape if it meant we were a stronger Grove. We're not. Even with you here, there are more weaknesses in the Weave than we can tend. We just take care of the worst, and hope nothing busts through until we get enough people to fix everything properly. We would need at least ten or fifteen Grove members to be anything approaching a normal Grove.

"We've *had* to listen to our instincts and wing it in order to just *survive* for so long. We barely keep one step ahead of the next catastrophe, and call it a win. It's all Robert's known since he was introduced to summoning. He was instrumental in stopping the very real threat last fall. Of course we've had to improvise."

"I don't see what this has to do with your *ex*-apprentice's viability." Thad glowered at me. "And I will not accept the argument that improvisation justifies his complete disregard of Grove authority."

Hearing my words out loud had helped me know my own mind, at least where Robert was concerned. He was the hurt, lonely kid. I was the adult. Time to start acting like it.

I took a deep breath and tried again. "Robert is used to being alone. His parents died, he doesn't have relatives...to him, I am the Grove. You were a stranger, trying to *execute* him for something he doesn't completely understand. There's something else, too. Robert is one of the most innately powerful summoners I've ever known. If he had wanted to kill you back in that factory, he absolutely could have. But Robert's a decent kid. He didn't want to. He worked so hard last year to undo the accidental harm he'd done with his summoning. He is not savage, or uncontrolled, or even that immature. That's not to say he doesn't have prickles."

My mind made up, I started looking for a place to turn the car around. "He does. He also has a knee-jerk reaction that adults are usually out to screw with him from his years in the foster-care system.

Which you just reinforced." I found a convenient traffic signal and turned the car around, heading back the way we'd just come.

"Where are you going? We need to go straight back to headquarters," Thad snapped. "I'm not done talking with you."

"Well, I'm done talking to you," I said, my insides doing a little uneasy flop. Hearing myself say it made me realize it was really true. Robert expected everyone to abandon him. And to him, it looked like everyone had just lived up to his expectations. I couldn't let that stand. I really, really couldn't.

"No matter how broken you may think me to be, I have to go find my apprentice. He is a good, loyal kid, and I won't let the Grove throw him away like this. Not ever. Someday, you may even be glad. When that time comes, I'll try not to say 'I told you so.'"

Better late than never seemed to be the motto of my life lately, and I wasn't happy about it.

"How do you even think you'll find him? Neither of us has any idea where he is."

I bared my teeth at him in an unfriendly grin in the rearview mirror that turned to a grimace as he stared at me with wide, distrustful eyes.

"I'll improvise. You might want to summon yourself some clothes."

ROBERT

WELL, that could have gone better.

As far as I could tell, I had managed to piss off Grace, the Grove hierarchy, the cops, my foster parents, and a demon. I continued to drive away just about everyone in my life. So there was that.

I didn't know whether Grace was facing the same execution I had just avoided; Grove politics were always a little murky to me. I was, however, pretty sure that Neilsen wasn't going to be the last high muckity-muck to try to kill me. I didn't *think* I'd killed him back, but honestly, at this point, who knew?

As I drove Neilsen's car away from the factory towards my Volvo, I pondered my next move. Attempting to contact Grace might bring more heat down on her. Same problem arose if I went to Amy or Matt. Carlenos still had the Feds coming down on him, and I don't think he was too happy with me after last night.

Heck, *I* wasn't too happy with me after last night. The hangover came back with a vengeance once the adrenaline rush of my fight with Neilsen wore off. The morning light pounded its way through my eyes and into the back of my skull.

I drove the Volvo through the streets of Spokane Valley, back to Shawna's place. Jake was leaning against the hood of my car as I pulled up. I exited Neilsen's rig, and Jake tossed me a half-hearted wave. I wasn't the only one feeling like hell, it seemed.

"Where the fuck did you get that car?" Jake asked.

"Uh, not sure. Weird night last night."

The front door to the house opened. Shawna stepped out into the morning, wearing flannel pajamas. She waved at me, her mouth quirked into half a smile. I waved back. I wasn't sure at the moment what, exactly, my social obligations were to Shawna; should I go talk to her, or was the wave enough? As I pondered this, she solved my dilemma by slipping back into the house and closing the door behind her.

"So, things went well last night?" Jake asked slyly, eying the door.

"Huh? Oh, uh...Shawna. Right." Had that only been last night?

Jake tossed his elbow into my side. "Of course Shawna. I hear she's an absolute tiger in the sack. Dish, man. How was it?"

I was, under no circumstances, going to tell Jake that it was two seconds long and followed immediately by a stream of vomit. It was clear to me that he'd already asked Shawna, and if she hadn't told him, I wasn't going to. I understood that Shawna and I weren't going to form any kind of lasting relationship, but it looked like she was going to keep silent about the embarrassing details of our encounter. There was one plus for the day.

"Fine, fine," I lied.

"Fine? Just fine? You're telling me you hit the hay with one of the sluttiest girls in the Valley and it was only *fine?* Bullshit, fucker. Dish with the details."

This was not a conversation I wanted to be having at the moment.

"I don't know what you want, Jake. I was drunk, she was drunk, we had sex, it was fine. You really want me to hit you with imagery? Besides, I'm not going to kiss and tell. Shawna's a nice girl, and it's not cool to call her slutty. Bragging on things just makes that worse for her." I owed Shawna at least that much of a defense, even if I would have preferred to remain silent.

"Oh, fuck you. That's a self-applied descriptor. Shawna's *proud* of it. So come on, dish."

"If she's so proud, then I'm sure you've already got all the details from her." Jake's eyes slid away from mine on this one. Checkmate.

"Look, man, I hit it with some chick, I *always* make with the details to you."

"True. Regardless of how I try to make you *stop*."

Jake rolled his eyes. A short silence fell. "So, what'd the cops do to you?" he asked.

"Me? Took me to the tank for a night, held me, let me go."

"They give you the rental car?"

"Uh, no. Picked that up on my own." I briefly considered turning the rental back in for Neilsen, then decided that he could get hit with the late fees all on his own. Screw him.

"What about the rest of you?" I asked. "Cops haul everyone off?"

"Fuck, man. They left Shawna here 'cause it's her house. I saw the cars coming, managed to hide out back." He jerked his head. "Everyone else was either arrested or told to go away. Willy's going to be doing time; he still had most of his stash on him."

I failed to be concerned about Willy's fate. My own was enough to deal with at the moment.

"Jake, it's been a blast. I'm out," I said, trying to keep my voice level and failing.

"Whoa, man. What the fuck? Why are we getting all morose and shit? Cops busted a party, big deal. It's not the end of the word."

I couldn't even meet his eyes.

"Rob? It's not the end of the world, right? Robert?" Jake's voice began to shake slightly.

I let it hang there for a minute, then brought my eyes up in a gray stare.

"Shit, man. Tell me that doesn't mean what I think it does." His voice was rising to a fever pitch; I decided to let him off the hook.

"No, man. Not the end of the whole world. I just...I may be going away for a while."

"How long is a while?"

"Not sure. I've got some shit to do. Once I settle things from graduation, it'll be safe for me to head back to Donald and Francene's."

"Settle things? Those wolf-things looked pretty settled, man."

"But there's the guy who sent them," I said, meeting Jake's eyes. "Them, and the Cornuprocyon—raccoon demon thing—from the mall last year. This guy's after me, Jake, in a bad way. It's past time I went after him."

Jake raised an eyebrow and stared at me.

"You have got to be fucking kidding me. He's after *you*, so you're going to *him*? Does that sound just fucking moronic to anyone else here, or is it just me?"

"Just you," I said, a half-grin on my face. "Look, I've won every time he's hit me so far. But anytime it happens, people around me die. The people in the mall, the cops on the freeway, and now graduation. He comes after me, I win, but other people die. Time for me to go after him."

Jake shook his head slowly. "What does Grace say?"

"Grace is—not around anymore."

"So? You're not going to at least fucking ask her?"

"I wouldn't even know where to start."

"How are you going after this fucker, then? I mean, isn't she kind of your high grand muckity-muck?"

"He gave me his address." My left hand rubbed the tag in my pocket. "I'm just going to swing by."

"Hey, Robert. No shit. Be careful, ok, man?"

"Yeah."

"You need anything?"

"Oh, so many things. Nothing you can do, though." I sat down behind the wheel of the Volvo.

"Fine." Jake held out his hand in a closed fist. "You need me, you know where to find me."

I rapped my knuckles against his. "Yeah. Later."

"Later," he said, and I pulled the Volvo away.

When I looked back, he was still staring at me.

~

FRANCENE WAS NOT ENTIRELY conscious when I entered her hospital room. I had waited until I knew that Donald was at work, leaving her alone. I didn't really know what I was going to say to her, but I owed her a goodbye.

By the way her eyelids fluttered, they had her on some pretty potent painkillers. She struggled to open her eyes as I approached her bedside. My hand went out to grasp hers; she gave it a feeble squeeze. An oxygen mask covered her mouth, and all sorts of tubes ran from various places on her body.

I squeezed her hand back and sat by her bedside, wordless for a time. Eventually, I broke the silence.

"Hey, Francene." I tried to keep my voice soft and level. She squeezed my hand again in reply. "I'm sorry for what happened. Donald probably told you it was my fault, and he's right. But—" I broke off, my throat closing against my will. "Anyway, I just wanted to stop by one last time and tell you I really appreciate everything you did for me. Not just this," I said, gesturing to incorporate her current predicament, "but, well, everything. You were a good mom. I was just a rather nasty son. I'm sorry."

I bowed my head and closed my eyes, then made to rise. Her hand closed on mine with a strength I did not think she had. She whispered something into her mask, but it was too soft for me to hear.

I brought up my Sense. This was important.

"Say that again?"

I felt the vibrations in the air as she began to speak. Sound is nothing more than finely tuned kinetic force; with my Sense focused on her, I could hear the soft whispers plainly.

"You could...never...be a bad son."

I choked a little. There was no response I could make. I sat, staring at the mess I had made of my foster mother, and lowered my head to her bedside, releasing my grip on her hand. She brought her trembling arm up and stroked the hair on the back of my head. My

Sense felt each gash on her broken body, but it also felt her heart race as I reached my right arm out to delicately embrace her.

There are a lot of things there are no words for. I had no idea how to tell her what she had done for me. By stepping in front of the Lycaon, she hadn't saved my life, but she'd reminded me what it was to have a mother. I couldn't tell her how overwhelmed I was to be accepted into her life. All I could bring myself to do was sit there and submit to her gentle ministrations, my tears wetting her bedspread.

After...I don't know how long. I lost track. But after a while, I composed myself and looked her in the eye. "I'm going to go take care of this," I said. "There's a man. Well, no. There's a *thing* that's sending these attacks, and I'm going to stop it. I just wanted to come tell you goodbye before I did."

Her eyebrows raised a little. "Dangerous?" she whispered.

I smiled with a confidence that I did not deserve. "Yes, but that's nothing new. I'm pretty dangerous, myself."

She smiled at me. "I saw. With the...wolves."

"I thought you were unconscious. You saw that whole fight?"

She nodded, coughing.

"Whoa, slow down. Don't hurt yourself. If you saw that, then..."

She nodded again. Damn, I'd hoped Donald had kept that a secret. Apparently he hadn't needed to.

"So you know this is my fault, then."

She shook her head. "You...protected. Not your...fault," she coughed out.

"And knowing that, you're still ok with me?"

She nodded.

"Why?"

She gestured at me with a finger, bringing me in closer to her masked face. Then she raised her arm, shaking, and rapped her knuckles against my skull with what little force she could muster.

"Ow!" I exclaimed, more in surprise than pain.

"Don't...ask that. Ever. Because," she said, then coughed. She struggled for a moment, then lay back and took a deep breath. Her eyes locked onto mine, her brow furrowed with effort, and she spoke in the first clear tone of the day.

"*You are my son.*"

There was little I could say in response to that. It had been so long since I'd had a mother that I didn't know how.

I nodded and stood up, wiping the tear from my eye.

"I'm going to be fine. I'll be back, and I'll come see you in a bit."

She smiled. Her head lolled back on her pillow, her eyes closing. Her breathing became slow and steady as sleep overtook her. I stayed and watched until I knew she was out.

Then I left. On the way out, I upped my Sense and snagged a bag of blood from a refrigerator on the other side of a wall. I was going to need it.

THE GYMNASIUM WASN'T CORDONED OFF by police tape, but it was still locked by the school. A paper sign taped to the door of the gym read "Closed for Repairs." I extended my Sense and popped the lock free of the door.

Inside was a mess. The floor had been cracked in several places. The bleachers I'd shattered with the Lycaon remained in splinters. The chairs and stage from graduation had been put away; the room had returned from being the place of graduation to the place where basketball gets played.

I extended my Sense as Uncle Herman had taught me, and found what I was looking for at the back of the gym where the Lycaon had emerged. As at the factory, the Weave was weakened here. The whole structure of it had been strained, first by Cythymau's insertion of the Lycaon, and then by my frenzied grappling. I felt the Weave's frayed edges around me.

Good. That would make this easier.

I pulled Cythymau's "address" from my pocket and stared at it. The last time I'd been in his world, I'd almost been strapped to a board and used as a battery for his summons. Of course, the last time I was in his world, I didn't have nearly the polish using my Sense that I did now. The last time I was in his world, I'd come from the middle of a knock-down fight to the death with a raging Cornuprocyon. And the last time I was in his world, I'd almost saved Andrea.

Almost.

I still remembered unlacing the straps that bound her to Cythymau's rune-covered board. Her eyes had fluttered, and hope had just begun to dawn on her face when I was summoned back to this world by Grace. I hadn't saved her—I'd left her behind. Grace didn't care too much about that, but I did. I knew what it was like to be left behind, and it was slowly killing me that I'd done that to someone else.

No more.

I ripped open the heavy plastic bag of human blood I had stolen from the hospital. Normally, stealing essential medical supplies would have given me a guilty conscience, but not today. Not now. This blood was intended to save a life; a life it would save.

I knelt in front of the tear in the Weave, placed the tag exactly at its base, and coated it with the blood. It flared in my Sense, drawing me inward. My focus bent toward it; the rest of the world paled a little bit to my Sense. Normally, I can't focus entirely on a rune set. With the runes Cythymau had prepared, I could barely notice anything else.

Which explains why I almost missed the tiny thread of power punching through my Sense to grab at the tag.

I shielded the tag at the last moment, batting the power away. I recognized it, of course. Interacting directly, Sense-to-Sense, is far more intimate than simply looking at someone's face. When my power touched Grace's, I *felt* who she was, and she felt me.

I stood up. Grace stood framed in the doorway to the gym. Blood dripped from her magnetic rune board; her bandolier was half-loaded. She was dirty and her skirt was wrinkled. Her face and hands were scratched and rough, and her hair was even more disheveled than normal.

Another figure brushed by her, his hand on the top of her chest, pushing her back.

"Mr. Lorents, this ends here and now," Neilsen said in his crisp, officious voice.

I didn't miss a beat. Before, when Neilsen and I had fought, I'd been surprised, confused, and afraid. This time, I was just angry.

I summoned a section of bleachers into the air and let them fall. Grabbing the force from them, I wrapped it around myself and hurtled toward him. With my fist wrapped in the remaining force, I gut-punched Neilsen as hard as I could.

The air rushed out of him. He doubled up, holding his gut, his face flushing. I grabbed him by the back of his head and, using no magical force at all, simply slammed his face directly into the floorboards. He lay on the ground, his face bleeding and his arms still wrapped about his stomach. Using the Sense in that condition would require a Herculean effort; I felt pretty sure Thad was out of Herculean efforts for the day.

"So, how's your research assignment going?" I asked Grace in an overly conversational, almost sing-song tone.

Grace shook her head. "Robert, you're not helping anything here. I think I know what's on that tag. You go through with this, you're going to be in a world of trouble."

I couldn't help it; I laughed at her. "A world of trouble? A *world of trouble?* Tell me, oh my master, what exactly *the fuck* this world is, then."

Her eyebrows lifted, then a grimace settled onto her lips. I kept at it. I was angry, and Grace was once again the convenient target. I let the emotions of everything that had happened since graduation, since before graduation, rip through me.

They carried me on a tide of words that I rode into Grace with the force of a tsunami. I knew, somewhere in my rational mind, that I shouldn't take it out on her, but she was *there*. By her simple presence, she became the focus for everything in my life that was currently against the wall.

"Your precious *Grove* decided it was better to put me down like a rabid dog." I pointed at Neilsen, still writhing on the ground. "Your boy there attacked me, and when his magic wasn't good enough he just shot me. I've been busted by the cops, the summoners are trying to kill me, my mother is on her deathbed, and my foster father has thrown me out of the house. My ex-girlfriend and the boy we both risked our lives for last fall are dead. So if I'm headed for *a world of trouble* then I guess I'm going to feel right-the-fuck at home."

Grace sighed. Her shoulders slumped. She looked *tired.*

"Robert, we'll have to straighten things out between you and the Grove. I'm not sure how we do that yet, but punching a hole in the Weave isn't going to help your cause any. We've gone up against Cythymau before; you know as well as I do that it's going to take more than we have. You barely got out alive last time, and this time you won't have a Cornuprocyon handy to make a last-ditch cheap shot with."

"Last time I almost—*almost*—rescued Andrea. She's been strapped to that board for God knows how long, and she's still there. He's got her plugged in like a battery. I had the straps halfway off, I *could have saved her,* but you pulled me back before I did."

Grace hung her head for a moment. "I know," she said quietly, then raised her head to look me in the eyes. "And if I'd known what was going on over there, I would have waited. But I didn't. I just pulled you back as soon as I could. As it is, I'm glad I got you back. We'll find a way to rescue Andrea, but it's going to take more than just you. Just us."

"Well, I don't see the rest of your precious Grove members lining up for the posse. Matt couldn't fight his way out of a paper bag and Amy's so scared of a fight she throws me to the wolves every time. As for getting help from the outside, I think that's pretty much fucked at the moment, given that every other Grove member is *trying to kill me.* I'm alone. I'm always going to be alone. People don't stay with me. You get reassigned, Jake starts hanging out with his druggie friends, my fosties either kick me out or, hey, new twist—I get them killed. Well, I'm not like the rest of you assholes. I'm not going to leave. I can't. Andrea's still there, and I'm going to get her."

I paused to take a breath. The gravity of what I was about to say hit me even in my tide of rage. My voice dropped to barely above a whisper.

"And you can't stop me."

That one landed. Grace's face turned pale as her eyes met mine. I wasn't going to let her interfere, and master or not, she knew tussling with me would be difficult. I didn't want to fight her, but I might not have a choice. I let my anger flow into my Sense. The Weave around me strained with the pull of it, and the rune tag flared brightly. I saw Grace's fingers flying across her rune board and her eyes locked on mine.

Then I slammed my massive, anger-driven Sense straight at the tag behind me.

The Weave tore into a frayed, gaping hole in the Universe. No clean portal like Grace had made, this. Grace would have some work to do before she could come after me, and time being what it was in Cythymau's world, I didn't think she could pull it off fast enough to stop me.

Or rather, in time to make me hurt her.

I turned my back on Grace as she'd done to me all year. Then I stepped through the ragged tear in reality and began my quest to rescue the girl.

GRACE

IF I'D HAD a beverage in hand when Robert opened his so-called "portal," I would have done a spit-take. As it was, I stared with slack jaw and mental stutter at the jagged, gaping hole in reality he had opened. Reality on the far side of the gym split open like one of Gallagher's melons. My skin went cold just watching it. For a fraction of a second, Robert was visible on the other side, walking stoically away from the tear he'd made. Then the time difference swept him away.

My arguments hadn't been able to reach him, and now—well, now he was truly far beyond my reach.

I repeated it to myself in an attempt to try and accept what had just happened. My apprentice had walked away from me through a hole in reality that he'd created. This was no tidy, precise connection between two Weaves. Robert's method twisted, mashed, and mangled the Weave into doing what he wanted.

As I stood dumbfounded—for what seemed like an eternity but was probably more like two or three seconds—the rift began to grow. Hungry fingers of instability crept farther up the wall, spreading into the ceiling. The rift consumed the far side of the gym like an ugly blemish, warping the entire area behind where the graduation stage had been. Beyond, the interior of classrooms on the second floor became exposed like a diorama.

That side of the room didn't even look like a gymnasium anymore. The basketball hoop, bleachers, and school pennants had already been sucked out by the imbalance between the Weaves.

I had to fix it before it became permanent or, god forbid, even more unstable. It really made no difference whether I knew *how* I was ultimately going to do that, or not.

Keeping an eye on the giant crater Robert's power had made in the Weave, I stepped over to the tag he had used. My eyes just about fell out of my head. It was an archaic formation with the runes Kano, Jera, Othila, and Dagaz overlying and melding with each other instead of linking. It shouldn't have worked. When I'd been in school, I'd been told that formations such as the one I was looking at pre-dated humans using runes to summon, and while they could be an interesting window into the minds of summoning's ancestors, and certainly be seen as the roots of summoning today, they were not "usable or functional" in practical summons work. Their overlapping forms made them much too imprecise to actually use as guides for the Sense. Which seemed like a no-brainer. Or so I'd thought.

With each rune overlying each other like that, the tag *should* have been a jumble of meaningless lines. I shouldn't have been able to make out the individual runes at all. And yet, with my Sense I could not only see each rune, I could feel Robert's residual power clinging to them, combining them to punch through to their corresponding Weave. I couldn't explain how the tag worked, and I sure as hell didn't know any Visitant Pacts linked to a Weave that used runes like that, but at least it gave me somewhere to start disentangling the effects the crude summons inflicted on *our* Weave.

I blinked, yelling at myself to think and *do something*. Thad would be no help, since he was still unconscious on the floor.

Purple moss crept out of the rift and started to cover the floor in front of the tear. Instinctually I reached into my shoulder bag, pulling out my tags before I even decided which one I needed, or what I was going to do. Thank the gods for reflexes and muscle memory. I slapped the tags on the floor in front of me and shifted my feet into battle stance.

So... I'd never actually confronted a tear on this scale. No one in their right mind would ever intentionally inflict this much damage on one point in the Weave. Unfortunately, Robert had pretty much table-flipped. And he was walking straight into an obvious trap that would probably end him faster than the Grove Council could, or possibly do something worse.

He'd effectively kept me from going after him immediately. My first concern had to be stabilizing this tear. If I didn't, and it continued to spread, there was every possibility that the two Weaves could intermesh to a point where separating them would be impossible, giving Cythymau and any number of other undesirables a permanent hole to exploit. That was, of course, assuming Cythymau didn't just stroll through the tear before then. With every second over here equating to several hours on the other side, I just couldn't be sure how long I had. Taking a steadying breath, I arranged the runes on my board and splashed a vial of blood across them, sending my Sense into the damaged Weave.

What I found made me swear, loud and long, my fingers dancing over my rune board as they realigned and re-blooded new rune phrases. Robert hadn't just brought together this Weave and Cythymau's. Like a wadded map, he had brought the two points he wanted together, but he had smooshed several other Weaves together in the middle as well. Counting our Weave, this "portal" was open to four Weaves and all of their denizens. Not to mention that all of them were currently out of balance and trying to reach equilibrium by either pushing something into our reality or sucking something into theirs.

A cold sweat broke out across my forehead as I worked feverishly over my runes, trying to simultaneously separate and mend the worst of the damage. I had a Visitor expressway in front of me, wide open to multiple parts unknown.

It's for times like this that I really should learn more languages.

There just weren't enough swear words in the English language alone to honor the epic level of shit Robert had just opened up.

On the stupid-teenage-recklessness scale, this one was definitely up there. I scowled at Thad's limp form still sprawled beside me. Not that this guy had helped matters any.

Even as I began balancing and tying off the connection to the first unknown Weave, a swarm of small, winged Visitors swooped through the tear in a cloud of dark, sleek, bodies. *Of course* they weren't coming from the Weave I almost had under control. Sweat began to pour down my forehead, stinging my eyes as I struggled to maintain my focus.

"Why can't anything ever be *easy?*"

I finished my summons, disentangling the first Weave from the rest and sealing it away from ours. That was one Weave less to worry about, but since it was not the one that was currently flooding the room with Visitors, the relief was minimal. I brought my right hand up to wipe my forehead, smearing blood on my face but clearing some of the sweat.

I took a deep breath, my fingers rearranging the runes so I could pinpoint exactly which of the Weaves my new friends were coming from. *Not Cythymau's. Thank the stars.* I released a shaky breath and started closing the tear in their home Weave. Letting them leave the gym into the world wouldn't work; I glanced around the room. At least the doors were all closed and the thick walls didn't have any windows. I still needed more hands. Turns out it's impossible to mend the Weave and try to contain all these Visitors at the same time. Or any of their friends that might still come through the rift.

I stretched a foot out to the side and nudged Thad's prone form with my shoe, still trying to disentangle the big snarl of broken Weaves. "Hey, I could really use some help here." Thad groaned in response, his eyes clenched shut. Not a lot of help there.

The swarm of Visitors had made it to the far end of the room. Not finding an outlet, they were now swinging back in a wide arc toward us, screeching out of mouths full of jagged, carnivorous teeth. Damn. So much for my hope that these suckers were benign. I abandoned the mending summoning and started thinking defensively as my fingers danced over my rune board.

I also kicked Thad again. "I need help *now!* Wake up your lazy ass, you smarmy politician, and save your own skin! I can't"—I flung another quick kick into his upper shoulder—"do—"

Surely the third kick would be the charm? "Everything myself!" I gave up and dropped into a crouch, my fingers working frantically over my rune board. The headache that had never really gone away redoubled as I started to power the summons, reminding me that I had been demanding a lot of my Sense already today.

Just as the summons went off, something punched my ankle, throwing me off balance and totally destroying my focus. I managed to catch myself on one knee, so I didn't face-plant. Swearing, I looked to see if the summons had gone off.

Please let it have gone off.

"What the fuck do you think you are doing? If you kick me one more time, I swear I'll—" Thad glared at me viciously, his hand still fisted, completely unaware of the swarm of winged doom bearing down on us. He was answered by a deluge of sticky, tar-sands crude pouring down over the swarm of demons. They and the crude hit the floor at the same time in a flood of reverberating sound and sludge. The mucky oil coated them, sticking them to the floor and gumming up their wings. They flopped and screeched and didn't move one inch closer to us. It was a scene that would give an environmentalist nightmares for years. But effective. The crud stuck them to the floor better than quicksand.

"*That's* what I'm doing," I answered. "Glad you could join me. Now do something useful for once. Since you seem confident in throwing down with Robert, I'm really hoping you still have a trick or two left in there somewhere. We're going to need them."

I reset my runes and started disentangling Weaves again. The rift was starting to stabilize, at least. It no longer sent new fingers of growth out in all directions. One point for me. As I started closing away the first alternate weave, the purple moss stopped creeping forward from the portal, and started to be overgrown with tall yellow grasses. The breeze that swayed them definitely didn't originate from here. Damn.

The exact moment our situation actually fell into place for Thad became obvious as his face slackened with shock and then turned a pasty shade of green. Although, to be fair, part of his queasiness may have been from the punching and kicking he'd been through today. Not *all* of it.

Thad sat up where I'd left him, staring with a stunned, somewhat glassy expression at the large rift. It had stopped expanding and sucking in objects from the gym, which I took to mean my makeshift summons had worked, at least for the moment. No new cracks formed in the gymnasium walls and the floor had stopped vibrating and pitching under our feet. I blooded my bracelets and checked again. The three unknown Weaves were still sealed off, leaving this Weave and Cythymau's in a tentative and fragile balance.

An area of swaying yellow grasses still spilled from the tear onto the gym floor. On the other side of the rift they continued in an endless plain under a blue, cloudless sky.

I pulled a notepad from my pocket and scribbled a note to Amy, asking her to come pick Thad up and make sure he got to a doctor. Right now worrying about our recent fight was a luxury I couldn't afford. Amy had been truly angry with me earlier in the day. Still, she was my only friend left in town. Thad might be the "director" now, but with a rift like this, I wanted to know that someone I trusted was on-scene.

After a moment I scribbled, *Gone after Robert. Don't follow us. If we don't return within half an hour, seal the rift. We're probably long gone or captured by then anyway.*

Taking a deep breath, I piffed the note off to Amy. I'd stabilized the Weave as much as possible, alerted Amy and Matt, and now I had no excuses left to stop me from stepping through that portal after Robert.

Oh, there were insurmountable odds, sure.

I might not come back.

I might not even find Robert.

Simple things like that have never stopped a Moore, even before

Uncle John set foot in Portugal or died at the Battle of Corunna back in 1809. Since it had already come to this, it'd be a shame to be the one to break with the family tradition.

Lips curling upward, I quipped to myself, "Well, I've always said I wanted to travel. Today seems as good as any other to start, I guess." I've found its always better to walk into a doomed situation with a sense of bravado and a joke on my lips. Hearing my own voice made me feel a little better about it, at least. *Once more into the breach, Gracie.*

I walked toward the tear and through the swaying grasses. As I stepped through, Thad came out of his stupor. "What—what—where are you going? Come back at once!"

Much too late. My feet already stood on the earth on the other side, though it wasn't really "earth" at all. Thad, Amy, and Matt would just have to make do on their own. The only way to deal with this new development that wasn't one hundred percent catastrophic would be to find my wayward apprentice before Cythymau. I just hoped I still had time.

Time to break my habit of arriving late to Robert's parties.

ROBERT

At least this time I was expecting it.

I knew, this time, the change in the world would be both instant and a little disorienting.

Last time I took this trip, I'd been running for my life as Rick the Cornuprocyon chased me down a strip of I-90. I hadn't actually noticed the portal until I was already through it. This time, I knew to watch my feet, and I stepped through slowly. That let me keep my balance as I began my intrusion onto Cythymau's territory.

With a start, I noticed that several of the bleachers from the gymnasium had come through the portal with me. They sat at angles on the hilltop amid the yellow grass. As I stared at them, I heard a loud crash from behind me. I spun, and saw the shattered remains of a glass backboard. I winced; the school wasn't going to be happy with this kind of damage.

At least they couldn't stop me from graduating.

I also saw that the portal was gone. I'd expected that. The time difference between the worlds doesn't actually stop; it just makes the portal skip frames in Cythymau's world. Last time, Rick had been hot on my heels when I entered, but I'd had time for a nice nap and a little supper before he caught me.

The portal would open back up in several hours, but until then I had a head start. Even if Grace followed me through, she wouldn't be able to stop me before I got to Cythymau's cave. I had just enough time to go rescue Andrea and get back. By the time Grace could do anything about it, this would be over and done with, one way or another.

I smiled, and set off for Cythyma—

Wait.

I looked around. The strangely yellow grass was here, but I hadn't seen that rock face last time. Well, years in this world had potentially gone by since I was here; maybe there was an erosion issue. I set off for Cythymau's cave.

As I hiked, the scenery began to look more and more unfamiliar. After a while, I realized I'd covered twice the distance, give or take, between the portal and Cythymau's cave.

I wasn't hiking towards Cythymau's cave at all. This new portal was in a different spot in the world than the last one. I was, in fact, lost in an alien world. I'd hit the right planet, but had no idea if I had managed to land on the right continent, let alone within walking distance of the cave.

Okay, maybe I'd missed a step in my planning.

IT MADE SENSE, in retrospect, that the portal hadn't shown up in the same spot. After all, it was Cythymau who gave me that rune set. He may have set it to show up where it did.

If that was the case, then why hadn't I already been attacked?

Maybe the location of the portal in this world depended on the location of the portal at home? In that case, Cythymau had sent the Lycaon to the school from the hilltop I'd appeared on. Actually, I'd been using that existing weakness in both Weaves to punch through, so that seemed very likely. Good chance, then, that I was somewhere in the right vicinity to find Cythymau. I wouldn't have to cross an entire hemisphere to get to my goal.

That thought comforted me, so I clung to it as I walked.

Cythymau's world was not so different from ours. Trees occasionally rose from the ground, and though I didn't recognize their species, I did recognize that they were trees. A breeze flowed over me, the air cool and damp but not cold. The dirt felt, largely, like dirt.

Most of the plants, however, were yellow. Not dying; they were still alive and supple, but yellow. It was as though that was the most convenient color to absorb light from their sun, though I didn't discern much of a difference in the color of the sun.

It was daylight when I started out. The last time I'd been here, I'd come at night. The sight of the stars in completely alien configurations had taken my breath away, and driven home that I was not, in fact, in Kansas anymore.

Today, the sun was out. It floated in the air, disappointingly boring, a single yellow orb that could have been the sun on Earth. It wasn't, of course, but it could have been. I admit here that I was a little sad that it wasn't a different color, or maybe a binary star system, or something really cool. Nope, Cythymau's world had a simple, yellow orb.

Alas.

Once I descended the hill, I entered what appeared to be an old-growth forest of some sort. I say old-growth simply because of the girth of the trees, but really I have no idea how old they were. They were big, though. These are the kinds of trees that, on Earth, you'd expect to see a hippy living in.

Their bark felt hard. Solid. I ran my hand over it, and it was smoother than my standard impression of tree bark. Rapping my knuckles against it produced a hard, almost metallic sound, which rather satisfied my desire to see something weird and alien. The trees were spaced well apart and the ground underneath was brown, with a covering of leaves that had turned a dark red before falling. The occasional bush grew in places where the sunlight cracked through the trees, but the limited undergrowth was easy to contend with.

The problem with being alone and lost in an alien forest without supplies, other than the obvious ones, is that you have to confront yourself. Now that I was cooling off, I realized that I hadn't treated Grace fairly. She'd been trying to help me, and I'd blown her off. Now I was stuck in an alien world, and I didn't have my master supporting me. Worst of all, it was my fault.

Damn it.

I'd been so pissed that she'd left me alone that when she tried to get near me, I'd gone off alone. *Brilliant, Lorents.* I added it to the list of interpersonal relationships I'd tossed into a blender lately. I hadn't done too well by my friends, foster parents, teachers, fellow summoners, or random people. In fact, as I looked back at my actions, I had been something of a selfish prick.

I didn't like admitting that, but I couldn't help it. I moped. There's really not a better word for my emotional state. I'm not proud of it, but I really began to feel sorry for myself. After all, it was beginning to feel like anyone who gave a damn about me got hurt, and anyone I tried to keep near me ran away. Or died. Or both. My pace slowed, my head bowed, and I began kicking small stones when I saw them.

The sun rose higher in the sky, then began to drop down. I had no timekeeping device, and so could not honestly say how quickly a day on this world passed. I was getting hungry, though. Back at the factory, I'd prepared for an expedition into a foreign world, but once Neilsen had come at me I'd simply left. There were some berries on the bushes, but I decided that I'd have to be a lot hungrier before I chanced those. Uncle Herman had taught me to tell poisonous berries from safe ones, but if he knew the species I saw here, he hadn't taught them to me.

I'd signed on for a quick rescue mission: come in, save the girl, deal a crippling blow to the power of the demon who'd been harassing us, then get out. Now I was hungry, tired, dejected, and lost.

And I was no closer to rescuing Andrea than I'd been back on Earth.

~

THE VILLAGE CAME AS A SURPRISE.

When I first saw it through the trees, I thought it my salvation. Stone cottages, nestled next to each other in a cozy, English-countryside look, peeked through the trees at me. I imagined a warm fire and, with any luck, a meal. My stomach growled in anticipation. I began to step faster, images of comfort in my head.

Once I got closer, the balloon of hope dragging my spirits upward deflated. The cottages were stone-walled, but their roofs were simply gone. This wasn't an active village; this was the long-dead stone ruins of a village. Two rows of cottages and the crumbling remains of a larger building still stood, but the furniture within had long since rotted away.

The homes were neatly built one-room affairs. I imagined them having a thatched roof at one point. The gray stone forming the walls looked rough-hewn, but the floor had been smoothed and leveled before the weather had pocked it. A hearth was built into one wall of each cottage, with the crumbling remnants of a chimney rising from it.

The gray of twilight began to veil everything, and my skin began to bump up in the cold. I was wearing the jeans and t-shirt of June, but it felt like November. As my body began to shiver uncontrollably, I began to think less about rescuing someone else and more about living through the coming night.

I'd been raised in close contact with a crazy mountain-man. Uncle Herman had been a stickler for teaching outdoor skills. At the time, I'd thought it was all kind of a game. After all, why learn to start a fire by rubbing sticks if you could just light a match?

Now that I sat out here, freezing, I chuckled over *that* particular argument. Thanks, Uncle Herman. The number of times he has saved my life with what he taught me is pretty staggering.

Granted, it had been a long time since the two of us had gone camping. Still, I knew I needed shelter. I found a cottage with a decent-looking hearth and began to gather spare wood from the nearby forest. The wood weighed more than I was used to; the dark grain ran so tight that I had to squint to make it out. Even so, it wasn't hard to use the Sense to summon portions of wood apart from each other.

Ignition was a problem. In my Sense, I could summon things smoothly. Fire, though, I would need to use runes for. As soon as I did that, my peculiar brand of summoning would mark my location to Cythymau almost as clearly as if I'd given him GPS coordinates. And that was just Cythymau; this was the world with beasts like the Cornuprocyon, who lived on a summoner's energy. Even if I didn't pull Cythymau down on me, I might call one of Rick's cousins to dinner. Or worse, more than one. A whole...pack? Herd? What was the word for a group of raccoons? Gaze? Regardless, it would suck.

Best not to chance it. If I tried to use my Sense alone to start the fire, I would end up pulling heat from around me. I'd never tried that, and I wasn't sure on the math, but I didn't want to end up freezing myself while trying to start the fire.

No, this was going to have to happen the old-fashioned way. A medium-sized stick would serve as a hand drill. I unlaced one of my sneakers and wrapped the lace around my thumbs, then around the flat end of the stick. My Sense effectively hollowed out a small crevice in the wood, then filled it with sawdust. The point of the stick fit into the hole, and the shoelace forced it on down. I leaned into it, pressuring stick against wood, and began rubbing the stick in my hands, twisting it against the wood like a drill.

In the movies, this process takes about thirty seconds. A tendril of smoke rises, the hero blows on it, and fire suddenly blossoms in his hands. He kindles it, shouts out his victory, then does a celebratory dance. Triumphant music plays.

Usually I'm a little susceptible to the myth that the movies give us, but not this time. Herman had made me do this any time we went camping, and I knew it was painful. It failed to shock me when the stick jumped from the hole and I slammed my knuckles down against the wood before I could pull back. That almost always happened.

No, the rubbing-wood process takes a little longer than it does in the movies, and there are false starts to contend with. No sooner had I gotten a tendril of smoke than I blew it out, and returned to my rubbing, cussing at the wood in front of me. My hands were starting to go numb as the cold continued to set in, grabbing at my exposed extremities with its icy touch. I remembered that Jack London story about building a fire, and started to get a little worried. If I took any longer on this, I was going to end up frozen to death like that dude.

The next time I saw smoke, I didn't stop with the friction immediately. I kept rubbing, and the smoke grew thicker. Excited, I pressed down hard and rubbed frantically. When a thicker cloud of smoke rose up from my sawdust I leaned down and blew.

A flicker from deep inside rewarded my efforts. The fire began to blossom. Quickly I laid the wood down and stacked kindling over the top of it, then bigger pieces over that. The warmth from the flames gave me a basic, primal sort of joy. I had made fire. I didn't dance, but some of that triumphant music did play a bit of itself in the back of my head.

I had fire, and I had shelter. Two out of three isn't bad, right?

I LAY AGAINST THE WALL, considering how badly I had screwed myself. On reflection, blowing off everyone, then jumping half-cocked into a foreign world where an immensely powerful spirit waited to enslave me felt like a plan with a couple of holes in it.

It should have hurt. I was prepared to, once again, feel sorry for myself. I was shivering and starving on the floor of a roofless primitive hut, and I had done nothing to rescue the girl I had come for. I knew I had failed, and I knew that tomorrow I would hike back to the portal and wait for it to open. I would re-enter my own world, head hung, apologize to Grace, let her deal with Thad, and then try to get to the nearest buffet. My mission would be chalked up as yet another Robert Lorents failure. I braced myself to feel the overwhelming sense of depression that usually accompanied such things.

I didn't.

Instead, it just seemed goofy. This had been *stupid*. I had shredded the Weave back home all so I could jump into this one and starve myself. Brilliant, Lorents. Three points. I had screwed the pooch *so hard* on this one, and I alone was to blame. The only thing to do was to laugh, because there was no one around to be mad at.

Andrea was still here. I needed to do something about that. I needed Grace's help. Tomorrow, I would need to retrace my steps back to the portal and wait for it to open so I could get home. I would talk this over with Grace, get her to come with me. She could use the runes to detect Cythymau's location.

It might not hurt to bring along a backpack with a sleeping bag and some food while I was at it.

Sleeping without a bag next to a fire is an interesting experience. Not fun, but interesting. One side of the body is invariably too hot. The other one risks frostbite. I slept in fifteen-minute segments, turning myself as though I were on a rotisserie.

During one such turn, a sound took me by surprise. Somewhere beyond the village a rush of air went *woomph*.

A chill ran up my spine. I *knew* that sound. It haunted some of my worst nightmares. It was the sound of a Cornuprocyon projecting its telekinetic force downward in a kind of jump. Somewhere out there was a beast that looked like a giant, red-orange cross between a raccoon and a hedgehog, with the ability to generate the telekinetic force of a freight train into a focused blast. It also had a massive, chitinous club of a tail; my ribs ached in remembered pain.

And it ate summoners.

The thud of a thirty-foot-long raccoon demon landing in the middle of the street broke the night's silence. I moved quietly away from my fire, hoping to hide from the beast. My night vision had been wrecked by staring at the flame; I tripped on the uneven floor of the ruined cottage. I fell with a loud thump, and an involuntary "Oomph" escaped from my lips before I could stop it.

I tried to even out my breathing, but my heart rate was accelerating. Full fight-or-flight was starting to kick in, right when I wanted to hold still.

A brief memory of my paralyzed reaction the first time I'd heard that *woomph* flashed through me. I cocked a half-smile. Why couldn't I be like *that* again?

A rustle moved up the street. I pictured the quills of the giant, raccoon-looking demon clacking softly against each other as it moved. Its actual footsteps were light, but I could hear them if I held my breath. Its breathing was short and fast, like a beast trying to get a scent.

Oh good: scent. And I was afraid this would be *easy.*

I extended my Sense. As I did so, the snuffling sound stopped—not good. I began piling broken pieces of stonework next to me for use as weapons, not that they would do much good. These things were a league farther above the Lycaon I had taken care of at graduation.

I reconciled myself to the fact that, if it detected me, I was dead. I resolved that I would put up a fight, but I knew what a Cornuprocyon was capable of. Going mano-a-mano with one was suicide.

The *woomph* filled the night again. A flare of sparks erupted from the fire I had left behind as the wind from the Cornuprocyon's jump hit the coals. He was airborne again, and I didn't know where. I hoped it was away from me, from this place.

That hope died when, with a thunderous crash, the Cornuprocyon came down in front of me, crushing the walls of the cottage underneath it, its muzzle less than a foot from my face.

GRACE

STEPPING through the portal gave me a shock akin to plunging into the Puget Sound in February. My skin pebbled with goose bumps and my eyes watered.

I left the polished wooden flooring of the gym behind and came out on slightly damp, uneven ground. My balance went out from under me and I stumbled before getting my feet back under control. Robert was nowhere to be seen, but given the time dilation between the two Weaves, that didn't shock me. A whole string of cuss words passed my lips on my next exhalation anyway.

It was just that kind of day.

Smoothing my hair back from my face into my customary low ponytail, I took a better look at my surroundings. The tear had opened on top of a gentle sloping hill with waving yellow grass. The sun hung heavy in the middle of the sky. I turned slowly in a circle, trying to spot anything out of the ordinary to tell me which way Robert had gone. Broken bleachers, limp banners, and shattered glass littered the hill, giving a surreal vibe to the scenery. The glass crunched under my feet as I threaded my way between the mangled bleachers.

I had to find Robert first, and that meant finding him *fast*. And if Cythymau already had him... I'd deal with that reality when I saw it.

This time, summoning wasn't an option to find Robert. The chances that he'd failed to alert Cythymau to his presence with this ham-handed portal were pretty astronomically low. Which meant Robert and the demon would actually be hunting each other. But that didn't mean I had to tip off the opposition about more than one person using his invitation.

If I started summoning now, I'd lose my chance at surprising Cythymau. Much like Robert attracting Rick last summer, it would leave a trace in the Weave that would signal my presence. Not to mention, that trace could then be used to pinpoint *my* location. I didn't relish going one-on-one with him on his home turf with no preparation if I could help it. I'd keep the small advantage surprise gave me as long as I could, thank you very much.

The tear I'd stepped through vanished completely as if it had never been there. It would open when the timelines between the two Weaves lined up again. Based on Robert's experience here last time, that would likely be several hours. Unfortunately this tear would beckon like a beacon to Cythymau, and Robert was already out there somewhere. Sticking around to find out the exact interval during which moving between the two Weaves became possible wouldn't be an option.

There were no paths or obvious signs to tell me which way Robert had gone, so I figured I'd just head down and see what I found. I tried to remember everything he'd told me about Cythymau's cave and this world. There was another hill in the distance that might be large enough to hide a cave, in what I guessed was a westerly direction. Or at least it would have been west on Earth, judging by the sun. Who knew if an alien world like this one even had a magnetic north? I took a deep breath and started walking.

Travelling by foot with no real idea of when you'll find what you're looking for is problematic, since you have much better odds of running into something you *don't want* while simultaneously providing yourself with way too much time for introspection.

I'd really and truly burned my bridges with Thad and the Cooperative Council by stepping through the tear. The reaction when we tried to step back through into our world defied my attempts at speculation. Nothing good would happen, though.

But really, that worry should be way down on a list of problems that had to be overcome before going home would even be an issue. For example, even assuming I managed to find Robert, we still had to evade Cythymau long enough to make it back to the mess I'd just left behind in our own Weave.

Since I'd followed Robert through without any supplies or plans, it was pretty optimistic to assume I could survive long enough to find him, let alone make it back home. But I also couldn't leave Robert here by himself. Even if he didn't die, he'd only become another prisoner, making Cythymau even more powerful. We'd been playing right into his hands this whole time.

I made it to the next hill with no incident, but I couldn't find anything like a cave opening. Really, from up close, it was more of a butte than a normal hill. The rock loomed above the grasses, rough and white.

Still, it was going to be the best vantage point for miles around.

Shielding my eyes from the lowering sun, I gazed up toward the top of the cliff face. The sandy dirt slid easily under my shoes where it wasn't held down by the clumps of grass as I tried to climb up. After the third false start, which left my right knee scraped and bloody, I looked for an alternate way up. Following the base of the butte around, I eventually found a jagged route that worked its way upward. I squinted up at it critically. It was only about two hand-spans wide, and would require some tricky handholds farther up, but I just might be able to use it to get to the top.

I worked up my courage and tied my skirt around my hips in a giant knot before putting my foot gingerly on the first foothold. The rock under my feet was covered in a film of silt that slid under my weight and made my balance even more precarious. I slid my left foot out to the side and dragged my weight after it, desperately keeping my center of gravity above the balls of my feet by leaning forward and grappling any rock protuberances with desperate hands.

I crabbed my ways sideways and up in a very long, very arduous climb to the top of the cliff, gouging my fingers into the rough face and clinging to it with all my might.

What seemed like two centuries later, with my legs and arms burning, my lungs heaving, I flopped myself down on the summit. The prickly yellow grass tickled my back as I lay sprawled and panting, the blue sky spinning. I would have given my left arm for a bottle of water and a towel.

Finally catching my breath, I struggled to my feet and gazed down on the land around the butte. The grassy rolling hills continued for some distance, but I could also see clusters of trees, and what might be mountains off in the distance. Turning away from the edge of the cliff, I gazed behind me.

"Son of a bitch." After the summit of the cliff, the side of the hill I hadn't been able to see from my approach sloped gently downward. In contrast to the hellish ascent I'd just made, if I'd continued around the base, I would have eventually been able to leisurely stroll up the back slope. Wasn't that just peachy.

Along the top of the hill were spindly trees, and off to the right, three oblong rocks stuck up about six feet from the grassy earth.

Something about them seemed out of place, so I walked closer to get a better look. The rocks were white, like the cliff face. I ran my hands over their surface, and realized what was troubling me. They were worn but much too smooth, and very hard compared to the cliff's rough, jagged stone. The corners of these stones were also artificially even. Not rounded, like you'd expect of something that had been worn by wind, rain, or sand, but sharply curved, like the stone had been molded somehow.

Using my hands as scoops, I cleared dirt away. About four inches down the stones were fused together into an angular base. My brow wrinkling with surprise, I cleared more soil away.

The base was roughly rectangular in shape, and went down quite a bit farther into the hillside. I gave up at about eighteen inches, but it showed no sign of ending soon. I did find some markings that may or may not have not been etchings, or they could just have been wear from other rocks. It had been buried in the ground, after all. Without the ability to summon away the years of erosion and silt or clean out the grooves, I couldn't really tell. There was too much caked soil to effectively get it off with just my hands.

On a hunch, I ran my hand through the dirt around the strange formation, trying to find anything that felt similar. Nothing. I kept looking, feeling around in the soil and grass on my hands and knees. About three feet to the south of the strange formation, I hit pay dirt. Or pay *rock*, really. Excited, I began digging to expose my new find, ignoring the cuts and scrapes that rapidly began to accumulate on my hands. My method of excavation was not ideal, but I reminded myself it was better than alerting Cythymau.

Repeatedly.

Hard labor is not usually my shtick, but if today was anything to go by, I'd better get used to it.

The stones I uncovered were uneven and broken, but it looked like there had been a paved path that led right to the strange rock columns sticking out above the cliff face. Every few feet the gleam of white rock poked up through the waving grass. Which meant that maybe the three rocks had significance to something that used the paths.

If it had been a simple trade route, the stones could be some kind of way marker. But if so, shouldn't there be holes, or something that stuck out to differentiate which one this was? Also, short of leading down onto the grass plain, there really wasn't any other sign of habitation that I could see from the top of the hill.

So really, I still had no idea why the columns or broken road were here. I opted to believe it was for religious reasons, the old anthropologist fallback position and in-joke. Either way, following the ruins of this road through the grass to see where it led seemed like my best option. If I got lucky, maybe I'd find shelter before dark.

The sun that had been low in the sky when I arrived was rapidly approaching the horizon. I could really use a light, or a coat, but I didn't trust summoning anything here. Not without a damn good reason. I had no idea if this world's Weave worked differently, or how far the noise of my summoning would travel. Directly to Cythymau wasn't that far-fetched. Or, considering his hobby of collecting summoners, and that this Weave was his home, he could have left surprises and traps for unwary summoners.

This was also Rick's home world. I knew for a fact the Cornuprocyon could Sense power shifts in the Weave. When I'd talked to my Uncle John last summer, he'd indicated that the Weave Rick came from would be full of beasts with similar eating habits. Since Rick's favorite food was summoner, I really didn't want to run into any of his relatives. Cythymau was a big enough predator on his own.

I felt stripped almost bare without my summoning, stumbling along the remains of some ancient thoroughfare just like some vanilla human. I hadn't really thought about how often I use my Sense and runes to bring things to me until I suddenly couldn't. Truly, using summoning, I'd have a number of ways to locate Robert and shortcut this really long and draining hike. I tried not to worry about the nearly one-hundred-percent likelihood that Cythymau was using those same methods to find Robert as I limped along this stupid road.

My current strategy bet on the fact that Cythymau seemed to be playing a really long game. If I were him, I'd wait until Robert was hungry, weak, and in no shape to fight back when I swooped in to seize him.

I hoped I was right.

I had to be right.

Otherwise, Robert and I had been screwed since the moment we stepped foot into this world, and I didn't know what I was doing here. Not that I had good grasp on how I expected to save the two of us and Andrea anyway. But I was a Moore, and I was already here. Last-ditch efforts and ingenuity are my family's specialty. I mean, look how Uncle John shook up the British military's Light Infantry.

Since we were stuck in a strange Weave, we might as well save Robert's fantasy girl while we escaped. Who knew when there'd be another chance?

The wind picked up, bringing with it the chill of approaching night. I hugged my arms around my middle and picked up my pace. Squinting at the skyline, I estimated I had maybe an hour, no more than two, before the sun went down for good. Better find somewhere to brave the night before then.

The grasses gave way to a sparse stand of trees. More of the rock pavers showed where the trees' limbs sheltered the old road from the elements. I followed them through the trees as the path started to slope downward. It terminated suddenly under another steep hillside crowned by another tall oblong column of stone.

Just past the first column, the ground sloped downward before changing to a circular depression bordered by fifteen-foot-tall standing stones. I immediately thought of pictures I had seen of Stonehenge and simulations I'd seen of the original stone circles at Avebury in England. This henge had no lintel stones, but its similarities were eerie. I stepped gingerly down the slope, over a small ring of mounded earth that encompassed the clearing, and then hopped a slight ditch before ending up inside the stone circle.

The surface of the columns appeared rough and pitted as well as covered with a purple lichen in some places. Faintly, I could see traces of what may once have been etchings covering the stones, but the weather had worn them down. I couldn't see what they originally were meant to be.

The columns themselves exuded a sense of ancient times. I put my palm flat against the surface of the nearest one, savoring the feel of something so old. Then I frowned as my fingers twitched. It felt like... runes? I squinted at the old stone but I still couldn't be sure. Besides, what would runes be doing here?

Thanks to my rune board, my fingers were trained to find rune shapes without having to look; I sometimes joked I could read better with my fingers than my eyes, but I'd never really believed it.

I set both hands against the old stone and closed my eyes, extending my Sense. Overlaid runes like the ones on Cythymau's calling card from the gym flared under my fingers, some of them brilliantly, others dark, indistinct and broken. Even without my Sense extended, my fingers told me they definitely rested across a Wunjo rune. With my Sense, it became entwined with a Thurisaz and Uruz like a runic knot.

Depending on context, that combination of runes might usually mean "strong protection for the people," but so far I hadn't seen any sign of life here. I hadn't even run into any of Rick's kind yet. Robert hadn't mentioned running into life besides Cythymau and Andrea when he was here before.

If there were people here once, where the hell were they now?

I must have been off in my estimation of how this sun moved, because the light began to fade as I stood there feeling for runes. However, I didn't necessarily need it. I was trusting to my Sense and tactile sensation to make out the inscription. The stone was too worn to decipher the runes by sight alone. In places it was so faded that even my clever fingers, aided by my Sense, couldn't make out what the rune was supposed to be. Or perhaps there were runes so archaic they weren't recorded in our Weave. Or there could even be specific runes only used in this Weave. Either way, in places the runes suddenly melted away or devolved into unrecognizable forms. Even so, I was still starting to see a narrative. I wasn't sure this was a summoning. It read more like...a history.

I moved from stone to stone, feeling out the archaic compound runes and chaining them together, sometimes going back to retrace the runes I'd already read based on the runes I thought I'd found on the next one. With runes, context is absolutely everything.

Digging through my cavernous shoulder bag, I drew out a few blank tags and a pencil. I wrote down all the runes I had managed to make out, leaving gaps for the ones I hadn't, and attempted to trace the ones I didn't know with the tag and a slanted pencil. It worked much like when you take a rubbing from a leaf or a weathered gravestone. The images came out grainy and poor, but the vague outline of the unknown runes was there, and still just as cryptic. I finished the last of my notes, and realized, to my surprise, that the sun was well under the horizon, probably had been for hours, and it had grown bitingly cold.

I fished a pair of driving gloves, a rolled-up cashmere traveling shawl, and a keychain pen-light out of my bag. Given that I still hadn't managed to find anywhere sheltered to spend the night, I figured I'd better at least try to keep moving. The traveling shawl was much bigger than it needed to be on my small frame, almost big enough to mimic a throw blanket, but I didn't want to take chances.

The wind was blowing, and carried a hint of smoke. I decided to head out against it in hopes that I would come across some sort of inhabited structure. And if that inhabitant turned out to be Cythymau—well, I'd always been a fan of the cheap shot.

Worried that I'd freeze if I stopped, I walked for most of the night. I wouldn't have thought that thin tendril of smoke could carry so far, but this was an alien planet after all. I wondered what that said about the composition of the air here. Obviously I hadn't died the minute I step through the portable, so it contained oxygen. But what other gases might be making up the atmosphere, I had no clue.

The smell of smoke drew me down into what, at first, appeared to be a little village. My footsteps quickened as I wondered what type of life forms lived here. The glimmer that would eventually be the sun sparked on the far horizon.

I peeked my head in the first door I came to, and quickly realized that along with no door, the stone-sided structure had no roof. The smoke was definitely coming from somewhere nearby, though. I followed the row of houses into a small deserted square.

Part of the stonework of a corner building looked like it had fallen pretty recently. I pointed my pen-light at it. A flash of color against the pavement caught my eye, and I stepped closer for a better look. Stooping, I picked up an all-too-familiar orange and red quill from the stone and dried mud debris. As much as I didn't want to even think about it, a Cornuprocyon had been here, and probably not all that long ago. I stood up straight, scanning the square for any signs of immediate danger. All seemed quiet.

Cythymau or no, if I was going to face off with a Cornuprocyon on its home turf, I needed all the advantages I could think of. I pulled my rune board out of my bag and made sure it was firmly strapped to my right arm. This would probably get ugly fast.

∿

I WALKED the entire length of the village without running into the Cornuprocyon. The scattered remains of the fire that had drawn me here lay smoking in the hearth of a hut on the far side of the village. The inhabitant was not there. Call me crazy, but since Cythymau reportedly had cozy chambers in his cave, I doubted he would be squatting in a ruin.

A thick swath of early morning dew coated everything. A large area that had been wiped mostly dry seemed to indicate that something large had exited the village to the northwest.

I couldn't help it. I went to check it out.

As I rounded the last hut, headed toward the clearing behind the village, the *woomph* of a Cornuprocyon's leap sounded close by.

Instinctively I crouched, my hand hovering over my rune tiles. I expected one of Rick's cousins to come down right on top of me. Nothing happened.

The clearing behind the buildings consisted of an overgrown jumble of weeds and rock. At one point it appeared to have housed something more perishable than the stone huts. Bits of jagged, fragmented wood still stuck up from the ground like broken teeth. At the edges of the field were five man-sized boulders in a widely spaced pentagon. A giant raccoon demon didn't seem to be hiding behind any of them.

I slowly started to straighten up, part of me wondering if my long night of walking and stress had translated into hearing phantom noises. A yell dropped me back into a crouch, and I thumbed open a vial, just in case.

Robert rounded a boulder, whooping at the top of his lungs, looking back over his shoulder. He suddenly spun and repelled a burst of kinetic energy, sending it back in the direction he'd just come from. A second *woomph* sounded. A Cornuprocyon suddenly appeared high above the boulder, generating kinetic force in its mouth. It flung the energy at Robert's fleeing back.

Not just any Cornuprocyon, either. From the size of that demon, it looked like our nemesis from last fall, *the* Rick himself, had found Robert after all.

I ran forward on an intercept course before my brain even had time to finish processing what I was seeing.

Robert needed help. I could give him that.

I skidded to a halt between the two of them—directly in the path of the ball of force, and wondered what I was doing there or what I expected to summon. This wasn't Earth. The wide range of force-absorbing rubbers or plastics I had access to at home just didn't exist here. Or if they did, I had no idea where to find them on short notice.

In desperation I found the runes for water and crafted an aqueous barrier in front of me. The ball of kinetic energy blasted into it with the smashing force of a wrecking ball. Water sprayed everywhere, deluging me, sticking my clothing to my skin in a chilly cocoon, but it diffused the impact.

My fingers ran over my runes, feeling out their shapes as I raced to come up with the next move. Maybe if I could draw his attention to one of the other Sense-fed beasts that lived on this world we might have a chance. I sent my Sense out through the runes, looking for another Cornuprocyon, or a Lycaon, or anything that wasn't us.

Robert ran back in from my right, shouting something. My ears buzzed, full of water. His frantic expression and rapid pointing at Rick indicated he was trying to communicate something urgent to me. My water-logged ears couldn't make out what he was saying. I braced my feet, ready to summon a Lycaon and make a run for it. The Cornuprocyon leaped over me straight at Robert. Landed next to him smoothly, and…cocked its head back at me?

Robert's face broke out in a grin. The two of them loped over to me. My hand hovered frozen above my rune board. Robert gripped my shoulder urgently, pointing in the Cornuprocyon's direction, still smiling. I shook my head, draining the water out of my ears. I coughed, clearing my throat, barely able to tear my eyes away from the Cornuprocyon long enough to meet Robert's gaze.

"Say that again? What's going on here? What were you doing?"

If anything, Robert's grin got even bigger.

"He followed me home. Can I keep him?"

ROBERT

Look, how was I supposed to know Grace was going to get in the middle of our game of force-ball catch?

I struggled not to laugh as we stood there. The expression on her face was priceless. The corners of her mouth set into a grimace, and her eyes locked onto mine in a narrow glare. It was hard to take her seriously, though, because she had absolutely drenched herself. Her blouse, her skirt, and her hair all dripped into the pool of water at her feet, and her sodden state did not help her to appear threatening.

The tattered remains of her dignity and my willpower were simultaneously shattered when Rick gave the left side of her face a swiping lick. Grace leaped backward, startled. I doubled over laughing.

It had been a while since I'd had a true, gut-busting laugh. The cynical self-abuse from last night just wasn't the same. It's amazing how the human mind needs that once in a while. Ever since graduation, I'd been so self-absorbed that I'd forgotten to see the funny. Watching Rick, the Raccoon Demon from Hell, lick Grace's face with all the enthusiasm of your average Labrador—that was the funny broadsiding me in the head. I clutched at my stomach and laughed until it hurt.

"I'm glad you're enjoying this."

"Sorry, sorry—I"—*snerkt*—"couldn't"—*gasp*—"help it. You should see yourself."

"Yes, I'm sure it's all very entertaining. You have a fire around here, right?"

"Yeah, got it built against a wall back there. Rick here provided breakfast in the form of some sort of herbivore. It's no Thai duck curry, but it's food."

"Few things in existence are Thai duck curry. I'll take it."

I gestured toward the cottage I'd made my shelter, then stepped behind Grace to scratch Rick behind the ears. I think it's a universal truth—animals love to be stroked behind the ears. Dogs, cats, rabbits, and now, apparently, Cornuprocyons. Some things remain constant regardless of scale. Rick leaned toward me with his bulky head, trying to rub back in a gesture of what I presumed was affection. I leaped back instead, dodging out of the way of Rick's spines. I was going to have to dull those down if he wanted to do *that* all the time.

Rick took my sudden movement as an invitation to play some more and immediately went into a crouch with his forelegs, then began hopping back and forth, waiting for me to do something. I shook my head.

"No, boy. Not now. I'm going to talk to Grace for a bit. You stay here and be good, ok?"

Rick drooped his head.

"He understands you?" Grace asked behind me.

"Not sure," I said. "He seems to get the general gist of things. There's some sort of connection between us. I think when I broke Cythymau's bond, I got a little of it on me. I can't control him like Cythymau could, but he basically listens to me and does roughly what I tell him. He's more like a well-trained dog than anything else."

"Why didn't he just eat you?"

I blushed a bit. "Um—he did. A little. He was really quite hungry when he found me. I fed him—a bit."

"You fed him?"

"A bit."

"How?"

"Through the bond. I think that's how Cythymau was controlling him."

"And *what* did you feed him?"

"Well...um..." I hedged here. It had seemed so natural when I'd done it, but now that Grace was staring at me. "Me?"

She quirked an eyebrow.

"Not *all* of me, obviously. But some. I'm down to about a forty-foot Sense radius."

"Robert, you amaze me. The very moment I think you've done the most reckless thing imaginable, that you seem to have found the most profoundly impulsive act, you manage to surmount it. You fed yourself to a Cornuprocyon. Words, beyond these, fail me."

"It's growing back! And it's not like it hurt or anything. I'll be back to full power, in time. Or in time to feed him again, I suppose."

"*Again?*"

"Well...yeah. I mean, I haven't seen the pet owner's guide on these things, but I'm pretty sure you have to feed them more than once."

"I think you may be having some sort of dire neurological event. This is *Rick* you're talking about. Remember Rick? Responsible for the death of untold civilians in the Spokane Valley Mall, half of the law enforcement officers of Spokane County, and the *entire* Spokane Grove? By the way, that last includes not only your Uncle Herman but also Matt's *whole family.* This is an insane killing machine. It is not, under any circumstances, a *pet.*"

"Well, he *was* an insane killing machine. Now he's just a big, mostly sane animal who loves me."

"Robert, you can't—"

"*He loves me,* Grace. Unconditionally. If I have to live over here instead of back home to get that, so be it." My voice hardened. I'd been having fun up until now, but this was important. Rick's affection was genuine. It had surprised me at first, but I could feel it through the bond. Rick knew who I was, knew I had freed him, and loved me for it. I could ask for nothing else from him.

"If you want a puppy—"

"Too late. Got better now." I smiled at her. I have to admit, part of the fun here was how much this irritated Grace.

She sighed.

"Look at it this way. Best. Guard dog. Ever."

Grace snorted. "Any guard dog that levels your house while defending it has failed in his basic objective."

"Hmm. Okay, point conceded. He's still awesome."

Grace's eyes rolled in the universal gesture of the parental figure who has given up. I'd won this round, and I knew it. Not that it was ever in doubt.

BREAKFAST CONSISTED of hacked-off chunks of half-chewed, unseasoned carcass of—well, of something, roasted over a fire. Rick had sensed my hunger, and had dutifully run down some form of game for me last night. He hadn't been too delicate bringing it back; identification was a moot point by the time I got my hands on it.

Still, it was food, and while a bit on the gamey side, it tasted delicious after a day of not eating anything at all. Grace tore into it herself, though after the first couple of bites her face scrunched up in disapproval.

"Hey, if you want to put anything else on the menu, get it yourself," I said.

Grace shook her head. "I know, I know. I'd kill for just a bit of salt, though."

I had no response for this, so I merely shrugged. We finished our meal in silence and took the roasted hunk of meat off the spit to wait for lunch.

"All right," Grace said. "Have you slept yet?" She began draining the remaining corpse of blood, refilling a number of empty vials on her bandolier.

"Yeah. Rick gave me a bit of a scare last night—"

"I'll bet."

"—but once I realized he was friendly, he made a pretty good watchman. He fetched dinner, then looked out for me while I caught some zees. Not too comfortable with only the fire for warmth, but I got something."

"Better than me, then. I'm going to rest here for a while, and then we're heading back to the portal and getting out of here."

This startled me. I had forgotten that Grace was probably not here to rescue Andrea. I had gotten so wrapped up in last night's plan to convince her to help that I'd totally forgotten I hadn't actually done it yet.

We had been laughing and talking with each other as normal. Up until this point, it felt as though things had never gone wrong between us. It had been a lovely illusion, but Grace had shattered it. I lifted my eyes to stare her down.

"No."

"No? You still want to attack Cythymau, the two…" She glanced at Rick. "Well, the three of us? Alone? How's that going to work?"

"Last time Rick and I got him to a draw, and it was just the two of us. I'm better, now, and we've got you as well. I put the odds in our favor, actually."

"Really? A draw? That's not how you described it when we talked about it afterward."

"Well, maybe not a draw. But we both lived. So there's that."

"You lived because I summoned you out. Cythymau's got his own power plus Andrea's, and it was enough to enslave Rick. That's some juice, and it's not all summoning. There's magic in there that I don't know, and that means it scares me."

"*It scares me too!*" This came out louder than I had intended. "I know how dangerous he is. You're right; I probably don't have too much of a chance. Last time he let me into his cave out of faux kindness, trying to trick me into getting onto that slab and letting him strap me down. I know he wants to enslave me like he's done Andrea, and that's terrifying."

I took a breath.

"But I left her behind. Do you *know* what it's like to be the one left behind? I do. I've never been anything else, except this once. Everyone leaves me behind. My parents did it. My fosties have all done it. Francene tried not to, and now she's in a hospital. You left me behind when you went to Vegas and when you fought the cops. Your boy Thaddeus just wants to kill me. At least he's honest."

I was beginning to choke up a bit. I stood up and began pacing by the fire. Grace simply watched, letting me work through it on my own.

"And I know you didn't do it to hurt me. I know Francene was trying to help me, not abandon me. I know my parents didn't die just to leave me alone. It's not their fault, but that's not the point. The point is that *they left me alone.* At the end of the day, that's what there's been for me. People leaving me. And I have to tell you, it hurts like hell when they do."

I shook my head. Grace's eyes were on me, her head cocked to the side. She wasn't smiling, but nor was she angry. Her hands were clasped in her lap as she sat next to the fire, and she simply listened.

"Point is, I can't do that to someone else. Andrea saw me. She *saw* me. For one brief, fleeting moment in God-knows-how-long, someone was there for her. And then I left her behind. It may not have been my choice, or my fault, but I left her behind. I know how much it hurts when others do that to me; I won't do it to someone else."

"Why now? You've had all winter to do this, so why now?"

"Haven't been able to cross the worlds on my own until now. That, and I really did need to train through the winter. I've got a fighting chance now. Sure, Cythymau's powerful, but if I can get him inside forty feet, I think I can match his raw strength. Add to that the fact that I've got Rick here as backup, and if I can get the drop on him, I can do this."

Grace waited patiently. Not too patiently; I noticed her biting the side of her lip. I knew she saw the flaws in my plan, and I knew she wanted to see if I saw them too. I'd been training with her long enough to realize when she was giving me enough rope to hang myself. I did see the flaws; I just didn't want to admit them. Still, it was best to get it over with.

"Of course, I don't know where Cythymau is, or what kind of

defenses are on the outside of his cave, or—well, really anything. It's been years in this world since I've been here. Decades, probably. I don't know where I am, and I don't know where he is. By this point, he knows I'm in the world; he probably felt that portal opening. I'm betting the only thing that saved me from an immediate ambush was the location of the portal—in from the gym and not the aluminum plant. On the whole, getting the drop on him is going to be tough."

"Not to mention," Grace said, "that he can control the beasts in this world. We've seen him send more than one through a portal at a time. There's every chance he has his own backup. Plus, I think 'a little tough' is a gross understatement. You've been playing *games* with Rick here that involve large amounts of summoning energy. Now, Cythymau's not here strapping you to a board as we speak, and so I think we can assume that your use of the Sense fades into the background animal summons that happen in this place. But did you even *think* of that possibility before you started playing with your new pet here?"

I hadn't. I hung my head. Grace was right; that had been a risk, and one I'd known damn well before I got caught up in Rick's ebullience. The emotions along that bond must run two ways.

Back on track. "But now you're here. That's another factor he can't see coming. You and me, working together like back in the day—"

"By 'back in the day' I presume you mean a couple of months ago."

"Whatever. You and me can tag-team him, get him on the ropes, and get Andrea out of there. We get her, we cut his connection, and he gets weaker. Then we've got him."

"Do you have any idea how much weaker he gets? How much his power relies on Andrea being on that slab?"

"Um...no..."

"So by 'got him,' what you mean is 'we will have weakened his power by some theoretical amount?'"

"So it's a working theory."

"No. That theory is not, in fact, 'working.' It's a wild guess, not a theory."

"Doesn't matter. I'm getting Andrea back, or I'm going to die trying."

"Well, that's the problem." Grace paused, her eyes fixed on me. "There's actually a third option. Cythymau gets you on a slab, and his power increases. Then he comes after the world the two of us are supposed to be protecting, bigger and badder than before."

I didn't want to admit it, but Grace was right; *that* was the worst case scenario. It was also the one point I was ready for.

"Not if I don't let him. If it looks like I'm in a losing fight, I'll take myself out first. I can't promise you I'll win. I *can* promise you that I'm getting Andrea back, or I'm going to die trying."

Our eyes locked. Grace wasn't happy with this pronouncement, but I wasn't going to back down. After a long, hard staring match, she let out a heavy sigh.

"You are one crazy kid. You know that, right?"

I took that as her way of relenting, and smiled at her. Then I raised one of my shoulders in a half-shrug and spread my hands open and palm up in a what-can-you-do? gesture.

"Okay, look. If we're going to do this—"

"We?"

"Yes, we. After your little speech about leaving people behind, you think I could just take off and let you do this alone? I still think it's stupid, but you've convinced me. So if we're going to do this, we're going to need some intel. Where is the cave, how far, what's outside of it, where are things we can use, et cetera." Grace pulled her rune board out of her bag but didn't strap it on. Instead, she held it in her lap and rearranged some of her tiles on it. A dab of blood from one of her vials, and she closed her eyes.

"The Weave here constantly thrums with low-level activity. The amount of Sense-like magic going on is kind of astounding; it feels like a natural part of animal life here. That's definitely what saved you and your games from notice." Grace shot me a meaningful look to drive the point home.

"The only source of major disruptions in this world's Weave are something exactly in the direction of the portal you ripped open, and...another one over that way. The first is, of course, going to be that nasty portal. Messy work on that, by the way."

"That was the goal."

Grace cocked an eyebrow at me, then shook her head. "If the first one is the portal, then we need to look at the second. I don't know how far, but that's the direction. I'm going to catch my own zees. You head in that direction, slowly. Don't draw attention to yourself. Take a gander, see what we're up against, and we'll talk about what to do when you get back."

I nodded. Grace laid her head back against the wall and promptly closed her eyes. Within seconds, she was lightly snoring.

I shook my head quietly, amazed at her ability to nod off like that. Then I started in the direction she had pointed out. After several paces, I realized I was not alone.

I turned to face Rick. "Look, boy, you can't come with me."

Rick's head ducked down. His big, red eyes looked at me in what, for him, must have been a begging puppy stare. The effect was a little disturbing.

"I'm trying to be sneaky on this one. You're, well..." I eyed the thirty-foot-long Cornuprocyon. "—not exactly Mr. Subtle."

At this point I heard the *woomph,* and Rick was up and over the wall of the nearest cottage. A forest of his spines was clearly visible over the wall. His club tail cracked against first one wall, then another, as he wagged it back and forth.

"Rick, I can both see and hear you right now."

The tail wagging stopped.

"Stay here with Grace. Protect her. Don't eat her. Understand?"

Rick climbed over the wall and gave my face a good licking. I took that as a yes and gave him a scratch behind his ears. "Good boy. I'll see you in a bit." Head bowed, he turned away from me, shooting me one last look over his shoulder. I chuckled at him, then left our little camp.

～

IT WAS good to have a plan. I just wished it didn't lead me up the side of a mountain.

Grace had pointed me in the direction I needed to go. By using my Sense to feel the reference points around me, I could generally keep myself pointed in a straight line. I didn't dare deviate from that line, though; that was a good way to get lost again.

As a result, I found myself staring up at a rock face and wondering what exactly I was going to do about it. The side of a mountain was simply exposed, a sheer face hundreds of feet high. Standing on a pile of scree below, I stared upward and gulped.

Uncle Herman had taught me a lot about wilderness survival in general, but rock climbing had never been a topic. I'd asked him once, and his response was to call anyone who wanted to ascend the direct side of a rock face a damned fool. To his mind, there really wasn't a good reason to be stuck doing such an activity, and so his advice when I asked had always been "just go around."

That wasn't an option this time. I had to go straight up the side of this thing, and I had to do it without making too much noise. Granted, I could probably simply summon some steps right out of the thing, but that was bound to get a little noisy. For all I knew, Cythymau was in earshot, and so that wasn't the course I wanted to take.

The Sense was an aid, though. As I stepped onto my first footholds, I could use it to find the nearest handhold and Sense whether there was any fault in the stone underneath that would cause it to, say, break off and send me hurtling downward. The face was very rough, providing ample handholds, and I am certain that for an experienced free-climber it would have been laughably easy. For me, though, it was a long and nerve-wracking process.

My Sense could not compensate for my physical failings here. Band nerds tend to take the bare minimum in terms of physical education in high school, and I was no exception. Gyms were places one went to get picked on by the jocks; they were to be avoided at all costs. Thus, halfway up the side of the cliff face, my muscles began to cramp up on me. I risked some noise at that point and summoned a chunk of rock away from the face of the mountain, hollowing out a small sitting area to rest in.

The stone I had sent into the abyss clattered harmlessly to the ground below. No immediate threat showed up to kill me, and I concluded I was safe. I took my seat and leaned back, allowing my strained muscles to relax. As I did, I admired the vista this height provided me. Over the treetops and plains of yellow grass I could see the ruins of the hamlet where Grace was probably still sleeping.

I'm not sure how long I rested there on the side of the world, but my arms regained some semblance of mobility and I resumed my climb. I let my Sense slip from me; simply keeping it up was more effort than I could expend. I stopped twice more to rest on the way up, briefly using my Sense to create another sitting area. The sun was high in the sky when I clumsily flopped my way over the top of the cliff.

And found myself face to snarling face with another of this world's oversized beasts.

This was neither Lycaon nor Cornuprocyon. It looked more like a man-sized, jet-black squirrel. Much smaller than either of those bruisers, it was still far larger than its earth-based counterpart could ever be. Its face hovered less than a foot away, and its red, swirling eyes met mine for a brief second.

That red—I had seen the same color in Rick's eyes last fall, and in the Lycaon's eyes during graduation. This was one of Cythymau's beasts. I brought my Sense back up, getting ready to fight.

Then it turned, sprinting away from me on all fours.

This surprised me; I had been braced for an attack. Then I realized what was happening. Squirrel-thing wasn't here to fight; he was an early detection system. I rolled painfully to my feet and began to give chase, my overworked muscles protesting after the climb up the mountainside.

The squirrel demon had about an eighty-foot lead on me, down on all fours and moving fast. I upped my Sense but there was very little force to steal to get moving, and nothing heavy presented itself on this grassy mountaintop for me to generate that force with. My dead sprint was barely keeping pace; I had the distinct impression that my body was going to give out first.

There was a very slight breeze up here. I tried funneling it behind me to increase my speed, but even the pressure of a forty-foot half-circle's worth of magical sail boosted my pace only slightly. The net effect between this and my tiring body was simply maintaining speed, not gaining. I needed something more.

The squirrel was approaching the summit. I didn't know what was on the other side, but I didn't want it getting a clear vista. Now or never, then.

I reached down with my Sense and grabbed a small, round pebble from under the layers of grass and topsoil. Summoning it to my hand, I funneled my force sail in to a fine point. At that concentration, the force was far more violent, and I applied it to the pebble, sending it rocketing at Squirrel Thing.

Almost instantly, the squirrel dropped to the ground, rolling not once but twice. Crouching low to stay below the horizon, I crawled up to the body, panting hard. My pebble had entered into the back of the head and blown out the front, dropping the thing instantly. Like the Lycaon, these beasts must not have a lot in the way of defenses.

Then I crept slowly up to the horizon and peered out over the valley below.

I did not enjoy the view.

GRACE

I CAME SLOWLY out of an exhausted sleep, not sure what had awakened me. I cracked my eyes open, squinting against the mid-morning sun. An awkward kink in my back nagged me as I struggled up onto an elbow. For a moment I was at a loss, trying to remember where and why I'd been sleeping outdoors. The pop of the campfire and smoky smell of the bland mystery meat filtered in slowly. Right. I was in Cythymau's world, and Robert was out scouting. I had his promise to be very cautious, which meant he'd probably left—

Turning my head in sudden concern, I came face to face with a snuffling Cornuprocyon snout and accompanying carnivorous teeth. Adrenaline crackled through me, jerking me up onto my elbows.

Rick immediately backed up two steps, sitting in a half-crouch, with tension in every line of his body, much like mine.

I sat up and narrowed my eyes at him suspiciously. He returned my gaze with a wary look of his own. He considered me for a few seconds, shook himself, then padded over to the other side of the campfire with a studied air of nonchalance before yawning and stretching out all thirty feet of his large frame. All while keeping one eye firmly fixed on me. I wasn't fooled.

Rick might be afraid of me, or he may have gotten hungry enough he was checking out a potential snack. Impossible to know for sure.

"We promised Robert we'd play nice," I told Rick in a guarded tone, rather stupidly, since I didn't have Robert's bond with him. There's no way Rick understood me. "You can't eat me, and I'm not going to punish you for anything that happened while you were under Cythymau's control. Robert seems to believe you wouldn't have done any of it otherwise, so I'm giving you the benefit of the doubt. But that's only so long as you don't eat me. Just saying. You attack me, and all bets are off."

Needless to say, I wouldn't be sleeping now. I gathered myself and reached over to my bag, looking for my notes from the henge.

Rick yelped and backed away from the fire, his spiked coat standing on end, his eyes on my hand where it disappeared into the bag. I sighed and pulled it back out empty.

Okay, he had a point. Not the smartest thing right now, pulling out a sheet of runes, endangering our fragile truce.

"Fine." I eyed the hulking raccoon as he huffed and settled back down on his side of the fire, fixing me with an aggrieved look. "Let's hope your friend gets back pretty soon. Otherwise, it's going to be a long morning."

I WAS AMUSING myself plaiting a long rope from the supple yellow grasses, coiling it next to me, when Robert walked back into camp. I didn't know what we'd use the rope for, but it's always useful. Plus, if I'd continued the staring contest with Rick *all* morning, no doubt I'd be well past crazy by now. The rope already extended nearly twenty feet, and the tensile strength of the woven grass fibers turned out to be surprisingly robust.

Rick bounded up to Robert, licked his face, and tried to rub up against him. Robert must have been expecting it, because he dodged the quills while scratching Rick behind his ears. Rick's tongue lolled out in a grin of happiness that would have been cute—if wasn't so out of place with the whole summoner-eating monster thing.

Then another thought struck me. The Cornuprocyon might be smiling, but Robert wasn't.

I tied off the rope and put my hands in my lap, rubbing my palms against my knees. "So did you find Cythymau's cave?" I resisted tapping my fingers against my kneecaps as I waited.

"Oh, I found it, all right." Robert's voice was flat. "I also found out it's surrounded by hundreds of Rick's cousins and their friends. Cythymau has a whole army of Ricks and other creatures just waiting for us. No wonder we haven't been running into much out in the wild. He's got most—if not all—of them under his control."

"You're sure none of them saw you?"

"Something saw me, but I'm pretty sure I killed it before it could get much information back to Cythymau."

"Still, it's safe to assume that Cythymau will know for sure that you're closing in. We can only hope he'll assume you came alone. We may be able to use that to our advantage. What's the land like around Cythymau's cave?"

Robert found a long, straight stick from a nearby tree, and sat for moment staring into the flames as he charred the end. With his foot he cleared the dirt away from one of the large flat stones that formed the wide hearth of the fire pit. On the extreme left edge of it he drew a circle.

"This is the village. I went in a straight line from here to here, climbing up a rocky mountainous area." He dragged his stick to the right and drew another circle. From the second circle's right edge, he drew another line downward. "I stopped here, which overlooks a wide valley that meets up with several more mountainous regions here and here."

He drew two more circles at slight angles to the one representing the village, on the top and bottom of his map so the points formed a shallow triangle. "A small valley divides all three of these mountains, and then opens into this wide plain in front of where I was." He took a deep breath and drew a fourth circle at the bottom right of the crude map. "On the other edge of this plain here is where Cythymau's cave is set into the side of the foothill. There are hundreds and hundreds of beasts like Rick between us and Andrea right now."

His mouth set in a grim line as he contemplated the map he'd drawn. I knew he was calculating his chances of getting past them and not liking his conclusions. As if to illustrate this point, he gestured with his stick at a spot on the left side of us, not even on his map.

"The portal to home is all the way back here."

I gestured decisively at the mountain he'd drawn at the top of the map. "Tell me more about this mountain here."

"The face pointed toward Cythymau's cave is pretty steep, but not impassable." He jabbed his stick at the top of the circle. "This face is not quite sheer, but it would be a heck of a thing to get up or climb down. The easiest way up it is probably here." He tapped the left arc of the circle with his stick.

"And it connects to the plain and Cythymau's cave through these valleys here and here?" I asked, pointing. Robert obligingly drew his stick down the left and right of the circle in curving snaking lines to represent the valleys around the mountain and hooked them up with the plain.

"More like this."

"What about the mountain there?" I asked, pointing at the bottom of the map. He drew in the valleys and indicated where they met up with the plain and the gathered forces. Then he marked both the steepest face, and the most likely route to the top.

I nodded, a seed of a plan beginning to form in my brain.

"This army of beasts," I said slowly. "You said there are hundreds of them. Did you get a good look at what kind they are?"

"As good a look as I could without going down there and seeing if they wanted to go for a walk." Robert shot me a considering glance.

"Can you give me a closer count?"

"I dunno, more than two hundred, probably less than three. I didn't stick around too long once I killed Cythymau's lookout. Seemed more prudent to get back here ASAP."

I flashed him a grin. "I didn't think you knew the meaning of prudent. Are you sure you're not some clever disguise meant to look like Robert? Maybe I'd better go double-check and make sure that the real you wasn't captured on that ledge after all."

"Ha, ha. I'm reckless, not stupid," he retorted.

"Fair enough." I stuck my tongue out at him. "I could debate the line between reckless and stupid all day, but then I'd be a hypocrite. My family is not known for prudence either." I smiled at him to take the sting from the words. Robert groaned.

Another thought struck me. "You didn't see anything down there that could fly?"

"No, I don't think so. I wasn't there very long, though."

"There's such a thing as too clever. This time, it just may get us out of this. We'll beat Cythymau with his own trap. We have work to do." I picked up a handful of the loose grass I'd been weaving into rope, and started threading it together into a square mat.

Robert gave me a quizzical look, but I just gave him my best cryptic smile.

"Time for a little bait-and-switch."

I STOOD atop a rocky promontory at the summit of the mountain opposite the plain where Cythymau's forces gathered. I shaded my eyes against the sun, watching the animalistic demons mill below me. For the opening gambit of this showdown, I'd positioned myself on the highest point, directly across from the field full of Cythymau's army and the entrance to his cave where Andrea presumably lay. The goal here was to get everything down there to chase me while Robert rescued Andrea. No sweat right?

My skirt was cut and sewn together into rough trousers, and I had the sore and pricked fingers to prove it. I'd blackened my skirt and blouse to a suitably dark if somewhat streaky color with soot. My hair had been stuffed under a tight cap made from woven grass. From a distance, it was just possible to mistake me for a teenage boy with a fondness for black. Or at least, that was my hope.

From this vantage point, high above the plain full of creatures, it was hard to distinguish any detail from the milling beasts below. I knew from Robert's report that in addition to Cornuprocyons and Lycaon, I would need to lure away giant Frankenstein-squirrels and various other hulking, mutant saber-tooth carnivores. Let's call them the bear-ferrets and the beaked-terrors.

The most important thing at the moment was that none of the horde of demons appeared to have wings. In the time we'd observed them, nothing seemed to indicate that any of the creatures were above animal intelligence, either. Cythymau appeared to be controlling them much as he had Rick last fall. To get through this, we'd need to use that to our advantage. I'd chosen my position—with the steep but not impassable slope in front of me—because their instinctual response should be to charge up the incline at me.

Robert and I had already made all the preparations we could.

No time like the present to find out if they worked.

I smoothed a rune tag across one of the rocks sticking up from the mountain floor. I pulled a vial out of my bag and stared at it. After helping me set up my tags and traps, Robert had given himself a small cut at my request to obtain the dark blood that now sloshed against the clear glass. Three more identical small vials were clipped to the strap of my bag above my usual vials. Disguising my summoning with Robert's blood was the cornerstone of my diversionary tactic, so if Cythymau didn't bite...

I breathed a little prayer to any spirits that might be listening and smeared part of the contents of the vial across the tag.

Focusing on my carefully drawn runes, I used Robert's blood to channel the loudest summons my Sense could muster. It went off, lighting the Weave up with my location like a beacon. The kinetic force I'd summoned slammed into the side of the hill below me. Robert's blood *should* overlay my Sense and mimic the traces of power his personal magic usually left in the Weave. That was the theory.

A churning avalanche of dirt, branches, and rock came loose from the side of the mountain and slid down toward the host of beasts. It blindsided a few, burying them in a fraction of a second as they howled and clawed, attempting to get free. I'd purposefully constructed the summons to seem clumsy; a naïve, desperate, unfocused attempt to take the group out all at once. The creatures the ploy *did* manage to take out were just bonus. That should get Cythymau's attention.

Most of the beasts in the path of the landslide still managed to evade it with relative ease. One of the Cornuprocyons didn't even bother to move. It just deflected the dirt and rock with nonchalance that made my stomach flip-flop. I did not look forward to meeting Rick's cousins at closer range, and secretly I hoped that their power level would be significantly reduced without Rick's access to the all-you-can-eat summoner buffet. They were less juiced, but not as weak as I'd hoped. Joy.

As the dust from the landslide started to settle, the horde of demons lifted their heads in a perfectly uniform motion. It resembled a pack of feral dogs catching an elusive smell on the wind. They all turned their red, malevolent eyes on me. The hairs on the back of my neck stood on end; goose bumps slowly raised on my arms. The Lycaon howled, the sound reverberating across the mountain continuously like a struck bell. I had a fraction of a second to marvel at the noise before the horde ran forward in a frothing wave of teeth, claws, and lethal intent.

With the Lycaon in the lead, the rest of the host wheeled and began swarming in behind, headed straight for the foot of the mountainous peak I stood atop. Cythymau got a good look at me, silhouetted at the top of the mountain, through their eyes.

I powered another summons with Robert's blood, uprooting several trees, sending them careening down the slope at the advancing horde. My supply of Robert's blood was very limited, for obvious reasons, but my summoning display had to be as impressive and as loud as possible if the ploy had any hope of sticking. I'd never, ever tried to mask my summoning with someone else's blood before, so we were in new territory here. The necessity for this type of summoning tactic just didn't come up in the normal scheme of things. Of course, my circumstances for the last year had been anything *but* normal.

Uncle Herman's notes about the potency and distinctive qualities of one's own blood had given me the idea. Not that he'd ever described doing something like this. I'd gone far out on my own wild theory here.

Fortunately, based on the number of demons that had just swarmed my direction, it seemed to be working. For now.

I watched for a few more precious seconds to be sure the bulk of the demonic army committed to the chase. The first few Lycaon were starting to claw their way up the slope below me before I moved. I spun around the clump of rock and trees behind me, running up and over the pinnacle of the summit as fast I could. I ducked into a clump of trees, dodging low-hanging branches, running for my next cluster of tags.

After a few seconds I risked a glance behind me and saw the first Lycaon cresting the top of the mountain. I forced my legs to move faster, smearing my hand with Robert's blood. The next tag was on a tree to my left at chest height. I darted my hand out, slamming it into the tag. The force ripped it off the tree as I powered the runes. Shooting another glance backward, now I could see the Cornuprocyons—and coming next, a small humanoid figure, directing their actions from the rear.

Perfection. Absolute fucking win.

My lips pulled upward in a fierce grin. Cythymau had taken the bait. He didn't want to let a prize like Robert slip through his fingers again, and was making sure there were no mistakes this time by coming himself. Now that I had confirmation he was here, it was time to put the *whole* plan into action. I traced my next rune tag, triggering my first trap. A heavy fall of rock rumbled toward the demons, bouncing and careening down the mountain face with shuddering impact. The line of Lycaon charging up the slope in the lead swerved in panic. Several of them miscalculated, dodged into a rock's unpredictable bounce, and were flung back with a crunch and a whimper.

I winced. If I could have gotten Robert, Andrea, and myself out of this Weave without injuring them, I would have. But while they were under the demon's control they were just too lethal to leave alone. Rick had proven that time and time again during our last confrontation. They would kill both Robert and me without blinking.

Plus, I still wasn't entirely sure how much of the threat they represented was their predator nature, and how much was Cythymau's influence. If I left a bunch of them uninjured at our back and it turned out Cythymau had been using natural tendencies as something he could control, we could still be swarmed under.

I'd preplanned my route across the top of the mountain with tags pasted against the back sides of several large trees. I coated my hand with the rest of Robert's blood from the first vial and slapped the tag as I ran past. It pulled the tree out of the ground and laid it across the path behind me. From a distance, it should look as though I had flung out a hand and used nothing but my Sense to uproot the trees in Robert-style.

The Weave hummed with the feel of Robert's power. Intent on pursuit, the Lycaon howled in stereo. Cythymau's hooting laughter underlay their calls like an eerie ghost. A shiver crawled down my spine. I gathered myself for another burst of speed.

I dodged around a tree out of his line of sight, and placed another tree in the path of the oncoming Lycaon. Threading my way through the branches and trunks, I made sure to keep just far enough ahead of the demons that they only lost sight of me completely for a few seconds at a time. Usually, just long enough for me to activate another tag and add a burst of speed. I was burning through the second vial of Robert's blood at a record pace.

The next tag opened a series of gaping water-pits in my wake and finished off the vial. I discarded it with a flick of my wrist, listening with relief to the splooshes erupting behind me. I unclipped the third vial of Robert's blood and thumbed it open. Only one small vial remained on my bag strap.

Cythymau knew the terrain around here, but even so I was betting that the chance of catching Robert could lure him into overextending himself. I triggered a spiked pit trap under the two Cornuprocyons that had taken the lead, forcing the two behind them to skid to a stop and swerve around to avoid its gaping width.

Next, I threw down several sections of braided rope tethered to two stone weights on each end. My improvised bolo entangled the feet of the Cornuprocyons. Enmeshed in their quills, it drew them up short and forced them to take the time to figure out how to burst their way out by force.

The smaller, beaked-ferret demons slithered under the thrashing Cornuprocyons with barely a pause. I triggered another tag. Magma spurted up from the ground, sweeping their feet out from under them in a fiery swath. It hurled small demons back into the Cornuprocyons in burning, writhing confusion. It wasn't pretty to watch, and I reminded myself of the deputies and civilians Rick had killed last fall, and all of the recent graduates who had died because of demons just like these.

One Cornuprocyon managed to evade all the traps, either through luck or Cythymau's instruction. It cleared the smoking lava with a familiar *woomph* and landed just short of my heels, swiping at me with the curved claws of one paw.

I triggered one last tag, hitting the Cornuprocyon with a wave of boiling mud and ash lahar, sweeping it away from me. The wave of lahar sped down the hillside, carrying the enveloped Cornuprocyon with it and bowling through its fellows.

I'd finally reached the crest of the mountain's reverse slope. In front of me lay a steep descent covered in waving yellow grass. I skidded into scrubby yellow brush near the ledge and yanked out the square, grass-woven mat hidden underneath. Really, technically, it was a woven grass sled. The Hawaiians thought of grass sleds way before me, so I can't take all the credit for a genius idea, but either way it was a damn good way to get down off a mountain fast without the usual swift fall, followed by death.

My desired landing zone lay straight ahead—on the horizontal plain. The vertical plane, well, that one could only be called a doozy. This moment represented the only chance to aim myself. It wouldn't be possible to steer this thing once in motion.

I double-checked my trajectory, launched into a running start, and took a leap of faith. By the time I'd settled more firmly on the mat's surface it had already carried me down the slope so fast that the wind snapped fiercely at my clothes and tried to rip off my cap.

I ended up with one hand in a death grip on the sled and one hand desperately trying to keep my hair hidden for as long as possible. Every second I could keep Cythymau chasing me was one more second that Robert and Andrea had to escape.

The howling of the Lycaon faded as I shot down the mountain. I'd aimed for a wide, flat area devoid of trees, but if I wasn't careful I would still come to a sudden, painful, arboreal stop.

I reached the plain and slid a good thirty feet before throwing myself off the sled, rolling to stop my momentum. Relieved of my mass, the sled slid a little farther and stopped.

Flopping onto my back, I was rewarded by the sight of Cythymau reaching the ledge, sketching a summons. He threw himself off the precipice I'd just left, streaking toward me like a man-shaped missile. The fur-lined edge of his leather armor flapped loudly but didn't slow his descent at all.

Presumably, his summons would stop him from hitting the ground with the usual finality that accompanies a hundred-and-fifty-foot fall off a mountain. I scrambled back, flailing to find the bushes that hid my rune board.

The jig was up, anyway. It would be too difficult to maintain the distance between me and Cythymau or his beasts now that we were on the flat. At this stage in the showdown, without my rune board, I'd truly be a sitting duck. I finally found it, then strapped it my arm with a now battle-hardened ease.

Turning, I watched with satisfaction the gleeful look on Cythymau's rune-etched face freeze as he fell toward me. His face slowly transformed into disbelief, then horror. His head jerked up to look over his shoulder at the mountain behind him, blocking the easy way back to his cave. He'd already committed himself to the jump; he couldn't stop now, but he could redirect his troops. He turned his face to glare at me, his hand going down to one of the blue tattoos on his chest and activating it. His descent slowed and, even in his shock, he landed with a sure grace that I envied.

A moment before, Cythymau had been sure of imminent victory, his blue-painted face set in the hard lines and cruel ambition of a conqueror. Now his facial muscles appeared stunned and slack, an expression of disbelief that appeared absolutely out of place and priceless on his features. No doubt it had been a century or three since anyone gave him as much trouble as Robert and I had managed to dish out in the last few months.

"Miss me?" I gave Cythymau my best Cheshire grin. "I know I wasn't invited, but I just couldn't resist gate-crashing. Surprise parties are just so much more fun, don't you think? I know you do."

ROBERT

I was one mountain over from where I had encountered the demonic squirrel thing. This slope was easier on its way up. Sure enough, another Squirrel Scout waited atop the peak. Unlike last time, though, I had brought backup. At a word from me, Rick hit it with a wave of kinetic force, then leapt at it, spinning in midair. His club of a tail hit the scout across the back, and with a sickening *crunch*, the top of the mountain was ours.

It wasn't much of a mountain, as mountains go. I remember watching some movie about Wales where a bunch of people were pissed off at a geologist who called their mountain a hill. My mountain was about as high as that one. It stood too high to be a hill, but too short to really be a mountain. The occasional tree sprouted from its crags, but for the most part the slope consisted of broken-off bits of rock and cliff faces from which the rock had broken.

Then the waiting began. The vast plain below was filled with Cythymau's beasts. In fact, it appeared even more populated than it had during my scouting mission. I figured Cythymau must be gathering them together in response to—

Well, to me. After all, it's not like my showing up here was a secret.

And had I been without Grace, I probably would have tried something much more direct and suicidal.

I've never been good at the waiting part. Rick, though, was positively agitated. He would try to poke his nose over the horizon to get a look at what was scaring me. By the way he paced, then scratched at/through nearby trees, he was even worse at this than I was. Keeping his massive bulk below the horizon turned out to keep me plenty occupied as we waited for our signal.

I didn't have my Sense raised when Grace picked her fight. I knew she was planning on doing it sloppily, to feel like me, but I didn't want to waste the effort of maintaining my Sense if I didn't have to. Still, I didn't need to feel the resonance in the Weave to notice Grace's opening move. The entire side of the mountain opposite me across the valley broke free, careening into the monsters below. The keening of pain rising throughout the valley replaced the crashing of rock. That, too, was drowned as, across the valley floor, a low-pitched growl took root. Every demon below rose to its feet, its eyes focused on the top of Grace's mountain.

Then, as if at some invisible signal, they broke for her all at once. I had been thinking of this gathering as Cythymau's army, but watching them swarm after Grace, I realized that "army" implied a kind of coordination simply not present among these beasts. What we dealt with could best be described as a "pack," or maybe a "swarm." They reacted to each other on instinct, not out of a sense of directed command.

As they started up the hill toward Grace, a small, blue-painted man stepped out of the cave.

He stretched out his back and shook his head like an athlete preparing for a competition. Then he took off, running for Grace's mountain. His speed gave no ground to the four-legged beasts running in front of him.

Good. Cythymau had taken the bait. He and his army, his swarm, hurtled away from his cave and toward my master.

What remained was bad enough. Outside of Cythymau's cave, and not responding to Grace at all, sat two Cornuprocyons. They didn't look as large as Rick; I was guessing that they had never eaten an entire Grove of summoners. From nose to tail, I guessed they had fifteen feet to Rick's thirty.

"Any relations of yours?" I asked Rick. He simply stared at me. "Well, we have to go through them regardless. How do we do this?"

Rick licked me across the face.

"You are not being helpful, boy. We don't have a lot of time here. You think we can take them?"

Rick *woomphed* his way up into the air, flinging himself over the mountainside in a dive that, for a lesser creature, would have been purely suicidal. He was outside of my Sense range before I even brought it up. Sighing, I started down the side of the mountain.

Extreme, Sense-aided cross-country was one of my earliest forms of summoning training, though I hadn't known it at the time. Uncle Herman made me run through his woods so many times that running pell-mell down the side of a mountain felt pretty natural. Down-hilling really isn't running; it's more of a serious of controlled leaps and slides. Without the aid of the Sense, it's doable, but it's one of those don't-try-this-at-home deals. Jumping off cliffs and sliding down the scree below might be a fast way to descend, but it's also a good way to break your ankle, leg, arm, neck...

With the Sense, even a skinny band geek can come off looking like a professional. I knew exactly where to jump and how to position my feet to catch just enough of the mountainside to slow me. As I descended, there was a moment in which I forgot where I was. I let go of the fact that we were an army of three up against an *actual* army, including a general more powerful than any of us, and instead I gave in to the simple joy of moving quickly through nature. I'm pretty sure that there is a deep, primal part of all of us that remembers running over rough terrain, because doing it makes you forget everything else that's going on.

I have a sneaking suspicion, however, that said instinct comes from our ancestors running *away* from large, dangerous threats, not *toward.* In this respect, my cavemen grandfathers and I differed somewhat.

I was running *into* the danger.

When I reached the bottom, Rick was already engaged on both sides and getting battered. Cornuprocyons don't manipulate the world the way summoners do; they can't move things around one way or another. They *create.* Rick could spontaneously generate a wave of force, and he could send it out from himself. If he blasted it in the right direction, it allowed him to make those leaps of his. If blasted outward, it could deflect incoming attacks.

But there was a time delay. With Rick, cranked up by his consumption of an entire Grove, it was little more than a second, but it was still enough. With two of his own kind to deal with, Rick was not getting the better end of the deal. One would generate an attack right after the other, and Rick couldn't deflect them both. Their force blasts weren't nearly as strong as Rick's, but they were keeping him on the defensive, and every other one was landing. Rick was tough, but he couldn't attack.

I didn't have a lot of time. I had no idea how long Grace was going to be able to keep that army running after her, but I knew that Cythymau would recognize the diversion as soon as he realized whom he'd been following. We'd set him up, and I didn't imagine that was going to make him all too happy with me. I needed to get Andrea and get out. If we were still here when he got back, at best, I'd end up as kibble for his army. At worst...

No time to think about that.

Here's a little guilty secret of mine: there is a part of me that loves these moments. The fact is, as a society we deal with some seriously inane crap every day, and we pretend it's important. We get bogged down in which girl likes me, what my classmates think about me, are the cops going to bust me for shoplifting, where am I going to go to school, how much money is in my trust account, do we know anyone who can buy that beer, who won the latest sporting event, what was my grade on my biology final? We pretend all of that is important, and we stress out over it constantly.

Otherwise, our lives would seem pretty meaningless. Hollow.

But every once in a while, you find something that actually has *real* meaning. And you want the rest of the world to be like that. Someone throws herself in front of an attack meant for you. Someone else gets herself chased by an army of beasts simply because she believes in you. That level of sacrifice, that kind of pain and joy, accompanies the things that are truly important in life. We don't expose ourselves to those things much. I'm not sure what would happen to us if we did.

But I can tell you this. For all that I'd been mad at Grace for dragging me into this war, in the moment I hurled myself across that field toward a snarling pile of death, I felt relieved.

All that other bullshit had simply fallen away from my shoulders. There was nothing—*nothing*—else in my life that I needed to worry about. My entire life boiled down to getting Andrea and getting out.

The Grove had their knickers in a bunch over me? Didn't matter. My (former) foster father had banished me from his home? Worthless. I had embarrassed myself in my first full-on attempt at sexual prowess? Eh, at least I'd had the attempt. In the clear light of impending violence, everything else that had been weighing on me simply lifted itself, freeing my mind to deal with the next split second.

I'd felt this kind of insane joy once before, as I stood on a bridge and waited for Rick to come kill me. Now I rushed to Rick's side, and the joy of having my life simplified, distilled down to my next breath, filled me. I laughed openly with the relief of it.

In my calmer moments, I realize that this makes me not entirely sane. That doesn't bother me; I'm not sure anyone is *entirely* sane.

I barreled at the Cornuprocyon-on-Cornuprocyon fight with reckless abandon. They had Rick encircled, and his big head whipped back and forth, trying to deal with both threats at once. Their attention was on the giant exemplar of their species, and they paid me little mind.

I could have slipped around them, but I wasn't sure how long Rick could last, and I didn't want to come out of the cave to the two of them standing on my new friend's corpse. Rick's swirling eye caught mine, and I smiled at him. He seemed to get my intent, because as I came within Sense-range of the Cornuprocyon on my side of him, he turned away and launched his own assault on the other.

The one I ran at blasted toward Rick, still not watching for me. That was its mistake. I had learned some tricks since fighting my last Cornuprocyon.

I took its blast for my own, wrapping the force away from Rick and steering it back around my body in a wide circuit. The last time I'd pulled this trick, I'd managed to knock Rick off his feet, and I'd been an amateur then. This time, I did it right; instead of simply hitting the Cornuprocyon with the kinetic energy, I shaped it. No longer the size of a freight train, I focused it down into a cone with a sharp point. It still had all the momentum of an eighteen-wheeler, but it wasn't the wild wave Cornuprocyons project. When it comes to breaking things, it's not sheer pounds you're looking for.

It's pounds-per-square-inch.

I drove the cone of force up under the Cornuprocyon's jaw before it had time to defend. The blow penetrated. The cone ripped through its flesh and skull with a quiet *crunch*, spraying fragments of bone, flesh, and gray matter around in a neat circular pattern.

The Cornuprocyon's club tail came around as though to hit me, but then twitched away. For a moment, I worried that my theory about brain destruction was off. It worked on everything from zombies to immortal Highlanders in the movies, but applying that rule to Cornuprocyons had been something of a guess.

A correct guess, as it turns out. The giant raccoon demon flopped to the ground and twitched, but made no further moves. I wasn't sure it was dead, but it was distinctly incapacitated. Good enough. I looked at the battle between Rick and the second guard, but Rick appeared to now have the upper edge in a one-on-one fight. His kinetic blasts were overwhelming its defenses, sending it sprawling. I got the impression Rick was enjoying this little vengeance, so I left him to it and turned into the cave.

Memory flooded me upon reaching the entrance. The cave had changed only slightly since last I had been inside. The same cozy little hearth, the bedding, the same pots and pans neatly ordered on the cave walls. I ran past it, my Sense raised and wary for ambush.

And there was Andrea, in all her naked, strapped glory. At least I was ready for it; I didn't take a minute to Sense-stare at the naked girl like I had last time. This time, I took less than a second. I promise. That cord of power was still attached to her, and it ran through the cave wall to the outside, where Cythymau was chasing Grace down.

She still lay strapped to the board in the side room of the cave. The wall Rick blew in last fall looked repaired. A second board lay next to her, the straps prepared. A shiver ran up my back. I knew who that was for.

"Hey," I whispered. I'm honestly not sure why I whispered; the sound of the Cornuprocyon vs. Cornuprocyon fight raging in front of the cave would have drowned all conversation from the outside. Still, I was on a semi-stealthy mission here. Whispering seemed appropriate. I dropped my Sense as I hurried to undo the straps.

Andrea simply lay there. I really hadn't expected much more than that, but it seemed important that I talk to her anyway.

"I've got a partner this time. Grace is out there, pulling Cythymau away from us." I worked the forehead strap loose first, just as I had done a year ago. As they had done then, Andrea's eyes snapped into focus on mine as soon as it was loose.

"Can you hear me?" I asked, moving my way down to her wrist strap. I began with the left, as I had so long ago. "I know it's been a while since last we met, but this time no half-measures. We're going to get you out of here, and we're going to do it right."

The left strap popped open, and the hand underneath began to flex. That had happened before as well.

I reached across the bound girl for the strap on her right. This was the point when, last time, Grace had summoned me back to Earth, and I had left Andrea behind. I popped the strap binding her right wrist free, and began working on the criss-crossed chest bands.

As I leaned across once again, I felt something cold at my throat.

"Ak y'r mynzuleth og hyrtundu," Andrea said, in a harsh whisper.

Okay, this was a bit of a hitch in my plan. She was holding some kind of a blade to my throat. Looking down, I saw a quick series of red runes drawn on the table with her left hand, the one I'd freed first. Blood was dripping from the hand holding the blade; she had cut her own hand with her nails to draw and feed the runes. She kept the blade on me with her left hand as her right began undoing the straps that bound her across the chest.

I might be able to get my Sense up and get rid of the knife, but that was a gamble. I was guessing hers was up by now, and there were good odds I was in its radius. Any move on my part to bring up my power could quickly be ended with a cut artery. Not worth risking.

"*Og hyrtundu!*" she commanded.

I could only respond by putting my hands in the air. I'd fantasized about being Andrea's knight in shining armor for almost a year. Now I wished I had at least a gorget.

I'd never really considered the possibility that Andrea spoke some language other than English. What was it? I knew it wasn't Spanish (and it took me two years of education to come to that stunning conclusion).

Still, moments like this are once-in-a-lifetime shots; when it comes, you have to, *have to*, say exactly the right thing. Screw it up, and you've damaged the course of your life forever.

"I'm Robert Lorents. I'm here to rescue you." Nailed it. I had been saving that one.

A quick eyebrow raised only slightly at that, and she shook her head. She finished with the straps binding her chest and waist and sat up, keeping the knife at my throat and her eyes locked on mine. She undid her knees, then each ankle separately. Then, forcing me to move by applying sharp pressure to my neck, she swung her legs down off the board. Immediately she staggered, the knife clattering from her grip. The effort of simply standing was too much for her body. I didn't know how long she'd been on that board, but clearly it had some kind of preservation ability. Watching her struggle to rise as her legs shook under her, I could tell it hadn't done enough. My gut twisted as the reality of Andrea's torture hit me anew.

I brought up my Sense and felt hers collide with mine. I squatted down and reached my hand toward her. She recoiled, her hand seeking the knife on the floor. Power rippled through her Sense. Before I could react, the knife was in her hand. That summons had been lightning-fast and precise, and it caught me napping. She drove the knife hard at my chest. I summoned the knife from her hand as it began to penetrate my skin. She managed to fight my summons long enough to make contact first, slicing through my shirt. A trickle of blood began to work its way down my chest.

"Hey—watch it!"

I stepped back. Her eyes bored into mine as she tried to summon the knife again. I was ready for it, though; her Sense locked up against mine. She staggered toward me, arms outstretched as though to grasp at my throat. Her Sense continued to batter against mine, but I could feel it weakening in her exhaustion.

I made no aggressive move. I didn't want to startle her any further. Her hands closed on my neck, but she didn't have the physical ability to grip with any strength. She stood there, hands wrapped around my throat, eyes meeting mine in a hardened stare and Sense flailing its last vain attempts against mine.

"Kill..." she said, gasping. English!

"You speak English?" I asked, carefully grasping her wrists and tugging her arms away from my neck. "You know, I'm the one saving you right now."

Her head cocked to the side, her eyelids narrowed in suspicion.

"Look, we don't have a lot of time. I have a way back to Earth, but we need to hurry up and get out of here." Slowly, I turned and wrapped her arm around my neck. Then I began guiding her toward the mouth of the cave.

Outside, Rick stood behind the corpse of the Cornuprocyon he had been fighting. When he saw me, he began bouncing back and forth on his forepaws, proud of the gift he was presenting.

Andrea screamed. Her voice ripped its way up through her lungs, keening her rage as her Sense flared against mine with renewed energy. I flinched back, then wrapped my Sense around hers like a calming blanket.

"No, Andrea, it's ok. He's a friend."

Her body coiled and tensed. What muscles she had went taut as she stared…but not at Rick. At the horizon.

When I looked, I realized what it was she saw.

There was no longer a stream of power running to Cythymau. And it looked like he'd noticed before I did, because his army was coming back.

GRACE

CYTHYMAU STOOD STILL where he'd landed just a few feet from me. For a frozen second he stared at me, his pack of writhing beasts flowing down the slope, milling behind him in stunned confusion. One thing was clear, I'd managed to lure them exactly where I'd wanted, far from Robert and his rescue effort. I stood between Cythymau and his goal.

Diversion successful. Go me.

So, here we were, cut off from everyone else and any hint of backup.

In the asset column, I had me, my Sense, any naturally occurring elements, and a few guardian spirits. Of course I was up against an ancient, megalomaniac demon with more juice in his little pinky than I probably had in my whole body. Great plan I'd come up with here.

Cythymau swept a contemptuous glance at my battle stance, his face cold and hard.

"Whuft! I do not have to dally with a gnat when a much bigger prize awaits me. This but delays the inevitable." With a quick, angry motion, he dug a small knife into his palm and smeared the blood across one of the runes on his chest. He spun, presenting his back to me as if I weren't a threat to him at all.

A Lycaon bounded over to him. He swung up on its back, holding onto the spikey black fur of its ruff with his fists, ignoring the blood still running down his hand.

Ok, I wasn't a big-time powerhouse like Robert, but I'm just as stubborn. Screw anyone who expected me to bow to the inevitable, or allowing anyone to insinuate a fight with me wouldn't even be worth the time.

Every second I could manage to delay Cythymau gave Robert another second to get Andrea out. My Sense may not have the same oomph behind it as Robert's, but I wasn't going to let Cythymau get away *that* easy.

Not that confronting him was a comfortable proposition, mind you.

Fear hovered in the back of my mind, waiting to pounce. It'd be easier to hold in check if I was doing something. I slid my foot behind me, scooting a bit farther back, my fingers flying over the runes on my board.

In the startling way of lava, the frothy magma I'd used for the diversion earlier had already cooled, but I had other uses for that pumice it had become. I summoned it to me, using kinetic energy to grind it into a fine powder before spreading it over the front ranks of demons. Cythymau managed to deflect it away from him and the Lycaon he rode, but the rest of the beasts went down, howling and pawing at their eyes. I still needed to slow down their boss.

Rearranging the runes on the board, I sent the remaining mud and ash lahar down the plain on a collision course with Cythymau and the demons that had avoided the cloud of ground pumice. Cythymau dodged facilely around the crest of the surging slurry of hot mud, evading my new ploy with mocking ease. With a wave of his hand, a few of the Cornuprocyons broke out of the pack and wheeled toward me.

That couldn't be good. In my favor, Lycaon that had been taken down by the pumice fragments were still pawing at their eyes, but the Cornuprocyons were starting to shake themselves free of the stinging particles and regain their footing.

Biting my lip, I tore the earth open just under Cythymau's feet. The Lycaon standing to either side of him yelped and scrambled to firmer ground on the far side. Cythymau himself barely glanced at it; the Lycaon he rode bounded clear with almost nonchalant dexterity.

Doing some quick mental math, I lined up the next set of familiar runes, but with a twist for this Weave, blooding them with a sure stroke of my thumb. A deluge of refrigerator-sized boulders fell in a curtain of destruction behind Cythymau. A chorus of howling and growling started in the ranks of the injured Lycaon.

The familiar *woomph* of the Cornuprocyons sounded as several veered off course to avoid the boulders. One was deflected by a blast of kinetic force and suddenly skewed sideways, taking out a row of demons that looked like giant, horror-house squirrels on steroids.

It also effectively turned the slope they'd just come down into rough, treacherous terrain, unstable and potentially crushing. I maintained my battle crouch on the other side of the newly torn earth and kept rearranging runes for my next summons as I waited for Cythymau's return move. I bit back four-letter words as he evaded the destruction and his Lycaon continued to delicately leap and bound over the debris, progressing rapidly back the way we'd come. That shouldn't have been a shocker, I guess, but a girl can hope.

I blooded the rune on my board and watched five trees come crashing down immediately in front of him, bouncing, rolling, and losing branches the whole way. One of the branches caught the Lycaon carrying Cythymau in the chest before he was able to completely deflect it. The giant demon-wolf staggered sideways.

Cythymau jerked his arm in irritation as the Lycaon regained its balance and took a bounding leap. It perched briefly on the ledge above me before cutting up and around the slope, back in the direction that would lead them closer to Robert and Andrea. I swore louder. I had to delay somehow. We needed more time.

I didn't have enough fingers to count the possible doomsday scenarios if Cythymau actually got his hands on Robert. In addition to the global calamity that would no doubt follow if he got loose, I had three very immediate, very personal reasons to make sure Cythymau didn't get what he wanted. Namely, the freedom of Andrea, Robert, and myself. Cythymau had already more than demonstrated how poorly he took care of his pets. No way would I stand aside as he bound Robert to his non-existent mercy.

"Oh, no, you don't. I may be easy, but I'm not that easy." I scanned the landscape, trying to memorize where every tree and rock lay. I might need them later. My hand went to my rune board, sliding the runes into place along with the compound runes for this Weave. I closed my eyes briefly, praying I was right, that the summons wouldn't fizzle.

Not shockingly, I'd never tried to summon a Guardian into a Weave that wasn't my own before. Hyctea popped into existence with an avian scream and then took a very confused look at the yellow waving grass around her. Her damaged feathers and wounds from the last battle had already healed.

The Lycaon leaped in unison, their claws extended toward me and jaws open. A flick of my wrist aligned the next rune set into place, and a wall of ice hurtled toward them. It took them in their chests, mid jump, and bore them back into the surrounding hillside with a tremendous impact. Hyctea gave a low, uncertain hoot, still swiveling her head around at the unfamiliar plant life. She hopped over to me. I put a reassuring hand on her neck and swung up onto her back.

"Fly, Hyctea!" I pointed after Cythymau. "Follow that Lycaon!" It wasn't quite the same as telling a taxi, to "Follow that car!" but still, I'd always wanted to try it. I hugged her neck tightly and braced myself. With a powerful flap of her wings, Hyctea surged into the air. Under my legs I could feel the power flowing through her muscular shoulders. I leaned forward to lessen my wind resistance and keep my body in line with hers.

Within seconds we had shot over the rocky hillside where Cythymau had disappeared. The landscape unfurled beneath us like a map. Cythymau had already rejoined his army of slavering death-beasts. They swarmed down the valley in front of us.

About five hundred feet ahead of them, the valley opened up into the plain. My best chance of stopping them by myself was to bottleneck them in the valley; I absolutely had to do it before they got to that wide plain, or I'd be screwed. Hugging Hyctea with my knees, I straightened up enough to be able to reach my rune board. With the added strain, my abused skirt and its crude stitching was starting to come apart. I'd be lucky if I wasn't half naked by the time this was over, though it wasn't really high on my priority list at the moment. Naked, alive, and free still sounded like a win.

The wind whistled in my ears. Every once and a while we rose or dropped suddenly with the beat of Hyctea's wings. Some part of my brain acknowledged that pulling a "Look Ma, no hands!" on top of a giant flying bird spirit just might be the epitome of a stupid, reckless act.

On the other hand, no risk, no gain, right?

Biting my lip in concentration, I got the runes lined up and reached for the next blood vial, thumbing the lid off in a gesture so routine to me I didn't even think about the slipstream whistling past us. Big mistake.

The wind grabbed the blood, and thanks to the shaky nature of my perch, it flew everywhere except my rune board. I had the tiles set, Sense fired up, and blood coating a rock on the ground below, but no blood on the summon. Cythymau was only about a hundred feet from the mouth of the valley and closing.

Swearing, I grabbed another vial and waited to open it until it was much closer to my board. The wind forced the blood backward toward my arm and down Hyctea's back. I ran my hand over her feathers, trying to pick up enough blood to at least power the summons. My hand came away coated and gross, but with the wind there was just no way to get enough of the rapidly-drying blood to the board while it was still wet.

Dried blood's like a spent battery. No juice. Plus, it's not like my blood supply here came close to being unlimited. I had fifteen vials left, and I would need every one of them to get us out of here. I needed the two currently uselessly spread over the ground too, but spilled milk and all that.

Every passing second brought me that much closer to not being able to get a summons off before Cythymau and the front ranks of his pack of doom reached the plain. They only had about fifty feet to go now. Any second they would pass the point of no return, and this summons would be pointless.

I don't actually like pain. When my high school science class tested blood types, I'd learned it's actually a challenge to stab oneself in the finger. It had been surprisingly difficult to push myself past that instinctual aversion to inflicting injury on my own body.

But I needed blood that wasn't going to lose potency under the force of the wind, and I needed it *now*. Squeezing my eyes shut against the pain, I bit down on the top of the webbing between my thumb and forefinger, swift and hard, until my mouth filled with the strong copper tang of blood. Not up to my usual gourmet tastes at all. The flavor engaged my gag reflex briefly, but I forced my Sense to focus on the summoning at hand. I'd only get one shot at this.

Wincing, I swiped my bleeding hand across the runes and focused on one of the biggest, most brute-force summons I'd ever tried. I was chasing a demon in an unfamiliar world, and I just didn't have the time or knowledge to fine-tune my formula as much as was my wont.

All the muscles under my scalp cramped at once. I thought my Sense would snap back in rebellion from the imprecise formula, causing the summons to fizzle. Despair and disappointment turned my stomach acid. My thumb throbbed.

The world held its breath, and all was still. Time slowed down in front of me. I could see each strike of the Lycaon's paws against the turf, a monster-squirrel slowly turning its head toward me, and the Cornuprocyons launching upward. I watched the air pressure from their pounces blasting leaves off the ground in slow, tumbling cartwheels along the earth.

Cythymau hunched over the lead Lycaon's back, urging it forward like a grotesque parody of the classical hero charging to the rescue. He looked statuesque, almost noble in a warped way, and absolutely unbeatable. Tears came to my eyes; I couldn't look away. The summoning strained, and something in my head tore in two. I'd never tried to brute force something like this before; I didn't actually know if my Sense would be strong enough to pull it off. Through the wash of red dancing in my vision, I struggled to hold onto the summons.

Screaming into Hyctea's bloody feathers, I refused to give up. Black crowded in at the edge of my vision; I scrabbled to see Cythymau at the head of the charge.

Panting with the pain, disoriented, dimly I heard a rumble. It grew louder, and then suddenly the valley walls collapsed inward in a cataclysmic avalanche of earth, mud, rock and trees. It started with one small stone tumbling at the top of the valley and turned into a massive rush of pulverized rock and dirt. It swept downward, obscuring the valley in a mighty tide of churning debris. More and more of the walls collapsed, filling the whole valley with thunder. I squeezed my eyes shut against a wave of nausea that seemed to slosh back and forth between my head and stomach.

"Forward, Hyctea," I whispered. "We need to get ahead of them before they get free." I clutched her sticky feathers in suddenly trembling hands. Focus, Grace. My stomach churned again, bringing the stinging tang of acid into my mouth. No doubt I'd pushed my Sense past its rather meager limits this time.

I put my fingers to the rune board. Their familiar shapes felt almost painful under my suddenly clammy and over-sensitized skin.

Yep, not good. I'd definitely injured something. But I just had to hold it together until we got through the portal. I took a deep breath and held it, trying to channel the pain away from my surface thoughts.

To help Robert, I needed to be able to summon. To summon, I needed to focus. To focus, I *needed* to be able to push my pain to the side. At least until we were back in our own world. Then Thad could shoot me for all I cared. But I couldn't afford to let myself go. Not until then.

Taking another deep breath, I let a warm rush of resolve and strength expand my chest. I didn't know how I'd do it, but I would get Robert and Andrea out of here. Cythymau would not have them. Not now, not ever.

The pain dwindled to a knot of discomfort at the back of my neck. I was aware it was there and demanding attention, but for now I could ignore it. I forced my eyes open against the too-bright glare around me. Hyctea sped over the rubble in the valley. Under the settling dust, I could already see movement as things started to force their way up through the debris. A Cornuprocyon burst free, showering bits of rock, dirt, and splinters in all directions.

He must have been mid-air when the slide hit, so he'd been buried near the top. With any luck, Cythymau was at the very bottom, still digging his way out from under several tons of earth and rock.

I didn't have any hope that he'd been crushed; his mastery of runes was much more extensive than mine. The chances that he didn't have a defensive summon prepped by the time the rockslide hit approached zero. But that was ok. My goal had never been to take him out, just slow him down. Well, I'd managed to do that.

Hyctea swooped closer to the mouth of the valley where the Cornuprocyon had broken free. I swiped my bloody thumb across my rune board. A tingling prickle ran over my skin, raising goose bumps, and the pain in my head returned three-fold, driving my breath out in an audible blast.

The gout of lava I'd summoned over the Cornuprocyon popped into existence, but in a much smaller quantity than I expected. Rather than encasing him and a good portion of the valley around him in the molten rock, I splashed a little on his back. The rest was easily deflected by his kinetic shields, coating a small section of the debris. A few small fires started, but nothing like the blanket of fire and quickly hardening rock I'd planned.

My head felt like it was full of fire instead. I dragged more air into my lungs and tried to tamp down the pain like before. Carefully, I slid together the runes mixing earth, ash, and water and threw a heavy crust of thick cement-like lahar over the top of the landslide. As I slid my thumb over the runes and powered the summon, black and red dots swam in my vision and pressure squeezed my head like a vice.

"Find Robert, Hyctea," I mumbled. "We have to get there first."

Hyctea pumped her powerful wings, sending us swiftly in the direction where Andrea and Robert would be waiting for the portal.

I lowered my face into her feathers and gave myself to the pain for a bit. I didn't think I'd get a chance to later.

GRACE

With Hyctea's help, I managed to catch up to Robert and Andrea before Cythymau's demon horde dug itself out of the rock slide. I kept looking over my shoulder, expecting Cythymau appear at any moment, but so far the coast remained clear. I thanked Hyctea for her help and dismissed her back to her own Weave. I'd already asked too much of my Guardians recently; asking one giant owl spirit to go up against a horde of demons alone was something even I wouldn't do.

Robert and I stood on top of the hill where the portal would open, our backs to the area where we expected it to appear. We knew from last summer that the time dilation between the two Weaves meant that while it was open continuously in our home Weave, in this one it only opened at specific time intervals. Much like the first movie cameras only catching ten frames per second, the portal was only open here for snapshots of time. The problem was, we only had a rough estimate of when it would open. Sometime soon. *Exactly* when, well, that was beyond me.

Robert's body radiated tension and nervous energy. Rick, next to him, growled low in his chest, his bristly coat standing on end and his tail raised menacingly. Andrea sat wrapped in a dingy gray blanket I'd summoned out of Cythymau's stronghold, her torso slumped over her folded legs with one bright, pale arm wound round her knees, her fiery red hair spilling down to meet the yellow grass. I wasn't sure if she was unconscious, or if it was just too much for her to keep her head upright after being strapped to a board like a side of beef for so long. Either way, I doubted she'd be much help in the coming fight.

Not to mention, if I was absolutely honest with myself, neither was I. Powering the little tags I'd just placed around the clearing to bring boulders, trees, and some of the stone obelisks to fortify this spot had made my head want to disintegrate. I'd never heard of someone straining her Sense to the point it couldn't be used, but apparently it existed. Some instinct told me I'd been dancing awfully close to that line. Much more, and I was pretty sure I'd be just as useless in this showdown as Andrea.

Oh, who was I kidding? I was probably so close to useless already that the distinction really didn't matter. I was out of plans, and really had no idea how we were going to get out of this one. Again.

Robert walked around the inner perimeter, whipping up some rough earthworks. He'd made a wide ditch with his Sense and was lining it with broken glass from the gym and hastily sharpened wooden points. I hadn't bought us enough time for anything else. Shattered bleachers had been heaped together in front of us to create some shelter before curving them around to our left and right. It wasn't enough for a true barricade, but it did narrow the available ways to attack us and serve as a crude fortification.

At our back was a stand of trees and a high rock wall made from standing stones I'd stolen with the tags. I'd made Robert place the pillars very carefully, so I still knew in what order they went back into the circle we'd taken them from. They were just too handy not to use. Assuming we made it out of here alive, I promised myself I'd come back and get a full transcription of all the runes etched on their surface.

Rick growled, his quills bristling. Robert came to stand next to him, putting a hand carefully beside his muzzle. Already dreading what I would see, I turned to look.

Cythymau had gathered his forces at the far edge of the plain in front of our position. Their shadows hung low on the edge of the horizon like a nightmare waiting to happen. I started to count the shifting beasts, and gave up when I reached two hundred. No matter the exact number, if he sent all of that at us at once, we were totally, unmistakably screwed.

I took another deep breath and held it in. Those breathing exercises I'd learned over the last few months in dealing with Robert were actually coming in really handy today. Go figure.

If I concentrated on the air moving in and out of my lungs hard enough, it forced the bongo drums currently thrumming between my temples into temporary submission. So far, it didn't look like Robert had picked up on just how bad off I was. I wanted to keep it that way until we got out of here. He needed to look after his own skin, and Andrea's next.

Me, well, I wasn't about to actually let the kid look after the adult. That's just not how I rolled. Still, I wasn't suicidal. Unless I needed to step in, I'd let Robert prove just how much he'd learned over these last few months. After all, kids have their pride too.

Really, we needed a miracle. Praying for a miraculous stroke of genius had become as natural to me since last year as saying something like, "Looks like it might rain today."

I wondered what that said about my life recently.

Still, I held to the belief that it was always much better to make your own miracle than wait for one. Or in this case, *coach* your own teen miracle. And his thirty-foot raccoon-demon pet.

We just needed one more win.

As if hearing my thoughts, the first dark forms at the edge of the plain detached themselves from the rest and started running toward our position. Looking at the mass of beasts swarming over the field below us, laughter started to bubble up from my queasy stomach. The four of us seemed pitifully insignificant against those numbers, but apparently Cythymau wasn't taking any chances.

I gave Robert a toothy grin, fueled almost entirely on bravado. "This is it. You ready to hold this ground, no matter what?" I raised an eyebrow at him.

He flashed me a wide smile as he rolled his shoulders and cracked his knuckles. He was obviously riding high on the success of springing Andrea. He'd need to watch out, though. The next step was a doozy.

"Rick and I have this. Cythymau wasn't planning on me having him on our side. Just you wait and see." His fists clenched; his jaw set defiantly.

"In that case, shall I just sit back and watch? You don't need your teacher anymore? Glad to hear it. Andrea and I'll just chill here and wait for the portal, I guess."

I flopped down next to Andrea and stretched my arms above my head in a carefree gesture. Sure, my heart was hammering and my head felt like it might not stay attached to my body, but the kid didn't need to know that.

Robert fixed me with a suspicious glower. Rick, next to him, gave a shuddering exhalation that could only be taken as an offended humph.

"You do that," he said rather shortly. "Rick and I are a team now. We got this."

Something tickled the back of my throat that I refused to acknowledge might—just might—be tears. He looked so grown-up all of a sudden that I couldn't resist adding one last worthless piece of advice.

"Don't get cocky. Cythymau's not going to let Andrea or you go easily. Be sure to watch your back."

"Right. Good thing someone's already got my back." Robert shot me a look that barely stopped short of rolling his eyes, before turning and fixing his attention on the first wave of advancing beasts. That wave definitely wouldn't be the last.

Robert and Rick positioned themselves to the right and left of our makeshift barrier and waited.

A horde of Lycaon reached the barricade first, flowing over the ground like something out of a nightmare, clawing up the hill on their way toward us. I felt Robert extend his Sense. He diverted several of them before they even reached the barricade by sending a deluge of rock and dirt down on top of them, then pushed the whole mess back with a blast of crushing kinetic force.

Rick rumbled, deep in his chest. The familiar *woomph* of his kinetic attack filled the air, only this time that brutal force was directed point-blank at our attackers rather than at us. It caught the other half of the first wave and knocked them back, twitching and sprawling on the ground. Their cries of outrage, pain, and defiance tore the air in a wrenching cacophony.

Cythymau might be the general of this attack, but he hung back on the horizon, out of Robert's range. It was his demon-beasts that bore the brunt. If we wanted to live, defeat or capture was not an option. That didn't mean I enjoyed watching Rick and Robert kill and crush bones, no matter how efficient they were at it.

More Cornuprocyons followed, leaping over or, in some cases, onto, the fallen Lycaon. They sent a blast of kinetic energy careening at our crude barricade in an attempt to destroy our makeshift shelter.

Robert, his face focused, intent, caught the kinetic force in his Sense and turned it back on them, releasing it with a natural flick of his hand that looked entirely subconscious. I doubted he even realized he'd done it.

We were surrounded by a malignant plague of teeth and claws, flying debris, and sudden blasts of kinetic force. All the demons were bent on one thing—making sure Cythymau got what he wanted. Rick waded farther into the fray, slamming that huge chitinous tail into the front ranks and accumulating an impressive pile of unconscious animals around him.

Robert and Rick worked in unison, like some elaborate dance. Robert would fend off an attack and turn it back on its instigator; Rick would come down like a giant cleanup crew, slashing with teeth and claws before clearing swaths with a swing of his giant spiked tail.

A crafty Lycaon circled behind Robert, just outside his Sense, readying himself for a pounce. Before it could leap, a spiky orange freight train, fondly known as Rick, T-boned it with extreme prejudice. Rick pounded the Lycaon into the ground with one final, spiteful swing of his tail. Then he pulverized the ground around them with a completely unnecessary blast of kinetic force for good measure before bellowing his displeasure at the now very vanquished attacker.

Robert glanced to the side, saw Rick had his flank well under control, and kept fending off the seemingly endless flow of beasts. A flood of relief turned my mouth sour at the same time a warm rush of pride swelled in my chest.

He was working with the Weave, bending it to his will, but not bashing it like he'd been wont to do recently. He had himself under control and his calm showed in the precision and efficiency of his strikes. Under his eyes, lines of fatigue had started to form, and a wrinkle between his brows told me this extended battle wasn't as easy as it appeared to be, but he hadn't boasted. He and Rick had this under control. Despite the desperation of our position, I could see he had matured. I'll even admit it—it gave me a warm fuzzy.

Maybe I wasn't such a bad mentor after all. He seemed to be turning out ok. He'd be all right. Some day in the future he would be a pillar of support for others.

Cythymau himself still hung back from the fight, content to send more and more foot troops. It wasn't hard to see he was trying to wear us down before coming in and finishing us off himself. I wished I knew when the portal would open. If Cythymau didn't already have that knowledge, I'd eat my hat. If I'd had one right now, that is.

Robert flipped a kinetic attack back on a Cornuprocyon, stunning it. Rick swept in from the side, smashing his tail into its face with an audible crack. It slumped to the ground.

There came a sudden silence as we all looked around and realized the onslaught had paused for now. The ground in front of our barricade was littered with unmoving bodies. Like any battlefield, it was gory, horrific, and pathetically wasteful. I looked at Rick as he and Robert jogged back toward Andrea and me, wondering how much of the attack was due to the beasts' feral nature, and how much of their feral nature only existed because Cythymau had gotten hold of them. There was a good possibility we had just killed a host of beasts who were just as trapped as ourselves, and part of me mourned that.

Robert flopped down cross-legged across from me. His clothes had become stained with sweat and blood, and his breath wheezed slightly as he panted for air. Rick lay down next to him, never taking his eyes off the horizon where the next attack would form.

Andrea hadn't moved during the whole fight except for the slight twitch of her shoulders that let me know she still breathed. I eyed her with concern, but until we got her out of here, we had many other priorities. Speaking of which...

"We have a problem," I told Robert, still absorbed in my thoughts. He chortled weakly. I realized how incongruous that sounded and raised rueful eyes to meet his. Despite the exhaustion in his face, he still went for the joke.

"You don't say, Teach. And here I thought we were all having fun. Granted, we probably won't be too popular with any animal rights groups, but this is the ultimate in big game hunting, right here."

"Sorry, poor choice of words." I smiled. "I should have said we have *another* problem."

Robert groaned. "I want to be an ostrich right now. Or a turtle. In my next life, I'm going to be one of those things, and tell everyone to go fuck off."

"I hate to break it to you, but even if you ignore the shit that goes on, it doesn't mean it's not happening. It just means your IQ isn't high enough to tell the difference until it's already run you over."

"I still think I could get used to a lower IQ. Or maybe I'll be an amoeba instead. I can just float through life, and no one will even know I'm there unless they get a high-powered microscope." He leaned back, resting his weight on his hands, and tipped his head back to look at the sky.

I looked up with him and blew out a deep breath. "When that portal opens, very little time will have gone by on the other side. When I left, I sent a note to Amy and Matt. But we can't assume they will be there yet."

"No matter what world we're in, there's no backup." Robert sighed. "Let me guess. Once we're through, the time difference makes it so we can't close it before Cythymau and his hordes come through."

"Exactly. With the time gap, anything that follows us through will be right on our heels." I huffed out a huge sigh.

Robert considered this, his brow wrinkled. "Isn't that Director Thad guy still there? If it's just a few of these foot troops, then between him and Rick, we should be able to hold them off long enough for us to close it. These guys aren't nearly as uber-juiced as Rick was last fall. Or at least, as long as none of us get eaten, they aren't." He frowned and moved his head from side to side, cracking his neck.

I shook my head. "Do you want to gamble on Cythymau *not* showing up once this thing opens? That seems overly optimistic. Besides, do you even remember how badly you beat Thad before we left? I wouldn't count on him being completely vertical, let alone mobile enough to fight."

Robert winced, grimacing before grunting an acknowledgment.

"We should both start thinking about how we can make sure Cythymau and friends stay in this Weave instead of following through on their no-doubt-imminent travel plans."

Typically teenager, Robert responded, *"Now* who sounds overly optimistic?" Rick stood up, rumbling low in his chest, his quills rising. I followed his gaze with the sour weight of foreboding.

"Overly optimistic or not, get your gray matter on it, because we don't have long before we'll be back in the thick of it. Looks like they're forming back up."

Not that Robert actually needed me to tell him that. Hundreds of beasts that hadn't been there seconds before milled on the edge of the flat in a restless, shifting mass, waiting for some kind of signal.

Robert sighed and rose to his feet, dusting his hands against his jeans. I got to my feet more slowly, joints aching, my head still about the size and temperament of an over-used bongo drum.

Andrea still hadn't moved. She made a mighty fine impersonation of a statue.

The beasts started streaming across the plain at us. My stomach dropped into my shoes. They'd formed into a rough V with the point facing toward us, and two rows back from the apex of it sat Cythymau himself. He rode astride a Lycaon; the cruel grin on his blue-runed face brimming with glee was a given even if I couldn't see it from that far away.

My facial muscles hardened into a grimace I could feel. Robert's face turned a little paler under his tan. He caught Rick's eye; in unison they moved toward the front of the barricade.

Cythymau pulled up just short of the earthworks and the crumpled forms of the fallen. The first line of beasts rushed our fortifications. His hooting laughter hovered over us. I swear the temperature dropped about five degrees.

Rick pounced, blasting one Lycaon with a wall of force before body--checking another. Robert followed him quickly, redirecting the force from a snarling beaked-terror into one of the giant dire-chipmunks, swiftly following that up by grabbing a long sharp branch with his Sense. He forced the branch into the beaked-terror's eye, up into its brain in a truly gory, but effective, way. It dropped the demon like a sack of bricks.

A thin, wounded scream cut the air as a stick figure with a gray blanket and streaming red hair flew up between Robert and Rick, vaulting the downed beaked-terror as if it were no more than a low gate. For a confused second, my brain refused to comprehend what it was seeing. Andrea moved? And that fast? She was going to confront Robert over killing the beaked-terror? He'd killed many more in the first wave of attacks with no reaction from her.

And then she was past him, sprinting well outside the range of his Sense. What the heck?

In the glimpse I'd caught of it, her face had transformed into a mask of fear, hatred, and anger, her tears glossing her contorted cheeks and mouth into an illusion of wood and marble. It reminded me of the rictus of a death mask. I looked ahead of her and tried to figure out what had her attention. Then swore for probably the millionth time today. She was headed straight for Cythyamau; it seemed he was the only demon that existed on that battlefield for her.

My feet moved without thought. I ran after her. I couldn't be as fast, but I might be able to cause a diversion, some kind of delay so

Robert or Rick might have a chance at stopping her, bringing her back. If she died now, this whole thing, this whole bloody mess was for nothing. I closed my eyes and reached for my rune tiles, acidic worry clenching my stomach. What the heck were we supposed to do now?

A Cornuprocyon blasted her with kinetic energy from the right. Still snared by the sight of Cythymau, she didn't even try to defend. I winced, expecting to watch her frail body go tumbling. Then Rick was there, blocking the blast with his own. He countered with a pained roar and the *woomph* of his telekinetic leap, pouncing on the attacker.

Andrea didn't even appear to notice Rick. Her gaze remained locked on Cythymau.

The little blue man sat his Lycaon with a relaxed, satisfied smile that seemed to say everything was going as he wanted—no, predicted, even. His actions broadcast confidence that he didn't even have to move and everything would still go his way. He could claim all his toys without breaking a sweat.

I was with Andrea on one thing.

FUCK. THAT.

Pulling in a deep breath, I marshaled what little Sense I had left and lined up the runes for a summons. I took little pieces of volcanic glass and dropped them on the beasts in front of Andrea from so high up they were at terminal velocity on impact. It wasn't much, but I just needed Cythymau and his ranks to be busy with something other than the wild-eyed madwoman currently charging at them. I ran as fast as I could after her, still rearranging the runes on my board.

I sent my Sense flowing through the runes. As expected, the saw blade rending my skull redoubled, clouding my vision with sparks and flashes of light. I held steady as best I could, praying to all the spirits I knew, to my ancestors, that I could hold out just a bit longer.

The glass fell like rain on Cythymau's forces, shredding hides, piercing scalps, and lacerating eyes and mouths. Cornuprocyons, Lycaon, those dire-chipmunks, and the beaked-terrors clawed and rolled and galloped trying to get away from the cutting deluge.

Andrea looked primed to charge into the glass herself. Fortunately, I wasn't the only one trying to catch up with her.

Robert bounded toward her and shoved his elbow into her side, knocking her flat about twenty feet from the first glass shards, well before she reached the bucking Lycaon carrying Cythymau.

Cythymau had created a shield around himself, protecting his skin from the glass, but either he hadn't protected his mount nearly as well as himself, or with all the pain and blood, the Lycaon couldn't tell the difference. Cythymau was currently occupied with trying to bring its wild movements under control.

Panting, Robert grabbed Andrea's shoulder, looking for the best avenue of escape. I could tell his Sense was working overtime by the number of projectiles that were deflected and then redirected back at the writhing masses of Cythymau's beasts.

Robert looked at me, his brow wrinkled in pain and stubborn determination as a feral Andrea kicked, clawed, and bit him far worse than any of the attacking demons had managed to.

Her eyes might still be directed toward Cythyamau, but obviously part of her anger now pummeled Robert.

Yep, that's my apprentice all right. Run to the rescue first, think about how to get out of it later. He might have the equivalent of great cosmic power, but without a plan to back it up…

The portal opened at the top of the hill, releasing a blast of stale gym air. My head whipped toward it on reflex, and I barely missed getting taken out by a bear-ferret swiping at me from behind. It did a double take too, and Rick took the opportunity to pound it into the ground with a vindictive downward swipe from his chitinous tail.

Cythymau finally brought his struggling mount under control and gave the telepathic command to break off the fight. Every single monstrous demon on the plain who could still move started loping toward that damn portal at what I like to call leisurely-but-deceptively-fast-we're-still-totally-fucked-speed.

Cythymau's lips curved upward with a pleased malice that made my spine itch. He rode toward us and the portal on his Lycaon mount, just as if he had all the time in the world. His easy pace and relaxed pose exuded smug confidence that nothing we did could keep him away from our Weave. He was going to follow us through the portal to Spokane and start a new power base, fueled by my friends, my colleagues. Paid for with Robert's and Andrea's lives.

Or so he thought.

I reached into the very bottom of my bag and closed my hand around a summoning scroll I hadn't expected to use here. Hadn't expected to use at all, ever, really. The times when it would be an appropriate show of force were very few and far between, after all.

Closing my eyes against a sudden flow of cowardly tears, I remembered the sunny afternoon at the cabin where Matt, Robert, and I talked about the importance of runes…and other things. Things that people with a lot of knowledge and just a spark of Sense could do. I took a deep breath and lowered my head for a second.

Or at least, people like me.

Part of my mind told me that the nascent idea forming in my brain equated to an act of madness.

But as a solution to Cythymau's imminent plans, it was so clean. So *very* clean, and it protected everyone. Robert, Andrea, the Spokane and Seattle Groves, and with very little exaggeration, maybe even the world. And it was something *I knew I could do.*

I skidded to a halt beside Robert and knocked Andrea out with a brisk chop to the base of her skull. Her head lolled. Robert's jaw went slack. He stared at me with wide, shocked eyes.

"Self-defense classes," I explained tersely. "We need to move." I shoved him toward our makeshift barricade. "Do me a favor and get yourself and Andrea over to the portal and through it."

"What? I'm not leaving you behind!" He jerked to a stop. "Either you go with us, or none of us go." His jaw already had that stubborn tilt I'd come to know so well in recent months. I sighed, grabbed his arm, and shook it. He needed to take me seriously; we didn't have time for this.

"I have a plan. But I need you and Andrea to be clear. And I need my hands free." I rummaged in my bag, bringing out the last vial of blood and the long tube of butcher paper held closed by a shoelace. I slung the strap around Robert's neck and rested the bag on Andrea's lap.

Rick shoulder-blocked a bear-ferret away from us, then leaped into the air, landing in front of three more, effectively blocking the rest from us. He bristled his quills in a show of force, clearly telling them they'd have to go through him first. He'd bought us a little space, and with it some time.

I caught and held Robert's gaze. "There are things in my bag and Grove Book that Cythymau must not get his hands on. I'm counting on you to get it out. You set out to save the girl. Now do it, and let me worry about how to keep Cythymau from following us through. *I* have a plan." I bopped him over the head with the tube and waggled the blood vial at him. He gave me a look that clearly stated he didn't think this was the correct time to be goofing around.

Moreover, he wasn't convinced. I guess he *had* seen some of my other plans... So how to convince him?

I considered his face with its mouth turned down in disapproval, his brow furrowed, throwing his cheeks into stark relief. I had a sudden vision of how he'd look fully grown up, ten or so years from now. To keep that intact, I'd truly do anything. Rick bellowed a challenge at the bear-ferret he was fighting and started backing toward us. Even if Robert didn't think he'd agreed yet, apparently Rick did. At least the whole political debacle at home wouldn't be *my* problem anymore. Silver linings, right?

I felt my lips turn up at Robert's disgruntled expression. I gave him my best shit-eating, summoner-frightening grin. After all, when else was I going to get a chance to pull this baby out?

"I'm the teacher, remember? We'll save the world. Again. All you have worry about is saving the girl. That is, if. You. Move. Your. Butt. *Now.* Cythymau isn't going to wait for you to make up your mind."

I gave him another shove, waving the tube of paper jauntily as he glanced uncertainly over his shoulder.

Robert zig-zagged with Andrea back and to the left as Rick fended off another attack from a dire-squirrel.

Given all the promises I'd just made to Robert, I'd better make sure he and Andrea made it to the portal first. I rolled out the long scroll of butcher paper onto the ground in front of me. The cramped rows of compound runes stared up at me.

Cythymau was still loping toward me at a leisurely you're-obviously-so-fucked-I-don't-even-have-to-exert-myself-pace—and behind me, the portal. With a flick of my thumb, I uncapped the vial of blood, grinning at him like a madwoman. I'd bet he wouldn't see this one coming. I dropped to one knee and threw the blood over the length of the butcher paper, sending my Sense into the runes.

My Sense stretched into the Weave, following the runes through the portal into our home Weave. It flowed in a rush through the runes and into the gym, streaming through the yellow grasses until they turned into the fine wood grain and wax of the gym floor, and then back out of the school and through tile, asphalt, dirt, rock, cement, water, and lead. I stretched myself from continent to continent, seeking the target runes, creeping into each one until I became a web strung through the whole Weave, fine as spider silk and just as strong. For a moment I held the whole Weave in me, or it held me. I'd already pushed past my limits, and it strained every part of my being to hold on to the hundreds of complex runes this summons required.

I ground my teeth against the pain and turned my head, slitting open my eyes to watch Robert run through the portal carrying Andrea. Rick followed at his heels, fending off stray attacks. Cythymau was almost upon me. I locked eyes with him and flashed a defiant grin.

The first Lycaon would be at the portal in a few seconds more. I couldn't wait longer; I had to trust Robert would be able to protect himself and Andrea with that immense Sense he'd been gifted with. Our time together had been bumpy, but truly a gift to both of us.

Closing my eyes, I reached into myself and surrendered my concentration to my Sense. For just a moment, I existed in a hundred different locations on the other side of the rift, refining and separating one gram of pure U-235 from the heart of each of my targeted power plants. The immense density of the uranium weighed down my Sense, but I'd been precise in my calculations to bring it back to me. Even with my weakened and overworked Sense, I could still do this.

This was our last hope. I didn't have enough strength left in me to save our Weave, Robert, or Andrea from Cythymau any other way. But this, this could be my final fuck-you to the demon who'd turned my once well-ordered life completely upside down for over a year. If I had one regret, it was that there was no time and no energy left to summon my duck curry. I had faith that Robert would live well. Maybe he'd eat a plate for me in remembrance.

I commanded my tattered Sense to reel back in, to come back and be whole once again. Reaching into all my reserves, ignoring the black, yellow, and red dots swimming through my battered mind, I brought the U-235 together at exactly the same time in the same place. For a fraction of a second I saw the reaction take hold, the light intensely white and beautiful. The earth trembled. The explosion took me and my triumphant tears along with it.

ROBERT

THE COMPLEXITY of Grace's summons was staggering. I Sensed her power entering the portal, a woven braid of hundreds of strands. Once through, it blossomed, each strand heading in a different direction. It had a peculiar kind of beauty; it felt like *being* a waterfall as it hits the stones. To those of you without the Sense, talking about it is like explaining red to a blind man. It doesn't translate, but the sheer *artistry* behind what she did took my breath away.

It felt like listening to Paul Gonsalves play in Ellington's band at Newport. Being in the presence of perfection is a rarity; savor it if you ever get the chance.

It wasn't until I Sensed the first chunk of metal that I figured out which scroll she'd pulled out of her bag. Radiation, as it turns out, just feels...weird. Everything around the first chunk she brought in seemed just a little fuzzy. The small piece was super-dense, but I couldn't tell exactly where its borders were; bits and pieces of it streamed outward. It felt like pouring an entire packet of popping sugar candy into my mouth at once.

She was bringing in uranium, and lots of it. U-235. Pure. I Sensed her through the portal, and felt the crooked grin on her face. Her eyes were locked on Cythymau, and I knew she wasn't coming back.

I also knew it was far too late to stop her. With a choked sob, I dove past the portal, dragging Andrea with me.

Out of the corner of my eye I saw Thaddeus still on the ground. He wasn't in a direct line with the portal, but he was still going to take a big chunk of the blast. He looked to be conscious. I shouted a quick "Fire in the hole!" at him; he was going to have to watch out for himself.

Rick, sensing my fear, dove on top of Andrea and me. He caught most of his weight himself, but he still covered our bodies with his. Breathing would quickly become an issue if this held long-term, but I didn't plan on breathing for the next several seconds anyway. I was grateful for the cover.

We were back and away from the portal, and it only took in a small portion of the blast, like a pinhole letting light into a dark room. It dissipated through the gymnasium, but even that was enough to deafen me for several seconds afterward. The sound, even with the dispersion and underneath Rick, came on like a brick wall, and I felt it in my gut.

I almost panicked then, waiting for the heat and the noise to consume me, but I kept my focus. I used my Sense to redirect as much as possible away from the three of us, but I couldn't hold that much heat and force away; I could only lessen the blow. For several seconds I lay there on top of Andrea and under Rick, and then the weight of Rick's body lifted and I took a deep breath.

The air smelled foul. Black soot coated the walls of the gym. In front of Thaddeus was a large chunk of concrete, which had taken the force of the blast for him. He had been a little more skilled than I at redirecting the heat away from himself, but his clothing had burnt to charred tatters and his skin was blistered where it wasn't red. He'd set his face in a stoic mask over his pain, his breathing controlled.

I wasn't exactly Thad's biggest fan. Still, it's hard not to respect a guy that can be stoic about something like that. I nodded slowly at him. He didn't seem to notice.

Rick had been burnt bald, his skin charred black. I felt his pain through the bond, and directed what I could of my Sense to him. He ate it greedily, his regeneration beginning to replace dead flesh with new, pink growth. Orange spines began to grow from his hide.

I patted his head gently. "Good boy," I said in a soft voice. "Thank you." His red eyes glowed and swirled brighter. I smiled at him, then looked down at Andrea.

The blanket had been lost somewhere in the fighting, and she was once again nude. I must have been getting used to it, because the first thing I looked for was injuries instead of breasts.

For me, this was real progress.

She was panting, like me, but appeared unhurt. Her eyes flicked around the room nervously. I held out my hand to help her to her feet, but she shrank from it and stood up on her own power, totally unashamed of her nakedness. Quickly she took two steps away from me, dropping into a defensive crouch.

I didn't know what to say. Instead, I shook my head and turned away. She would calm down on her own. I'd seen that look on the faces of other foster kids, the look of someone for whom attention means imminent violence. The best thing to do for kids like that was give them their space.

I stepped around toward the portal, hoping; I even convinced myself to *expect* that when I looked through I would see my mentor in some sort of a defensive working, smiling that toothy grin of hers and flipping me some comment about how she'd always wanted to try that.

That's not what I saw.

I didn't see much of anything at all. The landscape had been laid bare. There were no bodies, though I'd stacked them up around the portal as best I could during the fight. The defenses we had erected were simply gone. The portal, once above solid ground, was now several feet higher. A crater had formed in the top of the hill, with no vegetation anywhere to be seen.

I saw no sign of Grace. Cythymau had either died with her or fled, but the epicenter of the crater was exactly where Grace had been standing. She was gone.

I dropped to one knee, tears rolling down my face. Once again, I had left someone behind. I hadn't saved anyone; I'd only managed to trade Grace's life for Andrea's. I looked at her, at what I had bought at the price of my mentor's life. She still sat in a defensive crouch, her face twisted up in the anger that comes from deep, deep fear.

Rick nuzzled me in the side, lapping at my face with his tongue. I reached my hand out, patting his muzzle. "Yeah. I know. One last job to do."

Wearily, I pulled my Sense back from Rick; he whimpered but let it go freely. I took a deep breath and tried to concentrate.

It was hard. Thoughts of Grace kept ramming at my consciousness, tearing my focus away from my already-overworked Sense and down into grief. I wanted to break down and wail, beat the floor with my fists, but I couldn't. This portal remained, still growing, and Thaddeus was in no condition to do anything about it. This was on me.

Slowly I discarded thoughts of my dead friend. I pulled in my Sense and let it bring what comfort it could. I bent my mind to the task, reaching out into the Weave and knitting it together. Carefully, I closed the curtain on the crater that was sure to be Grace's last memorial.

Then I stood there, letting my Sense drop back into Rick's waiting hunger. I hung my aching head and let the grief take me.

At the far end of the gym, Thaddeus Neilsen rose to his feet.

"Mr. Lorents," he said, calmly. "I take it you have decided to face your just punishment, then?" His naked skin still bubbled with those puffy, irradiated blisters; he must have been running on pure adrenaline. I wasn't sure whether he was going to live, in the long term, but he was keeping his voice even and controlled. The effect was disturbing in a way that shouting simply wouldn't have been.

I think I knew, even then, that Grace's death was on me. Deep down, I knew that burden was on my shoulders. But there are some things that it kills you to admit out loud, and this one was far too fresh. Thaddeus had pushed me to these extremes, and I decided it was going to be easier to be angry with him than to confront my feelings for myself. There is nothing quite so immediately therapeutic as blaming someone else for your own problems.

In other words, I did not maintain the same control over my voice as Neilsen had. I'd like to tell you that it came out in a measured pace, but the fact is I broke into an angry wave. The anger was an ointment for my grief, removing the pain of it, even if only temporarily.

"Mr. Neilsen. You and I have disagreed twice now. Twice. Neither time has ended well for you. This time, the worst thing you could possibly do to yourself is win."

"You're stalling, Lorents."

"Nope. I just think you need all the truth. Do you see this beast to my right?" Rick was ten feet high and thirty feet long. Missing him would have been pretty hard. "You know what he is?"

Neilsen stared at Rick blankly.

"Oh, come on, Mr. Neilsen," I said, my voice taking on a mocking, bitter hardness. "After all, you've read my file. You know what happened last fall. You know all about Rick here."

Neilsen's eyes widened a bit.

"You know that Grace and I almost died fighting him together; that he is basically invulnerable, regenerates what damage he does take, is warded from summoning attacks to his internals, and can project a wave of force that would make Union Pacific jealous. And you know that he eats summoners."

Neilsen gave me a short, jerky nod.

"Well, you're going to learn some new things about him, now. The first is that he's bonded to me. Something to do with the hold Cythymau had on him, and how I broke it. The second is, I'm pretty sure he goes back to status quo if I die. And, third and finally, he isn't going to let you kill me anyway. The thing is, I don't want to kill you. But Rick here? Well, you make him angry and you're not a precious life to him. You're just breakfast."

I was snarling by now, really getting into the rhythm of it. Hey, the guy already had orders to kill me; it's not like I was going to piss him off *more*.

"Now, I'm going up to the cabin, because Rick isn't really built for city life. Andrea here will be coming with me. *You* are going to file a report with the Grove about how compliant I am, and how you want to train me further. You're also going to get a medical summoner out here for us, because I'm sure we've all just been irradiated. Once the adrenaline wears off, I imagine we're going to be pretty sick." The radiation didn't seem to surprise him, but I had managed to knock him off balance with something else.

"You want *me* to train you? What about Ms. Moore?"

And that took it away from me. The wind left my sails, and I gulped. I lowered my head, unable to talk. I struggled to hold back the tears, but it was hopeless. They poured out of me without my permission, turning me back into a child just as I was trying to intimidate the hit man in front of me.

"Oh," was all he said, staring at me.

Once I'd recovered, my voice softened. "You should also probably put in your report how Grace died saving everyone in this reality. I think that needs mentioning."

"Did she? You weren't exactly chummy a couple of seconds ago." His eyes carried a suggestion with them, one I could have used to spark my anger. My river of tears had carried the edge off it, though, and what came out was simply war-weary.

"It was a couple of seconds for you; it was a full day for us. I'll give you the full story later and elsewhere."

I turned toward Andrea. "Come on. We're going home."

"And who is *she?*" asked Neilsen. *Damn it,* would his adrenaline never give out? He had to be going into shock, but he still held himself as though he was wearing a business suit. I gave him points for toughness, then subtracted them for obstinacy.

"She's...a friend. Andrea. We got her out. We can talk once we're *out of here,*" I said over my shoulder, then turned to Andrea. "Let's go."

"Home?" she asked. Her voice was quiet, but it held a hard edge.

"Well, *my* home. A little cabin in the woods. We're back on Earth now. We're safe."

Slowly, Andrea nodded, and dropped her guard—enough to move. That'd work for now.

I led Rick and Andrea past the collapsing Director of the Spokane Grove. When I reached the double doors exiting the gymnasium, I turned to look at him. "Oh, one more thing. If you ever—*ever*—accuse me of killing Grace again, I will choke you to death with your own testicles. I'm not a medical summoner, but I'm pretty sure I could pull it off."

I turned back to leave, then paused for a moment and looked back one last time.

"Congratulations on your appointment, Director."

A QUICK STOP IN THE GIRLS' locker room yielded an old basketball uniform. It wasn't much, but it was something for Andrea to wear. She sniffed at it first, then donned it hesitantly. I turned my back while she did—a useless gesture, given that I'd been fine staring at her naked. Still, the old habits die hard. When a girl's changing clothes in the same room as you, you turn your back.

Rick was regenerated by the time we emerged back into the hallway.

We walked through the school, with his spines scraping the ceiling tiles. I didn't bother worrying about that; given the current state of the gym, the school could replace a couple of ceiling tiles too.

"Hey, boy," I said to him, "remember when Grace put you underground?"

Rick cowered away from me. Grace had once opened up a five-hundred-foot-deep pit underneath him, then dropped the five-hundred-foot column of earth and rock she'd removed back on top of him. I couldn't imagine it had been pleasant for him.

"Well, you got out of that. I'm guessing you're a pretty good tunneler, right?"

Rick began bouncing his forepaws back and forth excitedly. The tiles of the ceiling gave up the ghost completely and showered him in particles of crushed foamboard. In spite of myself, I chuckled.

"Okay. Is that how you got around last fall?'

Rick licked me.

"Can you do it again? We're still in the middle of the city, and I don't know how to get you out to the cabin without you getting noticed."

Rick responded by nudging me to one side. His *woomph* echoed through the hallway, and the floor gave way immediately. I didn't have my Sense up, but from the look of the shrapnel spinning up and away from the impact point he'd put a bit of English on his force. It wasn't as powerful as his previous blasts, but the twisting turned it into a rather effective drill.

"Okay, buddy. I'll see you back at the cabin." I sent an image of the cabin and a general direction through the bond. Once he was close enough, he'd find me. He'd done it once already.

Rick's disappearance underneath the school revealed two figures at the far end of the hall. They were taking cover behind the end of the locker rows. The light was dim, and I couldn't see their faces, but one of them sent me a harsh whisper.

"Robert!"

Andrea looked at them, confused and edgy. She stepped away from me and started to drop back into the defensive crouch that seemed to be her default position. I stood in the middle of the hallway and said clearly, "It's safe. Rick's fine." Then I turned to her and said, in a lower voice, "It's safe. They're fine."

Matt and Amy stepped out from behind the lockers. "Rick? Safe?" asked Amy.

"Long story," I said. "But yeah, he's ok. As long as I'm alive, anyway."

They both stared at me. I probably looked like a wreck.

"You should see the other guy," I said. "Actually, you probably should. Thaddeus is in there, and he looks a lot worse than I do. I'd make it quick; you don't want spend much time in the gym right now. The rad count is going to be pretty high in there for a while."

Their eyes widened. "Did Grace—" Matt began.

"Yeah. She used it. Took out Cythymau's army, may have gotten Cythymau himself. But she did it pretty close to the portal."

279

Matt let out a low whistle. Amy stared at me. No one said anything; they both knew what that meant.

Without a word, Amy reached out and embraced me. I relaxed and let my head rest on her shoulders, simply accepting the hug. I wrapped my right arm around her waist, and we held each other. Matt joined in from the side after a moment; my left arm went up around his neck. We simply stayed like that for several seconds before I straightened to my full height.

During the group hug, Andrea had relaxed her posture, but she hadn't come any closer to these strange new people. I broke off the hug and gestured at her.

"Amy, this is Andrea. Andrea, this is Amy. Amy was Grace's best friend. She's not going to hurt you."

Andrea's eyes were wide as Amy extended her hand for a shake. Her muscles tensed, but Amy was good at soothing tense nerves, and simply smiled back at her. "Come on, sweetie. Let's get you taken care of."

Andrea continued to stare for a second, then looked at me. I nodded at her; she looked back at Amy, gesturing for her to lead the way. Andrea still wasn't letting anyone behind her.

As the two girls left, Matt looked at me. "How you holding up?" he asked.

"It's still setting in. Look, can I cadge a ride from you? I've got somewhere to go."

Matt cocked his head slightly sideways, then nodded. We had started toward the exit when my knees buckled. He caught me before I fell.

"Sorry," I said. "It's been a long day."

"I'll bet. You should get some sleep."

"Yeah. But first, this one thing."

Matt shook his head. "Ok, brother. But then you're going back to the cabin and hitting the hay."

"No problems there," I said.

We strode out the doors of my high school for the last time.

I didn't look back.

~

ACCORDING TO PACIFIC STANDARD TIME, I had only been away from Francene's hospital room for a little more than an hour. Donald was at her side, her hand in his. She was asleep.

Judging by the mirror over the sink, I looked haggard. My clothing was torn, my eyes droopy. Donald's face grew pale as I stalked toward Francene, then it hardened.

So did mine.

I wasn't in the mood for a confrontation. I was exhausted and grumpy. Trying to use my Sense in this condition would have been nigh impossible. But Donald didn't need to know that. I met his eyes and stared him down, willing the pain and fear I had felt over the last week to fill them and project outward.

Before, he had thrown me out for his and Francene's safety. I understood that, then. But Cythymau was no longer a threat, and this insufferable little bigot of a man was not going to stop me from seeing my self-appointed mother. He wasn't happy about it. His eyes widened and he rocked back slightly in his chair, flinching away from a power I didn't actually have at the moment. I kept the stare on him, boring him down, daring him to complain about my presence. He didn't say anything.

I picked up a chair from the far side of the room and gently placed it down on Francene's other side. I took her other hand, held it, then leaned back in my chair and stared at her face.

I was home.

GRACE

I TOOK another swig of my extra-tall mojito and relaxed onto the beach lounge. My bare legs stretched out in front of me as I watched the sun dance off the waves. From here, the ocean was a shocking blue, the sand down the beach blindingly white in contrast. I wore a one-piece swimsuit with a floral wraparound skirt; chunky, over-large sunglasses; and a floppy, wide hat. My hair was pulled back in its customary low ponytail, but I'd stuck a large hyacinth flower behind my ear as a nod to my festive mood.

Redwood stood next to me, his branches soaking in the brilliant sunlight, allowing me some shade. His roots were sunk deep into the warm sand as he basked in the warmth of the beach; his needles glinted like emeralds in the bright wash of sun. Both of us were content to enjoy the companionable silence and listen to the waves.

I set the tall, frosted mojito glass down on a little table next to my lounge. A tray laden with sliced pineapple, papayas, mangos, and kiwis sat next to it. Stretching my arms up, I laced my fingers together and rested the back of my head against my palms.

This. This was the life. Or the afterlife, really.

A light breeze off the waves moderated the sun's heat into a drowsy blanket of comfort. The waves tempted me, but I was too pleasantly content to bother getting up right now.

I was blissfully warm, without a care in the world. I reached a lazy arm out and drained the last of the mojito. Like magic, Jorge, the cabana boy, appeared in my peripheral vision, carrying another frosted mojito glass. His browned abs glistened under the bright caress of the sun, his straw hat charmingly out of place over his tanned, youthful face.

I unabashedly enjoyed the show from under half-open eyelids as he carried my new beverage toward my bastion of repose.

I was just lifting a languid hand up to accept the new offering when I felt a sharp tug on my spine. "What the heck?" I spluttered, jerking upright, bumping Jorge's outstretched hand with my flailing arm and splashing my new drink in an arc onto the sand, my eyes flying open.

"Hmm?" Redwood opened one drowsy eye to look down at me.

"My back is cramping, almost like something's yanking at me. It feels like whatever it is, it's trying to rip out my spine." I put my free hand on my back, just to verify that my vertebrae were not currently bursting out of my body. Warm, supple skin met my fingers. Everything seemed to be normal. My back was not suddenly developing an exoskeleton.

"Oh, ho!" Redwood chortled. "Does it feel like being pulled upward and uprooted?"

"Kind of, I guess. I think it feels more like being a fish on a hook, if the hook was wrapped around my spine," I grumbled. Redwood startled me by letting out a thunderous laugh.

"Welcome to the club. Now you'll get a taste of the other side of the coin after all these years." The bark around Redwood's eyes crinkled as he smiled at me knowingly.

"What do you mean?" I asked suspiciously, as the spasm in my spine became even more insistent. I actually felt unstable, as if the force of the stitch in my back was beginning to lift me off my beach recliner.

"*You* of all people should know what's going on, Little Sister.

You're a spirit now. What do *you* think is happening?" Redwood laughed. "See you when you get back."

Oh.

"But I didn't sign up to be a Guardian!" I spluttered in futile protest.

Redwood waved a branch in cheerful and noncommittal farewell as the beach disappeared below me. I soared up into that cloudless sky, reeled in by some irresistible force.

THE COOL ROOM I dropped into was a jarring change after the sunlit beach, the flooring chilly under my bare feet. I glanced around in confusion, expecting it to be somewhere familiar, but I didn't recognize the furnishings. It was also a lot darker in here than it had been on the beach, which wasn't helping. I took of my sunglasses and waited for my eyes to adjust to the dimmer light, then turned to see who had the gall to summon *me*. I hadn't signed up for this shit. Give me back my beach and cabana boys, dammit. I had *earned* that afterlife.

It took me a moment to locate the schmuck who'd summoned me. He stood next to the closed door that led out of the room, the rune phrases that had summoned me still laid out in front of him and wet with blood. He stood almost motionless in the gloom, half hidden by a tall potted plant, which is why I'd missed him on my first glance around.

I stalked up to the hapless summoner who'd called me, my bare feet slapping against the cold of the floor.

"Just who do you think you're summoning?" I snapped. I stopped in front of him and jabbed a finger accusingly somewhere around his belly button. He flinched slightly but didn't respond. I pulled his larger frame out into the light with a new strength I hadn't known I possessed.

He loomed over me, taller than I remembered, but very familiar.

"Hullo, Grace," Robert offered, his lips curling up in a half-apologetic, half-sheepish smile.

My anger evaporated slowly, and I let out a long-suffering sigh. In addition to being taller, Robert looked older in small ways. I wondered how long I'd actually been gone. It felt like just a few days for me.

Which reminded me that my incredibly pleasant afterlife had recently been cut short by this very person. I frowned at him, my irritation stirring.

"I can see I called at a bad time. Nice hat," Robert said, eyeing me dubiously. I looked down at my swimsuit and back up, daring him to say anything further about my attire or lack thereof. He visibly choked down some comment under the force of my stare and settled for, "It's good to see you."

"Look." I put my hand on my hip and regarded my former apprentice somewhat glumly. "I never really had time to go into it with everything we had going on, but Ancestral Spirits have to sign up for this kind of thing. *I* never did. It's good to see you too, but you can't just go summoning any spirit willy-nilly like this. How did you even figure out *how* to summon me?"

"It's a long story. It wasn't easy, if you're worried that some other summoner might do the same thing."

"No, Robert. That lovely thought hadn't occurred to me. But I guess it has now. Thanks for that. Since you've got my attention, why don't you tell me exactly how you managed to summon me without a Visitant Pact, and then I'll go back to my 'vacation,' and you will never do this again."

"I can't do that. I mean, I can tell you how I managed to summon you, but you can't go back. Not yet. Please."

He had my attention with that "Please." The Robert I knew didn't ask for things easily, and definitely didn't ask people to stick around when they'd indicated they had somewhere else to be.

Which may be why the next words came out of my mouth before I even had a chance to think them through.

"I'm sure I'll regret asking this, but why not?"

He regarded me silently for a moment, and then said five words that changed everything.

"Because I need your help."

Damn. At some point this kid had learned my weakness.

So much for my afterlife. I'd been right. I regretted this already.